ROBERT B. PARKER

PLAYMATES

VIKING

VIKING

Published by the Penguin Group
27 Wrights Lane, London W8 5TZ, England
Viking Penguin Inc., 40 West 23rd Street, New York, New York 10010, USA
Penguin Books Australia Ltd, Ringwood, Victoria, Australia
Penguin Books Canada Ltd. 2801 John Street, Markham, Ontario, Canada L3R 1B4
Penguin Books (NZ) Ltd, 182–190 Wairau Road, Auckland 10, New Zealand

Penguin Books Ltd, Registered Offices: Harmondsworth, Middlesex, England

First published in the USA by G. P. Putnam's Sons, New York 1989
First published in Great Britain by Viking 1990
1 3 5 7 9 10 8 6 4 2

Printed in Great Britain by
Richard Clay Ltd, Bungay, Suffolk

A CIP catalogue record for this book is available from the British Library

ISBN 0-670-82986-2

For Joan

1

Vince Haller invited me to lunch at the Clarendon Club on Commonwealth Avenue with the Chairman of the Board of Trustees of Taft University, Haller's alma mater.

"No sneakers," Haller told me. "No jeans, no open shirts with that idiotic gold chain you wear that's at least six years out of fashion."

"Susan gave it to me," I said.

"Sure," Haller said and gave me a look I'd seen him give witnesses during cross examination. It was a look that said *you are a bigger simp than Michael Jackson.*

Which is why, on the last day of February, I was strolling up Commonwealth in my gray suit wearing a blue oxford shirt with a traditional roll in the collar, and a yellow silk tie that whispered *power*. My cordovan loafers gleamed with polish, and I had a brand new Browning 9mm on my belt just back of my right hip. The Browning was flat and the holster canted forward so that the gun snuggled into the hollow over my right kidney and didn't disturb the rakish drape of my suit. I was dressed to the nines, armed to the teeth, ready to lunch with the WASPs. If I hadn't been me, I'd have wished I were.

Haller was waiting for me in the entry hall. He was wearing a double breasted camel hair coat, and a winter vacation tan that seemed even darker around his gray hair and mustache. Haller said, "Spenser," in his big courtroom voice, and put out his hand. I took it. A retainer in a black suit took Haller's coat and hung it for him, and Haller and I went up the stairs toward the main dining room.

The Clarendon Club looked as it should. Twenty foot ceilings, curving marble staircase, dark oak paneling. It had been once the enclave of Bostonians of English descent, a redoubt outside of which the masses had huddled in appropriate exclusion. Now it was an ecumenical enclave, accepting anyone with money and pretending they were WASPs.

Baron Morton was waiting for us at a table. He stood when we approached. Haller introduced us and we shook hands and sat down.

"Drink to start, Mr. Spenser?" Morton said.

"Sure," I said.

A white-coated waiter was instantly there. I ordered beer, Morton had Chivas-and-soda-tall-with-a-twist, Haller had a martini. The waiter scuttled off to get the drinks and I sat back to wait. I knew how this would go. Morton would fiddle around for a while, Haller would prompt him, and after a bit he'd tell me why we were having lunch.

"So you're a detective," Morton said. Haller's eyes were sweeping the room, picking out former clients and prospective clients; much of his work was criminal, but Vince was always alert.

"Yes," I said.

"How does one get into that line?"

"I was a cop and after a while I decided to go on my own," I said.

"Spenser had a little trouble conforming," Haller said. "He's, as I told you, Baron, a bit of a free spirit."

"Like a stormy kestrel," I said.

The waiter brought the drinks.

Morton took a dip into his and said, "Stormy kestrel, by God!" He laughed and shook his head. "What kind of living can someone make doing this, if I'm not being too nosy."

"Varies," I said. "Averages out to sufficient."

"Is there much danger?"

"Just enough," I said.

Morton smiled. The waiter handed out menus.

We ordered lunch.

"So what do you need from Spenser?" Haller said.

Morton looked apologetic. "I should be getting to the point, shouldn't I?"

I smiled politely.

"Just that I was so interested. I mean, you know, a private eye and all that."

I flattened my upper lip over my front teeth and said, "You ever stood out in the rain with your guts beat out?"

It sounded exactly like Humphrey Bogart. Morton looked at me blankly.

Haller said, "Spenser thinks he does impressions."

"Oh," Morton said. "Well, ah, I need some help on a fairly delicate matter."

The waiter brought our lunch. Chicken pot pie for Morton. Scrod for Haller. Red flannel hash for me. I drank some Sam Adams.

"You're familiar with Taft University?" Morton said.

"Yes."

"I'm the Chairman of the Board of Trustees, at Taft."

I put some ketchup on my hash.

"Do you follow college basketball, Mr. Spenser?"

"Some. I like the pros better."

"Well, Taft, as perhaps you know, is a major basketball power. Not only in the east, but nationally."

"Made the final four, couple years ago," I said.

"Yes, and we're ranked in the top twenty again this year," Morton said.

"Kid, Dwayne Woodcock, is a piece of work," Haller said.

"Yes," Morton said. "Best power forward in the country."

"So what can I do for you," I said. "You looking for a point guard?"

Morton took in some air, slowly, and let it out slowly, through his nose.

"I guess I'll have to finally say it," he said.

I drank some Sam Adams and ate some hash.

"There's rumors of point shaving," Morton said.

"Ah," I said.

"The student newspaper first reported it, and a couple

of sportswriters have said something about it to Brad Walker."

"Who's Walker?" I said.

"The A.D."

"How about the coach?"

"People don't like to give Dixie bad news. He reacts, ah, poorly to bad news," Morton said.

"Tends to kill the messenger," Haller said. He'd finished his scrod and was nearly through his second martini. It always puzzled me he could have that kind of lunch and then go into court and win cases.

"So no one's asked the coach," I said.

"No," Morton said.

"Anyone ask the players?"

"No. Dixie doesn't like people upsetting the players," Morton said.

"Does the college paper say where it got its rumor?"

Morton shook his head. "Kids say they're protecting their sources."

"How about the sportswriters?"

"Well, we haven't actually pressed this very far, Mr. Spenser. We didn't want to lend credence to the rumor, and we didn't want to encourage the rumors to circulate, if you see what I mean."

"So what is it you want me to do?"

"We want you to track the allegations down, establish their truth or falsity, put the matter to rest."

"What if they're true?" I said.

"If they are true we will turn the matter over to the district attorney. The university is not prepared to cover up illegal things," Morton said. "We care about our student athletes, and we care about a winning program at Taft. But we also care about rule of law."

"I may have to annoy your coach," I said.

"I understand. He's a difficult, proud, volatile personality; but don't misjudge him. Dixie Dunham is a good man."

"We'll get along fine," I said.

Haller made a noise in his throat and then coughed into his clenched fist. Morton glanced at him and said nothing.

"If we can agree on the costs, are you willing to sign on for this?" Morton said.

"Sure," I said. "My fee increases twenty percent, though, if your coach is mean to me."

"Mr. Spenser," Morton said, "I can't promise . . ."

"He's kidding," Haller said. "He does that a lot."

"Oh, of course. Well, let's talk money."

We did. It wasn't hard, and when it was over I was employed again.

"Am I working for you, Mr. Morton, or the University?" I said.

"You are employed by the Board of Trustees and empowered to act on their behalf." He glanced at Haller for confirmation.

"Baron," Haller said. "It doesn't make any difference how you say it. He'll do what he wants to."

"Well, we will need a contract spelling out the parameters of the job, I think," Morton said.

"Sure," I said.

Haller made the sound in his throat again.

"I'll have the corporate counsel draft up something," Morton said.

"Fine," I said. "Are you the one I talk with when I need some access, or whatever?"

"If you'll come by the University, I'll introduce you to our President," Morton said. "He will be more effective in seeing that you get what you need."

The waiter came with the bill, and Morton discreetly signed it.

"Perhaps you could meet me at the President's office tomorrow," Morton said, "and we can talk about details and meet President Cort."

"What excitement," I said.

2

President Adrian Cort was a tall guy with a big Adam's apple and very energetic eyes. He told me I'd have full access to any information or facility I needed at the University, though he hoped I would find no need to be intrusive, and that the students and Coach Dunham both would be treated respectfully. I promised to do my best. He asked if I wanted someone to show me around the campus, and I said I'd rather wander on my own. Then we all said good bye. Morton and Cort called each other Baron and Adrian.

Alone at last, I strolled over toward the campus police station, walking extra softly in case Coach Dunham was in the area. From a cop at the desk I got a map of the campus, and took a one-hour stroll of orientation. Taft University occupies about forty acres west of Boston in a town called Walford. It had grown rapidly since the Second World War and the core campus of ivy-covered brick buildings had been extensively augmented with a variety of architectural styles that blended like pieces from different puzzles. The dominant feel was of brutish slabs and confusion.

I found the Taft Daily Collegian in the Student Union Building on the second floor, looking out over the long narrow quadrangle that led to the angular glass and granite library. It was early afternoon. The thaw had departed and the hard sun was without warmth as it glinted on the snowy campus.

The newspaper office was busy. It looked like a small daily newspaper office, which it was, except that the staff was younger. A young woman wearing pink Reeboks directed me to the sports department in the far corner of the room, where three desks were pushed together to define a sort of horseshoe space underneath sports glossies stuck to the wall with map tacks. Most of the photographs had curled up around the single tack that held them. At one of the desks a young blond kid with a ragged crew cut was working on an Apple word processor. He wore jeans and a white shirt buttoned to the neck and he kept typing when I arrived at his desk. I consulted the list of names that President Cort had given me. Actually Cort hadn't given me the list. He'd spoken to his secretary and she had given it to me.

"Barry Ames?" I said.

The kid didn't look up. He kept typing, his eyes on the screen, but he paused long enough to raise his right hand for a moment and waggle it at me in a gesture that said, *wait*. He continued typing for maybe another full minute while I waited. Then he paused and looked up.

"Who was it you wanted?" he asked.

"Barry Ames," I said.

"That's me," he said. "Sorry to put you on hold like that, but when you're hot, you like to get it down before you lose it."

"Certainly," I said. "My name is Spenser, and the University has asked me to look into the question of point shaving by your basketball team."

"Are you a cop?"

"Private," I said.

"Holy shit, a private eye?"

"You wrote the column in which the allegation about point shaving was made, Barry?" It was the oldest of cop tricks. Use the guy's first name when you talk to him. He doesn't know yours, puts him slightly on the defensive.

"Why do you want to know?" Barry said.

"Because I want to know where you heard the rumor."

"That's privileged," Barry said.

"Barry, I'm too old to listen to horse shit. You made an allegation of criminal behavior based on hearsay. That in itself is irresponsible, maybe libelous."

"And maybe I want to talk to my lawyer," Barry said. Calling him by his first name had really softened him up.

"Let me put this another way," I said. "You printed a rumor that your team was shaving points. What did you expect would happen next?"

"That someone would investigate, for crissake," Barry was outraged.

"Right," I said.

Barry opened his mouth, and then paused, and then did a smart thing: he closed it.

I nodded encouragingly.

"Well, I still can't tell you my sources," Barry said.

"Is it a reliable source?" I said.

"It was a girl who dated one of the team guys."

"She should know," I said.

"She didn't say she knew. She just said she'd heard some-body sort of hint at it, you know, joking."

"Who was she dating?"

Barry shook his head. "I won't tell you. I'm not going to get her in trouble."

"Why would she get in trouble?" I said.

Barry shook his head some more.

"At the moment no one's talking about prosecuting on this thing, but if they do, and your rumor is correct, then you're going to get asked this question again under the threat of a contempt citation," I said. "Then it's grown up time, kid."

"You think I'm a kid and a kid doesn't know shit, don't you," Barry said.

"Exactly," I said.

A number of Barry's colleagues had gathered silently about during this interplay. None of them seemed to be rooting for me.

"Whyn't you get off his case, Mister," said a young woman with very large pink-rimmed glasses.

"You happen to know the source of his rumor?" I said.

"No, but if I did, I wouldn't tell you."

I looked at the rest of the kids, slowly, one at a time. Nobody said anything.

"What's too bad," I said, "is you've fastened on to the

wrong principle. The heart of the business is not protecting your sources. It's spreading the truth."

None of them said anything except one in the back, who said, "Yeaa!" And another kid said, "It's Lou Grant."

Then a girl giggled and three or four others laughed. It is hard to remain dignified when being laughed at by a group of adolescents. I succeeded, however. I left without giving them the finger.

3

The "Taft Basketball Program" looks like *Life* magazine. It's in full color. It has biographies of all the players on both sides, pictures of everybody, individual statistics, and a history of the rivalry, which was Georgetown on a program Cort's secretary had given me. I had it rolled up and stuck in my left hip pocket when I drifted into the Taft field house and took a seat in the empty stands above the basketball court, put my feet up on the seats in front of me and spread out to watch the Taft Falcons practice. They were running switch drills in opposite corners of the floor under a couple of assistant coaches, and the head coach, Dixie Dunham, moved back and forth, commenting, correcting, reviling.

"Awright," Dunham was screaming. "Everybody around me down here." The group at the far left of the court came down to the far right end where Dunham was standing.

"Okay," Dunham said, "Dwayne, you got the ball. You pass off to Dennis, come down here, set the pick. Dennis, you go off and pick to the right. Now . . . okay, . . . Robert, what do you do?"

"Fight through the pick, Coach."

"And if you do, and Kenny thinks you're going to switch, what happens?"

There was silence for a moment.

"What the fuck happens?" Dunham's voice went up an octave.

"Both guys guarding Dennis," Dwayne said. "I roll to the basket."

"That's right. Come on, boys, is Dwayne the only one of you thinking? So what do you learn from that? What's the lesson we take. What does my system say about that?"

"We got to talk to each other," Robert said.

"Check," Dunham said, "and double check. That, Robert, is the sixty-four-thousand-dollar key. You got to talk. I don't care whether you switch, or you fight through the pick. Both of you got to know what the other guy's doing, otherwise, what? Kenny, what?"

"Two for them, Coach."

"You bet your ass." Dunham clapped his hands. "Okay, Frank, Billy, take them back, let's work on it some more."

Dunham was a legend. Certainly he was one of the two or three best college basketball coaches in the country. He was also a man of legendary temper and intensity and had sat out a five-game suspension a couple of years ago when he had gone into the stands after a heckler. Since he was six feet five and weighed maybe 225, when he went after the heckler it constituted a genuine threat. According to the program he'd been a small forward at Canisius, had averaged eight points, three assists and four rebounds a game, in a college career during which Canisius had won seventy and lost eighteen. He'd coached at Seton Hall, and then at Marquette, before he'd come to Taft, and he'd always won.

I sat quietly in the stands, one of maybe five or six people watching practice, and learning the players by comparing their pictures on last week's program with the faces on the court. In maybe twenty-five minutes I had them all memorized and attached to names.

I watched them scrimmage. I watched Dunham go into a frenzy at one point and send them all to the locker room, only to bring them back out of the locker room two minutes after they'd gone in. Finally the practice wound down and the players were shooting free throws at several baskets around the court.

Dunham turned away from this and looked up at me in the stands. Then he walked straight up the stairs from the court and over to me.

"What the fuck are you doing?" he said.

"What a clever way to ask," I said.

"I want to know what you're doing here," he said. "You're not a student."

"Now you don't know that," I said. "I might have stayed back a lot."

"Look, I'm not here to bullshit with you. You give me straight answers or I'll have your ass thrown out of this gym."

"Okay," I said. "I'm a spy from Syracuse. I've learned your secret, talk to each other on the switches."

"Listen to me, buster. And listen good," Dunham said. "I spotted you with the program half an hour ago. Why are you studying my players?"

I was laughing. " 'Listen to me, buster, and listen good'?" I said. "For crissake, Dixie."

Dunham glared at me for five seconds and then his face began to crease into a slowly widening grin.

"Shit," he said. "I talk that way all the time."

I shook my head.

Dunham said, "I still want to know what you're doing here." His face was mixed laughter and anger. "And I can still by God kick your ass if I have to."

I was still laughing, though it had calmed some and I kept it inside where it only made a murmur in my chest.

"Not if you fight like you talk," I said.

It is hard to be a tough guy when the intended victim is laughing at you. Dixie wasn't used to being laughed at. He wasn't quite sure what to do. The fact that he was half laughing too tended to compromise his position.

"Look," I said, and then I couldn't resist it, "and look good," I said. And this time Dunham laughed, before I did. I tried again. "Dixie," I said, "what I'm doing here takes some explanation. If you'll stop yelling at me and sit down and listen you'll learn a lot."

Dixie stared at me for a bit and then said, "I got to get these kids showered and out of here. I'll meet you for a drink in an hour."

"Okay."

"Local place, the Lancaster Tap," Dunham said. "On College Ave."

"Saw it when I drove in today," I said.

Dunham looked at his watch. "Be there about six," he said, and turned away and marched down to the court and across it and into the corridor on the far side. The team ended practice the minute he entered the corridor and trailed in behind him. A couple of undergraduates, one of them female, began picking up the basketballs. It had been a long time since I played. But I could remember the feel of the ball, the control as you bounced it, your hand knowing the ball would come back and when and where, bouncing it again in control, pulling up, the ball resting mostly on the fingers, the shot, the arc, just as your hand had specified. *Swish* . . . Well, sometimes swish. Often, *Clang.*

4

Dixie was glaring at me again, across a scarred table in a booth at the Lancaster Tap. I had a draft beer, Dixie had a large Coke. Between us were menus. On the table top in front of me was carved RP + JH. The table top was covered with initials, but RP + JH was carved deeper, and looked more permanent.

Dixie was holding the large Coke in his right hand. He leveled his right forefinger at me.

"I'm here to tell you that's bullshit," Dixie said. "Not one of those boys would do that to me. Not one ever has and not one ever will."

I nodded. On the walnut paneled walls of the pub were pictures of Taft teams and players. There was a prominent picture of Dixie with the National Championship team.

"University rules for eligibility are a two point oh average. Mine is two point three. Every player graduates with his class. Every one. Kids know that once they've been in this program, they're part of this program for the rest of their lives. You unnerstand that? Whenever the Trail Blazers are in town, Troy Murphy comes over, helps out at practice, sits on the bench during a game. Still calls me Coach. When the Pistons cut Stevie Scott, who'd he call? I got him an assistant's job with Rollie at Villanova, one phone call."

A little of Dixie's Coke slopped over the edge of his glass. He put the glass down, wiped his hand with a napkin.

"This isn't a bunch of free-lance schoolyard assholes, Jack," Dixie said. "This is a team. This is a system. Greatest system ever devised to play this game. No way, you hear me? No way anybody is going to betray that system, no fucking way they're going to turn their backs on their team. No way any of those boys would turn his back on me."

Dixie had his intimidate-the-referee glare locked on me. I said, "I guess you don't think they're shaving points, Dixie."

"You are out of line, Buddy Boy." Dixie turned up the voltage on his stare. "And if I hear that kind of talk out of you or anyone else you're going to answer to me. You unnerstand me?"

I drank a little beer, wiped my mouth politely with the back of my hand, and smiled pleasantly.

"Dixie," I said, "establishing the truth of this point shaving stuff will require that I keep running in to you for a while. It's going to be a lot easier if we clear up something now. You're a big strong guy, and you're probably in shape. But I've been doing this most of my life and if we have a fight I will put you in the hospital."

Dixie stared at me without speaking, which was a relief. The Lancaster Tap was only half full. There were faculty-looking people having an early dinner, and a few parents with children dining out family style. It was the kind of place that would fill up later as the college kids came in to drink. There was only one booth full so far, at the opposite corner of the room. Drinking tequila with a Corona chaser, the kids were relatively subdued. As their ranks swelled I assumed they'd get noisier.

Dixie said, "How many times your nose been broken?"

"Several," I said.

The waitress came over to our table. She looked like Knute Rockne.

"You want to order, Coach?"

Dixie shook his head. "Not yet, Lila."

"That scar tissue around your eyes?" Dixie said.

I nodded.

"You used to fight."

I nodded.

"Any good?"

I nodded.

"Ever fight anybody I ever heard of?"

"Joe Walcott, once," I said. "In the Garden. He was way past it, and I was just coming along. They threw me in to give Joe an easy one."

"And?"

"It's one of the times my nose got busted."

"Did he have an easy fight?"

"Easier than I did," I said.

28

"How much you weigh when you were fighting?" Dixie said.

"Hundred ninety-two."

"How much you weigh now?"

"Two oh one."

"Stayed in shape," Dixie said.

"Yeah."

"I fight it all the time. I'm down to two twenty-five now, but it's a struggle."

I nodded. Dixie picked up his menu and began to study it. I looked at mine.

"Mixed grill's good here," Dixie said.

I nodded. The waitress returned and took out her order book.

"Mixed grill, Coach?" she said.

"You bet, Lila, and another Coke."

She wrote it down eagerly and looked at me like I shouldn't dawdle. I ordered a club sandwich.

Lila lumbered off with the orders.

"You think I didn't see the column in the *Collegian?* Dumb ass kid writes it, what's his name?"

"Barry Ames," I said.

"Yeah, *Ames' Games* he calls it. Thinks he's Roger Angell."

"Most people aren't."

"This jerk isn't," Dixie said.

"So you knew there was talk of point shaving," I said. "You talk to the players?"

"I told them, 'Boys, anyone says that to you, you let me know, and I'll nail his ass up on the door of my office.' "

"You didn't ask them if it was so?"

"I tole you," Dixie said. "It ain't so."

"Dixie," I said, "somebody's got to ask them."

Dixie tilted his head back and let the ice cubes drain from his glass into his mouth. He crunched them with his teeth and rolled the fragments around in his mouth for a minute and then talked around the ice.

"We beat Syracuse Monday and we take the Conference championship. The playoffs come up in another week. Our first eight are as good as anybody's and we got one legitimate all-American. We don't get hurt and we could go the whole way. We don't have the stud in the middle, but Dwayne offsets that considerably."

Lila came back and slapped a green salad down in front of Dixie. It was sloshed with orange-colored dressing. Dixie swallowed his ice.

"You mind?" he said.

I shook my head and Dixie began to eat the salad. He acted like it was good.

"You figure that a point shaving investigation, even if it turns out to be groundless, will screw these kids' heads up," I said.

Dixie put his fork down and looked up from his salad.

"You know goddamned well it will," he said.

"I don't suppose they could shave points without you knowing it," I said.

Dixie snorted. Lila came with his mixed grill. There was a lamb chop, a kidney, a sausage, two strips of bacon, and a small minute steak. On the side was a large mound of french fries and a saucer of cubed carrots. Dixie sprinkled half a cellar of pepper on the carrots. Lila put my club sandwich in front of me. Her body language suggested that she found me unworthy to eat with the coach.

"Nobody's saying they're losing games, Dixie. Just beating the spread."

"You stay away from those boys, Spenser. You stay out of my gym, you stay away from my kids. Not one of them will talk to you."

"Because you told them not to."

"Because I told them not to. We've worked too hard to have you screw up our season now with some harebrained dip shit investigation so you can make a few bucks off the University."

"I can't do it, Dixie."

Dixie was silent for a while. The room was filling up. All the spots at the bar were full and most of the booths. The people at the bar were mostly Walford townies. The booths were full of college kids.

"Spenser, I swing a lot of weight around here," Dixie said. "You keep pressing this thing and I'll use some of it."

"Okay if I finish my sandwich," I said.

That was as far as I got with Dixie Dunham. I finished my club sandwich. He finished his mixed grill. He paid and when we left in silence I knew nothing I hadn't known when I came in. Maybe a little less.

5

"Why not talk with the best player," Susan said. We were in my kitchen, Susan sipping coffee at my counter while I was attempting johnny cake for the third time, trying to get the batter thick enough to form cakes on the griddle.

"Because the coach can intimidate him less?"

"Maybe. Have they got a best player?"

"Dwayne Woodcock," I said.

"If he disobeys the coach what would be the punishment?"

"He doesn't play."

"And if he doesn't play does the team go down the tubes, or whatever revolting sports cliché fits?"

"The team suffers," I said. "Don't shrinks use clichés?"

"It would not be appropriate," Susan said and smiled at me as Mephistopheles might have smiled at Faust.

"Worth a try," I said. The johnny cake had been on the

griddle nearly ten minutes and was holding its shape, although it had spread out to be a bigger cake than I had in mind. I edged the spatula under it and when it was loose I flipped it carefully. The shape held.

"What are those doughballs you're cooking?" Susan said.

I shook my head sadly. "You Jewesses know nothing about honest down-home cooking," I said. "This is johnny cake, rich in history and tradition, favored by goyim in this part of the country for three hundred years."

Susan shrugged. "Vot do day know from fency cooking?" she said.

"I seem to remember that punch line in slightly different form," I said.

"I destroyed the alliteration," she said.

I pressed down on the johnny cake with the spatula. It did not sizzle. I slid it onto a plate and put it on the counter in front of Susan. I spread on a bit of butter and splashed on some dark amber Vermont maple syrup. I cut a piece for her and held it out.

"Take a bite," I said. "Learn something."

She nibbled it off the fork with a bright flash of teeth and chewed thoughtfully.

"Fried mush?" she said.

"Well, maybe a distant cousin," I said. "It's white cornmeal, mostly. Originated with the Indians."

"Can I have some lox with it," Susan said.

Susan managed to eat three johnny cakes, without lox, and I put away four, and two cups of coffee. Susan was wearing the white silk peignoir I braved Victoria's Secret to buy her for Christmas. She had no makeup on and I could tell what she'd looked like when she was a little girl. Except when she looked at me. The eyes were not those of a little girl. The eyes had seen life intimately and clearly.

"Gee," I said, "that robe seems to fall open very revealingly."

"Must be a design flaw," Susan said.

"Well, I certainly wouldn't have bought it if I'd known it was a second," I said.

"The thought of you in Victoria's Secret is heart warming, though," Susan said.

"I blushed," I said.

"Good to know you can," Susan said and got up and started putting on her makeup. I cleaned up breakfast and went to shower and shave.

Two hours later, with the johnny cake still sticking to my ribs, I fell into step across the Taft Quadrangle with Dwayne Woodcock. At six feet nine and 255 pounds Dwayne was the premier power forward in the country; he was also probably the number one pick in the NBA draft next year, and, according to the papers, a fair head case. Most men his size played center in college and switched to forward in the pros. The Taft center in fact was six foot seven, but Dwayne had made that condition when he came to Taft. He would be the power forward, giving him a four-year start on his pro position. Walking beside him was walking in the shade.

"Dwayne Woodcock?" I said.

He looked down at me silently and, after a moment, nodded.

"My name is Spenser. I need to talk with you for a moment."

"Know who you are, man."

"You on your way to class?"

Woodcock smiled and shook his head. "Breakfast."

"Good, mind if I join you?"

"Coach says I ain't supposed to talk with you," Dwayne said. There was no apology in his voice, or embarrassment. He was just reporting a fact to me.

"You always do what Coach says?"

"Don't do what nobody says, man. Do what Dwayne Woodcock says." Again the smile, genuine, but not friendly, condescending, as if to say he would overlook the fact that I was a short old white guy. It was probably hard not to seem condescending if you were Dwayne's size. You looked down from above the everyday world.

"So what does Dwayne Woodcock say about having breakfast with me?" I said.

"Free country, man, you want to walk along, okay with me."

As we walked across the campus a hundred people said hello to Dwayne. He was friendly but regal.

"So what you want to talk about, man?"

"Didn't Coach tell you?"

Dwayne smiled again. "Naw. Coach don't do a lot of telling. He just say stay the fuck away from you and not to talk with you."

"What happens if you do talk with me?"

"Me? Nothing."

"How about somebody else?" I said.

" 'My way or highway,' Coach always say."

"How come nothing happens to you?"

"Man, don't you know nothing? Coach wants that final

four so bad, he eat shit to get there. I don't play, he don't get it."

"Well, I'm a detective and the University has hired me to see if there's any truth to the rumors of point shaving."

Dwayne frowned down at me.

"You what?" he said. And I realized I'd gone too fast for him.

"I'm a private detective," I said. I'd feed it to him in small bits.

"Like fucking Magnum, PI?"

"Just like him, except I do it in Boston."

"What kind of wheels you got, man?"

"I'm driving a Jeep for the winter," I said. "Love that four by four." I also drove it in the spring and summer and fall and would drive it for a number of seasons to come.

"You carrying, man?"

"Sure." I opened my coat to let him see the Browning. "The University hired me."

"The University," Dwayne said. "This place? You working for this place?"

"Un huh. They heard that there was point shaving going on."

"Point shaving? They hired you to investigate fucking point shaving?"

"Yeah. Article awhile ago in the college paper about it. You see it?"

Dwayne shook his head. "No, man. I never read that shit."

We reached one of the campus dining rooms and went in. It was in a lovely Georgian brick building with a big, small-paned picture window that looked out onto the quadrangle. Inside was mostly white walls and quarry tile. Dwayne had four fried eggs, over easy, two orders of bacon, home fries, four pieces of white toast, two large orange juices, and two containers of milk. I had coffee. Regular, two sugars. I would have had decaf but I didn't want Dwayne to think I was a sissy. The dining room was nearly full, but Dwayne led me to a section marked Faculty Only where there were plenty of seats. We sat at a table for four and Dwayne spread his food out over most of it.

"So, man, what you want to talk about?"

"There's a rumor that some of the players on the Taft basketball team are getting paid off for shaving points," I said. "Can you tell me anything about that?"

"How come you talking to me, man?"

"Because I know that Dixie told his players not to talk with me and I figured maybe you'd be the only one with balls enough to do it anyway."

"Dwayne Woodcock talk to whoever he fucking wants," Dwayne said.

"What I figured," I said. "So what do you think?"

"Nobody throwing no games, man," Dwayne said.

"I know. But are they keeping the score down so that someone can beat the point spread?"

Dwayne shook his head. "No chance, man."

"Would you know it if they were?"

"Shit, man, I know everything going on out there. Dwayne Woodcock born playing this game, you know? Who say we dogging it?"

37

"Just a rumor, printed in the college paper."

"Who start the rumor?"

"Some guy was kidding about it in front of his girlfriend, or so they say at the paper."

"School paper?"

"Yeah, the *Taft Collegian*."

"Shit, they don't matter."

I shrugged.

"Who the girlfriend?" Dwayne said.

"They didn't know."

"Who you talk to over that newspaper?"

"Kid named Barry Ames." Dwayne could find out easily enough. I might as well earn points by telling him. I liked his interest.

Dwayne shook his head. "Never heard of him."

We were quiet for a moment while I drank a little coffee and Dwayne ate.

"So, maybe you wasting your time here. Broad probably didn't understand what the guy was joking about. Probably some kind of basketball joke and she don't get it."

"Maybe," I said.

"You keep hanging around, man, annoying us, everybody gonna get pissed off at you."

I nodded. "Happens a lot," I said.

"You understand what I'm saying to you, man? Dwayne Woodcock don't blow smoke."

"That's not what Smoke tells everybody," I said.

Dwayne gave me the hard schoolyard stare.

"You fucking with me, man?"

"Yeah."

"You fucking with Dwayne Woodcock, you fucking with the wrong man."

"Who would be the right one?" I said.

Dwayne had no food left. He surveyed the table to make sure he hadn't missed anything. Then he stood up. Looking down at me, he said, "You remember what I tell you, man. You keep snooping around, you going to wish you hadn't." Then he turned and stalked off.

I gave his back a grim look as he went.

"Oh yeah," I said.

6

In the spirit of experiment I checked out the coeds as I
walked across campus and concluded that I was still able
to respond to twenty-year-old women, but preferred them
older. At the President's office I consulted with Ms. Merriman, the President's secretary. She, for instance, was
older.

"I need a copy of Dwayne Woodcock's transcript, academic record, whatever; any documentation on him that
the University has."

Ms. Merriman frowned.

"It's not policy to show material like that without the
student's authorization."

Ms. Merriman was very trim and well dressed. She was
maybe forty-five with a tight body and short black very
curly hair. She wore an engagement ring on the wrong
hand and no wedding ring. Her dark blue tailored suit

must have set her back about $600. She treated me like some sort of distinguished barbarian, like the king of a very important cannibal nation who still wore a bone in his nose.

"We'll find a way," I said.

"You feel it's necessary?"

"I have no idea," I said. "Detective stuff doesn't really lend itself to 'policy' decisions. Detective stuff is pretty much weaseling around and finding out anything you can and then sitting down afterward and figuring out what's worth knowing."

"I don't know. I don't feel right about it."

"Why don't you consult with President Cort."

Her eyes widened. "Well, he's in an important meeting right now . . ."

"Something crucial?" I said. "Like whether full professors should be required to show up at all?"

"Mr. Spenser, please."

"Or whether a book that sells can be considered favorably in the course of a tenure decision."

"Mr. Spenser. Running a large university like this one is a serious administrative challenge. President Cort's time is as important as any executive's."

"I rest my case," I said. "But let's not argue. Let's compromise. Call up somebody and get me Dwayne's file."

"President Cort did say you should have our full support."

I nodded encouragement.

"All right, these are unusual circumstances. I'll call the registrar's office."

"God," I said, "you're beautiful when you're decisive."

"Oh, please," she said. But she went to the phone and called. In about fifteen minutes an undergraduate-looking kid showed up with a manila envelope and handed it to Ms. Merriman. She opened it, saw that it was what she'd ordered, closed it again and handed it to me.

"I hope you'll return that straight here once you are through with it."

"Right here," I said. I gave her the complete smile. The one where my eyes crinkle at the corners and two deep dimples appear in my cheeks. Women often tore off their underwear and threw it at me when I gave them the complete smile.

Ms. Merriman didn't.

I left the office and found the library and settled into a yellow oak chair with arms, near a window in the reading room.

According to the transcript of his grades Dwayne was a B – , C + student. He was on full scholarship, had been before the Dean for two incidents of fighting and a charge of larceny. The charge, apparently brought by another student, was dropped. There were several evaluations of Dwayne from his academic counselor, a woman named Madelaine Roth, Ph.D. The evaluations all stressed Dwayne's native intelligence despite his impoverished background. According to the transcript Dwayne had grown up in the Bedford-Stuyvesant section of Brooklyn, had a mother and four sisters, all on welfare. No father.

I settled back a little deeper in the chair and put my feet up on the window ledge and watched the students move across the campus. Most of them were noisy and oddly dressed and looked hung over. A few were carefully dressed, some of the girls wore eye shadow, many of the girls wore very tight jeans. I rolled my head a little on my neck to loosen my shoulders. The sun coming through the windows fell warmly on my back.

Dwayne had seemed too easy to talk to. He'd seemed too interested in who knew what. Or maybe I just thought so because I wanted to. Because it would be a place to start. Either way the transcript didn't tell me much. I swung my feet off the window sill and stood and brought the transcript back to Ms. Merriman.

7

Lennie Seltzer still had the back booth in the Yorktown Tavern on Mass. Ave. He was normally there from ten in the morning till four in the afternoon, sipping beer, reading newspapers, taking bets, getting up to use the pay phone on the back wall next to the rest rooms. His hair was shiny slick and parted in the middle. His face was pale and smooth. His three-piece suit had a fine windowpane plaid in pale blue running through the gray sharkskin fabric. He was getting plumper as time passed and a lot of the plumpness settled as he sat each day sipping beer. On the table in front of him were the *New York Daily News*, the *Globe* and the *Herald*. To his right, on the table against the wall, a portable computer screen stared grayly at me.

Lennie was tipping his beer glass delicately toward his lips when I slid into the booth opposite him. He held the glass with his thumb and first two fingers. His ring finger and pinkie were extended. He drank only a little of the beer and set the glass back down.

"Spenser," he said and made a gesture to the bartender.

"Lennie, you've moved into the age of tomorrow," I said.

The bartender brought over a shot of whiskey and a draft beer in a tall thick glass. I hated a shot of whiskey, but every time I saw Lennie he ordered it for me. Over the years the shot had upgraded. Now it was Irish whiskey, at least. When I first knew him it was Old Thompson.

"Computer's a wonderful thing, buddy. Got all my files in there, plug it into a phone jack, dial up everything I need. I have to close quickly, I just unplug it, fold it up and off I go."

"You think it's immoral, Lennie, to take a nap during the day?"

Lennie shook his head. "Hell, no. I take one every afternoon. I get home about four thirty, lie down for an hour, on my back, peaceful, get up, take a shower, couple a highballs, sets you up for the night, you know? Take the old lady to Jimmy's, maybe, Doyle's in JP, fish dinner, bottle a wine. The nap's the key to it."

"I need to know the line on every Taft basketball game this year," I said. "And the final score."

Lennie looked at me for a little longer than was comfortable.

"You think somebody's been dicking with the spread over there?"

"I don't know. I'm trying to find out."

"You know something you got to tell me," Lennie said. "It's business, you know. I mean if something's not kosher I could get flushed on one of those games."

"I know. All I got now is rumors. Everybody connected with the team denies it. I come up with anything, I'll tell you. In confidence."

"Confidence is part of being a bookie, buddy, you know that. I don't talk about anything I don't need to."

"Can you get me the line?" I said. "I can get the scores from the newspaper file at the library if I have to."

"You come to the right place," Lennie said. "I can get you both in about ten minutes." He tapped the gray screen. "I used to have it all on slips of paper."

"Hard to flush that thing down the toilet," I said.

"No need. Unplug it and there's nothing on me. No evidence unless they search my home and access the computer." Lennie grinned. "Besides, cops don't try too hard with me."

He turned on the machine and punched in a few codes. The screen turned black and printing came up on it in star wars green. Lennie gazed at it for a moment, took another delicate sip of beer, put the glass down carefully and punched some new keys.

Lennie reached under the table and came up with a slim, tan briefcase. He opened it, took out a yellow legal-sized pad, selected a pen from among the several that were clipped to one of the pockets. He put the pen on the table top beside the pad, closed the briefcase, put it back under the table and punched some more keys. This time he copied down the information on display, punched some more, wrote some more. After about fifteen minutes, Lennie had a couple of columns of dates and numbers on his pad. He put the cap on his pen, put it down, punched away the

46

display, turned off the terminal, and the computer screen went gray.

"Okay," Lennie said. "This column the date of the game. This column the point spread. This column the score."

A bartender came over with a fresh glass of beer for Lennie and took away the empty glass. Lennie took the cap off his pen and ran down the columns of numbers like an accountant scanning a tax form.

"Here," he said, and put a check mark next to one of the dates. "And here," he said, "and here." When he was through there were six games checked.

"Here's the games where they beat the spread," Lennie said. "Could happen, and be legit. Basketball's hard to handicap."

"I know," I said. "The Nets beat the Celtics at the Garden this year."

Lennie nodded vigorously. "Exactly," he said.

I finished off my whiskey and stared at the beer. My head was beginning to feel thick and my face felt a little separate from the world, as if there were a transparent layer of insulation on it. Be a nice title for a novel, I thought, *Boilermakers in the Afternoon.* I took the sheet of yellow paper and folded it and put it into my shirt pocket.

"You still with that Jewish broad?" Lennie said.

"Susan," I said. "Susan Silverman."

"You gonna get married?"

"You never know," I said.

"You marry a Jew, and you and me be like lunsmen."

"Oy vay," I said.

8

I had to promise Ms. Merriman the right of first refusal on my sex life, but I managed to get her to call the athletic director on my behalf and tell him that the President wanted me to have tapes of six Taft basketball games. The A.D. told her that Dixie would have a fit if he found out, and Ms. Merriman said that Coach Dunham worked for the University and not the other way around and should he hear of it and complain he should be directed to her.

"What if Dixie calls you up and yells at you," I said.

"We are not here to service the basketball team," Ms. Merriman said.

"Good to know," I said.

"Yes," Ms. Merriman said.

By early afternoon I was lying on Susan's bed in her place watching the tape of late January's game between

Taft and Seton Hall, on her VCR. Taft had been favored by seven and had won by three. I tried to watch away from the ball, at who was blocking out, who was rebounding, who was tight up on his man in the pressure man-to-man that Dixie insisted on in the age of zone. It's hard to watch basketball that way, even if you've played, even if you know the game. We are conditioned by television so to watch the ball. We tend not to notice weak side help, and who doubles down in the middle.

I watched the game through once without seeing anything that got my attention. This was going to take awhile. I watched the game through again, focusing for a while on one player, then another. The films were scouting films, not television, so they showed more of the court and spent less time fixed on the ball, and they didn't cover the time outs or half time, so the films only took a little more than an hour to watch. By three in the afternoon I'd watched Seton Hall twice and had concluded that I needed help. Also lunch.

For help I called a guy I knew named Tommy Christopher. He'd played at DePaul and then with the Celtics and had coached for six years at Providence College. When he was playing he'd had a good business manager and now Tommy mostly played golf, and a little poker, did a few commercials, and worked out at the Harbor Health Club, where he and I and Hawk now and then did some steam together.

I called the Harbor Health Club and left a message for Tommy to call me at Susan's.

"What's going on?" Henry said. "An afternooner?"

"More deadly than the adder's sting," I said, "is the foul mouth of an unusually short gym owner."

"I'm not unusually short," Henry said. "I'm just muscular for my height."

"Hell, yes," I said. "If you weighed twenty pounds you'd be just right."

We hung up and I looked into lunch. Susan seemed to me the most beautiful and intelligent woman I'd ever met. She had great warmth and compassion and humor. She had a top-of-the-line body, and strength of character and an appropriate sexual appetite. But as a larder keeper she ranked somewhat below Old Mother Hubbard. In her refrigerator was a plastic bag of raw cauliflower, a half empty carton of Dannon tropical fruit yogurt, a single round of whole wheat Syrian bread, which was unwrapped and had begun to fossilize, a jar of mayonnaise and a lemon. In her cupboard was a package of Rye Wafers, a jar of instant decaf, a loaf of whole wheat bread and, shamefully, a jar of all-natural peanut butter.

"Ah ha," I said. I boiled some water, made two peanut butter sandwiches, poured the hot water over a spoonful of decaf crystals, stirred twice, put the spoon in the sink and settled down at Susan's counter. Bon appétit.

While I was enjoying my second sandwich, Tommy Christopher called.

"Henry says you want to see me," Tommy said. "Said you needed help. I said you needed more help than I could give you."

"Susan's working on that," I said. "I need you to watch some basketball with me."

I explained what I had and what I wanted and Tommy said he'd come over.

"How many games are we going to watch?" Tommy said.

"Six," I said.

"I'll bring some beer," Tommy said.

Susan got through with her last patient at six and came upstairs from her office to find Tommy and me sprawled on her bed staring at the tapes. I had a notebook and wrote down what Tommy said.

"See that," Tommy was saying, "run it again. See Woodcock, he olés the forward on the weak side, and the guy comes in and takes the rebound and jams it."

"This is what you do all day?" Susan said. "I thought you were out fighting crime."

I hit the pause button. "Things are not what they seem," I said.

"I've heard that," Susan said.

9

We stopped watching after another hour that night and ate Chinese food that Susan had called out for and I had fetched. Then Tommy went home, and I stayed. Two nights in a row. Zowie.

Friday Tommy came in at nine and we settled in on the bed again and watched Taft against Pittsburgh.

"There," Tommy said. "Tubbs didn't fill the lane on the break, see on the left. So Davis takes it to the basket and draws the defender and has no place to lay it off and gets stuffed. He shouldn't have gone up in the air until he knew he had something to do with the ball, but it's reasonable to expect somebody to be filling that left hand lane. Then they'd have had a three on two." I scribbled in my notebook.

"Woodcock again," Tommy said. "You can see that play's set up for a pick. Stop, run it back. See the guard with the ball. He's yelling out a play. Okay, see, he comes out of the corner, loops around the perimeter, looking for the pick, and Woodcock is slow setting it. So Davis's got to back off and set up something else, and, see, they don't make the forty-five-second clock."

Benefiting from yesterday's learning experience, I had laid in a supply of smoked turkey sandwiches from the Mt. Auburn Market, and at noon we broke for a couple of them, each, with Cape Cod potato chips and Sam Adams beer; and back to the tapes.

"See, there's the same play that Woodcock fucked up this morning against Pittsburgh," Tommy said. "Look at this pick. Jesus Christ!"

I was sitting up on the edge of the bed so I wouldn't nod off.

"Okay, now here's another one. Run this back about ten seconds. Okay, there. Okay. It's Woodcock again. Simple give and go. The guard, what's his name, Davis, is going to find Woodcock in the corner, and then, the simplest play in basketball, he cuts for the basket. See. He loses his man. Amazing how often it works. He's free, the Temple center is too far toward Woodcock. And Woodcock holds the ball."

"Did he see him?"

"Spenser," Tommy said. "They've run that give and go twenty times in these tapes. They've run it twenty thousand times in their lives. Guy in the corner knows, *knows* there's going to be a cutter."

I turned it back and ran it again.

"See," Tommy said. "The minute he gets the ball, he

dips his shoulders like he's going to drive. He never looks for the cutter, even though he's double teamed, and Taft has to pull it out and start over."

"Wouldn't any coaching staff see this reviewing the films?"

"If they were looking for it. And, face it, if you're coaching Taft, you're not looking for Dwayne Woodcock as a key to your loss, you know. He's probably the best player in the country."

"But if you did notice it," I said.

"You write it off as 'Dwayne's a known head case anyway.' Passing off is not the strongest part of his game."

"And," I said, "unless you see it as part of a pattern, and you were looking for the pattern, it wouldn't seem like anything but a break in concentration."

Tommy nodded. The tapes rolled on.

At four fifteen in the afternoon we finished the last tape.

"I say it's Woodcock," Tommy said. "And he's smart about it. He's not missing lay ups and foul shots. He's just slowing down their game, keeps the score a few baskets lower. And he's so good that if they are in danger of losing because of that he can explode for five hoops in a row. I mean there isn't anyone in college ball that can stop him when he makes up his mind to drive."

"What he's doing is keeping his teammates from scoring as much," I said.

Tommy nodded approvingly. "Exactly," he said. "That's exactly what he does. Misses a pass, sets a sloppy pick, doesn't roll to the basket, doesn't block out underneath, is a step slow filling the lane. Usually the result is that another guy doesn't score."

"And," I said, "since they're winning most of these games, no one is questioning the outcome. Anyone else?"

"Maybe number eleven, what's his name."

"Davis," I said.

"There's nothing here I can swear to," Tommy said. "Can't take shit like this into court, but Woodcock, for sure. Maybe the other kid."

Tommy and I had one more beer and talked about the kinds of picks Wayne Embry used to set, and Wes Unseld. Then he went home and I packed the tapes back to the A.D.'s office at Taft.

It had gotten dark as I drove home. The commuter traffic was headed the other way. Susan was having dinner with friends tonight. I was playing a Matt Dennis tape in my car and planning supper. Fresh crabmeat, maybe, sautéed in olive oil and white wine with red and yellow and green peppers, and mushrooms, and served over rice. Or I could pound out some chicken thigh cutlets and marinate them in lemon juice and tarragon and a drop of virgin olive oil and cook them on my new Jenn-Air indoor grill. I could have a couple more beers while I waited for them to marinate, and I could eat them with some broccoli and maybe boiled red potatoes. I'd put a honey mustard dressing on the broccoli. Or maybe some tortellini . . . I parked in front of my place on Marlborough Street and went in. It was still and a little close. I opened the living room window a crack and ran through my choices again. I opted for the crab. Later there was a movie on cable, *Zulu*, one of my favorites. And the Celtics were playing Milwaukee, if I could stand any more basketball. The apartment echoed with a kind of spacious stillness, and the smell of spring evening seeped in through the open window. I'd been alone a lot in my life and I never tired of it.

"It's you, Dwayne," I said aloud. "You're shaving points."

I peeked in to see how the potatoes were doing in their pan, and shook the broccoli in its colander to get the last bits of water off.

"And shall I ruin your life by proving it?"

Nobody else said anything. So I added the crabmeat to the simmering pan and stirred it.

10

The next morning I went over to my office and typed up my notes from yesterday. I did pretty well with two fingers and some correction fluid, and by 11 A.M. I had a very convincing outline of the games in which Taft didn't make the spread, and what Dwayne Woodcock had done in each one.

It was a grand March day. The sun was bright yellow, the snow was gone, the wind still carried some chill, but around the base of the buildings, in bark mulched beds, crocuses were beginning to appear. *Nature's first green is crocus.* I had Dwayne's class schedule, and it told me he had an American History class that let out at one. I was at the door waiting when it did, but Dwayne wasn't one of the kids that came out. I strolled over to the cafeteria, where we'd had breakfast, but Dwayne wasn't there either.

I walked from the cafeteria to the President's office and fixed my sensitive blue eyes on the dread Ms. Merriman. I saw no signs of sexual tension when I did so. Odd.

"Good afternoon, Ms. Merriman."

"Mr. Spenser."

"May I call you by your first name, Ms. Merriman. We are, after all, destined to be working closely on this matter."

"Are we really," Ms. Merriman said. "My first name is June."

"June, do you suppose you could get me Dwayne Woodcock's address?"

June did not ask me my first name; probably too shy.

"Mr. Spenser," she said, "I serve this President and this university and President Cort has instructed me to help you as necessary. But I also want you to know that I disapprove personally, and very sincerely, of the degree to which you are invading the privacy of one of our students."

"Ah, June, 'tis a devious job I do. What was that address?"

"I'll call the housing office," she said. There was a little blush of red along her cheekbones. She spent maybe two minutes on the phone and when she hung up she handed me a piece of notepaper with an address on it.

"He lives off campus," June said.

I took the paper. "Thanks, June. You don't have a husband named Ward, do you?"

"I am not married," June said.

"Divorced?"

"Yes."

"Lot of that going around," I said. "Man's a fool."

"I don't believe my private life is part of this investigation, is it?"

"Good point," I said.

Dwayne Woodcock lived in a condominium complex a five-minute walk from the Taft campus. It was a cluster of pseudo-Cape Cod-looking buildings of two or three stories, asymmetrically jumbled at different heights and angles, sided with weathered shingles, with white trim and brightly colored front doors. Dwayne's was cranberry. I rang the bell and in a minute Dwayne opened the door. He was barefoot and wearing gray sweat pants. His massive upper torso was shirtless.

"What do you want, man?"

"Got something to show you, Dwayne. Invite me in."

"What you got?"

"Not on the doorstep, Dwayne, for crissake. Show a little class."

Dwayne jerked his head and stepped away from the door. I went into a small entry hall with a staircase rising right. Straight ahead was the living room. On the coffee table in front of the white couch was a half gallon carton of orange juice. To my right a twenty-five-inch television set was on. Dwayne was watching "Sonya Live in L.A." To my left in an oversized green leather armchair was a black girl with corn rowed hair wearing a large maroon silk man's bathrobe. Her legs were tucked under her. She was drinking coffee from a large mug that had a picture of Opus the penguin on it. She held the mug in both hands and looked at me without expression across the top of it.

"Hello," I said.

59

She nodded behind the mug.

Dwayne didn't introduce us. "What you got to show me," he said.

"My name's Spenser," I said to the black girl.

"Chantel," she said.

"Nice to meet you, Chantel."

"Cut the bullshit, Spenser," Dwayne said. "What you got to show me?"

I handed him my outline.

"What's this?" Dwayne said.

"Read it," I said. "Then we'll talk."

Dwayne looked at the paper. I waited. Chantel sipped her coffee. Sonya and her guests chatted on and on. I looked at Dwayne. There was something funny about the way he looked at the paper. Suddenly I realized what it was. He wasn't moving his eyes. There were three sheets stapled together. He was still looking at the top sheet and his eyes weren't moving back and forth across the page as he read.

Finally Dwayne handed the typescript to Chantel.

"Here, babe, what you think of this?" he said.

Chantel took the paper with one hand and looked at it as she continued to sip from her coffee mug.

" 'Bout you, Dwayne," she said, " 'bout some games you played this year and what you did in them."

Dwayne turned his hard look on me again. "How come you writing stuff up about me?"

I had a suspicion. "You read it, Dwayne, it should be pretty clear."

"It pretty clear to you, Chantel?" Dwayne said.

"Dwayne, you know I don't know a lot about basketball." Chantel was reading more closely. She set her coffee mug down to turn the page, flipping it over its single staple and letting it hang down from the corner. "Say you didn't get a rebound in some game against B.C."

"Hey," Dwayne said, "how come you writing that shit about Dwayne?"

"I love it when you refer to yourself in the third person," I said.

Dwayne frowned. "You gonna answer my question, man?"

"Dwayne," I said. "Can you read?"

"Dwayne Woodcock don't got to answer no bullshit questions from you, man."

"You can't, can you?" I said.

"Fuck off, man."

Dwayne was standing close to me, blocking the sun.

I ignored him and looked at Chantel. "He can't, can he, Chantel," I said.

Chantel said softly, "He can read a little. I'm trying to teach him."

"Shut up, Chantel. Don't tell this honkie motherfucker nothing."

Chantel's gaze was steady on Dwayne for a long moment. She opened her mouth and then decided not to speak and closed it. Dwayne turned toward me.

"You tell anybody 'bout this and I'm going to kill your motherfucking ass," he said.

"I shouldn't have to tell anyone, Dwayne. This is a goddamned college. You've been here four years. They should know."

"You hear what I'm saying?" Dwayne said.

"You and Chantel go over the stuff I gave you, Dwayne. It says when and how I think you shaved some points. When you've got it, and you want to talk about it, give me a call." I gave Chantel a card.

She looked at me with her steady gaze for a moment. "What you going to do?" she said. "You going to tell?"

"Never mind, Chantel. He ain't gonna do shit, he knows what's good for him." Dwayne put his hand on my shoulder to turn me toward him. I felt the little switch go that always went when people put their hands on me. I went with the direction Dwayne was trying to turn me, but I went much faster than he had in mind and as I came spinning around I brought my right arm up outside his and gave him a sharp chop with my forearm behind his elbow. With the force of my turning weight behind it, the blow slapped his arm across his chest like a loose tiller. I was right behind it and with my chest pressed against his flattened arm and my face very close to his chin, I said, "Don't make a bad mistake."

I could feel his body get rigid. I kept pressing against him. It pinned his right arm and I could feel what he was going to do before he did it.

"Hey, man," Dwayne said, "what's wrong with you?"

I looked up the nearly nine inches between my eyes and his. His eyes were soft. They weren't scared. They were hurt. I stepped away, keeping my right foot back of my left, and my left shoulder turned slightly toward Dwayne. I could feel the air going in and out of my chest in big slow breaths.

"You crazy, man," Dwayne said, "fucking with Dwayne

Woodcock? You crazy?" The voice was angry, street tough, Bed-Sty tough. But the eyes were hurt. The eyes were a kid who'd been startled and felt bad.

"No touching," I said. "You and Chantel talk and let me know." I stepped past Dwayne carefully and went out the front door and closed it softly behind me.

11

"The kid can't read," I said to Susan. "He's a senior in college, carrying a C+ average, and he can't read."

We were having dinner in Rocco's in the Transportation Building and I was halfway through a vodka martini on the rocks with a twist.

"You mentioned that," Susan said. "Twice on the ride over."

"It is outrageous," I said. "Nobody ever noticed?"

"Nobody ever cared," Susan said.

The waiter came to take our order. Susan decided on sweet and sour Thai soup and roast pheasant. I ordered black bean cake and Peking Duck.

"Isn't this the most spectacular room you've seen?" Susan said.

I nodded. "There's an academic adviser. Just for the team. Lot of major college teams have them. Try to keep the kids on time to graduate and such."

Susan nodded encouragingly as she gazed around the high-ceilinged trompe l'oeil faux art decor.

"Academic adviser says Dwayne's intellectually gifted despite an impoverished childhood."

"Could be," Susan said.

"Sure, but the kid can't goddamn read. Don't you think someone might someplace make mention of that? He's twenty-one years old and in his senior year in college and he can't read."

"You mentioned that. Who are you mad at?"

I took a pleasing swallow of my martini. More than two and I got a headache, but one before dinner was just right, sometimes.

"I'm mad at his teachers, his academic counselor, him."

"Yes," Susan said. "Him too. He knows he can't read and hasn't corrected it."

"Hard for a kid like Dwayne to admit," I said.

"Yes," Susan said. "Maybe too hard. He needs help."

"There's a girlfriend, Chantel."

"Excuse me?"

"Chantel, she says she's trying to teach him."

Susan said, "Way back, first grade, second grade, when he was trying to learn to read, he got passed over. He never broke the code."

"Meaning?"

The waiter brought the first course.

"Meaning that most of us learned to read phonetically. You can probably remember a teacher telling you to sound it out."

I nodded. The black bean cake had a slice of cob smoked ham on it, and a fried egg.

"For whatever reason, people who never learned to read never quite got the sound it out part. They know letters have sounds. Most can read a little. Words like *men*, *stop*, *rest room*, *beer*, words that they've seen so often they have become kind of pictographs. But they come to a word like, oh, *transportation*, and they are stuck. They try to make sense of the sounds a little," Susan did a halting imitation, "and then give up. They never learned the code and they never learned the rules. There are lots of rules, many of which we don't even think of."

"Like two vowels, separated by a consonant the first vowel is usually long . . . *sale*, *gale*, *pale*," I said.

"Very good," Susan said. "Or the business that *ph* is normally pronounced like *f*. If you didn't know that you'd have an awful time. Of course he could be dyslexic."

"Can you be dyslexic and be the best basketball player in the country?" I said.

"Probably not," Susan said. "Frequently, though not always, dyslexia affects your balance. A standard dyslexia diagnostic test for kids is to ask them to walk a balance beam."

"Soup good?" I said.

"Yes, taste it," Susan said. She held out a spoonful and I slurped it in. I gestured at my bean cake. Susan smiled and shook her head.

"I haven't the heart," she said.

"No wonder I love you."

The waiter came by to ask if I wished another martini. I said no.

"So," Susan said, "what are you going to do, sweet cakes?"

"Eat all my Peking Duck as soon as it arrives," I said.

"What are you going to do about Dwayne and the point stuff and the fact that he can't read?"

"I was planning on consulting you for advice," I said.

The waiter took away our plates and brought the entrées.

"What's the girlfriend like?" Susan said. "Chanteuse."

"Chantel," I said. "Hard to say. I only saw her that once and most of the time I was seeing her, Dwayne was breathing fire on my neck."

"He is, I understand, six feet nine inches tall?"

"Yes."

"And he weighs in excess of two hundred and fifty pounds?"

I nodded.

"How's your neck?" Susan said.

"I was wearing my collar stylishly up, at the time, " I said.

"Fashionable," Susan murmured, "yet practical."

I put a slice of duck on a pancake, brushed on the hoisin sauce with the scallion brush, put the scallion on top of the duck, folded the pancake over and took a bite. Not too big a bite. If I ate normally I always had my plate cleaned while Susan was still getting her knife and fork in position. Susan carefully cut a small piece of pheasant and moved it to her mouth and chewed slowly. She swallowed. I started a second pancake.

"I don't know what you should do about Dwayne," Susan said. "One option would be to do what you were hired to do."

"Report to the President that a viewing of the game films tells me that he shaved points in the following games?"

Susan nodded.

"Won't help the kid much."

"You weren't hired to help the kid."

"Kid grew up in one of the meanest ghettos in the world. He's gotten through almost four years at a major eastern university. He's going to have a pro career, unless he gets hurt, that will make him maybe a million dollars a year. Along the way he's acquired a nice girlfriend."

"And if you do what you're hired to do that all goes to hell," Susan said.

"Except maybe the girlfriend."

Susan smiled at me slowly. "That's what it really is, isn't it?" she said. "You are one of the three or four most romantic diddles in the world, and because this guy has a young woman who you think will stand by her man, you want to adopt them both."

"There's no such thing as a bad boy," I said.

"Sure," Susan said. "He ain't heavy, he's my brother." Her eyes were full of laughter, and something else, as she looked at me over the rim of her brandy alexander.

"A romantic diddle?"

"It's the first word that came to mind," she said.

"And yet you find me physically compelling."

"I find you compelling in every way," Susan said. And I knew what the something else was in her eyes.

"Even though I'm a romantic diddle?"

"Especially," Susan said, "because of that."

"So you agree that I should look into things a little more before I toot the whistle on the kid."

"I agree, I approve and, more than that, I knew before

the conversation began that you weren't going to 'toot the whistle.' "

"Nobody likes a know-it-all," I said.

Susan put her hand out and laid it on top of mine. "Somebody does," she said.

12

I was sitting in my office with my feet up, thinking about Dwayne Woodcock and Chantel and point shaving and illiteracy and the backside of the new young paralegal who'd opened an office across the hall. The door to my office was open in case the paralegal wanted to stroll down the hall. A fine-looking black-haired man with a ruddy face walked in. He was wearing pale brown boaters and starched acid-washed jeans and a green polo shirt with the collar up. His jacket was silk tweed, dark brown and nipped in at the waist. His thick black hair was longish and brushed back on each side. A gold medallion on a thick gold chain showed at his throat. On his left hand was a big ring with a blue stone that looked like a high school or college ring. His sunglasses hung against his chest on a cord.

"How ya doing," he said when he came in.

"Fine," I said. I kept one eye peeled on the hallway.

"Got a few minutes?" he said.

"Sure." The accent was New York.

"Mind if I close the door?"

I sighed. "No," I said brightly, "go ahead."

He closed it and then turned and sat down in my client chair. He was about my height and slender. His hands were square and pale with a lot of black hair on the backs. The nails were manicured. I could smell cologne. There was a yellow silk handkerchief in the breast pocket of his jacket. He had the jacket sleeves pushed up over his forearms. On the left wrist was a gold Rolex.

"Nice office," he said.

"Compared to what?"

"Compared to working out of a packing crate in Canarsie," he said. "You mind if I smoke?"

I shook my head. He took a pigskin cigarette case out of his coat pocket, and a round gold lighter. He took out a cigarette, offered the open case to me. I shook my head. He snapped the case closed, dropped it into his side pocket, snapped a flame from the lighter, put the cigarette into his mouth and lit it, automatically shielding the flame as if the wind were blowing. He took in smoke and let it out through his nose as he dropped the lighter back into the pocket with the cigarettes. Then he leaned back in the chair and stretched his feet in front of him and surveyed my office some more. He nodded approvingly.

"Nice little set up," he said.

I tried to look humble.

"Must make a pretty nice living with a set up like this."

I looked at the closed door.

I said, "I don't mean to seem impatient, but for the last hour I've been trying to get a look at the young woman across the hall and she usually walks by about this time."

He glanced over his shoulder at the closed door and then back at me, pausing a moment to figure out if he was being kidded. Then he grinned.

"Hey, pal, I never blame a man for hustling."

He took the cigarette out of his mouth oddly, with the palm facing away and the back of his hand closest to his face. He held the cigarette between his first two fingers, keeping the lighted end cupped slightly toward his palm.

"I'll make it quick," he said.

"Thank you," I said.

"We got a problem, you and me. Not the kind of problem can't be worked out. Couple of successful guys, a little good will, you scratch my back I scratch yours, everything is jake with a little effort."

I waited. He made himself even more comfortable in my client chair.

"My name is Bobby Deegan," he said.

I nodded.

"I'm in business in Brooklyn," Deegan said. "And I got some business interests up here."

I waited some more. He smoked some of his cigarette.

"Business been going good," he said, "and I'm showing a nice profit, but the interests up here are, ah . . . coming into conflict with your interests."

I leaned back on my spring chair and folded my hands across my stomach like Scattergood Baines and smiled.

Deegan smiled back at me.

"Dwayne Woodcock," he said.

"Dwayne Woodcock," I said.

We smiled happily at each other.

Outside in the corridor, through the closed door, I heard the sharp tap of high-heeled shoes walk past my door. Deegan heard it too.

"Balls," I said.

"Sorry," Deegan said.

"Always tomorrow," I said.

"With luck," Bobby Deegan said.

He let his gaze rest on me hard, steady, the hardcase stare. I waited.

After enough time Deegan laughed. "Big yard stare ain't going to do it, huh?"

"Been inside?" I said.

Bobby shrugged. It was a yes shrug. "So what are we going to do about Dwayne?" he said.

"I was thinking of teaching him to read," I said.

"He can't read?" Deegan said.

"No," I said.

Deegan shook his head and made a silent whistle. "Any other plans?"

I was getting tired of people asking me what I was going to do about Dwayne Woodcock.

"I don't know," I said. I'd read somewhere that if you were patient and didn't get mad and let people talk eventually they'd say something. I was skeptical, but I was experimenting.

Deegan looked around for an ashtray, saw one on the top of my file cabinet, stood, walked over, and stubbed out the cigarette.

"Don't smoke yourself, huh?" he said.

"Quit in 1963," I said.

"Good for you," Deegan said. "I been trying for a couple of years."

I didn't say anything.

"You're not helping," Deegan said.

"No," I said. "I'm not."

"Okay," he said. "It can go a couple of ways. One way is we give you a nice fee for deciding that Wayne isn't shaving anything but his face. The college likes that, Dwayne likes that, Coach likes that, we like it. Nobody doesn't like it." Deegan gave me a big grin.

"And the other way?"

"We put you in the ground," Deegan said. His voice was pleasant.

"Eek," I said.

"Sure, sure," Deegan said. "I know you're tough. We talked to a couple guys we know up here. But think about it. What's worth dying for here? You take Dwayne down, you ruin a kid's life that ain't got many options. And you probably get killed in the deal. Who gets hurt if you walk around it?" You get some bread for your trouble. Dwayne gets to be a big star in the NBA instead of a small time hoodlum in Bed-Sty. And who gets hurt? Team wins that should win, fans are happy. You think the college wants you to find out that there's points being shaved? Dwayne's a good kid, pal. Why fuck him up?"

"How much you willing to give me?" I said.

Deegan glanced around my office again. "Two bills," he said.

I shook my head.

"How much you want?" Deegan said.

"Two hundred thirty-eight billion," I said.

Deegan was silent for a moment, then he grinned slowly. "Well, like the old joke, we've established what you are, now we're just haggling over price."

"Be a long haggle," I said.

Deegan nodded. "Option two's looking better," he said.

We sat for a moment quietly while Deegan lit another cigarette.

"So what are you going to do?" Deegan said.

"Hell, Bobby, I don't know. I was trying to figure that out when you came in and distracted me."

"I thought you was trying to get a look at some broad's ass," Deegan said.

"That too," I said.

Deegan rose. "Okay, pal. You think about it some more, and I'll check back with you. Try not to be too fucking stupid."

"I been trying for years," I said. "Usually it doesn't work out."

Deegan laughed and walked to the door. He opened it and stopped and looked back at me.

"You know we mean it," he said.

"Sure," I said.

Deegan shrugged and started out.

"Leave the door open," I said. "I didn't hear her come back yet."

13

Maybe a minute after Deegan left, the paralegal across the hall came back from wherever she'd been. *Worth the wait.*

I put my feet up on my desk and looked at the toes of my Reeboks. *Okay.* I knew that Dwayne was shaving points for some New York guys of whom Bobby Deegan was one. Maybe Danny Davis. Deegan hadn't mentioned him, but he had no reason to. I hadn't talked to Davis. Bobby had no reason to think he was a suspect. But the kid at the school paper had said the story source was somebody's girlfriend, and I was willing to bet it hadn't been Chantel. Which meant at least one of the others was in on it. *So what?* If I decided to take Dwayne down, anyone else involved would have to go down too. If I let Dwayne off, they got off too. No point thinking about them at the moment. The thing was, a lot of Deegan's arguments were right. Some bookies took a bath, but otherwise nobody much suffered from point shaving. The integrity of the game maybe suffered, but that was too abstract for me.

Outside my door the corridor was still. All around me people were working away on bills of sale, and order forms and service calls. No one had time to be hanging around the corridor, not if they were going to get ahead, or be number one, or not get fired. Actually it was probably Dwayne who got hurt. Shaving points couldn't do much for your self-respect unless you got a good feeling from slipping one by the establishment. It would make a guy like Deegan feel good. He was a nearly ideal wiseguy. He'd love the shiftiness, the hustle of it, the smart money he was making. I didn't think Dwayne was like Deegan . . . *He might want to be.* Who knew. So was I going to bust Dwayne for his own good? *Hurts me more than it does you, Dwayne.*

"Shit," I said.

I owed Baron Morton and Taft University the job I'd agreed to do when they hired me. I owed Dwayne Woodcock nothing. He was an arrogant kid, but he was sullen. *Okay. So I don't turn the kid in.*

I got up and looked out my office window at the still bleak spring. Berkeley Street was washed in a pale yellow sun. On the corner of Boylston, opposite me, a young woman walked with two short gray woolly dogs on a pair of leashes. She held the leashes in one hand and carried a pooper scooper in the other. The task was a challenge to her. The dogs, who looked straight from a Disney movie, were crisscrossing in front of her tangling their leashes, and the young woman was trying to untangle them without letting go of the pooper scooper.

"You think you've got problems," I said.

I sat back down and began admiring the toes of my shoes again. I couldn't just walk away from it. I couldn't blow the whistle on Dwayne yet, but I couldn't leave Deegan and company in place either, and there was the matter of literacy. I figured Deegan wouldn't try to shoot me for the moment. If I was killed while investigating point shaving it would produce just the result they were trying to avoid. If they were logical. I picked up the Taft file from my desk and flipped through it looking at my notes. Madelaine Roth, Ph.D.

I got up and put on my leather jacket and went out and closed the office door behind me. When in doubt do something; and hope that if you keep doing it you'll come to understand what it is. Across the hall the door to the paralegal office was open. She was at her desk thumbing through *The Harvard Law Review*. She looked up as I stepped out of my office, and smiled. I smiled back and gave her the kind of wave where you hold your hand still and wiggle your fingers. She wiggled back.

Enthralled.

14

Madelaine Roth had high cheekbones and very pale skin and a mass of auburn hair. She sat in her office wearing a dark blue silk dress splattered with red flowers, crossed her legs and let her swivel chair tilt back behind her big blond desk. The wall was covered with pictures of the Taft basketball team, clippings, letters from former players and announcements of summer tutorial offerings, new courses, new academic regulations and her three degrees, each separately framed in blond wood that matched her desk. There were bookcases on two walls filled mostly with paperback books that had the look of required reading. Her desktop was covered with papers. Her big round blue-rimmed glasses lay among the papers. There were two ballpoint pens and a red pencil among the papers as well.

"I read the article in the student newspaper, Mr. Spenser," she said. "And really, unfounded allegations, rumors,

79

unnamed sources. It is simply amazing how much these students refuse to learn."

"Amazing in fact," I said. "Did you ever notice that Dwayne Woodcock can't read?"

Madelaine's face flushed and her dark blue eyes rounded and then narrowed almost at once.

"I beg your pardon," she said.

"I said have you ever noticed that Dwayne Woodcock can't read?"

She shook her head. Her face was still flushed.

"That's, that's simply, ah, crazy. Dwayne's a senior in college, of course he can read. Why on earth would you say he can't."

"I gave him a few pages of typescript to read and he couldn't read it."

"Well, for heaven's sake, it's like the old voter literacy tests in Mississippi, you ask someone to read a complicated technical report and when they can't, or perhaps simply won't, you assume they're illiterate."

"It was a discussion of several basketball games in which he played," I said.

Her face was very red now, and she shook her head firmly. "Literacy testing is quite a complex specialty, Mr. Spenser. I suspect that you were not entirely qualified. I wonder if Dwayne were white if you'd be so quick to assume illiteracy."

"Some of my best friends are jigaboos," I said.

Dr. Roth looked like she'd swallowed a hairbrush.

"Mr. Spenser, I assume you're trying to joke; but the racial cliché is offensive."

"I'm feeling offensive, Dr. Roth. I am sitting here being bullshitted in patronizing tones, and we both know you know he's illiterate."

"I'm afraid that's enough, Mr. Spenser. You'll have to leave." Madelaine spoke with as much dignity as one could who was blushing scarlet.

"That's silly, Madelaine," I said. "This is a testable hypothesis. Kicking me out won't protect you from embarrassment when Dwayne's illiteracy becomes public knowledge and people ask you how come you're writing these rave reviews of his academic performance."

"I feel no embarrassment in trying to help a poor black boy to stay in school. Would you have me send him back to the ghetto?"

"So you know he can't read," I said.

"I know his skills are not, perhaps, what they should be, granted, but would he be better off back in that environment? The boy has a future here."

"He'd probably rather be called a man," I said.

"I know about calling black people 'boy,' " Madelaine said. "But he is a boy."

"Not on a basketball court," I said.

"But otherwise," Madelaine said. "He's not a grown man. He's a boy."

"Why do you say so?" I said.

"For God's sake," Madelaine said. "He can't even read."

I smiled. Madelaine looked at me, puzzled; why was I smiling? I smiled some more. The room was quiet. Madelaine frowned. Then the light went on. Had she not been flushed she would have flushed.

"Well, not just because he can't read," Madelaine said. It was weak, and she knew it, but like a lot of academics I had met she kept chewing at it. She was so used to manipulating meaning with language that both became relative. As if you could make falsehood true by richly said restatement. Academics are not first rate at saying *I was wrong.*

"What are the other aspects of his boy-ness?" I said, finally.

Madelaine opened her mouth, closed it, took a long breath. "This is pointless," she said. "I do not have the time to sit here and argue with some redneck detective."

"We're not arguing, Dr. Roth. I'm trying to educate you, and you're resisting. We can't just let Dwayne's illiteracy go," I said, "because we think he won't need to be able to read or because we think he can't or won't learn. Those assumptions, Doc, are racist, and it's what's wrong with this whole deal. This kid has gone through sixteen years of education, public and private, and he can't read, and no one has bothered about that."

"You just called him a kid," Madelaine said. She was sullen now.

"He is a kid. He hasn't got the shrewdness or the strength to admit he can't read and get help so that he can. He thinks he's going to make so much dough playing basketball that he won't ever have to read. He'll get a smart agent. And he'll be entirely dependent on him. And when Dwayne's about thirty-four, thirty-five, he won't be making any more money playing basketball, and so he won't have an agent and then what's he going to do? Manage his affairs?"

"But you were dreadful to me when I called him a boy."

"Dreadful's a little strong," I said.

"I'm not a racist," she said.

"What's in a name," I said. "But when I came in here, I wasn't sure what to do with Dwayne. Now I am. And it's you that showed me. I'm going to treat him like a man."

"Does that mean you're going to turn him in?" Madelaine said.

"I don't know," I said. "But whatever I do I'm going to treat him like he's responsible for himself and his life."

"And what about me?" she said.

"What about you?"

"Are you going to tell that he can't read?"

I stared at her.

"It would be very hurtful to my professional standing," she said.

She was leaning forward in her chair now, her hands resting on the edge of her desk. Her mouth was open and her tongue moved rapidly back and forth over her lower lip.

I was still staring.

"Holy Christ," I said.

15

Hawk and I tried to have dinner together once a week or so just as if we were regular people. After a session with Madelaine Roth, Hawk looked a lot more regular to me than he used to. We had a table against the wall in a storefront place called the East Coast Grill in Inman Square, where all the cooking was done over an open barbecue pit in the back, by a guy in a red baseball cap. I ordered the ribs, Hawk asked for grilled tuna.

"Don't dare order the ribs, do you?" I said.

"Heard it came with a wedge of watermelon," Hawk said.

"Your national cuisine," I said.

We were drinking Lone Star beer, in respect to the barbecue, and the first one went quickly. As we drank, people glanced covertly at Hawk. He was wearing white leather pants and a black silk shirt. His shaved head gleamed, and

his movements were almost balletic: economical and sur-
gically exact. He never moved for no reason. He never
spoke to make conversation. His white leather jacket hung
on the back of the chair, and if you paid attention to stuff
like that, you could see where it hung a little lopsided from
the weight of the gun in the right hand pocket. When he
brought the beer glass to his lips you could see the muscles
in his upper arm swell, stretching the silk of his shirt sleeve.
The waitress brought us a second beer.

Hawk said, "Guy named Bobby Deegan came by to see
me."

"Bobby gets around," I said.

"You know him?" Hawk said.

"Came by my office this morning," I said. "Urged me to
lay off a thing I was looking into."

"S'pose you said, 'sho nuff, Bobby,' " Hawk said.

"I was going to," I said. "But my chin was trembling so
bad it was hard to talk."

"Ah," Hawk said. "That why Bobby looking to have you
clipped."

"Clipped?"

"Un huh."

"A sweetie like me?"

"Un huh."

"Gee," I said. "I thought I'd won him over."

"Guess not," Hawk said. "Bobby come in to Henry's
looking for me. Said he needed some pest removal work
done. Heard I was in that business."

I shook my head. "Pest removal," I said. "That hurts."

"Can see why it would," Hawk said.

The waitress came and brought ribs for me and tuna for Hawk. On the plate with my ribs were some beans, some watermelon and a big piece of cornbread.

Hawk looked at the slab of ribs. "Mighta made an error," Hawk said.

"Tuna's good for you," I said.

"Sure," Hawk said. "So I ask Bobby where he heard that, and he said, guy he'd done some business with in town. I say 'gimme a name.' He say . . ." Hawk smiled happily, " 'Gerry Broz.' "

I said, "A blast from the past."

Hawk cut a morsel off his tuna and inspected it. It was pink, as promised. Hawk nodded his head once and put the tuna into his mouth and chewed. He nodded once again, and swallowed.

"So I figure the guy's probably straight, using Joe's kid's name, anybody can know Joe's, but most folks don't know 'bout Gerry."

"So I say what's the pest's name, and he say you."

I was struggling happily with my ribs. Normally I ended up with barbecue sauce in my socks when I ate ribs, but I always figured they were worth it.

"What's he paying?" I said when I could.

"Five bills," Hawk said.

"For crissake," I said, "Harry Cotton was offering that, when, seven, eight years ago."

"Yeah, well, Bobby's out of town, he don't know 'bout you. So, I say, 'You tell Gerry who you want hit?' And he say, 'No, what's the difference?' and I say, 'No difference.' "

Hawk ate a couple of grilled vegetables. I ate some beans. Hawk drank some beer, patted his lips carefully with his napkin, put it back on his lap.

"So Bobby say, 'Well?' And I say, 'Well what?' and Bobby say, 'You want the job?' and I say, 'no.' And Bobby say, 'How come?' and I just look at him for a while and Bobby say, 'Well, okay, fine, you don't want it.' And I just looking at him and he say, 'You got any suggestions?' and I say, 'no' and Bobby takes a walk."

I shook my head. "Five grand," I said. "That's insulting."

"Hey," Hawk said, "I just reporting the news."

I nodded. My ribs were gone, also the beans and the watermelon and the cornbread. Also my beer. I'd done another good job at the table.

"These are serious guys," I said. "Bobby came into my office this morning, offered a bribe, made a threat, neither one worked, so he went right out and found you."

"And when I said no he probably went on and found somebody else not as good," Hawk said. He was working on his supper now that it was my turn to talk.

"The only one as good would be me," I said, "and I wouldn't do it either."

"Still, they probably find some people willing," Hawk said. "Not everybody know better."

"Sucker born every minute," I said.

"What you into?" Hawk said.

"Basketball," I said.

"The national sport," Hawk said, "of ma people. Better tell me about it."

I did. While I did, Hawk finished his meal, the waiter
came and cleared it and brought dessert menus.

"The bread pudding with whiskey sauce," I said to
Hawk.

Hawk held up two fingers to the waiter and said, "Bread
pudding."

We were eating the pudding by the time I got to Madelaine Roth. And I finished with Madelaine and the pudding at about the same time.

"What you think 'bout Bobby," Hawk said when I got
through.

"I think that cheerful, pally act is a very thin veneer over
a very tough guy," I said.

Hawk nodded. "Yeah," he said. "How 'bout I cruise
around with you a while. Might meet me some adventur-
ous coeds."

"Yeah," I said, "might be able to help me get Dwayne's
attention too."

"Or Chantel's," Hawk said.

"Hawk," I said, "Dwayne is, you gotta remember, approximately the size of Harlem."

"There's that," Hawk said.

"Besides, I think we're trying to help him," I said.

"What's this we, white man? You the helper, I just along
to see how it goes."

"Mr. Warm," I said.

The waiter brought the check. Hawk picked it up, looked
at it and handed it to me.

16

The next time I went to see Dwayne Woodcock, Hawk came with me. We found Dwayne in the spa in the Student Union drinking a Coke in a booth with two other kids. I recognized them. One was Kenny Green, the off guard, and a reserve forward named Daryl Pope. Dwayne looked up and said something to the other two. There was some laughter.

"Dwayne," I said. "We need to talk."

Dwayne was playing to his friends. "I don't need to talk, man. You need to talk whyn't you go someplace and talk?" He made the last word stretch. Hawk came up and leaned against the corner of the booth. All three kids looked at Hawk uneasily.

"I had a chat with Bobby Deegan," I said.

Everyone at the table got a little stiffer when I said Deegan's name.

"I don't know nobody by that name, man," Dwayne said. "Sounds like some dumb fucking Irishman to me."

Dwayne's buddies laughed along with him.

"Don't that sound like that to you?" Dwayne said.

"Sounds like that to me," one of his buddies said.

I looked at Hawk. I was getting tired of college kids. Dwayne was especially easy to get tired of.

"Want me to shoot one?" Hawk said.

All three turned and looked at him.

"Who you talking to, man?" Dwayne said.

Hawk turned his head slowly and looked at him, carefully. Then he looked at the other two, just as carefully.

Basketball players are big, and it's been years since they were reedy. There was nothing in Hawk's look that I could see that was anything but neutrally interested. He didn't say anything. But when he was through looking at them, all three kids had stopped laughing. Green and Pope looked at Dwayne, he looked back at Hawk for a minute, and then looked at me.

"You bring some fucking dude around, say he's going to shoot us?"

"Dude," I said to Hawk.

"Talks like all those bad-ass black guys on television, don't he," Hawk said.

"Heart of the ghetto," I said, "pulse beat of the streets."

Hawk leaned a little forward toward Dwayne and spoke softly.

"You had best excuse yourself from your friends, young man, and allow us to speak with you. We have your best interest at heart."

Hawk's eyes were steady on Dwayne.

Finally Dwayne said, "Man, shit. I may's well get this over. You guys give us couple minutes. Get these fucking people out of my hair."

"We be over at the counter, Dwayne," Pope said.

"Sure," Dwayne said. "I'll catch you in a minute."

When they were gone I slid into the booth opposite Dwayne. Hawk sat beside me.

"Whatcha want?" Dwayne said.

"I think I want to help you," I said.

"Dwayne don't need help. Dwayne can carry the weight, you know?"

"What weight you carrying, Dwayne?"

"Whatever fuckin' weight you think you going to talk about. Dwayne Woodcock don't need no motherfucking help, man."

"You need help, Dwayne," I said. "You can't read, and you can't write, and some hard guys from New York got hold of your balls."

"Bullshit, man . . ."

"You don't think they got hold of your balls. You think you're making some easy bread, and no one gets hurt. But one of these days you'll try to walk away, and, whoa, sonovagun, they got a firm grip on your nads, and they're starting to squeeze."

"Nobody gonna squeeze Dwayne's balls," he said, "no dumb Irish fucker like Deegan. No honkie motherfucker like you, either."

Dwayne took a big breath. "Don't need advice from no honkie motherfucker, either," he said.

"Yes you do," Hawk said. "You need advice wherever you can find it." His voice was quiet. "And this is about the best place. It's also about the last place. You don't get help, and pretty soon advice ain't going to matter. You going to belong to Bobby Deegan, or the cops. Or you going to be dead."

"Whyn't you just leave this alone," Dwayne said.

Hawk's voice was still soft. "He ain't going to do that. He doesn't leave things alone. You can trust him. You can trust me. Lot of men don't meet two people they can trust in their whole lives."

Dwayne didn't say anything. He just shook his head. Hawk and I were silent. Pope and Green stood at the counter, looking at us, ready to jump in. Dwayne kept shaking his head.

I waited.

Finally Dwayne said, "Bobby say he was going to talk with you."

I nodded. Next to me Hawk was in absolute repose. His hands on the table before him were perfectly still. He was looking at Dwayne. He had an expression of mild interest.

"Bobby say he going to talk with you and take care of it."

"He didn't take care of it," I said.

"He will," Dwayne said, and got up, which in itself was fairly impressive, and walked out of the spa with his two buddies in trail.

I looked at Hawk.

"Big," he said.

"From the neck down," I said.

Hawk shrugged. "You could turn him in," he said.

I shook my head.

Hawk grinned. "Figured that would be too simple for you."

Classes broke and a swarm of undergraduates filled the spa. Hawk and I left the booth and pushed through them out onto the quadrangle.

"Where's Gerry in this deal?" I said.

"Broz?"

"Yeah. He sent Deegan to you."

"Figure Deegan's from New York," Hawk said.

"And he knows Gerry Broz," I said.

"Maybe we ought to find out how," Hawk said.

"Joe won't like that," I said.

Hawked grinned again. "Yikes," he said.

"Makes your blood run cold, doesn't it," I said. "But once we find out what's it going to do for me?"

"Know that when we find out," Hawk said.

I nodded.

"What else you got?"

I shrugged. "Got Dixie," I said.

"The coach? Thought he found you annoying."

"Hard to believe, isn't it," I said. "But he can put pressure on the kid that you and I can't."

Hawk's face brightened. "By sitting him down," Hawk said.

"Yes. If I can persuade Dixie to bench Dwayne until he cooperates we might have something."

"Means you've got to convince Dixie that Dwayne's doing what you say," Hawk said.

"And Dixie would rather get a case of clap than talk to me," I said.

"Amen to that," Hawk said.

17

I walked into Dixie Dunham's office in the gym on a March morning that felt like January. There was snow, and wind and a windchill factor. I had the lining zipped back into my leather jacket.

"What the fuck are you doing here?" Dixie said when he saw me.

I put my gym bag down on his desk and took the game tapes out of it. I put them on the desk in front of him. They were the six games where Taft beat the spread. I took out a copy of the running transcript that Tommy Christopher and I had put together.

"Read that," I said, "and watch the tapes and you'll know that Dwayne Woodcock's influencing the point spread."

"Where'd you get those tapes? I didn't authorize those tapes to anyone."

"I showed the transcript to Dwayne and he couldn't read it," I said.

"I told you, you sonovabitch, I told you to stay away from my players." Dixie shoved his swivel chair back behind his desk and stood up. "You trying to rig this goddamn tournament, come in here and fuck with my players' heads? You bastard, you're the one rigging the spread. I told you, I explicitly fucking told you . . ."

"Goddamn it, Dixie," I said, "shut up."

Dixie was so startled that someone would say that to him that he shut up. For a moment.

I charged into that moment. "You got a kid here, he's not just one of your players, he's also a real actual kid, and he's in trouble and you don't give a rat's ass about it. You're so goddamned busy being a coaching legend that you're going to let him slide right into the sewer."

Dixie's face was red.

"People don't talk to me that way," he said. His voice was tight as if he had trouble forcing it through his throat.

"People don't usually talk to you any way," I said. "You're such a goddamned windbag they don't get a chance."

Dixie came around the corner of the desk in a rush and threw a looping right-handed punch at me. It was like watching the slow curving swoop of a Frisbee. When it got close I turned my head to the left and let his fist soar majestically on past. Then I drove a left hook into his solar plexus, turning on the ball of my right foot and getting a lot of my weight behind it.

Dixie said "oof," and he folded like a camp stool and staggered back against his desk trying to get his breath.

I didn't say anything. I waited. Dixie got enough wind in him in a short time to lunge off the desk at me again. As he came I took a quick shuffle step left and put a right hook into the same spot, pivoting this time the other way and getting even more weight behind it. Dixie staggered back, doubled over again, leaned against the desk and then slid slowly to the floor, his legs stretching out before him with no strength in them, a look of puzzlement on his face. I knew the feeling. Dixie sat there, his arms wrapped across his stomach, bent forward, trying to get air, for maybe a full minute, while I waited without saying anything. Finally he could breathe. He put both hands flat on the floor and supported himself while he sat straighter, still on the floor, and his eyes began to focus on me.

"You got a punch like a mule," Dixie said.

"Like the kick of a mule," I said. "Get it right."

Dixie nodded without speaking. Then he pulled his legs toward him and twisted and got them under him and rose to one knee, holding on to the desk, rested a minute and then boosted himself up onto both feet and stood there, leaning forward, his hands palm down on his desk, his shoulders hunched, his back to me. He breathed for a while and then finally rolled himself around along the desk edge until he had turned and faced me. He put one hand up, palm out.

"Ain't going to try again," he said. "Just getting my legs back."

I waited.

"Hoooeee," Dixie said.

"Yeah," I said.

"You warned me," he said.

"Yeah."

Dixie took a couple of deep breaths and arched his back. Then he went around his desk and got his chair and sat in it.

"Okay," he said. "What were you saying about Dwayne going down the chute?"

"Read the transcript," I said.

Dixie picked it up, opened his drawer, took out a pair of horn-rimmed half glasses, put them low on his nose and started to put his feet up. He stopped suddenly just after he started and put them back on the floor, and opened the folder and started to read. While he read, I looked around the room. It was classic gym cinder block, painted white. There was a picture of Dixie with Troy Murphy, who'd been an all-American point guard for Dixie and was now a star with the Portland Trail Blazers. But there weren't any others. No team pictures, no memorabilia. In the corner across from Dixie's desk was a big screen television set and a VCR on a yellow oak table. Three or four folding chairs leaned against the wall. I looked back at Dixie. He had one page flipped over and was reading the second one. I waited. Dixie flipped the second page. His face had no expression. Somewhere, faintly echoing off the cinder block, I could hear a basketball pounding on a floor.

Dixie finished the typescript. He put it down on his desk, reached out and assembled the videocassettes in a neat pile, stood carefully, and walked somewhat stiffly, carrying the tapes to the VCR. He arranged them in order, turned on the VCR and the TV, put a cassette into the VCR, punched

PLAY and walked back, slowly, to his desk. He lowered himself carefully into his chair and leaned back and began to watch the videotape. I leaned on the wall and watched it too, for maybe the fifth time.

Dixie watched the tapes, the way he'd read the transcript. There was no expression on his face. He had no reaction. He didn't say a word. When the first tape was over, he started to push himself up.

"Stay," I said. "I'll run the machine."

Dixie settled back into his chair. I went to the VCR and changed cassettes. When the last one was finished, it was midafternoon. I picked all the cassettes up and put them into the gym bag. Dixie still sat. Neither one of us made a sound. I went back to leaning on the wall. After a while Dixie swiveled his chair toward me.

"Dwayne's shaving points," Dixie said. "Maybe Danny Davis, too."

I nodded.

"You see what you want to see, I guess," Dixie said. "You say he can't read."

I nodded.

"Shit," Dixie said.

I leaned on the wall some more. Dixie sat. The sound of basketballs bouncing had stopped.

"What we going to do?" Dixie said. "East regionals start next Saturday."

"I don't know for sure what we're going to do," I said. "But I've got some goals. One, the kid's involved with New York wiseguys and I want to get him unhooked from them. Two, I want to be able to preserve his future. Three, I want him to learn to read."

"If we turn him in, his future is zero," Dixie said. "Pros won't touch him."

"I know," I said.

"Means you're going to cover up for him?"

"Yeah, I guess it does," I said. "How about you?"

Dixie shook his head. "He's the best player I ever had. Better than Troy, even." Dixie jerked his head toward the picture on the wall.

I waited.

"People can't trust the score, any game goes to hell," he said.

I shifted shoulders against the wall.

"I don't know," Dixie said. "I don't know what to do."

"Let's take it a step at a time," I said. "Let's talk with the kid. If he'll admit it, then we can move on the guys who rigged him to do it."

"What if he denies it?" Dixie said.

"You tell him you looked at the tapes, you know he did it. If he still won't admit anything, you sit him down."

"Sit him down?" Dixie said the words very slowly, with space between them.

"Yeah."

"For how long?"

"Until he tells us what's going on. Until he names names."

"Jesus Christ," Dixie said. "I got the East regionals next week. We get through those I got the tourney at Salt Lake. In about three weeks I could be playing for the national championship."

"I didn't say my plan was fun," I said.

"Fun, my God. Can't we use the tapes for proof?"

"Probably not in court, but even so, we don't want to go to court. And if we did, what have we got? The fact that Dwayne, maybe Danny Davis, is shaving points. We don't have for whom. And *for whom* is what we need if we're going to pull this off without screwing the kid."

"So what are you going to do if he does tell you?" Dixie said. "You say you don't want to ruin the kid, so you can't go to the cops."

"Dixie," I said, "you got to understand this kind of work. I don't have a game plan. I sort of feel my way along. When I run into something I don't know, I try to find out. When I find out enough, then maybe there's a way to figure out what to do. And maybe there isn't. You can't know until you find out what there is to find out."

Dixie rocked slowly in his swivel chair. His hands were folded across his stomach, and he seemed to be studying his thumbnails. Finally, without looking up, Dixie said, "I'll talk with Dwayne."

I said, "You want me around?"

"No."

"Okay," I said. "Let me know."

"Yeah, I will."

I picked up my gym bag and started out the door.

"Spenser," Dixie said.

I stopped and turned my head.

"I didn't know he couldn't read," Dixie said.

"Makes you wonder how he maintained a two point three average, doesn't it," I said.

"Maybe we ought to find that out too," Dixie said.

"We will," I said.

18

Tuesday morning, Hawk and I went to see Gerry Broz. Gerry was a second generation thug, been to college, graduated into the old man's business. He spent every morning in a coffee shop near Oak Square in Brighton. He'd have breakfast, read the paper, drink some coffee, make a few phone calls, receive a few visitors. Joe still ran things, but Gerry was the crown prince.

"Joe's garbage," Hawk said as we were walking across Washington Street toward the B&D Coffee Shop. "And Gerry's nowhere near the man Joe is."

"I know," I said. "Cops will be glad when Gerry takes over. They figure the organization will turn into pot shards in about a year."

"Pot shards," Hawk said.

We opened the door to the coffee shop and went in. The air was steamy with the scent of coffee and bacon and cigarette smoke. There was a rusty-colored marble counter and four booths by the big front window. The place looked as if it had originally been built to be a variety store and been converted, home style, by either B or D or maybe both.

Gerry was in his booth, farthest from the door by the window. There was a thick guy with curly black hair sitting opposite him with his overcoat on.

The first time I met Gerry he was still an undergraduate, selling coke and blackmailing women when he wasn't studying for midterms. Now he was about twenty-seven and looked younger. He had a soft face and a limp black mustache. He'd put on some weight, none of it sinew, and he hadn't adjusted his wardrobe, so that while he wore very expensive clothes they were a little tight everywhere.

He spotted us when we came in and said something to the man across from him. The man across from him put one hand inside his coat as he turned and looked at us over his shoulder.

"What do you want, creep?" Gerry said.

"Gee, Gerry," I said, "getting porky hasn't improved your style any, has it?"

The man across from him had twisted himself around in the booth with one leg resting in the seat, so that he was fully facing us. Hawk stepped up to the counter and ordered two coffees.

"The gentleman there wants it on his tab," Hawk said. The counter woman nodded and shuffled after the coffee.

"I asked you a question," Gerry said.

"Commendable," I said. "So many people these days are

always talking *me, me, me,* but you've developed listening skills. You're a sensitive guy, Ger."

Hawk came over with a cup of coffee in a Styrofoam cup. I took it and had a small sip. Hawk went back and sat on a stool at the counter and leaned one elbow on the counter and watched.

"Love a Styrofoam cup, don't you, Ger?"

"Spenser, I know you think you're a fucking scream, but I don't, and I'm a busy man. You got something to say to me, say it. And get the fuck out of here."

"I want to talk with you, Gerry. Unlike everybody else in the world."

"Talk," Gerry said.

"Tell your gunboat to beat it," I said. "It's just me and you."

Gerry shrugged. He made a hand gesture at the counter.

"Over there, Jojo," he said. "For a minute."

Jojo slid out of the booth carefully, his hand still under his coat, his eyes flickering back and forth between me and Hawk. He took a stool beside Hawk.

"How's it going," Hawk said pleasantly.

Jojo shrugged. I slid into the booth across from Gerry.

"Okay, what do you want?" Gerry said.

"Bobby Deegan," I said.

"Who's he?"

It was a standard reaction for a guy like Gerry. If I'd said George Washington he'd have said the same thing. College hadn't helped Gerry all that much.

"My question exactly," I said.

"Why ask me?"

"Because Bobby mentioned your name to my associate," I tipped my head toward Hawk, "and suggested you were a tight personal friend."

Gerry raised both hands in front of him palm out.

"Never heard of the guy," he said.

"Bobby says he asked you to point him at a good hitter, and you sent him to Hawk."

Gerry pushed out his lower lip and shook his head.

"I was supposed to be the hittee," I said.

There was a little movement in Gerry's eyes for a moment and then nothing.

"Would I send a guy to Hawk if he wanted you hit?" Gerry said. "How stupid you think I am?"

"Awful stupid," I said. "Bobby didn't tell you who he wanted hit."

"Look, asshole," Gerry said. "I told you I don't know nothing about no Bobby Deegan. You unnerstand? Nothing."

"Gerry," I said, "I've known you since you were a boy."

"You're a pain in the ass. You been a pain in the ass to the old man and you're a pain in the ass to me. The old man let it slide. I don't know why. He does what he does. But I ain't going to let it slide. You hear me talking? You get in my way and you're going to sleep with the fishes." Gerry's voice was soft, but he leaned forward and his face was reddish-looking as he spoke.

I turned toward the counter.

"Hawk, you hear this conversation?" I said.

Hawk shook his head.

"Gerry says if I get in his way I'm going to sleep with the fishes."

Hawk's quiet face broke into a slow widening grin.

"Sleep with the fishes?" he said.

I was smiling too. "Yeah."

Hawk began to chuckle quietly and then to laugh and finally he bent over on his stool and pressed his hands against his stomach and laughed.

"Sleep with the fishes," he said, his voice shaking. "Sleep with the fucking fishes."

There was a slim black guy who looked like a cabbie sitting next to Hawk at the counter, and in another booth there were two Irish-looking women, who had probably walked the kids to school and were on their way home. All three studiously ignored the hilarity.

"Guppies," I said to Gerry, "could I sleep with some guppies? I always sort of liked guppies."

Gerry was redder than before. He jerked his head at Jojo and said, "Let's get the fuck out of here."

Jojo slid off the stool and stood by the booth as Gerry edged out of the booth and stood up.

"Does this mean you're not going to tell me about Bobby Deegan?" I said.

"Fuck you," Gerry said, and stomped out of the coffee shop. Jojo barely got to the door in time to hold it for him. Through the window I saw them get into a charcoal gray Mercedes sedan, Jojo behind the wheel, and drive away.

Hawk got off the stool and stood beside me looking through the window.

"Not productive," I said.

"Counterproductive," Hawk said. "Now we got to worry about Bobby Deegan putting a hit on you cause you screwing up his scam, and we got to worry about Gerry putting a hit on you cause you hurt his feelings."

"Had to ask," I said.

"Sure," Hawk said.

"Hurting Gerry Broz's feelings isn't a bad day's work," I said.

"True," Hawk said.

19

I was back on paralegal watch when Chantel knocked on the frame of the open door. I put my feet on the floor and stood.

"Come in," I said.

She was wearing black stockings and a red leather mini skirt and a silver gray silk blouse with the top three buttons open. Her high-heeled shoes were gray and she wore a silver gray duster open over her outfit. She walked in slowly, looking at my office the way people look around at a museum. She stopped maybe two feet in front of my desk, holding her black alligator purse in front of her thighs with both hands. Her hair wasn't corn rowed today, it framed her head in soft black curls. She wore eye makeup and red lipstick, and probably more subtle stuff that I didn't know about. She looked maybe twenty years old and she was beautiful.

"I . . ." she started and stopped. She looked back at the open door. "Can I close the door?" she said.

I came around the desk.

"I will," I said.

I went and shut the door and came back and pulled one of the client chairs a little closer to her.

"Sit down, please," I said.

She looked at the chair and then at the closed door. Her movements were all slow, as if she had to think through each one before she made it. She looked at me again and then at the chair and then carefully smoothed her skirt against the backs of her thighs with her left hand and sat down. She sat upright, forward in her chair, her knees together, both feet on the floor, side by side.

I went around my desk and sat down and smiled at her. Encouraging. Supportive. Attentive. Entirely without sexual or racial prejudice. She could tell me anything.

She did not smile back. She gazed at me without any affect at all that I could discern. She held her purse now in her lap with both hands.

We sat and looked at one another. The steam knocked for a moment in the pipes and then stopped. I heard heels clack in the corridor again.

"Dwayne don't know I'm here," she said. Her quiet gaze didn't move. "He be really pissed off if he knew."

I nodded. Nice to hear a human voice again.

We were quiet some more. She turned the purse once in her lap so that the open end now faced her. Too bad I didn't smoke. The heels in the hall clacked back from wherever they had clacked before.

"Excuse me," Chantel said. "I don't mean to just stare like this, but I'm shy around white people until I know them."

I nodded again.

"I don't know many white people," she said. "Even at Taft I stay mostly with other black people."

"You live with Dwayne?"

"Yes, since the end of sophomore year."

"You going to get married, you think?"

"Un huh. After graduation. Dwayne probably going to be drafted by the Clippers so we probably going to move to LA."

"You mind?" I said.

"No," Chantel said. "Me and Dwayne be fine anywhere."

I nodded. "How's his reading coming?"

Chantel shrugged. We sat and looked quietly some more. She didn't seem to be uncomfortable with the silence. I wasn't either. I'd heard too many silences to get uncomfortable.

"You told anybody?" Chantel said.

"About Dwayne can't read? No, nobody that you'd care about."

"How 'bout the other thing?"

"Same answer," I said.

Chantel nodded, as much to herself as to me. I waited.

"You married?" Chantel said.

"Not quite," I said.

"You got somebody?"

"Yes."

She nodded again, as if I'd passed some kind of test.

"What you going to do?" she said.

"I can't seem to help Dwayne from Dwayne's end," I said. "So I'm going to try to go back door. I'm going to bust his connection and see if I can spring him free."

"Dwayne's a boy," she said. "I know we not supposed to say 'boy.' We supposed to talk that man child shit; but it's true. He looks like a man, and he's good as any man, but he hasn't grown up at all."

"He's been a star so long he's never had a chance to," I said.

Chantel nodded her head four or five times rapidly. "Yes," she said, "that's right, and he always been bigger and stronger than everybody and he never had to, you know, do stuff he didn't like, do stuff he wasn't too good at."

"Like reading and writing," I said.

"That's right," Chantel said. "He wasn't so good at that so he just didn't do it. He so good at other stuff that he don't have to do it."

"What happens when you try to teach him?" I said.

"He get mad," Chantel said. "No, he don't get mad. That's not right." Chantel paused for a moment and looked out my window while she thought. She pushed her lower lip. And frowned just slightly. I wanted to pick her up and kiss her on the forehead.

"He gets embarrassed," she said.

"Yeah," I said.

"He is very proud," Chantel said. "He got this whole Dwayne Woodcock thing he got to live up to and protect and be, and it cost him a whole lot to do that all the time."

"You grow up with him, Chantel?"

She shook her head. "No, he from Brooklyn; I grew up in Germantown. You know, Philly. Met him here, freshman year."

"Damn lucky thing for him that you did," I said.

"Why you say that?" Chantel said.

"Because you are a woman and a half, Chantel. What's your last name?"

"deRosier," she said. "Chantel deRosier."

"What would you like me to do, Chantel?"

Her gaze was steady and unembarrassed on my face.

"I want you to help us," she said.

"Chantel, I will help you do anything you want forever," I said. "Where would you like me to start?"

She shook her head. "They are bad people he's with," she said. "They don't care about him. They call him 'big guy' and they tell him how terrific he is and they pretend to be scared of him cause he's so big and so good. But they aren't scared. And they don't think he's a man like them. They think they've got this here poor nigger boy by the nose."

Chantel's eyes were shiny, maybe a little damp.

"And they have," I said.

She nodded. "Yeah, they have, and he doesn't know it. He think they the cat's ass. They got cars, they got money, they take us to restaurants and clubs, and give us clothes."

"They treat you good?" I said.

"They treat me like I'm Dwayne's piece of ass," she said softly. "And Dwayne don't seem to notice."

I stood up from my chair and turned and looked out the

window for a moment, down at Boylston Street and the people moving by. I looked across at the trees in very early flower outside the building that used to be Bonwit's and was going to be Louis'. Right below me a young man in a tuxedo passed carrying a cluster of balloons that read HAPPY BIRTHDAY KATIE KROCK. He crossed Boylston with the balloons and headed on down Berkeley toward the river.

I turned back around and looked at Chantel. She was crying, though not very much.

I said, "Whatever comes out of this, Chantel, I'm going to do three things. I'm going to save Dwayne's ass, I am going to see to it that no one involved will treat you like anyone's piece of anything, and I'm going to make the bastards wish they hadn't treated you like that to start with."

"I'm not, you know," she said.

"Dwayne's piece of ass?"

"Yeah. He loves me. I love him. We got each other. We got a space nobody can come in. When we sleep together that's making love, it's not no piece of ass thing."

"I know," I said.

"How you know that?" Chantel said.

"Because that's the kind of woman you are," I said.

She nodded, the movement of her head barely perceptible.

"How you going to save him?" she said.

"Like I said, I'm going to go after Bobby Deegan."

"You get them it going to get Dwayne in trouble."

"I know, that's the part I haven't figured out yet," I said. "Be nice to get some feedback from Dwayne."

Chantel shrugged and looked at her lap.

"How much they paying him?" I said.

"I don't know. Dwayne never talks about that."

"Who's in on it with him?"

"On the team?"

"Yeah."

Chantel looked down and shook her head again.

"Don't know, or won't say?"

"Won't," Chantel said.

I nodded. "Okay," I said. "We figure it's Danny Davis."

Chantel didn't move.

"You know anything that will help?"

"Mr. Deegan got a friend named Gerry," she said.

"Gerry Broz?"

"Don't know his last name. White guy, scraggly mustache. Kinda fat . . . not really fat, just sort of flabby-looking."

"That's Gerry," I said. "You know what he's got to do with this?"

"No," Chantel said. "I just see them together when we go out. They talk to Dwayne. Dwayne don't want me talking to them. He knows I don't like them. He's afraid I'll say something bad."

"Dwayne likes them?" I said.

"He likes Mr. Deegan," she said. "I don't think he likes Gerry so much."

"Most people don't," I said.

"Dwayne don't like white people exactly, but he likes them to like him, you know? He needs to have them think he's a big man."

"And Deegan makes him feel good?"

113

Chantel leaned a little forward toward me.

"Yes. Mr. Deegan got money, and he acts like he got money. He know what to do in restaurants and how to talk to headwaiters and what to tip the hat check girl, you know, that kind of man. Real sure of himself. Confident, seems nice, but very aggressive too, like a big success."

"Dwayne likes that?" I said.

"Dwayne been a star most of his life but he been poor most of his life too and where he lived was all black people like where I lived. But his was poorer. We weren't poor. And you'd see all these cool white guys on TV, and you didn't really think about it, and if you did you wouldn't admit it, but being a success got kind of mixed up with being white, or being like a white person, or having white people like you. Mr. Deegan is what Dwayne thinks he ought to be."

"He is better than that, Chantel, or you wouldn't love him."

"He needs to know he better than that," Chantel said. "He got to see that Mr. Deegan is a sleaze with nice manners."

"Okay," I said. "I think I've got it. I show Dwayne that Deegan's a sleaze, prove to Dwayne that he himself is not a sleaze, get Deegan off his back, keep anyone from finding out he shaved points, teach him to read and write and not let anyone know that he can't."

For the first time since I'd seen her, Chantel smiled.

"Yes," she said, "that's exactly it."

"And on the seventh day I'll rest," I said.

20

I got the call from Dwayne on my office phone at four thirty on a cold drizzly Thursday afternoon. Hawk was with me. We'd spent most of the last hour trying to figure out how to deal with the mess Dwayne was in, and we weren't making much progress. We were in the middle of a five-minute break devoted to a discussion of the paralegal's backside when the phone rang and I answered it.

"I need to see you," Dwayne said.

"How come?" I said.

"I been thinking 'bout what you said and I was wrong to get mad," Dwayne said. "I need to talk with you without anybody seeing me."

"I'll meet you," I said.

"Gotta be private, man. Nobody better see me."

"Wherever you want," I said.

"You know the parking garage by the Aquarium?" Dwayne said.

"Yes," I said. "On Milk Street."

"I be on the top level at six thirty," Dwayne said. "You come in your car and I'll get in."

"Six thirty," I said.

"Don't tell nobody," Dwayne said and hung up.

I said, "Dwayne wants me to meet him on the top level of the parking garage on Milk Street by the Aquarium."

"When?"

"Six thirty. Says he's changed his mind about me being a honkie motherfucker."

"He actually say that?" Hawk said.

"Well, he implied it," I said.

"Hm," Hawk said. "What you think?"

"Could be true," I said. "Or he could be doing what he's told and when I get there whoever Deegan hired instead of you will jump out of a Cutlass Supreme and shoot a hole in me."

"Wonder which it'll be," Hawk said.

"Me too," I said.

We talked a little and observed the paralegal one more time as she closed up for the evening. Then Hawk left and I put my feet up on my desk and my hands behind my head and closed my eyes and thought about things. At six I let my feet down, unfolded my hands from behind my head and stood up. I had the Browning on my hip. I took it out, put it into the pocket of my leather trench coat, put the trench coat on and buttoned it up, turned the collar up, put on the tweed cap that Susan said made me look like Trevor Howard, and headed for the meeting with Dwayne, or whoever.

By six the rush hour traffic had congealed into jams on the Southeast Expressway and the tunnel and the Mystic River Bridge. At the turnpike tolls in Allston they were cursing one another. But in the city the streets were shiny with rain and almost empty. Later the people would come in from the suburbs for dinner, or to hang around Quincy Market with the collars turned up on their Lacoste shirts, but right now the city folks were having a couple of Manhattans before dinner, and I was driving from Back Bay to the waterfront in maybe five minutes, hitting the lights on Berkeley and at Leverett Circle and cruising along Atlantic Avenue by six fifteen. I was driving a black Cherokee that year, with tinted windows. I parked it across the street from the garage and sat looking through my tinted windows at the entrance. No point arriving early.

The rain along the waterfront was canted by the wind from the harbor and came in at about a sixty-degree angle against the windows on the driver's side. At the parking garage there was very little action. A car went in. Two came out. Guys with their ties loosened heading home late. Entry was an automatic gate and a ticket dispenser. At the exit was one attendant in her toll booth. At six twenty-nine I pulled across the street and took a ticket and drove into the garage. I wound up the rampways through the nearly empty garage to the top. There were seven or eight cars parked. I moved slowly down the empty aisle, the Browning out of my pocket now and on the seat beside me. At

117

the end of the aisle in front of me a Ford station wagon backed out of its slot and blocked the way.

Not an Oldsmobile Cutlass after all.

I looked in the rearview mirror. A Chevy Blazer with body rot and a plow hitch had backed out and blocked the aisle behind me. I suspected that Dwayne wasn't driving either car. I was right. The people in the Ford got out of the side away from me and stood behind the car. Behind me another two guys got out of the Blazer. One of them had a shotgun. None of them was Dwayne.

Nobody did anything. I sat. They stood. I picked up the Browning from the seat beside me and waited.

One of the men in front of me yelled, "Spenser."

I lowered my side window. "Yeah."

"Step out and we'll talk." He had one of those plastic Red Sox caps that has an adjustable strap and plastic mesh in the back. The hat crown was too high, and the brim was too short, and he'd done nothing to break it in or shape it, so it sat on top of his head like a saucepan.

"I can hear you from here," I said.

"I wasn't giving you a choice, stupid," the guy with the cap said. "We got you penned in and there's four of us. Get out of the car."

"That's the ugliest baseball cap I've ever seen," I said.

He put his left hand up toward it, then caught himself and rubbed his face instead.

"Have it your way," he said.

He and his pal, a very fat guy with an untrimmed black beard, came around the Ford. Each had a handgun. Behind me the two from the Blazer began to move toward

me. Behind them Hawk appeared and leaned over the hood
of the Blazer and sighted down the barrel of a twelve gauge
pump at their backs. The guys from the Blazer didn't see
him, but the guys from the Ford in front of me did. I slid
across the front seat and out the door on the passenger side
of the Cherokee. Blackbeard and the guy with the hat
raised their handguns to fire at Hawk. The big boom of
the shotgun came just as Blackbeard was slammed back
against the Ford. Over the hood of my car I shot the guy
in the baseball cap as he was shooting at Hawk and turned
and stepped to the back of the Cherokee before he hit the
ground and held my gun steady on the two guys from the
Blazer that Hawk had trained his shotgun on from behind.
Everyone froze.

In real time the whole sequence had probably taken ten
seconds. In the slow motion of crisis time it had unreeled
in ponderous elegance, and the crystalline immobility that
followed was intensified by the lingering smell of gunfire,
like an olfactory echo of the big bang.

"The set up got set up," I said.

Neither man moved.

"We can drill you," I said.

They knew that. The guns were their protection, but if
they used them they were dead. They knew that too.

Behind them Hawk said softly, "Put them down."

They still hesitated, but only for a moment. The guy
with the shotgun bent over carefully and placed it
on the ground. The other guy, just as carefully, put the
big .44 Mag he'd been carrying on the ground beside the
shotgun.

"Put your hands on the roof of the Blazer," I said. "Back away. Spread the legs. I bet you've done this before."

They did as I told them. Then I went to the front of the Cherokee and examined the two guys we'd shot. They were both dead. I walked back over to the quick and patted them down. The guy who'd carried the shotgun had a .25 automatic in the pocket of his leather jacket. I took it. When I stepped away, Hawk came around the Blazer, the shotgun resting butt forward, trigger guard up on his shoulder.

"They picked a good place," Hawk said.

"Yeah. Two gunshots and nothing happens. No cops. No sirens in the distance. One of you guys pick this place?" I said to the two on the Blazer. The one in the leather jacket said, "No. Frankie did." He made a small head gesture toward the two dead men.

I said, "You can get off the car now." The two men shuffled their feet in from the spread and stood straight and turned around.

"Let's discuss motivation," I said.

The guy in the leather jacket had a Miami Vice two-day growth of stubble. The other guy was dressed against the weather in one of those oversized short jackets with lots of lapels and collars and cuffs and epaulets and doodads. The zipper was diagonal across the front.

"Whaddya mean?" he said.

"Why did you try to kill me?" I said.

"We was just going to talk with you," he said.

"What about?"

The guy in the leather jacket said, "We was told to talk to you about staying away from Dwayne Woodcock."

"Who told you?" I said.

He looked at the ground. The guy in the fancy jacket looked at him.

Hawk said, "We already dumped two of you. You think we going to have a lot of trouble going four for four?"

Fancy jacket shook his head.

"Guy from New York hired us, give us five grand, said to rough you up and tell you lay off Dwayne Woodcock. Said if you were stubborn, or we thought the warning wouldn't stick, we was to kill you. He left it up to us."

I looked at Hawk. "Twelve fifty apiece?"

He smiled and shook his head. "That's embarrassing," he said.

"It's humiliating," I said. I looked back at the two hoods.

"Twelve fifty?" I said.

The one in the leather jacket shrugged. He was still staring at the floor.

"Why not," he said.

"Why not?" I said. "For crissake, think how I feel. Some guy thinks I'm only worth twelve fifty to whack? What kind of thing is that to learn about yourself."

Neither one said anything.

"Guy from New York named Deegan?" I said.

"He didn't say his name. He just gave us the money, told us what he wanted."

"How'd he find you?"

"Come into the bar where Frankie works, said he heard Frankie would do this kind of job."

"Worked," I said. "Frankie doesn't work there any-more."

"So Frankie says, sure, and he gets the rest of us and we come to do this."

"Who told Dwayne to call me?" I said.

"I dunno," Leather Jacket said. "Frankie just said you'd show up here around six-thirty. Said the New York guy told him."

I nodded. "Okay, beat it. You run into the New York guy tell him he needs to hire better than twelve fifty apiece."

"We didn't know he'd be here," the guy in the fancy jacket said. He looked at Hawk.

"If I knew you were in this price range," I said, "I wouldn't have bothered to bring him."

I jerked my head toward the Blazer.

"Screw," I said.

The two of them turned and got into the Blazer and pulled away. Hawk walked to his Jaguar, parked at the near end of the floor. He opened the trunk, put the shotgun in, closed the trunk, got into the car and backed out. He lowered his window.

"Thanks," I said.

"Twelve fifty," he said, and shook his head happily.

Then the window went up silently and the Jag slid away down the ramp.

21

The next day I went to see Dwayne. I found him at the field house. He had no classes and he was there with three other players shooting around.

I stood in the shadows at the top of the stands and looked down at him for a while. Two of the managers were there, retrieving balls, keeping the ball racks full. There was some banter, some hoots at a particularly bodacious jam. Davis, the point guard, was the butt of a lot of teasing.

"Hey, white shadow," Kenny Green yelled, "you stuff one." He had a spare net he'd picked up and was holding it open at knee level. Davis went behind his back, drove toward the basket and pulled up for an eighteen-foot jumper, which he swished.

"Hit one of them, Kenny," Davis said.

Green, who had never played more than eight feet away

from the basket, laughed and cut for the basket and Davis hit him with an alley oop and Green stuffed it.

Dwayne worked methodically around the perimeter shooting jump shots. One of the managers would pass him the ball and he would catch it and in the same motion go up for the shot. Every third or fourth time he'd fake the shot and drive. He did this without pause over and over again. He didn't do much talking, he seemed wholly focused on his workout.

I watched for maybe ten minutes and then moved on along the top aisle of the arena to Dixie's office. He was there. Tommy Christopher had told me that Dixie took Christmas morning off, unless there was a game.

"You got something?" he said.

"Nothing you'll like," I said.

"I haven't liked anything about you since you first walked in here," he said.

I sat in the chair across from him.

"Dwayne set me up last night to be shot," I said.

Dixie looked at me without any understanding.

"I mean he called me and arranged a meeting with me and when I showed up for it, there were four guys there and they tried to kill me."

Dixie shook his head slowly, persistently.

"Dwayne wasn't one of them?" Dixie said.

"No, but he arranged to have me there."

"He wouldn't do that," Dixie said.

"No, he just called and wanted to meet me in a parking garage and then decided not to come and, oddly enough, four guys happened to be there who want me to lay off this case and they had guns."

"Parking garage? There was a shooting last night at a parking garage on the waterfront."

I nodded.

"Jesus Christ," Dixie said, "was that you?"

I didn't answer.

"Jesus Christ," Dixie said again. "I . . . what are we going to do?"

"We're going to talk with Dwayne."

"Spenser, Dwayne's a good kid, he's a quality kid, he wouldn't . . . he must have been under pressure."

"We'll find out what kind of quality kid he is," I said. "So far he seems to me to be a loud-mouthed pain in the ass. I'm way out on a goddamned limb trying to save his neck."

"I know, I know, don't think I don't know that. But the kid is so great. We can't lose him. I mean he's a blow off the court sometimes, I see him in the interviews talking about himself in the third person. I know he can be irritating. But on the court . . . Spenser, he is the most coachable kid I ever had. He's got better work habits than I have. He listens, he does what I tell him, he practices more than anybody on the team. He stuck with the program for four years. He could have gone pro after his sophomore year. But he stayed here out of loyalty, out of respect for me and his teammates. Guys with talent like Dwayne, they can dog it through college, take the big pro contract, never really learn the game. Dwayne could pass more, maybe, but he's got all the fundamentals. He knows the game. He feels it. Spenser, the kid is a genius in his own way."

125

"Get him in here, Dixie. I'm now covering up point shaving and accessory to attempted murder for him. I need to find a handle on this thing or I'm going down with him."

"You didn't report the attempt to the cops?"

"No," I said. "I couldn't figure out how to do that and not get Dwayne dragged into it. *What were you doing in the garage? Why did you agree to go there? Why did these guys want to hit you?* Cops aren't dumb. Cops been lied to a lot in their career. They know about that."

"And if they find out it was you and you didn't report it?"

"Pretty well eliminates my chances for the gumshoe hall of fame," I said. "Get him in here."

Dixie nodded. He rose and walked past me to his office door and stuck his head out.

"Vicki," he said to his secretary, "tell Dwayne I want to see him, please."

Dixie came back around his desk and sat heavily in his swivel chair.

"Goddamn," he said. "Goddamn."

We were quiet while we waited for Dwayne. When he came in he filled the room. It was always startling to see Dwayne up close. When I wasn't with him, I forgot how big he was and tended to think of him in normal-sized terms. But in shorts and a tank top, with a towel draped over his shoulders, he was startling in his size. And more startling in his athleticism. He moved as gracefully as any corner back, and he was built like a good middleweight boxer, except that he was six feet nine inches tall. As he moved the muscles bunched and rolled under his skin.

"What's happening, Coach?" Dwayne saw me but didn't look again.

"Come in, Dwayne, close the door, sit down."

Dwayne did all three and looked at Dunham. Dixie put his hands behind his head and laced the fingers. He leaned back against the spring on the swivel chair and took in a breath and let it out.

"Dwayne," he said, "you gotta help us."

Dwayne's eyes shifted to me when Dixie said *us* and shifted back to the coach. He nodded.

"Sure," he said.

"Dwayne, you got to tell us what the hell is going on."

"I don't know what you mean, Coach."

"Yeah, you do. You been shaving points. Last night you set this man up to be murdered."

Dwayne's head was shaking back and forth in denial all the time Dixie talked.

"You called him," Dixie said, "you told him to meet you in a parking garage, and instead of you, when he got there he found some people with guns."

Dwayne's head continued to shake.

"They weren't . . . He said they wasn't . . ."

"Who?" I said to Dwayne.

Dwayne shook his head some more.

"Goddamn it, Dwayne," Dixie said. "Think a bit. This man is trying to help you. I'm trying to help you. Now, goddamn it, how we going to help you if you won't tell us what's going on?"

Dwayne was still shaking his head. He wasn't looking at Dixie anymore. He was looking down.

"You got a responsibility, Dwayne," Dixie said.

Dwayne didn't raise his eyes. His head was still now, and he gazed steadfastly at the floor.

"Dwayne, you got a responsibility to this program, to me, to the other guys on the team."

Dwayne was motionless.

"You owe it to yourself, Dwayne."

Dwayne raised his head and looked at Dixie.

"I can't, Coach," he said.

"Why not?" Dixie said.

The connection between Dwayne and Dixie was real and concentrated. I got a hint of why he was a great coach.

"I got other responsibilities," Dwayne said.

"Responsibilities? Who the Christ to?" Dixie was outraged.

Dwayne shook his head.

"More important than the program, Dwayne?"

Dwayne looked at the ground again. We were all quiet. In the outer office we could hear Vicki typing. I watched the quartz clock on the wall for a while. The second hand jerked around the dial in one-second increments.

"Dwayne," Dixie said, "I'm going to have to sit you down."

Dwayne's head raised slowly until his eyes were on Dixie's face.

Their eyes held each other. I was entirely extraneous.

"You got to help us to help you, or I can't play you," Dixie said.

"Tournament startin'," Dwayne mumbled.

"Yeah," Dixie said.

Dwayne looked at him some more. Then slowly he stood up. He looked down at Dixie, for a full breath cycle.

"I got to go," he said.

"You change your mind, Dwayne, you know where I am," Dixie said.

Dwayne nodded and turned slowly away. He carefully didn't look at me. He opened the door and went out and closed it carefully behind him. The silence in the room was majestic. Dixie slammed his open hand flat on his desktop.

"Damn," he said.

"Yeah," I said.

We sat some more.

"What's your chances in the NCAA Tournament without him?" I said.

"Slim and none," Dixie said.

"What are you going to tell the press?" I said.

"Nothing," Dixie said.

"They'll be all over you," I said.

"Like ticks on a bird dog," Dixie said.

22

We were at my place. Susan was taking a bath and I was in bed reading Roger Angell's new book. It was ten o'clock on a Friday night. The door was locked, my gun was on the bed table, the television was playing with the sound off. All was peaceful. Susan came from the bathroom wearing a large blue towel and drying herself with it as she walked.

"Is there a wonderful movie we can watch on cable?" she said.

"No," I said. "I think we'll have to make love."

"And have a late supper after?"

"We had supper," I said.

"No, we had dinner," Susan said.

"Of course," I said.

"Well, if 'tis to be done," Susan said, "better it be done quickly."

She dropped her towel and dove onto the bed. I dog-eared the page and put the book on the bed table beside the gun.

Susan made her bubbly little laugh, which, in a less stately woman, might have been construed as a giggle. She pulled the covers part way back and wiggled in under them.

"Oh good," she said. "The sheets are clean."

She pressed against me.

"And," she said with her near-giggle lurking under the words, "I think you're glad to see me."

"You shrinks," I said, "you don't miss a thing."

"Some things are easier to miss than others," she said.

"I beg your pardon," I said, and she inched her body up a bit against mine and pressed her open mouth against mine.

All smiles ceased.

Susan's energy was limitless. She worked out every day, often twice a day. Her body was strong and very flexible. I was in pretty good shape myself.

When it was over we lay pressed together, our bodies wet with perspiration, our breaths coming in big heaves, our lips still touching. Susan's eyes were closed.

"I never remember how strong you are," Susan said with her lips touching mine as she spoke, and her eyes still closed.

"It's because my heart is pure," I said.

"Bullshit," she said.

"Good point," I said.

We lay like that for a bit, quietly. Then Susan rolled

away from me and sat up without using her hands and got out of bed and walked across to the bedroom closet, where she kept a robe.

Eat your heart out, Paralegal.

She put on her robe of many colors and got one out for me. It was black, with a hood. I looked like Darth Vader in it. But Susan liked it. She draped it over the foot of the bed.

"What's for supper?" she said.

I put on my Darth Vader robe and went to the kitchen. When Susan came out of the bathroom I was peeling an avocado.

"That looks encouraging," she said. She came and sat at the counter on a high stool with a fluted back. I put a glass before her and poured in some Cristal Champagne. She smiled.

"To us," she said. We both drank some.

"You have always had wonderful taste in champagne and women," she said.

"The taste in women is instinctual," I said. "I learned the champagne from Hawk."

I finished the avocado and sliced it over endive leaves. I added some mango slices and put over it a dressing of first-press olive oil and lemon juice and honey. I put one plate in front of Susan and the other at my place and came around the counter.

Susan poured herself half a glass more of champagne and took a small bite of the avocado.

"Yum, yum," she said.

"It's only the beginning," I said.

"How is it going with Dwayne what's-his-name?" Susan said.

"Woodcock," I said. "It's going very badly."

Susan took a crescent of mango on her fork and dabbed it in the dressing and ate it in two small bites. Slowly.

"Tell me about it," she said when she was through chewing.

I did.

By the time I was through I had sliced some cob smoked turkey onto a plate with some tomato chutney. I checked the whole wheat biscuits in the oven.

"There needs to be a reason," Susan said. "Everything he cares about is pressing on him to act differently and yet he won't."

"I'm wondering, the kind of kid he is, is there some kind of jock ethic here?"

Susan clicked the rim of her champagne glass against her bottom teeth gently. I checked the biscuits again. They were golden. I took them out and put them on the counter to cool.

"Are you suggesting that he sees this gang of gamblers as his new team?" Susan said.

I shrugged. "Chantel says he thinks very highly of them. She says he needs white approval though he won't admit it, even to himself."

"Maybe why he's such a good player," Susan said. "Lot of white approval there."

"It helps that he's six feet nine and quicker than I."

"That quick . . ." Susan said. "Of course it helps. But there must be other people that tall and that quick who are not as good as Dwayne."

"I imagine."

"If so," Susan said, "won't Coach Dunham benching him change that?"

"Because Bobby Deegan and his outfit won't be so nice to Dwayne when he's riding the pines and can't help them shave points?" I said.

"Yes," Susan said.

I put the biscuits into a basket and put the platter of turkey and chutney on the counter. I got out some cranberry conserve that we had put up together last fall and set that next to the biscuits.

"I'm hoping for that," I said.

"But even if Dwayne turns against them finally," Susan said, "and tells you enough to put them out of business, how can you do it without exposing Dwayne?"

"I don't know," I said. "I was hoping if I drank enough champagne with you, I'd think of something."

"What you normally think of when you get drunk," Susan said, "will not do Dwayne any good at all."

"At least I'll be consistent," I said.

23

Susan went with me the next morning to Taft. It was a day when she didn't see patients, and she cancelled the class she taught at Tufts to join me.

"What is it exactly we're up to?" she said.

"We're going to look into the matter of Dwayne being a senior and unable to read," I said.

"And why are we doing that?"

"Because I don't know what else to do," I said. "Dwayne can't read and he's tied up in some kind of gambling scam. They're probably not connected, but since I don't know what to do about the gambling thing, I may as well look into the other thing."

Susan nodded.

"Better than doing nothing," I said.

Susan nodded again. "And where is Hawk?" she said.

"Around," I said.

"So how come I don't see him?"

"I don't know how he does that," I said. "But he can disappear if he needs to."

"But you know he's there," Susan said.

We were walking along a wide, hot, top path that curved up to the administration building.

"Yes."

"Because he said so?"

"Yes."

"And if those people try to kill you again and he's not there you're very likely dead."

"He's there," I said.

"Yes," Susan said.

We went up the wide granite steps and in through the Georgian entry of the administration building. There was a reception desk in the rotunda area and a long corridor that went straight through the building. We went past the desk and went halfway down the corridor and took some stairs to the left up to the second floor. Toward the back of the building on the second floor was Madelaine Roth's office.

Her door was open. She was at her desk talking on the phone. When she saw me she waved us in and gestured at the chairs in front of her desk.

"All right, Judy," she said. "Seven o'clock. Yes. Bye-bye."

She hung up and leaned forward over her desk and smiled at us.

"Dr. Roth," I said. "This is my, ah, associate, Dr. Silverman."

Madelaine stood and leaned across the desk and put her hand out. Susan half rose to take it. They shook hands and both sat down. Professional courtesy.

Madelaine sat back in her chair and put her palms together, making a steeple out of her fingers, and touched her lips with her fingertips. She said, "What is it today, Mr. Spenser."

"I'm still looking into the matter of Dwayne's illiteracy," I said.

She nodded, patiently, *this is my job, I have to put up with exasperating people.*

"How'd he get this far?" I said.

"I'm afraid I can't tell you," Madelaine said. "I am his academic adviser, but he has never been a student in a class with me. What strategies he employed to conceal the truth from us . . ." She turned her palms up and shrugged.

"What were his SATs like?"

"I don't really recall," Madelaine said. "It is, of course, confidential information."

I looked at Susan. "Confidential," I said.

"Isn't it always?"

I looked at the three degrees on the wall. B.A., Georgetown. M.A., Ph.D., Queens College, New York.

"Do you have Dwayne's class schedule for this year, and previous ones?" I said.

"Of course," Madelaine said.

"May I see the schedules?"

"What on earth for?"

"I am still looking for an answer. I am not getting anywhere with you. I thought I'd talk with his teachers."

"With his teachers?"

"Yeah."

"You can't do that," Madelaine said.

"Confidential?" Susan said.

"No, but, I mean you can't just walk around the University asking all Dwayne's teachers about why he can't read."

"Why not?" I said

"Well, I mean, you'd have to make appointments, and, well, they wouldn't . . . many of them wouldn't like it."

"Would they not wish to reach an understanding?" Susan said, "as to how a young man who can neither read nor write could get a passing grade in their courses?"

"Do you teach, Dr. Silverman?"

"I give a course at Tufts. Primarily I am in private practice as a psychotherapist."

"Well, with a Ph.D. you've certainly been in an academic setting long enough to know, with your teaching experience at Tufts also, how prickly the academic world can be about any threat, real or imagined, to academic freedom," Madelaine said.

Susan smiled. "What greater threat is there to academic freedom than illiteracy? To any kind of freedom?"

"You will offend a great many people," Madelaine said.

Susan smiled more widely. "My colleague will weather that, I think."

We all sat for a few moments.

Finally I said, "Do we get the schedules?"

Madelaine shook her head. "I'm sorry, I'm just not comfortable giving them to you."

"Well," I said, "at least you have a good reason."

I stood. Dr. Silverman stood. Dr. Roth did not.

"Wasn't it Dr. Johnson," I said, "who called academic freedom the last refuge of scoundrels?"

Dr. Roth said nothing. Dr. Silverman and I left.

We walked down the corridor and back down the stairs.

"Dr. Johnson said 'patriotism is the last refuge of a scoundrel,' " Susan said.

"I know, but does Dr. Roth know?" I said.

"Unlikely," Susan said.

President Cort's office was in the other wing of the administration building.

"I warn you," I said to Susan, "this woman is infatuated with me. So be prepared to smother your jealousy."

Susan yawned. "I'll do what I can," she said. We went into the President's office and June Merriman at her desk looked at me passionately.

"Oh, God," she said.

"This will be hard," Dr. Silverman murmured.

"June," I said. "This is my friend Susan Silverman."

Ms. Merriman smiled with her lips only and made a small nod of her head.

"We'll need a list of Dwayne Woodcock's teachers, June."

"May I ask why?" June said.

"June," I said. "I know you want to string this out so you may spend more precious minutes with me. But Dr. Silverman here is my honeybunch and she's alert to even the most subtle of love ploys."

"Please do not be offensive," she said.

139

"Oh, June," I said. "How transparent."

"You won't leave without the list, will you," she said.

"No," I said.

"I can call the registrar and have Dwayne's schedule over the past four years Xeroxed. You'll have to make the list yourself."

She then made her phone call, prefacing the request with the phrase, "President Cort wonders if you would . . ."

In an hour we were having a spot of lunch at the Lancaster Tap. In a manila envelope on the table beside my water glass were copies of Dwayne's classes over the past four years.

"And what are you going to do with all those class schedules?" Susan said.

"I'm going to talk to all his teachers."

Susan shook her head. "You are a piece of work," she said.

"Says so," I said "on ladies' room walls all over the country."

"No," Susan said. "It doesn't."

24

For the next week I interviewed professors. Susan came with me when she could on the assumption that she was more academic than I was and could add some insight. George Lyman Kittredge couldn't have added enough insight.

I was alone when I talked with J. Taylor Hack, Francis Calvert Dolbear Professor of American Civilization. Hack was tall and portly and well tailored except that his shoes weren't shined.

"Woodcock," he said. "No, I'm afraid I can't remember the boy."

"Took your course in The Frontier Hypothesis, last spring," I said.

Hack smiled graciously. "It's quite a popular course," he said. He dipped his head modestly. "I'm just not able to recall all of my students."

"Gee," I said. "That's too bad. I thought maybe because Dwayne is six feet nine inches tall and the best college basketball player in the world, you might have noticed him more than others."

"The best, really, how interesting. I don't pay much attention to basketball, I fear."

I was looking at my notes. "Dwayne got a B- in your course."

"Well, he did very well. It's rather a demanding course and for a, ah, basketball player to do that well, Dwayne must be an unusual young man."

"He can't read," I said.

"I beg your pardon."

"He can't read."

Hack was absolutely silent.

"Probably gotten an A," I said, "if he could read."

"It's not possible. Someone must have taken the exams for him," Hack said finally.

"Probably," I said. "And probably wrote his papers for him. You wouldn't have known if someone sat in for him during class?"

Hack paused a long time before he answered. Finally he said, "No, I wouldn't . . . there are forty or fifty people in this class, I give it every semester. I have two other classes each year. There're papers, and my own research."

"Anyone ever ask you to give his grades any special attention?" I said.

"No. Good God, no. No one would intrude on the grading process like that."

"Of course not," I said. "And you never heard of Dwayne Woodcock?"

"No."

"Amazing," I said.

"I do not," Hack said, "spend my time poring over the sports pages."

"I know who Frederick Jackson Turner is," I said.

"I don't see the relevance."

"There's a surprise," I said.

Susan was with me when we talked to a young assistant professor named Mary Ann Hedrick. She had an office about the size of a confessional, in the humanities building.

"Sure, I remember Dwayne," she said. "I had him in the American lit survey, two years ago. Who could forget him?"

"He's easy to notice," I said.

Mary Ann winked at Susan. "I'll say," she said.

"Was he in regular attendance?" I said.

"In class? Hell no. He showed up once in a while and he'd come to conference in my office when it was scheduled. But he had practice, and then he had games, and it's hard for a kid. The course is required, and I'm sure was about things that he had no interest in. Imagine him reading Emily Dickinson?"

"He couldn't read," I said.

"Excuse me."

"He couldn't read Emily Dickinson. He can't read."

"What do you mean he can't read?" Mary Ann said.

"He's illiterate," Susan said.

"God, aren't they all," Mary Ann said. "But you mean really, don't you?"

"Yes."

"Jesus Christ," she said. "What is he now? A senior?"

"Yes."

"And he can't read," she shook her head. "Don't we look like a collection of prime jerks," she said.

"Yes," I said. "You do."

"We're interested in how that happened," Susan said.

"It happens because nobody gives a goddamn. Me included. The students are the necessary evil in the teaching profession. Otherwise it's a pretty good deal. You don't work hard, you have a lot of time off. The pay's not much, but nobody hassles you. You can read and write and publish, pretty well unimpeded except for the students. Most of us don't like them much."

"Anybody ever pressure you to give Dwayne a better grade or whatever?" I said.

"No," she said. "What did I give him?"

I consulted my list. "C + ," I said.

"And he can't read," she said. "Boy, is this embarrassing or what?"

"Dwayne's embarrassed too," Susan said.

"I don't give exams, and I don't take attendance. I give them two papers a semester, and I work on grading them. But I don't like bluebook knowledge and I don't like teaching kids who are there only because they're compelled."

"So someone wrote Dwayne's papers for him," Susan said.

"Sure," Mary Ann said. "I don't remember him now, but I probably suspected it when they came in sounding like an Oxford honors thesis, but frankly I figure you get more teaching done by keeping them in school than by flunking them out. Besides, the truth, charging him with plagiarism and flunking him is a pain in the ass. It's easier to let it go."

"Why is it a pain in the ass?" Susan said.

"They come in and whine to you and swear they did it, but their roommate helped them, and . . ." Mary Ann made a push-it-all-away gesture with both hands. "I'm doing a book on Ellen Glasgow, and I like to work on it when I'm not teaching."

"No pressure not to catch him plagiarizing?" I said.

"None," she said. "That's the truth. What are you going to do about this?"

"I don't know," I said.

"Will you tell people?" Mary Ann said.

"It's what Dwayne wanted to know," I said.

"We're all ashamed of this," Mary Ann said.

"That's the easy part," I said.

Now and then I'd see Hawk, drifting across the street behind me. Parking at the other end of the block when I got out of my car. Motionless and barely real at the far end of a corridor as I stepped into someone's office. He was there, for a moment, with the morning light behind him when I went to see Harold Wagner.

Wagner taught Black History and had given Dwayne a D in the fall semester.

"He didn't do much," Wagner said. "And he didn't seem very interested."

"Do you know that he can't read?" I said.

"I don't know it," Wagner said. "But I suspected it. He

missed the midterm, and prevailed upon me to let him do a paper instead. He got an A on the paper. He said he was going to have to miss the final because of basketball. I said he'd have to make it up. I was skeptical about the paper. He missed two scheduled make-ups. He said an incomplete would make him ineligible to play. That Coach Dunham was a martinet, not his phrase, about such things. I knew what was riding on his having a good senior year. I said he could take a D for the course. His grades in his other courses were such that a D wouldn't make him ineligible."

"And that was it?" I said.

"No. I spoke to Dr. Roth, the academic coordinator for basketball. I said Dwayne was academically troubled. That I questioned his basic skills and that I thought perhaps he should be tested to see if we could help him."

"What did she say?"

"She said she thought I was unduly worried. That Dwayne had been doing well in other classes, but that she'd talk with him."

"She didn't press you to alter his grades?" I said.

Wagner shook his head. I thought about it for a minute.

"I didn't want to take away his chance," Wagner said. "There's not that many of us get a chance like Dwayne."

"I know," I said. "I got the same problem . . . among others."

"It is Dwayne's fault too," Wagner said.

"Yes. He knows he can't read. He hasn't done anything about it."

Wagner looked down at his hands for a moment. "Our fault too," he said.

"Yeah," I said. "It is."

25

So far as I could tell no one had conspired to keep Dwayne in school, although Dr. Roth kept bothering me. If Wagner had told her, and he didn't seem to be lying, she had not only her own knowledge, but the testimony of a professor. Why would she run the risk of covering it up at that stage? For herself, the help-out-the-poor-little-darkie attitude might explain it. But once someone else knew, would she jeopardize herself? Not the Madelaine that I knew.

I swiveled my office chair around and pulled my phone closer and dialed information in Washington, D.C. In maybe two minutes I had tracked down the registrar's office at Georgetown University. They had no Madelaine Roth. I called the alumni office. They had a Madelaine Reilly who had married Simon Roth in 1984. She was a member of the class of '82. They did not know the status of the marriage; but Simon Roth lived currently in Fullerton, California, and Mrs. Roth lived in Newton, Massachusetts. I hung up and went to my file cabinet in the corner so when the door opened it was concealed. Susan said it was the single ugliest piece of furniture she had ever personally seen, though a friend of hers who worked for Bedford Travel claimed to have seen an uglier piece in Paraguay in 1981. I got out my file on Meade Alexander and thumbed through it. Ah ha! Gerry Broz graduated from Georgetown in 1983. So they could easily have been acquainted. Pays to do business with a professional detective.

While I was on a hot streak I called a New York City cop I'd met a couple of years ago when I had worked for Patricia Utley. He wasn't in. He'd call me back.

The office felt stuffy. I opened the window a crack and then went and opened my office door to get some cross ventilation. Hawk was leaning on the door jamb across the hall talking with the paralegal. I left the door open and went back and sat at my desk and thought about what I was doing. After about fifteen minutes of running it back and forth it was clear that I didn't know what I was doing. What I had accomplished so far was to make people want to kill me. I'd gotten Dwayne in trouble with his coach. I had already found out what I'd been hired to find out, and I wasn't telling the people who'd hired me. I knew Dwayne was shaving points. I knew Deegan and others had put him up to it. I knew Deegan was connected to Gerry Broz, and I knew that Dwayne's academic adviser could be connected to Gerry Broz. And I could find that out in time, if she was, or if she wasn't. And I knew that the faculty at

Taft, by and large, didn't much care if Dwayne could read. What I didn't know was what good any of this did me, and how to get Dwayne out of the mess he was in without destroying his life.

I looked across the hall. Hawk had moved into the office and taken a seat next to the paralegal's desk. *Easy for him. All he had to do was follow me around and keep people from shooting me in the back.* I heard the paralegal laugh. *What's so goddamned funny? Probably be moving in with her Monday.* She laughed again, and the liquid hint of a giggle lurked in the laugh. *Probably wants me to be best man.*

The phone rang. I answered. A voice said, "This is Corsetti."

I said, "Remember me? The killing on Seventy-Seventh Street, guy named Rambeau?"

"Body'd been there about a week," Corsetti said.

"Yeah, that's it."

"What do you need," Corsetti said.

"I need to know about a guy named Bobby Deegan," I said. "Probably from Brooklyn."

"Why?"

I told him without naming any names but Deegan's.

"I don't know him," Corsetti said. "I'll check with Brooklyn and get back to you."

Across the hall Hawk's success continued.

In about forty-five minutes the phone rang. I answered.

"This is Detective Kevin Maguire," a voice said. "Detective Corsetti from Manhattan says you're looking for information on Bobby Deegan."

149

"I am."

"Okay. Deegan's been in twice. Once for grand theft auto when he was about nineteen. Once for hijacking a cigarette truck ten years later. He hasn't worked a day in his life. Been hustling since he got out of Queens College."

"Queens College?" I said.

"Yeah. Educated. Did a year of grad work there, too. Don't make no difference. He's a wiseguy. Grew up on the fringes of the Brooklyn mob. We can't prove it, but we're pretty sure he's one of the guys hit Joey Gallo."

"He married?"

"Yeah, lives in Far Rockaway, got a couple kids. But he fucks around. We're looking to get him for a cash room stickup at an OTB parlor in Manhattan."

"Who's he run with?" I said.

"Got a pencil?" he said.

"Yeah."

"Okay," he said, "known associates," and read a list of maybe a dozen names. None of them meant anything to me.

"You know any connections he has in Boston?" I said.

"No."

"What else you got to say about him?" I said.

"Bad news," Maguire said. "Got sort of college manners, you know, a breezy yuppie. Guy's crazy. Keep talking to you nice and shoot you in midsentence. You'd never know he didn't like you."

"He does his own work?"

"Sometimes. Sometimes contracts out. Doesn't mind doing it himself. Mostly it's what's convenient."

"Tell me about the betting parlor," I said.

"Last December. Four guys, went in with a key after closing. Tied up a couple cashiers, got seven hundred thousand or so in cash, small bills, no serials. Everybody in Brooklyn knows it was Deegan and his outfit, but nobody can tie it to him."

"Had somebody inside," I said.

"Everybody figures that, but we don't have anyone for that either. We talked to both cashiers until they turned gray, they don't have nothing to say. Two dozen people could have got a key legitimately, two thousand could have scooped it and made a dupe. Things ain't buttoned up really tight over there."

"Nobody's flashing money," I said.

"Deegan's been flashing money all his life. Story is he's made some heavy scores betting sports."

"That's the connection up here," I said. "He's rigging basketball games."

"Point shaving?"

"Yes."

"Can you get him on it?" Maguire said.

"Well, yes and no."

"What the hell's that mean?"

"Means I probably can take him down on the point shaving deal, but not without taking down some people I don't want to take down."

"They're involved with Deegan," Maguire said, "they deserve to go down too."

"All you need out of this is Deegan," I said.

"Any way we can," Maguire said. "Any other name, too, on that list I gave you."

"Name Madelaine Roth or Madelaine Reilly mean anything to you?" I said.

"Not right off," Maguire said. "She got something to do with Deegan?"

"I don't know. She was at Queens College, too, in grad school."

"Hey, there's a hot lead," Maguire said.

"She went to Georgetown same time as a local hood that Deegan's connected with."

"Jesus Christ," Maguire said. "You a campus cop?"

"She works at the school where the points are getting shaved."

Maguire was silent for a moment at the other end.

"Okay," he said. "I'll see if anybody knows her. Maybe she'll turn up on the computer. Goddamn thing must be good for something."

"Find something, let me know," I said.

"Yeah," Maguire said. "You too."

We hung up.

I observed Hawk's technique for a few moments, then I got out the phone book and looked up the paralegal's number and dialed. In a moment I heard the phone ring across the hall. She answered.

I said, "This is Spenser across the hall. There's an escaped sex fiend loose in the building. He's masquerading as a big good-looking black guy and I wondered if you'd seen him."

There was a pause.

"He's drawn obsessively to paralegals," I said.

"Does he rip off their clothes and do unspeakably kinky stuff?" she said.

"Often," I said.

"My God, he's here," she said.

"Want me to come over?"

"Hell no," she said. "Leave us alone."

She giggled again, blatantly now, into the phone.

"Oh hell," I said, "let me speak to him."

In a moment Hawk said, "Hello."

"I'm going down to Henry's and set new records on the Nautilus," I said. "If you're not at the moment of climax perhaps you'd care to stroll along and learn something."

I heard Hawk speak off the phone. "He worried," Hawk said, "that we at the moment of climax."

I hung up and headed out to the gym. The sex fiend joined me in the hall. "Jealousy an ugly thing," he said.

26

Without Dwayne, Taft won the Big East with an overtime at the buzzer victory over Syracuse and headed into the NCAA Tournament. Dwayne dressed for every game and sat on the end of the bench farthest from Dixie. The question was on the cover of *Sports Illustrated*, and the talk shows rang with it. Why isn't Dwayne Woodcock playing? Dwayne wasn't saying and neither was Dixie Dunham. The pro teams, Dixie said, were on his case worse than the press. Was there a reason that Dwayne shouldn't be drafted? Did he have a drug problem? Was there an injury? Taft's chances of getting to the final four without Dwayne were worse than my chances had been that day I fought Walcott.

Every day Dwayne showed up for practice. Every day he worked as hard as he always did. Nights he stayed in his condo with Chantel. Hawk and I had taken to trailing along behind him.

"Figure now that he ain't playing and can't help them," Hawk said, "might occur to them that he can hurt them."

"So we watch his back to protect him from people that you're watching my back to protect me from," I said.

"You get into weird shit," Hawk said.

We followed Dwayne around for most of that week when I saw Dixie after practice.

"Cort wants to see you," Dixie said. "Says if I see you to tell you to get on up to his office now."

"Gulp," I said.

Dixie kept on walking toward the locker room. Dwayne passed me without looking at me and went into the locker room behind Dixie. I left Hawk watching Dwayne and walked up across campus toward the President's office. I was aware that Hawk wasn't behind me and I could feel the muscles bunch in my shoulders as I walked across the unsheltered quadrangle.

In the outer office of President Cort, June Merriman looked pleased when I came in.

"Well, where have you been? President Cort has been trying to reach you for two days."

"Mostly I was home," I said, "playing with my knuckle knife collection."

"I'll tell the President you're here," she said. "Mr. Morton is with him! And Mr. Haller!"

"Wait, let me catch my breath," I said.

June pressed the intercom like someone lining up three cherries on a slot machine.

"Mr. Spenser has arrived," she said.

I couldn't hear the response, but she could and she said, "They'll see you right now," and stood and walked to the door to Cort's office and ushered me in, gladly.

Cort was at his desk looking serious. Morton was standing at the window gazing down at the campus. Haller was sitting on a couch against the wall with his feet on the coffee table. He looked amused.

Cort looked up at me for a long silent moment. Morton turned from the window frowning. I bore it stoutly.

"I'd like a full report, please," Cort said. He had on a double breasted gray pinstripe suit and a large silk foulard tie.

"I haven't found out anything," I said.

"That's your idea of a full report?"

"Often," I said, "I'm referred to as the great compressionist."

Haller recrossed his legs on the coffee table.

"You've practically pillaged our student personnel records. You badgered a large number of faculty members, Dwayne Woodcock is now on the bench, Taft is likely to lose the NCAA championship tournament. Neither Dwayne nor Coach Dunham will comment on this. The national press is in full cry." Cort's voice was a masterful example of emotion under firm control.

"Aw, hell," I said, "it wasn't much."

"You have charged that Dwayne cannot read," Cort said.

I didn't say anything.

Morton had his arms folded across his chest. He had on

a dark blue pinstriped double breasted suit with a large maroon silk tie.

"And you have nothing to report?" he said.

"Hard to believe, isn't it," I said.

"Mr. Spenser," Cort said, "we have been paying you to find out things that we want found out, not to disrupt this campus and annoy our faculty."

"No extra charge for that," I said. "It's a professional courtesy."

"There's nothing funny about this, Spenser," Morton said. "We want an accounting."

"Don't blame you," I said, "but I'm not going to give you one."

Morton looked at Haller. Cort looked at Haller.

Cort said, "Vince, do we not have a viable legal position here?"

Haller smiled. "Sure you do, Adrian. Everybody has a viable legal position everywhere in this great land, whatever that means. But in fact what you can do is fire him or accept his report. All other courses are, ah, counterproductive."

"Counterproductive," I said. "Vince, you been taking night courses?"

"Flippancy is no substitute for competence, Mr. Spenser," Cort said.

"That's too bad," I said. "I was hoping to get by on it."

Cort looked at Morton. Morton looked at Haller. Haller shrugged.

"You leave us no choice," Cort said. "I'm afraid we're

going to have to terminate our arrangement as of now. We will honor your expenses through this afternoon until five."

"Call it even," I said.

I turned and started for the door.

Haller said, "Wait a minute, Spenser." He turned to Cort and Morton. "You think firing him will get him out of your hair. It won't. He's got hold of something's tail, I know him. He's not going to let go until he pulls it out of its hole and sees what it is."

"He will no longer be welcome on this campus," Cort said.

Haller laughed. "You think he cares? He isn't welcome most places. He doesn't give a shit, Adrian, whether he's welcome or he isn't." Haller turned toward me. "Do you," he said.

I smiled enigmatically.

"What have you got, Spenser?"

I shook my head. "I don't quite know, Vince. No, that's not it. I do know. What I don't know is what the hell to do with it."

"And you won't talk about it," Haller said.

"No."

Haller shrugged. "He won't let go," he said to Cort and Morton.

"We hired him on your recommendation, Vince."

"And you didn't listen to the warnings that went with it," Haller said. "He's good. There isn't anyone as good, let alone better. But he does what the hell he is going to do and if you don't like it he doesn't care. I told you that. You hire Spenser and sometimes you get more than you hoped for and sometimes you don't like it. You remember those words?"

Cort was angry. "Enough," he said. "If there was a mistake made, now is the time to rectify it. You're fired, Mr. Spenser, and you are to be removed from campus by the university police if you are in any way an impediment to the business of this campus."

"I love it when you're angry," I said. "Your whole face lights up."

27

When Hawk and I got back to my office there was a message on my machine.

"This is Maguire in New York. Nothing in the computer or anywhere else on Madelaine Roth. But Deegan has a girlfriend in the Boston area. Slips out on the old lady every other week or so and goes up there. You get anything, let me know."

Hawk and I looked at each other.

"Okay," I said. "That's more coincidence than I'm ready to buy."

"Be odd," Hawk said, "if it ain't Madelaine."

"So she knows Broz from Georgetown, she knows Deegan from Queens College. When Deegan is looking for someone to scrag me, she puts him in touch with Broz."

"Education a wonderful thing," Hawk said.

"She's got to be in on the fix with Dwayne," I said.

Hawk was quiet.

"So if I follow her around, after a while she'll lead me to Deegan."

"What you going to do when you find him?" Hawk said.

"Don't screw this up," I said. "It's almost a plan."

Hawk nodded.

"Okay," I said, "you stick with Dwayne during the day. I'll try to get the campus police to cover him at night."

"Thought they didn't like you over there."

"Why should they be different," I said. "I'll call Haller, and have him talk to the college."

"Be a good idea if you did that with everybody."

"Let Haller speak for me?" I said.

"In every instance," Hawk said.

I called Haller.

"Vince," I said, "there's some chance, I don't know how great, that someone might try to kill Dwayne."

"He is caught up in something, isn't he?" Haller said.

"Hawk will cover him during the day, but he can't do it twenty-four hours. Can you get the campus cops to cover Dwayne when he's home?"

"Yes."

"Are they any good?" I said. "Like they have guns and stuff, don't they?"

"They're all right," Haller said. "It's a professional force."

"Get them to cover his house," I said, "from six at night to seven . . ." Hawk frowned at me, ". . . ah, make it eight, in the morning. Hawk will take him the rest of the time."

161

We hung up.

"Seven A.M.?" Hawk said. "Surely you jest."

"Hell, I was worried you'd be insulted when I said you couldn't do twenty-four hours."

"*Can,*" Hawk said, "is different than *want to.*"

"Sure," I said. "See if you can keep him alive till the campus cops get there."

When Hawk was gone I called Frank Belson.

"I need the make and plate number of a car registered to Madelaine Roth," I said.

"And you think I'm a registry inspector," Belson said.

"I figure you wanted to be, but flunked the test," I said.

"Only way to flunk that one is to die near the beginning of it," Belson said. "How do you spell Madelaine?"

I told him.

"Call you back," he said, "unless there's a crime or something, and I get distracted."

He hung up. I sat and waited. In fifteen minutes Belson called back.

"1988 Saab 900, silver gray, Mass. vanity plate says MAD," Belson said. "Anything else I can do for you before I go back to crime busting?"

"No," I said, "that's fine. I'll remember you at Christmas."

Belson hung up. I went down to get my car and drive to Taft.

28

I got back to Taft around three in the afternoon and began cruising the faculty and staff parking lot near the administration building. It didn't take long. I found the silver Saab with the MAD license plate in the second row three cars in, right behind the administrative building. There was a green triangular parking sticker on the right window near the door edge.

I parked my car in sight of the parking area in an area marked *Visitors* and waited. It was not a complicated intellectual process and I was able to handle it. The campus police did not open fire on me. A cruiser moved by me once and the cop looked at me with neither interest nor recognition. At 4:37 Madelaine came out of the administrative building wearing a full pleated skirt in sort of a pale violet plaid, high lavender boots, and a gray trench coat with the collar up and the belt knotted rather than buckled. She carried a big straw bag and a smaller purse of gray leather and she walked very briskly.

When she pulled out of the parking lot I cruised along behind her. We drove east, picked up Route 16 into Newton, turned left on Commonwealth and ended up at a series of condominium townhouses just up the road from the big Marriott where the Totem Pole used to be. I kept going past and watched her park and walk to her door. She went in. I U-turned 100 yards down and drove back and parked across the street in the parking lot of a complex of garden apartments where I could watch her door. Which I did until eleven forty-five and went home. She didn't come out, no one went in.

I did this for three nights, picking her up at work and following her home. One night she stopped at the Star Market in Newtonville, another night she stopped at a liquor store on the way home. That's all. She didn't see anyone or do anything. I figured that if she and Deegan were a matched pair sooner or later he'd come to her house or she'd go to his. I figured he wouldn't show up at the University, so that left my days free to sit around and think about becoming an abbot.

The fourth night was Friday, and I scored. I had been sitting in the apartment parking lot for maybe forty-five minutes when a cab pulled up and Deegan got out with an overnight bag in his hand. He went to the door and it opened and he stood for a moment with his arms wide and Madelaine came out and jumped against him and wrapped her legs around his waist. They kissed for a considerable time and then Deegan carried her into the house, still holding the overnight bag dangling kind of awkwardly from his left hand behind her back and slapping against her buttocks as Deegan walked. The door slammed shut behind them. Deegan had probably kicked it shut with his heel.

I speculated on what might happen next.

Whatever it was did not involve coming back out. At ten thirty I gave up and went home to bed. Deegan was going to stay the weekend. That seemed pretty clear. Probably had been back to New York to see his wife and count his money and, maybe, bring in a hitter from the Big Apple to deal with me. So I had access to him, I was pretty sure, for the next two days. If only it were pretty clear what I was going to do with him. It seemed time to consult with Susan and, perhaps, Hawk.

Susan was in pajamas when I arrived. But I wasn't fooled. Her hair wasn't up. She was waiting for me.

"Hey," she said, "how's it going?"

"Bobby Deegan just showed up at Madelaine's house and she ran over and jumped in his arms and wrapped her legs around his waist."

Susan smiled. Her face softened, "Hey, how's it going," she said.

"Yeah," I said. "We'd probably hurt ourselves doing that."

Susan went to the refrigerator and took out a low glass pitcher with a glass stirrer in it. It contained a pale chartreuse-colored fluid.

"Gimlets," she said.

"Gimlets?"

"Yes, I decided we ought to have something that was *our drink,*" she said.

"And you chose gimlets?"

"Yes, the color is so lovely."

I nodded.

"And we only drink them with each other, and we keep our pitcher and our two gimlet glasses by themselves and we don't drink anything else out of them." Susan's eyes were bright.

"I'll get a matched set for my place too," I said.

"Yes," she said.

"That's very romantic," I said.

"I thought so," Susan said.

"Wouldn't it be just as easy to jump into my arms and wrap your legs around my waist?"

Susan poured out a gimlet over ice and handed it to me.

"Drink the goddamn gimlet," she said.

"Right," I said, "it wouldn't be easier at all."

Susan leaned against me and I put my arms around her and one thing led to another and we left the gimlets half drunk on her kitchen counter.

Around midnight we were quiet. I lay on my back with my right arm outstretched. She had her head against my shoulder.

"Madelaine and Deegan are the keys to this," I said.

"Is that what we're going to do now? Talk about your case?"

I nodded.

"Then it must be they who prevent Dwayne from testifying," Susan said. "Unless you've missed a great deal, and you usually don't, there's no one else that could be."

"Yeah, but what have we got on him and how do I find out?"

"Without exposing Dwayne," she said.

"Sure, that's the goddamned kink in the rope. Otherwise I just give what I've got to Taft and let them take it to the D.A. and you and I can go to Chicago and have dinner at Le Perroquet."

"And a gimlet first?"

"The whole ball of wax," I said.

"Is that what we've been involved in tonight?" Susan said.

"Yes, tonight was the whole ball of wax," I said.

"And you call me romantic," Susan murmured.

"Shucks," I said.

We were quiet.

"Is there a way to bring them together?" Susan said.

"Dwayne, Madelaine and Deegan?" I said.

"Yes."

I shrugged. "Probably," I said, "though you've got to understand about Dwayne. If he's recalcitrant, it's heavy work."

"I know," Susan said, "I know. You've mentioned that he's big, but you and Hawk can probably reason with him."

"Say we get them together, what have we got then?"

Susan shook her head. "No way to know," she said. "Certainly no less than you've got right now."

"Very true," I said.

"And perhaps we'll have some insight into the relationship that we don't have now."

"We?"

"Yes," Susan said. "It's somewhat my line of work. Perhaps I might be able to add a useful observation."

"Perhaps you might," I said.

29

In the morning Susan called Chantel for me. I didn't want
Dwayne to answer and recognize my voice and hang up.

"Chantel?" Susan said.

Pause.

"Mr. Spenser calling, just a moment."

We were still in bed and Susan handed the phone across
her body to me.

"Chantel," I said.

Her voice was sleepy.

"What you want?"

"Can you talk?"

"Not much," she said.

"Okay, listen then."

"Un huh."

"I want Dwayne to see Bobby Deegan and Madelaine
Roth at an address in Newton I'm going to give you."

"I don't understand that, Ma'am." The "Ma'am" must have been diversionary.

"I'll be there, and Hawk, and my friend Dr. Silverman, the woman who just spoke to you."

"Un huh."

"So you've got to get him there under whatever pretext. What's a good time today?"

"Today?" Chantel sounded confused.

"Yes. This morning would be good. In an hour, say."

"We ain't even up yet," Chantel said.

"We need to do this quickly, Chantel. Can you get him there?"

"Yes," she said. "Two hours."

"Okay," I gave her the address and hung up.

"Kid's okay," I said to Susan. "No argument, no maybe. Just yes."

"And Hawk will meet us there?" Susan said.

"He's there now," I said. "I called him before you were awake."

"You awoke from an evening of rapture thinking business?"

"First I thought about the rapture," I said.

Susan nodded. "Hawk will make sure that Madelaine and her boyfriend don't leave," Susan said.

"Yes."

"Wise," Susan said, "though it came rather hard upon the heels of rapture."

"I'll make breakfast," I said, "and you can start getting ready."

"If I start getting ready now, I won't be able to hurry."

"I know," I said.

"I like to be in a hurry," Susan said.

"Puzzling, but true," I said. I got up and put on my Darth Vader robe. Susan slipped out of bed and walked naked toward the bathroom.

"Except when I take a bath," Susan said. "I like long slow baths."

"Among other things," I said. Susan looked at me the way she does, sort of sideways. She took her robe from a hanger in her closet and slipped it on. Susan was never naked except when there was occasion for it. She always looked a little relieved when she got into her robe.

I headed for the kitchen.

Susan and I had sweet potato pancakes and two cups of coffee each. Decaffeinated. No problem. I didn't miss real coffee at all. We cleaned up the dishes afterward and then Susan said, "My God, look at the time," and began to speed around her condo. I went into the bathroom and took a shower and came out and found a neutral corner in her bedroom and dressed and put my new Browning on my hip, slid past her into the living room and stayed out of the way until she was ready.

At nine fifteen we were on the Mass. Pike to Newton. We got off at West Newton and headed west on Washington to Commonwealth Ave. and west on Commonwealth to Madelaine's condo.

"I still say it would have been shorter," Susan was saying, "to go straight out to 128 and come back in."

"No hurry," I said. It was seventy-three degrees and sunny, an atypical late March day in Boston.

"Easy for you to say."

Hawk's Jag was parked in the apartment lot across the street from Madelaine's. I pulled in beside it and Hawk got out of his car and climbed in my back seat.

"They there," he said. "Deegan came out and took the paper off the front stoop about half hour ago."

"How are you, cutie," Susan said.

"Formidable," Hawk said.

Susan leaned back over the front seat, and Hawk leaned forward, and they kissed.

"The basketball star coming?" Hawk said.

"His girlfriend says she'll have him here at ten," I said.

"And when he get here, what is it we going to do, again?"

"We're going to bring him in and observe his interaction with Madelaine Roth and Bobby Deegan," I said.

"Interaction," Hawk said.

"They must be the people Dwayne's loyal to," Susan said. "Maybe we can get some sense of how or why."

"Besides, I can't think of anything else to do," I said.

"Could put them both in the river," Hawk said.

"Come on," I said. "Up here the river's almost swimmable again. Aren't you opposed to pollution?"

"We've done it before," Hawk said.

"The reasons were better," I said, "than any we've got now."

Hawk shrugged and leaned back against the seat.

"There need to be some reasons, Hawk," Susan said.

"Worried about reasons all my life, I be a long time dead by now," Hawk said.

"Yes," Susan said, "that's probably true."

Hawk grinned in the back seat.

"Don't make much difference to me, sweet potato," he said. "Kill them, interact with them, tell them about God. Whatever works. Or make you happy."

"How sweet," Susan said.

"There's Dwayne and Chantel," I said.

Across the street a bright red Trans Am slowed in front of Madelaine's condo and then swung into the lot in front and into an empty parking space. Susan and Hawk and I got out of the car and crossed Commonwealth and joined them. Chantel was in the driver's seat. Dwayne, looking a bit cramped, was in the passenger seat.

The car windows were down. Dwayne looked out at me and turned toward his girlfriend.

"What's he doing here, Chantel?"

"He's going to help us," she said.

"I don't want to have nothing to do with him," Dwayne said. "Let's get out of here."

Chantel shook her head and took the keys and stepped out of the car.

"Goddamn it, Chantel," Dwayne said. "Get your ass in here and drive this thing away."

"He's going to help us," Chantel said.

"That honkie motherfucker?" Dwayne said. "He the one got me benched."

"Honkie motherfucker," Hawk said. "He does know you."

"He'll help us," Chantel said.

"He'll help shit. Dwayne say get in here and drive, you fucking well better listen to Dwayne."

173

Chantel threw the keys into the car. "You want to go. You drive it away. This man going to help us, if you'd just let him, dope."

Dwayne's shoulders hunched, and his head sank. He seemed to shrink in on himself so that he looked like a huge black Richard Nixon, looking out under his eyebrows.

Chantel stepped around the car to the open window. "Okay," she said. "Okay." She patted Dwayne's face. "Okay. I'm not mad. I love you, and I want you to be helped."

Dwayne's head was hanging. He stared at the floorboards.

"You're not a dope, Dwayne. I just mad when I said that."

Dwayne nodded without looking up. "Let these people help us," Chantel said. "I trust them."

Dwayne nodded a little and slowly got out of the car and straightened up. He didn't say anything, but he looked at me with a blank implacable gaze that didn't seem to mean anything, though it was clearly not friendly.

"Wait here," I said to Chantel and Dwayne and Susan. Then I started for the front door and Hawk came with me.

He stood to one side of the door, and I stood to the other. Hawk's .44 Magnum was out, the long barrel resting lazily on his shoulder. I took the Browning off my hip. It looked sort of embarrassing next to the Mag. "Is that a siege weapon?" I said. Then I rang the bell. Nothing happened. I rang it again. Then I could hear footsteps and a female voice say something that was probably "I'm coming." The door opened and there was Madelaine in a blue-

and-white striped tank top and white shorts and leather sandals. I put the barrel of the Browning up under Madelaine's chin and said softly, "Where's Deegan?"

Madelaine's face stiffened and she said very slowly, "What?"

I pushed her backward and Hawk came behind me.

"Where's Deegan," I said again, softly.

"Patio," Madelaine said. And looked toward the back of the house.

The hallway went straight back along the right wall of the condo. The rooms all opened off to the left and a stairway rose halfway down the hall.

Hawk and I moved Madelaine down the hall ahead of us, and when we had about reached the staircase she seemed to come out of shock. She hollered, "Bobby." Hawk held her arm and I reached the door at about the time it opened. Deegan came in frowning in a lavender polo shirt and acid-washed jeans with a section of the *Globe* in his hand, his forefinger keeping the place.

"Bobby," I said, "how's it going?"

The muzzle of the Browning was right in front of his left eye as it adjusted to the interior light.

"What's this?" Deegan said and then as he looked at me, "Spenser? What's with the gun?" He looked past me at Hawk, who was still with Madelaine. A slow recognition moved across his face. "Shit," he said.

Hawk smiled at him in a friendly way.

"Let's all go in the living room," I said. "There's folks I want you to talk with."

"So," Deegan said, "knock on the fucking door, you

know? How come you got to bust in here waving a piece and scaring the shit out of Mad?"

"Just being safe," I said. "You did hire some people to ace me."

"Hey," Deegan said, and shrugged a New York shrug.

We went into the big white-painted living room. There was a fireplace at an angle across one corner, and some Scandinavian modern furniture in white pebbly material, and a big teak entertainment cabinet with TV and stereo and CD, and VCR, and maybe a hot tub.

Hawk stepped to the front door, and in a moment Susan and Chantel and Dwayne filed in. Madelaine said, "Dwayne?"

Deegan said nothing at all, but he looked at Dwayne. Susan leaned against the wall to the right of the door. Hawk leaned on the left door jamb, in the door. The Mag was back under his coat. I had put the Browning back on my hip. The only place Deegan could be carrying a piece would be in an ankle holster and Hawk or I would probably be able to spot him bending over and unlimbering. I went and leaned against the mantel of the fireplace.

"These are my friends Susan and Hawk," I said. "Hawk is the taller of the two."

"Better dancer, too," Hawk said.

Susan had already begun to concentrate. When she did, other things no longer impinged. She was watching Dwayne. Dwayne was looking at Deegan.

"I didn't know you was going to be here, Bobby," Dwayne said.

"No problem, Dwayne," Deegan said. "No problem."

I said, "Why, you are doubtless wondering, did I call this meeting."

No one said anything. Dwayne continued to watch Deegan.

I felt like Philo Vance.

"We are the components of a vexing problem," I said.

Peripherally I saw Hawk grin and say the word *vexing* silently.

"Usually the problem is you don't know what happened. Here I know what happened, I don't know what to do about it."

Everyone was watching me now, except Susan, who was watching Dwayne, and Hawk, who was watching Deegan.

"I know that Deegan stuck up an OTB in New York and started investing the money in a gambling scheme that involved point spread control by Dwayne. I know that Madelaine was the intermediary in the deal. I know that when I got involved and Bobby needed a shooter to take me out of it Madelaine put him in touch with her old school chum Gerry Broz, who without knowing the shootee recommended Hawk."

"Why not send the very best," Hawk said in a radio announcer voice with no hint of ethnicity.

"Hawk, being my frequent associate, reported this plan to me and hung around with me thereafter to help me foil it."

"You can't prove any of this," Deegan said.

"Might be able to prove the solicitation of a shooter," I said, "but your point is well taken. So far we can't prove anything much unless Dwayne is willing to talk about you."

"Dwayne is not a squealer," Deegan said.

Dwayne nodded silently.

"Or we could probably get this proved if we turned it all over to the D.A., but that would sink Dwayne."

"And you don't want to do that," Deegan said.

"No."

Chantel said, "I didn't know you was a friend of Mr. Deegan's, Dr. Roth."

"You know that, Dwayne?" I said.

Dwayne looked at Deegan. He didn't answer me.

"Did you know that they met at Queens College while they were both in grad school?"

Dwayne didn't move.

"You know she picked you out to help him control the spread?"

Madelaine said, "You don't know any of that, it's simply supposition."

"You pick Dwayne out for any special reason, Bobby?" I said.

Dwayne was frowning, slightly. Deegan didn't answer me. He simply shook his head.

"Makes sense, I suppose, to find a star you can buy."

The room was quiet. I didn't know where I was going, I was just trying to keep it going. I knew Deegan wouldn't say anything. He didn't know I wasn't wearing a wire.

"What made you think Bobby could buy him, Madelaine?"

"I don't know what you're driving at," she said.

"You steered Bobby, you must have. How does a Brooklyn wiseguy end up buying a Boston basketball player."

"I'm from Brooklyn," Dwayne said suddenly.

"Did you know Deegan before?" I said.

"No," Dwayne said.

I waited. No one else said anything.

"We from the same city," Dwayne said.

"That how you guys got together?" I said.

Dwayne looked back at Deegan. The arrogance and pizzazz were gone. Dwayne was scared and confused and trying to disappear in upon himself like a rabbit trapped in an open field.

"Didn't Dr. Roth introduce you?"

"You don't have to say a word, big guy," Deegan said. "These people got no right to be treating you and me like this. And they couldn't get away with it if they didn't have guns."

"Dwayne," Chantel said, "how you meet Mr. Deegan?"

Dwayne made a shushing sound with his hand at Chantel.

"You want to get up and walk out of here now, Mr. Deegan," Dwayne said, "you and Dr. Roth, I walk ahead of you. I don't give a fuck about these motherfuckers. Dwayne Woodcock want to leave, he leave and his friends go with him. You want, Mr. Deegan, I take you both out of here."

I liked him better then. It was a moment much better than the ones in which he sat looking at the floor. But I didn't like the development. Hawk and I weren't going to shoot him and he'd be a handful otherwise, with Deegan thrown in, who didn't look like a day at the beach himself. I would have thought of something, but Chantel saved me from it.

"They aren't your friends, Dwayne. Mr. Spenser's your friend. These people going to throw you away when they through."

"Dwayne," Deegan said, "have I ever lied to you? Have I ever given it to you any way but straight? You get out I'm going to represent you. I'm going to get you a deal with the Knicks, like Willis Reed never had, like Ewing never had. You know that. I know that. These people don't know. They don't matter, buddy. We matter."

"Let's walk out of here, Mr. Deegan," Dwayne said. In the doorway Hawk was motionless. The prospect of stopping a six-foot-nine-inch, two-hundred-fifty-five pound guy without shooting him seemed to present him no perplexities. He leaned against the jamb, his body loose, his face blank except for the hint of distant amusement that he almost always showed.

Chantel moved in front of Dwayne and took hold of his shirt with both hands. Her face as she stood was nearly level with his as he sat.

"No," she said, and her voice was scraping out of her throat. "No. You walk out with him and it's over for you. He's a crook. The cops want him. He's not going to get you a deal with the Knicks. You stay with me, Dwayne. You do what I say."

Dwayne said, "Don't you grab me, Chantel."

"I will," she said. "I gonna hang onto you so you won't drown. I won't let you drown with these people."

Dwayne said, "Chantel."

Chantel shook her head doggedly. She still hung onto Dwayne's shirt. He took her wrists and gently tried to pull her hands away. She hung on tighter.

"He going to ruin you, Dwayne." Intensity made her voice rasp. "Ruin you."

Deegan said, "Dwayne, you shut that little fucker up."

Dwayne still had hold of Chantel's wrists.

"She ain't no little fucker," he said, softly, a little embarrassed.

"Well, she's your broad," Deegan said. "Keep her quiet."

"See," Chantel said. "See what I am? See what he thinks of me? That what you think, Dwayne?"

Dwayne shook his head as if he had a bee in his ear.

"No," he said. Still soft, still a little embarrassed. "No, Chantel, you know I don't."

"He don't care about me. He don't care about you," Chantel said. "He just care about gambling and making money. He call her a little fucker?" Chantel tossed her chin at Madelaine who was sitting as far back in a white armless chair as the chair would let her.

"Dwayne," Deegan said, "you let her come between us and the dream is over. You understand? Now you shut her the fuck up, or someone else will have to."

The minute he said it Deegan knew it was a mistake. But it was out and he couldn't reel it back in. Dwayne's head came up and he looked at Deegan as if he were a sudden intrusion.

He said softly, "Let go, Chantel," and she did and he stood, his head nearly touching the ceiling. He looked down at Deegan. "Who gonna do that, Bobby?" he said.

"Hey, buddy," Deegan said, "I just mean we got to have quiet so we can talk. We can't have hysteria, you know?"

"Who gonna shut her up if I don't?" Dwayne said. There was no referring to himself in the third person now. No swagger; and there wasn't any petulance either, any sulky confusion. "You gonna do that, Bobby? You gonna have somebody do that, like you tried to do with this guy?" He jerked his head at me.

"Dwayne, cool it, big guy. You misunderstood me. Hey, if I offended Chantel, I'm sorry. Chantel. No harm intended, hon, none of us want to be talking out of turn."

"How long you been sleeping with her?" Dwayne said. He was looking at Madelaine, who managed to look frightened and embarrassed and angry and above it all at the same time. If I got a chance I would ask her how she did that.

"Hey, Dwayne, nice talk," Deegan said.

"How long, Bobby? You scoring her while she telling me that you be a good guy to meet cause you had important sports contacts in New York?"

"Dwayne," Deegan said. "You're talking yourself right into big trouble."

"What kind of trouble, Bobby?"

"The kind that will take you down too, Dwayne. Don't forget it. I go, you go."

"I been a stand up guy for you, Bobby," Dwayne said.

"Better keep it that way, Dwayne."

"No, I don't think so. I don't think you a stand up guy for me, Bobby."

"I'm not going alone, Dwayne. What you think you're

going to do? Tell everything you can think of about me and nobody'll notice that you've been shaving points. That you're on the fucking pad? Get sensible, kid. I go, you go."

"Guess we ain't as close as you said we was?" Dwayne said.

"Close enough to go down the shit chute together, buddy boy."

Dwayne took a long step and was directly in front of Deegan. Deegan tipped his head back to look up at him. "And don't think I'm scared of you, Jumbo. The bigger you are the better target you make."

Deegan stood up unhurriedly.

"I'm walking," he said.

From the doorway Hawk looked at me. Deegan stepped around Dwayne. Madelaine said, "Bobby?"

"You gonna shoot," Deegan said to me, "start now."

I shook my head.

"I got more than I hoped for already," I said.

Hawk stepped aside and Deegan walked out the door.

30

"Where you suppose he's going?" Hawk said.

"Probably down to the Marriott and sit in the lobby," I said.

"Embarrassing to stomp out and stand around outside on the street," Hawk said.

Madelaine was looking at us in her living room as if we didn't have tenure.

"You're in this, Madelaine," I said. "When Bobby goes you're going too."

She shook her head.

"Yes," I said. "You are the yenta in this thing. You knew Dwayne was a good prospect. He couldn't read. He needed money. He trusted you."

"I can read stuff," Dwayne said.

"You knew Bobby had money from knocking over that OTB parlor. You knew he was looking to do something with it, put it somewhere would give him a nice return, account for his affluence."

"I had nothing to do with that hold up," Madelaine said.

"But you knew it took place," I said.

"I . . ." She looked around the room and her eyes rested on Susan. "Can't you make him leave me alone?" she said.

"I can't make him do anything," Susan said. "It would be easiest if you told him."

"Genie's out of the bottle now, Mad," I said. "No corking it up. Sooner or later it's all going to get said."

She shook her head.

"You in this with Bobby, ain't you, Dr. Roth?" Dwayne said.

She kept shaking her head.

"Get out," she said. "Get out of my house."

I looked at Dwayne.

"You ready to tell me about it?"

He looked at Chantel and then at Madelaine. His eyes moved to Hawk and to Susan.

"I got to think," he said.

I started to speak. Out of Dwayne's view Susan shook her head. I stopped and then started again.

"Okay, Dwayne," I said.

Dwayne looked around the room again. Then he put his hand out and Chantel took it, and they left, walking past a motionless Hawk at the door.

Hawk looked at me. I nodded and he trailed behind them. If Deegan had been a danger before, he'd be a lot worse now.

"Are you going to leave?" Madelaine said. Her voice came out in a breathy rush. "Are you going to get out?"

I looked at her for maybe seven seconds.

"Sure," I said, and we left.

In the car I said to Susan, "Time to let Dwayne rest a little?"

"Yes," she said. "He'll come around. But he's giving up a male authority figure and it's hard for him. He needs a little time to find a new one."

"Be better if he didn't need one," I said.

"He's what," Susan said, "twenty-one? twenty-two?"

"Okay," I said.

"I watched him as all that went on," Susan said. "He looked at Deegan or you all the time we were there. One or the other of you. He was continuously aware of both of you and of the way either of you reacted to anything."

We were headed down Commonwealth Ave., past the Marriott and the canoe rental landing toward 128 and the Mass. Pike interchange.

"Deegan made a mistake when he threatened Chantel," I said.

"Yes," Susan said, "he did. And that's an encouraging sign. That his need for the young woman is strong enough to offset his need for the male authority figure."

"Might be something a little more than need," I said.

Susan turned her startling Technicolor smile on me.

"Love?"

"Maybe," I said.

"If love is more than need," Susan said, "or obsession or other pathological manifestations."

"You babes are such flighty romantics," I said.

I was looping around the complicated cloverleaf at the junction of Routes 30, 128, and 90.

"Is it love that made you go this way?" Susan said. "Because I think it's shorter?"

"No. This is stubbornness. I wish to prove to you that it's longer."

I dropped thirty-five cents into the automatic toll hopper and headed in the turnpike extension toward Boston.

"Love is what makes me care whether you know which way is shorter," I said.

She put her hand lightly on my thigh. I dropped my right hand on top of it and drove with my left.

"Professionally," Susan said, "I'm not at all sure that love, as such, is not simply a complex of human impulses: need, identification, possessiveness, fear of loneliness, impulse to replicate the family from which you sprang, sexual desire, anger, the desire to punish, the desire to be punished."

I didn't say anything. The Cherokee had tinted glass and with the windows closed the interior was quiet and cool. There weren't many cars out on a Sunday midday in late March, and the hum of the car's passage was all there was for sound.

"On the other hand . . ." I said.

"On the other hand I love you so much I could swoon," Susan said.

"Swoon?"

"Swoon."

"And the fact that Dwayne feels swoonie over Chantel," I said, "means he's capable of forming healthier attachments than the one with Deegan."

"I only said I was swoonie over you," Susan said. "I can't speak for Dwayne or Chantel. But the rest of it is right."

"Chantel says he needs white approval," I said.

"Yes, so a white male authority figure may even be more important to him than it would be to some," Susan said.

"What do you recommend?"

"Let Chantel work on him," Susan said. "Let him think about what's happened to him, and let him come to it himself. You don't want him to feel pushed or he's very likely to clam up and if you push him hard enough you can push him right back to Deegan. Deegan says things Dwayne likes to hear. You keep telling him unpleasant stuff."

"I keep telling him to grow up," I said.

"And that he's risking jail, and that he can't read, and that he should testify against a man who makes Dwayne feel like he's more important than oxygen," Susan said.

"Are you suggesting he doesn't enjoy that?"

"Only a suggestion," Susan said.

We went off at the Allston/Cambridge exit and wove through the silliest exit ever devised to Soldiers Field Road.

I looked at my watch. Susan glanced at hers and then turned to look out at the red brick Harvard buildings.

"Two minutes faster than my way," I said.

She turned and smiled at me a smile of infinite sweetness.

"Shut up," I said.

31

I was in Lt. Martin Quirk's office at Homicide. Quirk was there, and Frank Belson, and a young cop from Walford named Stuart Delaney, a former state cop named Le-Master, who was the Chief of the Taft U. police, and a guy from the Middlesex D.A.'s office named Arlett.

Quirk was sitting square in his chair behind his desk, his forearms resting on the desktop, his thick hands motionless on his blotter. Belson sat in a straight chair, tipped back against the wall to Quirk's left, smoking a cheap narrow cigar, with his hat on and tilted down over his forehead. The rest of us ranged in straight chairs in a semicircle facing Quirk. Quirk was looking at me.

"Why, you are perhaps asking yourself," Quirk said to me, "did Lt. Quirk invite me to his office at this time with these other gentlemen?"

"I assumed you were holding a crime stoppers seminar and wanted me to lecture," I said.

"Well, that's close," Quirk said. "Actually these gentlemen all wish to learn from you what the fuck is going on with Dwayne Woodcock?"

"So where do you come in?" I said.

"Because the Walford police asked me to pick you up and hold you for them, and I thought it might make more sense if we all got together and shared our thoughts on this matter."

"You're Homicide," I said.

Quirk looked at Belson. Belson looked up from under his hat brim.

"Man knows his cops, Marty," Belson said.

"Who's dead?" I said.

"We'll ask the questions," Arlett said to me, "if you don't mind."

I looked at Quirk. "We'll ask the questions?" I said.

Quirk shook his head.

"Kid named Danny Davis," Quirk said.

I felt a tickle of relief. It wasn't Dwayne.

"Lieutenant," Arlett said, "I'll conduct this interrogation."

Quirk looked at him for a moment. Nothing appeared to change in Quirk's face, but the room seemed very quiet. Then Quirk looked back at me.

"Somebody shot him behind the left ear outside the Taft field house," Quirk said, "and then shot him in the back of the head after he'd fallen and was lying face down. Big caliber gun, maybe .45 they tell me."

"And we know you know more than you're telling," Arlett said in a rush. I could see Belson smile slightly.

Quirk ignored Arlett. "And then," he said, "somebody apparently made a run at Woodcock, and your goomba, Hawk, ah, interceded."

"Shooter dead?" I said.

"Two of them," LeMaster said. "No I.D. on them. Delaney got prints and they're going to run it down for us at Ten-Ten."

"State Police Headquarters," Arlett said.

Belson's grin got a little wider.

"Gave us a statement," Delaney said, "and released Woodcock and the broad . . ."

"Chantel," I said.

"Yeah, Woodcock's broad."

I said, "She has a name. It's Chantel."

"Sure," Delaney said. "They support Hawk's statement that he acted in their defense."

"So what do you know about all of this?" Arlett said.

"Nothing," I said.

"Lieutenant, arrest him," Arlett said, "read him his rights and book him."

"Suspicion of murder?" Quirk said.

"Material witness, obstructing justice, anything you want. I want him in a cell thinking about this. Maybe his memory will improve."

"Didn't Robert Stack say that, in 'The Untouchables'?" I said.

"You're not as funny as you think you are," Arlett said.

"Yeah, sure he did," I said. "He said it to Bruce Gordon,

who was playing Frank Nitti, 'maybe your memory will improve,' he said. And . . ."

"Shut up," Arlett said.

"I bet you watched that all the time," I said. "I know it was Ness who said, 'we'll ask the questions.' "

"Spenser," Quirk said, "give it a rest."

"Farantino's got a bad caseload problem in Middlesex," Belson said, around his cigar. "Sends out the best he's got available."

Arlett turned toward Belson. "Sergeant, just what the hell is that supposed to mean?"

Belson's thin face with its permanent five o'clock shadow was sincere as he looked at Arlett.

"Trying to be supportive," he said.

Quirk stood up.

"You gentlemen wait here," he said. "Frank, Spenser, come with me."

He went around his desk and out the door of his office without waiting to see if we'd come.

We came. He went along through the squad room and out and down a corridor and in through a door marked OCU. It was another squad room, a little smaller than Homicide. We walked through toward a door that read SGT. MYLES HICKMAN, COMMANDER, and opened the door.

"Myles is on vacation," Quirk said.

He sat behind the desk and I sat in front and Belson closed the pebbly glass door and leaned on the wall beside it.

"Okay," Quirk said. "Arlett's an asshole, you know it, Frank knows it, I know it. He's new in the criminal division, he's insecure and he should be. So he tries to be tough and he don't know how. But the questions he's asking aren't questions that shouldn't be answered. And if he pushes me I'll have to arrest you for him. They'll hold you in Walford."

"For how long," I said.

"Until Haller gets there. If we bust you, I'll have Frank call him."

I got up and stood looking out at the nearly empty squad room. At the far end was a dark-haired cop with a thick mustache. His baseball jacket was hung on the back of his chair. He was wearing his gun in a shoulder holster and a set of handcuffs dangled as well from the strap under his arm. He had his feet up on the desk. He was wearing New Balance running shoes and jeans. He hunched his right shoulder up to hold the phone against his ear while he fumbled for something in the desk drawer.

"I should have had Davis covered too," I said.

The cop on the phone found a pad of yellow paper in the drawer and began to write on it with a ballpoint pen.

"And I simply didn't think of it," I said.

I turned and looked at Quirk and Belson.

"I didn't think of it."

"Too late now," Belson said.

I nodded.

"I know who had him killed, and I know who sponsored the run at Dwayne, and I know why, but I can't prove it."

"Give it to us," Quirk said. "Maybe we can prove it."

"Arlett's going to prove it?"

"They got some good people working out of there," Quirk said. "Stegman, Russo."

I nodded again.

"The other problem is I will have to implicate someone I don't want to implicate."

"Life's hard," Quirk said.

"Kid already knows that," I said. "I'm trying to make it a little easier."

"Woodcock?"

"I'm not going to say."

"What are you trying to do?" Quirk said.

"I'm trying to figure out a way to nab the son of a bitch who had Davis killed, without nabbing the kid he corrupted."

"You want to do this legal?" Quirk said.

"Doesn't make too much difference," I said.

"I didn't figure it did," Quirk said.

"But the kid's got to learn some stuff out of this," I said.

"Father Flanagan," Belson murmured.

"So you don't just ace the bad guy and call it even," Quirk said.

"No," I said.

"Not like you wouldn't do it," Quirk said.

"Not this time, at least," I said.

"You want to tell me the bad guy's name?" Quirk said.

"Informally?" I said.

Quirk laughed a little short laugh with his mouth closed.

"You mean will I tell Arlett?" he said.

I nodded.

"No," Quirk said.

"Okay. Guy named Bobby Deegan. New York wants him for knocking over an OTB parlor. He's been fixing Taft basketball games and was using Woodcock and, apparently, the Davis kid to beat the spread."

"I heard Taft hired you on that," Quirk said.

"And fired you," Belson said.

"And I got in there and stirred things up, and got so close to Deegan that he tried to hit me, and failed."

"Parking garage on Milk Street?" Quirk said.

I shrugged.

"And then he realized that the only people could put him away were the people he'd bought," I said.

"So he had them hit," Quirk said. "Except you figured he'd try for Woodcock, so you had Hawk there."

"Days," I said. "Dumb bastards had waited an hour they'd have had the campus cops to deal with instead of Hawk."

"Be my choice," Belson said.

"So you sink Deegan, and he takes Dwayne down with him," Quirk said.

"If we can keep him alive," I said.

"He's too hot," Quirk said. "Be hard to get anyone to try for him now. I wouldn't take the guards away, but I think you got a little time."

I nodded.

"So what are you going to do?" Quirk said.

"I'll think of something," I said.

"Too bad you didn't think of it before they killed Davis," Quirk said.

"Yeah," I said.

32

We went back to Quirk's office and teased Arlett for a while and then LeMaster and Delaney took me back to Walford in cuffs and stuck me in the Walford jail as a material witness. I was in for about two and a half hours before Haller came down with a writ and got me out.

The prisons in the state were sleeping four to a cell, but the town jails were as empty and quiet as a church on Wednesday. I alternated my time while I sat on the bare bunk between thinking about women I'd slept with and reanalyzing my all-time all-star baseball team. In recent years I'd replaced Brooks Robinson with Mike Schmidt and Marty Marion with Ozzie Smith. Now and then I wondered how the hell I ended up in jail in a case when I knew what happened and who did it and could probably prove it. But mostly I thought about women and baseball.

When I got back to my office it was late afternoon and

raining. I was wearing my leather jacket to keep my gun dry and I had my collar up when I walked in from the alley where I parked. When I got out of the elevator on the second floor the corridor had that gray look that indoors gets on days like this one, and the lights from open doors along the corridor made yellow splashes on the corridor floor. One of the open doors was mine. I unzipped my jacket before I went in.

Hawk was at my desk reading a book with his feet up. He was wearing lizard skin cowboy boots. He glanced at me over the book.

"Cops talk to you?" he said.

"Yeah," I said. "What are you reading?"

"Book by Stephen Hawking," Hawk said. " 'Bout the universe."

"Only that?" I said.

"Campus cops and Walford cops and some state cops all hanging around Dwayne," Hawk said. "Figured I wasn't needed."

"Tell me about the hit on Dwayne," I said.

"Two guys pull up about five, quarter of, park in front of the condo, walk up to Dwayne's place and ring the bell. Door opens and they go in quick. I figure I better go in right after them and I do. They in the living room with Dwayne and the girl."

"Chantel," I said.

"Un huh, and there's an Uzi showing, so I say 'How dee doo' and shoot the guy with the Uzi and his associate turn around with a hand gun and . . ." Hawk shrugged and made a shooting motion with the forefinger and thumb of his right hand, bringing the thumb down like a hammer falling.

"Chantel sort of moaning and got her face against Dwayne, and he hanging on to her like she gonna blow away, so I call the campus blue bellies and pretty soon there a lot of people there."

"Danny Davis got killed," I said. "They tell you that?"

"Yeah. Should a had him covered too," Hawk said.

"I know," I said.

"Can't think of everything," Hawk said.

"I'll say."

We looked at each other silently for a moment. Then Hawk nodded. I did too.

"What we going to do about this?" Hawk said.

"Dwayne will turn," I said.

"Better than dying," Hawk said.

"So we're going to have some leverage on Deegan," I said.

" 'Less Dwayne runs," Hawk said.

I looked at him.

"Think like Dwayne. You black, you look up to white people, but you scared of them. You don't trust them. All your life they been calling you nigger, acting like you don't matter. Now, he got his life on the line, his girlfriend's life on the line. He can trust the system, trust the white cops and the white judge to protect him, same system been telling him he don't matter for the last twenty-one years. Stand up to a white guy wants to kill him and count on the white system to protect him."

"Or," I said, "he can run. He can bury himself in the black ghetto of choice and hide for the rest of his life."

"What would you do?" Hawk said.

"Run for the ghetto," I said.

Hawk nodded.

"Can you watch him," I said.

"Can't watch him forever," Hawk said. Then he smiled. "Well, I could, but I don't want to."

"Stay with him a couple of days, give me time to try and put something together."

"You want me to stop him if he runs?" Hawk said.

"No," I said. "Just want to know where he runs to."

Hawk went to hang around outside of Dwayne's, and I went to my desk and sat down and called Detective Maguire in Brooklyn. Things were looking up; I got him.

"I'm going off duty, in fact I was supposed to go off a half hour ago," Maguire said.

"I thought you New York guys never slept," I said.

"We don't," Maguire said, "but we need time off for fucking. What do you want?"

I said, "If I got Deegan to turn on that OTB thing would you deal?"

"Maybe."

"If I got him to give you the rest of the outfit, can you get him immunity?"

"He turns on the rest of the outfit and he'll need witness protection. That's Feds."

"Will the federal attorney deal on this?"

"Ain't a federal crime," Maguire said. "Why's he give a shit?"

"That's up to you," I said, "convince him."

"Yeah?"

"Can you do that?" I said.

"Maybe."

"Why don't you look into it and find out," I said.

"How you going to get Deegan to turn?" Maguire said.

"That's my problem," I said. "You work on what he'll get if I do."

"Hey," Maguire said, "I gotta know you'll turn him. I'm not going to be walking around down here saying he's turned, and find out he hasn't, and end up looking like an asshole."

"Would anyone see the change?" I said.

"I mean it," Maguire said. "I'm not sticking my neck out on the word of some guy I never even met. I mean I talked to you twice on the phone, and you got me making deals with the federal attorney."

"Magic," I said, "isn't it."

"It's bullshit," Maguire said. "You gonna turn him or not?"

"I'll turn him," I said.

"You do and we'll talk," Maguire said. "We can work something out."

"Might get your picture in the *Daily News*," I said.

Maguire hung up without comment.

I swiveled around and looked at the rain washing down my window. Now I could discuss these things with Deegan. If I could find him. If he didn't shoot me when I did. If Dwayne would testify.

"I need a drink," I said out loud.

No one said no. So I sat in my chair, got out a bottle of Glenfiddich and a glass and poured some neat and sipped it and watched the rain as night settled in behind it.

33

I didn't have to find Bobby Deegan. He found me. I'd
been sitting maybe an hour and a half watching it rain
when he walked into my office without knocking. The
only light in the room was my desk lamp with the Tiffany
glass lamp shade that Susan had insisted would dress up
the whole office. When I heard the door open, I swung
around and opened the right hand drawer of the desk. I
kept a spare gun in there and it was always nice to have
it handy.

Deegan stood in the doorway with the light from the
corridor behind him. He wore an oversized, lightweight
trench coat with the collar up, and a gray tweed cap.

"I'm not here for trouble," Deegan said.

I waited.

"We need to talk," he said.

I nodded at the chair in front of my desk. He unbuttoned

his coat and sat down and stuck his legs out straight in front of him. I took a second glass out of the left hand drawer and put it on the desk and poured some Glenfiddich into it. Deegan leaned forward and took the glass and sniffed it and took a sip. He swallowed, and nodded his head.

"Single malt," he said.

We were quiet, the rain blurring down outside the window behind me.

"You're trouble," Deegan said.

"Nice of you to notice."

"Can't seem to get you out of the fucking way," Deegan said.

I nodded. We both sipped some scotch. Sipped thoughtfully, an ounce and a quarter of Glenfiddich will last half an evening.

"So what are we going to do about this mess?" Deegan said.

"I been giving that some thought," I said.

"Those were good people went after Dwayne," Deegan said. "Brooklyn guys. Guy Dwayne's size, you want the best."

I waited. Deegan would get to where he was going.

"You do them?" he said.

I shook my head.

"Black guy?"

I nodded.

"Gerry said he was good," Deegan said.

He was holding the glass of scotch in both hands in front of his chin, elbows resting on the arms of the chair. He rubbed his chin absently on the rim. I could hear the faint scratch of his beard against it. Deegan looked like a guy who would have to shave twice a day.

"Guys Gerry sent me for you didn't work out too good either," he said.

"Boston guys," I said.

Deegan nodded. He drank a little scotch. I pushed the bottle across the desk and he leaned forward and poured himself another inch, and pushed the bottle back across the desk to me. He leaned back in his chair again.

"I want out of this," he said.

"Un huh."

"I want to deal."

"What you got to deal with?" I said.

"I keep my trap shut about Dwayne," he said.

"And what do I do?"

"You walk," he said. "And I walk and nobody says nothing."

"And nobody shoots Dwayne?" I said.

"Nobody shoots him, nobody bribes him, nobody mentions his name again."

I leaned my head back against the padding on my chair. I was tired. Tired of Deegan, tired of Dwayne, tired of tough guys and cops and guns and deals. I was tired of almost everything but Susan.

"Whaddya think?" Deegan said.

I shook my head slowly, still against the back of my chair.

"No?" Deegan said. "Why no?"

"Davis," I said.

"Davis," Deegan said, "why do you give a fuck about Davis? You got nothing to do with Davis."

"Got to get something for Davis," I said.

Deegan took in a long breath and let it out and dipped his nose into the glass for a moment and swallowed.

"You got to get something for Davis," he said.

I nodded.

"How about getting dead for Davis?" Deegan said.

"Hard to do," I said.

Deegan nodded slowly. "Yeah," he said. "It is."

He drank again.

"But it's not impossible," he said.

"I can put you away on the gambling charge," I said. "Dwayne will testify. So will I. You're a known hoodlum. You'll be a long time gone."

The wind seemed to have shifted. I could hear the rain being driven at a slant against the window behind me.

"What do you want for Davis?" Deegan said.

"The rest of the OTB crew."

"OTB?"

"You and some other guys knocked over an Off Track Betting parlor in New York. I want the guys you did it with."

"I can't do that," Deegan said. "They'd fucking kill me."

"I'll get you a witness protection deal. You aren't prosecuted and the Feds will give you a new identity and relocate you."

"All to keep you from pushing this gambling thing?" he said.

"And I don't tell your wife about Madelaine," I said.

Deegan looked at me a long time without speaking.

"You are a hard fucking case," he said, "aren't you?"

The question was rhetorical. I didn't comment.

"For a fucking arrogant asshole kid, talks about himself in the third person," Deegan said.

"He's good at what he does," I said.

"So what the fuck is that to you?" Deegan said.

"Girlfriend's nice, too," I said.

"Chantel?"

"Yeah, she sees something in him."

"So what the fuck is *that* to you?" Deegan said.

"You want to deal, or not?" I said.

Deegan stood slowly, and put his whiskey glass on my desk and walked over to the wall to the right of my desk and stretched both hands above his head and leaned on the wall. He did a couple of push-aways on the wall and then turned and leaned his back against it.

"Who you dealing with in New York?" Deegan said.

I shook my head.

Deegan grinned. "Sure," he said. "Of course you won't say. You don't give a fucking inch on anything."

"You're not dead," I said.

Deegan raised his eyebrows. Then he walked to my desk and poured another shot for himself.

"You get it together in New York, names, promises, the works, in detail and then we'll talk again."

"Where do I reach you?" I said.

Deegan paused, thought about that for a moment, then shrugged.

"I'll be with Madelaine," he said.

"I'll be in touch," I said.

Deegan picked up the whiskey glass and tossed the rest of the scotch down. He put the glass on my desk again and turned and walked to my door. He tugged his collar up higher.

"Raining like a bastard," he said, and went out.

34

I spent the next day on the phone. I talked three or four times to Maguire in Brooklyn, and then twice to a guy from the New York Federal Attorney's office, a guy named Jennerette.

"Why don't you nail him for the gambling thing up there?" Jennerette said, "if it's so air tight."

"Because I'm trying to protect the player," I said.

"So why not let Deegan walk. He keeps quiet, you keep quiet?"

"Couple of reasons," I said. I'd already gone through them with Maguire and with the commander of the Brooklyn robbery squad. "He's walking around loose, with only the player to finger him, he might find it more sensible to ace the player. Also another kid died in this deal, kid named Danny Davis. I figure somebody has to pay dues for that."

"What's this kid Davis to you?" Jennerette said.

"Nothing," I said. "But somebody owes something for him; and I don't want the other kid to see Deegan walk away from this looking like a stand up guy."

"Witness protection isn't like doing time," Jennerette said.

"That's not it," I said. "I want my kid to see Deegan rat on his buddies."

There was silence on the phone.

"You want us to help you cover up a crime, so you can give some kid an object lesson?"

"You bet," I said.

Again silence on the phone.

"Why not try to get Deegan on the murder of this kid Davis?" Jennerette said.

"Expose my client," I said. "I'm trying to save this kid. He's got a future if I can save him."

"Mr. Fucking Rogers," Jennerette said.

"You get several guys that are better off the streets. Brooklyn cleans up a robbery that's been making them look bad. Witness Protection gets the chance to hang out with Bobby Deegan, always a treat. Who knows what you may find out once you get Deegan talking. Guy's a connected guy. You could end up on 'Nightline.' "

"Boss will end up on 'Nightline,' " Jennerette said. "Hold on a minute."

I could hear the phone being put down on the desk and the faint sounds of office noise: voices, other phones ringing, the tap, occasionally, of high-heeled shoes. There was maybe five minutes of this and then Jennerette came back on the phone.

"Okay," he said. "Deegan turns, and gives us the OTB job, we'll give him immunity and protection. If," Jennerette paused for the 'if' to sink in, "he delivers quality."

"But of course," I said.

"We'll be the judge of what's quality," he said.

"The rest of the crew in the OTB robbery," I said. "Is that quality?"

"Yes," Jennerette said.

"I'll get back to you," I said.

We hung up.

I went down to the alley back of my building and got my car and headed for Newton. It was nearly four in the afternoon and traffic was beginning to clog things. Boston was never meant for automobiles. The streets wound in the downtown section like cattle trails without any reasonable pattern and even in Back Bay, where the grid system had been applied when the old bay was filled in in the nineteenth century, the scale was too limited for automobiles in large number. In New York they drove faster, but for simple difficulty in getting from one part of town to another, Boston was, on a scale of ten, ten.

Storrow Drive would be standing still at this time. And so would the Mass. Pike. Shrewdly, I stayed off both and went straight out Commonwealth. So did everyone else. I hit every red light, and got to Newton at five thirty-five. Bobby and Madelaine were having cocktails. There was a pitcher of martinis on the coffee table. No one offered me one.

"Brooklyn will go for it," I told Deegan. He was sitting in a Barcalounger wearing a white cotton sweater over a crimson polo shirt, collar up. His acid-washed jeans were

carefully ironed and his Top-Siders were new. "You turn
on the OTB thing and they give you immunity and protection."

"And you?" he said. Madelaine sat on the foot of the
Barcalounger, near his ankles, her left hand resting on his
knee, sipping a martini from a thick lowball glass. She had
her shoes off but otherwise looked as if she'd just come
from work in a gray wrap-around dress.

"Me? You don't mention Dwayne, and he and I don't
mention you," I said. "Nobody ever fixed a Taft game."

"What happens about Davis?"

"I got no control over that," I said. "But if there's no
gambling case, I don't know how they'll make you for Davis."

"Danny Davis?" Madelaine said.

Deegan made a shushing motion with his hand.

"What about Danny?" Madelaine said. "Bobby, did
you . . ."

"Put a lid on it, Madelaine. How do you know this guy
hasn't got a wire?"

Madelaine looked as if she'd bitten into a sawdust donut.
Her mouth shut and stayed shut.

"He's not going down for it," I said, "but Bobby had
Danny Davis killed. Tried to have Dwayne killed. If he
were going down for it you'd probably be an accessory to
murder."

"I never . . ." she said, and that's as far as she got. Deegan leaned forward and grabbed her arm and yanked her
over, so that she was sprawled on top of him on the
lounger. With his face against hers, and his lips actually

touching her lips, he said, "Shut up, you understand that? Shut your fucking trap."

I could see by the whiteness of his knuckles that he was squeezing her arm hard. She squirmed, pulling at his fingers.

"You understand?" he said again in a hoarse voice, holding her head in place with his left hand.

"Yes," she whispered, and he let her go. She got up abruptly and went and stood near the fireplace rubbing her arm where he'd squeezed it.

"You say what you want," Deegan said to me calmly. "I'm not saying anything at all about any murder stuff, that's not part of this deal. I had nothing to do with any murders."

"I'm not wired, Bobby," I said. "And I just wanted Madelaine to know who she was sleeping with. But for the record the deal doesn't include any murders."

"Fine," Deegan said. "Who do I talk to?"

"I'll set it up," I said. "You'll be here?"

"Right here," Deegan said.

35

The next morning Dwayne bolted. He went into a washroom at the Lancaster Tap, opened the pebble glass window and went out and down the alley, leaving two campus cops having cheeseburgers and coffee and wondering what took Dwayne so long.

Chantel met him at the foot of the alley and they were off in the Trans Am, with Hawk behind them. He followed them to a house off Blue Hill Ave. near Mattapan Square. Watched them for a while until they settled in, and then he came and told me about it.

"You stuck with Chantel," I said. "You knew he wouldn't go without her."

Hawk nodded. "Dwayne can't drive," he said.

"He could have taken a cab," I said.

"Sure," Hawk said.

"Let's go see him," I said.

"Might make him run again," Hawk said. "I'm getting sick of chasing him."

"We need to talk," I said.

We went in Hawk's car. Out the expressway and onto Columbia Road toward Mattapan Square. Hawk was listening to an album by Kinky Friedman and the Texas Jewboys.

"What happened to Hugh Masekela?" I said.

"Next tape," Hawk said.

Hawk turned the Jag down Blue Hill Ave. and in another ten minutes we were pulling up in front of a three decker like a thousand others in Boston. Porches on the front of each floor with wooden railings. Shingle siding. Flat roof. The small yard out front was neatly trimmed. There were flowers in flower boxes on each floor. The house had been painted recently.

Hawk and I got out of the car. Everyone I saw was black, children mostly, and some older people. No one paid me any attention.

"First floor," Hawk said as we went up the steps to the porch. We went into the little entryway. The stairs went up the left side of the hall. There was a door in the right wall. I knocked. There were footsteps, and the door opened as far as the security chain inside would let it. A black woman looked out at us.

I said, "Hello, my name is Spenser, I'm here to see Dwayne."

"No Dwayne here," she said.

"Yes there is, Ma'am," Hawk said. "I know he's here. Trans Am parked in the garage."

"Ask Chantel," I said. "They'll see me."

The door closed. Hawk stepped back out onto the porch and looked down the driveway. After a minute or two the footsteps returned and the door opened. This time it was Chantel. She looked out at me. Hawk came back from the porch.

"Wait a minute," Chantel said.

She closed the door. The chain bolt slid off, and then the door opened. Chantel stepped back. We went into a den with a television, a braided rug on the floor, a daybed covered with a paisley throw, and a big leather armchair. Beyond the den was a big old kitchen, the kind that families would spend most of their time in. Chantel led us through the den and into the kitchen. There was a big square table against the wall opposite the big gas stove. There was another daybed in the kitchen, this one built in with a headboard of the same upright pine boards that formed the wainscot. At the foot of the daybed was a big old black leather rocking chair. The linoleum floor was covered with another braided rug. A door off the kitchen led to what appeared to be a dining room, another opened on a bedroom. At the far end of the kitchen was a bathroom and pantry. An old, portly black man stood at an easel in the middle of the kitchen floor under a bright fluorescent light, painting a landscape in oils. The woman who had opened the door sat at the oilcloth-covered table with Dwayne. There was coffee and the remains of a pumpkin pie on the table.

Dwayne looked up at me as Chantel brought us in.

"What you want?" he said.

Chantel went over and sat beside him. She had on a white shirt and jeans and low black boots. A scarlet scarf was knotted at her throat. Hawk went and leaned on the door jamb as he had at Madelaine's. There was no one could lean on a door like Hawk. When he was still he was entirely still. There was no real evidence he was alive when he leaned on the door jamb. You couldn't even see him breathe.

There was an empty chair at the table so I pulled it out and sat. The old guy at the easel ignored me. He had on a blue bib apron with paint stains on it, and he had a cigar clenched in his teeth. His brush moved in confident dabbing motions on the canvas.

"I think I got this thing fixed," I said to Dwayne.

Dwayne stared at me without comment. The woman got up and started to clear the table. She had on a yellow dress belted at the waist.

"Deegan was involved in a robbery in New York," I said. "To avoid prosecution on this gambling thing, he's going to testify against his associates in the robbery."

"So what's that mean for us?" Chantel said.

"Means you're clean. You can play basketball and sign with the Knicks for more than Ewing got—if the Clippers don't draft you—and live happily ever after."

"What about Bobby?" Dwayne said.

"After Bobby rats on his friends," I said, "he'll be in a witness protection program. New name, new place, new career. He won't have any chance, or any reason, to bother you," I said.

"How you get him to do that?" Dwayne said.

215

"Told him you'd testify against him on the gambling."

Dwayne stared at me. "I'd never squeal on nobody, man."

"He'd have killed you if we let him," I said.

"Don't matter about him," Dwayne said. "Matters 'bout me."

"You won't be a squealer even if the guy deserves to be squealed on," I said.

Dwayne thought about that for a minute, then nodded slowly.

"Man's what he is, not what other people are," he said.

"Sure," I said. "But you won't have to testify, so long as Bobby thinks you will."

"Ought to know I wouldn't," Dwayne said. "Dwayne Woodcock don't do no squealing."

"Fortunately, Bobby Deegan does," I said.

"Don't believe Bobby'll do that," Dwayne said.

"Did you believe he'd have somebody try to kill you?" I said.

"Don't have to be Bobby," Dwayne said.

Chantel made an angry little *tsh* sound, and Dwayne glanced at her. He didn't speak. But after he'd looked at Chantel for a moment he began to barely nod his head.

"Who else know we here?" Dwayne said.

"Just Hawk and me," I said.

"You going to tell?" Dwayne said.

"No," I said. "But you don't need to hide. Deegan's going to be wrapped up. You can play ball."

Dwayne shook his head.

"We going to stay here for a while," he said. "See what happens. See if it's like you say."

"Coach Dunham will want to talk," I said.

"Things be like you say," Dwayne said, "I call him in a while."

"There's another piece of the deal," I said.

Dwayne waited.

"You learn to read," I said.

"Nobody tell Dwayne Woodcock what he do and don't do."

I nodded my head at Hawk. "Man saved your life a while ago," I said.

Dwayne looked over at Hawk and nodded his head sharply once.

"You owe him," I said.

"Can't read," Hawk said, "you gonna be a dumb fuck all your life, excuse me, Chantel, and whitey gonna yank you around."

"He's right," Chantel said in a flat voice.

"Nobody call Dwayne Woodcock a dumb fuck," Dwayne said. He started to get up.

"Sit down, Dwayne," Hawk said. "We went to all this trouble to save your ass, I don't want to have to shoot you now."

Dwayne was on his feet staring at Hawk. Hawk remained as still on the door jamb as he had. The old guy kept painting. For all he cared we could have been on television.

Chantel said, "Dwayne, the man saved your life and mine. You know you got to learn to read. Both of them saved your life."

Dwayne stood for a long moment without speaking, then he sat back down.

"College will be able to arrange for a reading specialist," I said. "Coach Dunham can get that going."

Dwayne nodded.

"I want your word on it," I said.

Dwayne stared at me. I waited. Chantel banged her elbow into his upper arm.

"Dwayne," she said, making it two long syllables.

Dwayne still stared. Then he said, "You got it."

"Thank you," I said.

I looked at the painting the old guy was working on. It was mountains with a valley and a lake in the valley.

"White Mountains," he said. "New Hampshire."

"Un huh," I said and headed for the door. In the Jaguar, driving back up Blue Hill Ave. Hawk said, "Grateful motherfucker."

"Maybe he is," I said, "but can't show it."

"Or maybe he ain't," Hawk said.

36

Susan and I were having dinner at a place called Rarities in the Charles Hotel in Cambridge.

Outside the bank of picture windows Charles Square was beginning to look autumnal, and the first pumpkins and cornstalks were clustered around the display base of the Charles Square sign. Harvard students were back; parents, visiting, were lounging around the hotel lobby looking a little startled that they had kids in college.

"They convicted Deegan's friends today," I said.

She was reading the menu closely, peering through the crimson-rimmed twelve-dollar half glasses that she bought in Neiman Marcus.

"Bobby Deegan? Dwayne Woodcock's friend?" she said.

"Yeah, Bobby sang them all right into the state penal institution at Ossining."

"And Bobby?"

"Disappeared into the witness protection program."

"Do those work?" Susan said.

"They work if the guys after you have limited resources, and they work if the guy in the program isn't a dope. But most of them are dopes. They can't stay away from it. They knock over a crap game or they show up in Vegas on a gambling junket and someone recognizes them, or they get in a fight and someone hears about them."

"Do you think it will for Bobby Deegan?"

The waiter came solicitously by and took our order.

"Deegan's smart," I said, "but he's been a wiseguy his whole life. He's never held a job, except being a crook. They'll set him up with new identify, papers, some money, a house. And they'll place him in a job. Selling real estate, say, or being a short order cook; that kind of thing. And he'll go to work every day and after a while his boss will tell him to do something and Bobby won't want to and they'll come to words and Bobby will pop him on the nose and quit and pretty soon he's back into being a crook, and after a while somebody will recognize him, or he'll get busted, or whatever. If it's the mob after you, then you're in trouble, because they've got time and money and connections and no passion. Killing you is a wise management decision for them. Passion cools, except you and me, Hotpants, but wise business decisions by the mob are forever. His friends may forget about who put them away, or they may not."

The waiter brought Susan some sweetbreads with grilled fruit. For me he brought oysters.

"Hotpants?" Susan said.

"Yeah, that's why the oysters," I said.

Susan ate a very small bite of sweetbread.

"How is Dwayne?" she said.

"Fine," I said. "Surly, arrogant, uncommunicative, and the holder of a two-point-five-million contract over three years."

"Is Chantel with him?"

"Yes," I said.

"Good," Susan said. "Can he read?"

"Some," I said. "Chantel says he got to about third grade level over the summer."

"That's very good progress," Susan said. "It's only been, what, five months?"

"Yes."

I slurped an oyster and gestured with my wine list at the waiter.

"Gewürztraminer," I said. "The Trimbach."

He smiled approvingly and hustled off after the wine. Waiters smile approvingly if you order cough syrup. I finished my oysters. The waiter served the wine. Susan finished her sweetbreads. We each took a sip of wine. Around us the soft sound of conversation, the gentle noise of steaks being cut and soup being spooned. The light was soft and the encroaching September evening darkened the view through the windows.

"You can't stand Dwayne, can you?" Susan said.

"No," I said, "who could? Even Hawk doesn't like him and Hawk doesn't have feelings about anybody."

"Except you," Susan said.

"And you," I said.

"Chantel loves him," Susan said.

"Love's different," I said. "It doesn't alter 'where it alteration finds.' "

"I know," Susan said.

The waiter appeared with barbecued duck for Susan, venison for me.

"And yet you just stuck at it and wouldn't let Dwayne destroy himself even though they tried to kill you, and it was hard, and there was no reason to care about him."

"You think I shouldn't have?" I said.

"No, I think you should have. But, God, he's obnoxious."

"You have obnoxious patients," I said.

Susan smiled. "I'll say," she said.

"Dwayne is one of the best that ever lived at what he does," I said.

"Which is playing basketball," Susan said.

"Yes. Not brain surgery, but something."

"And?" Susan said.

"And I like Chantel," I said.

Susan smiled, and her smile widened as she looked at me. Then she picked up her wine glass and raised it toward me a little and held it for a moment.

"Is this a good omen?" I said.

"If I were you," she said, "I'd have more oysters."

A GUIDE TO CHAUCER'S LANGUAGE

A GUIDE TO CHAUCER'S LANGUAGE

DAVID BURNLEY

First published 1983 by
THE MACMILLAN PRESS LTD
Companies and representatives
throughout the world

ISBN 0 333 33531 7 (hc)
ISBN 0 333 33532 5 (pb)

Phototypeset by
WESSEX TYPESETTERS LTD
Frome, Somerset
Printed in Hong Kong

Contents

vi *Contents*

FOR HELEN

Abbreviations

Chaucer

CT	*The Canterbury Tales*
BD	*The Book of the Duchess*
HF	*The House of Fame*
AA	*Anelida and Arcite*
PF	*The Parliament of Fowls*
Bo	*Boece*
TC	*Troilus and Criseyde*
LGW	*The Legend of Good Women*
ABC	*An ABC*
Pity	*The Complaint unto Pity*
Lady	*A Complaint to his Lady*
Mars	*The Complaint of Mars*
Stedfastnesse	*Lak of Stedfastnesse*
W. Unc.	*Against Women Unconstant*
Complaint	*A Balade of Complaint*
RR	*The Romaunt of the Rose*

See the Preface for the significance of line references and the editions used.

Gower

CA   *Confessio Amantis*

Langland

PP   *Piers Plowman*

Other abbreviations

ANTS   The Anglo-Norman Text Society

Arch. Ling.   *Archivum Linguisticum*

ASE   *Anglo-Saxon England*

Chau. R.   *Chaucer Review*

CN   *Chaucer Newsletter*

EGS   *English and Germanic Studies*

EETS   The Early English Text Society

ES   *English Studies*

JEGP   *Journal of English and Germanic Philology*

JEL   *Journal of English Linguistics*

LSE   *Leeds Studies in English*

MLA   Modern Language Association

MED   *Middle English Dictionary*

MLQ   *Modern Language Quarterly*

MLR   *Modern Language Review*

MS   *Mediaeval Studies*

NED   *New English Dictionary*

NM   *Neuphilologische Mitteilungen*

NQ   *Notes and Queries*

OED   *Oxford English Dictionary*

PBA	*Proceedings of the British Academy*
Phil. Prag.	*Philologia Pragensia*
PLL	*Papers on Language and Literature*
PMLA	*Publications of the Modern Language Association*
RES	*Review of English Studies*
SATF	Société des Anciens Textes Français
SP	*Studies in Philology*
SN	*Studia Neophilologica*
TPS	*Transactions of the Philological Society*
TRHS	*Transactions of the Royal Historical Society*
UTQ	*University of Toronto Quarterly*
YES	*Yearbook of English Studies*

Preface

This is a book addressed rather to the reader of Chaucer than to the student of language; but its ideal audience would be that reader who would seek to make no distinction between the two activities, recognising the fact that the beginning of literary wisdom is in the knowledge of language. For such a reader, the word 'language' need not imply an excess of formal description, a complex of paradigms, or a conglomeration of statistics. Language for him is the bearer of meaning, and he hopes through its study to gain a fuller understanding of his text. This is by no means a simple matter because the text cannot be deciphered by the use of a grammar and a glossary as though it were a code. Just as the fossil leaf once flourished in a prehistoric forest, so the words preserved in a text are the immobilised testimony to a vital language system which has now disappeared. The text drew its original meaning from the place which its language held in this system, and the language system itself was significant by its use and history in the culture to which it belonged. Chaucer's language is, above all, a variety of Middle English of a kind used in London in the late fourteenth century, and this historical context is essential to its meaning.

The reference to language variety is one which recurs throughout this book, not only because variation is an essential descriptive quality of Chaucer's language, but also because that variation has important repercussions on the interpretation of his meaning. The possibility of choosing one linguistic form in preference to another in any given circumstance implies a potential for fine distinctions in stylistic nuance. To what extent could this potential be exploited? Just what are the distinctions implied by any such choice? Even near-contemporaries like Usk and Caxton could be unsure of the answers to these questions, so that modern attempts at answering them must often remain speculative. What is important is that the reader should recognise the dangers of over-confidence at the same time as the need to ask such questions. By asking them, some satisfactory answers will be found, and our understanding of Chaucer's poetry will be enriched. This book, therefore, is intended to be the kind of guide which encourages its reader to ask the right questions.

The book is divided into two parts: the first, concentrating upon the text, deals with problems of interpretation which are likely to be encountered in grammar and syntax. It also discusses the principles of text coherence. The second part deals with Chaucer's language and vocabulary in its broader contemporary context, discussing language use, style, and variety. Except where it would prejudice discussion, modern punctuation has been supplied to aid understanding of passages from Chaucer. Non-Chaucerian passages have been translated or glossed as necessary, but I have assumed that the less-experienced reader will be well enough served by his text or by the *Chaucer Glossary* (see Sources and Further Reading) not to need glosses of Chaucer quotations.

Indexes of words and of lines quoted are provided in order to facilitate the use of the book as a study aid. For convenience, line references relate to *The Works of Geoffrey Chaucer*, edited by F. N. Robinson, except that in references to the *Canterbury Tales* the lineation of Skeat's edition has been used, since this can readily be used both with Robinson's edition and with N. F. Blake's recent edition from the Hengwrt manuscript.

Although the book may be used for reference purposes, and indeed its two parts may be consulted individually, if read consecutively its chapters adumbrate a coherent conception of Chaucer's language as a variety of Middle English. This is an aspect of the book which may be expected to interest the more specialist reader, for whom extensive notes are given.

My thanks are due to my colleagues in Sheffield: in particular to Brian Donaghey for helpful discussion, and to John Johansen and Norman Blake for reading the typescript and making valuable suggestions for improvement. They are in no sense responsible for any errors which may have persisted. I am grateful too to Sandra Burton for finding time amid her other duties to produce the final typescript so efficiently. Not least, I should like to record my appreciation of the patience and understanding of my wife and children.

UNIVERSITY OF SHEFFIELD   JDB
AUGUST 1982

I should like to thank the authorities of the National Library of Wales both for supplying and for permission to reproduce photographs of part of Peniarth MS 392 ('the Hengwrt MS').

Map 1: Middle English Dialects

PART ONE
The Language of the Text

Preliminary Note

Chaucer died in October 1400 and within the next twenty years his works became widely read. Among these readers was one Thomas Hoccleve, a minor poet who claimed him as 'maister deere and fadir reverent', and who tried to preserve his memory by having Chaucer's portrait included in the manuscript of one of his own poems. However, it is not Hoccleve's devotion to Chaucer which concerns us here, but the job by which he earned his daily bread, and which he describes so poignantly in his *Regement of Princes*. He was in fact a scribe, a clerk in the Privy Seal office for nearly twenty-four years; one of an army of London scribes who, in the days before printing, spent their working lives laboriously copying documents by hand. People, he tells us, think it an easy job, but in fact it is exhausting and exacting:

A writer mot thre thynges to hym knytte,	*combine*
And in tho may be no disseuerance;	
Mynde, ee, and hand, non may fro othir flitte,	*eye, separate*
But in hem mot be ioynt continuance.	*must be joint*
The mynde al hoole with-outen variance	*entirely*
On þe ee and hand awayte moot alway,	*must be in attendance*
And þei two eek on hym; it is no nay.	
Who so schal wryte, may nat holde a tale	*gossip*
With hym and hym, ne synge this ne that;	
But al his wittes hoole, grete and smale,	
Ther must appere, and halden hem ther-at;	*be present*
And syn he speke may ne synge nat,	
But bothe two he nedes moot forbere	
His labour to hym is þe alengere.	*more tiresome*
	(995–1008)

Stooping over his copy damages the scribe's back and upsets his stomach, but most of all his eyes suffer. Nevertheless, Hoccleve occupied his leisure hours not only by writing his own poetry but by copying that of others in order to eke out a meagre salary. He was not alone in this, and indeed some scribes seem to have become specialists in copying the newly-fashionable English verse of Chaucer, Gower, and Langland: such copying was the only method of widely publishing a poet's work before the invention of printing.

Publication by scribal copying differs from that by the printing press in that, instead of the uniformity of the print-run, each scribal copy will reflect the skills or vagaries of its individual writer; and not all scribes maintained the perfect co-ordination of hand, mind, and eye recommended by Hoccleve. Their attention might wander, and they would omit, repeat, or re-phrase the words of the original. Sometimes – more consciously – they might feel that a text required explanation, so they would add it in the margin, from where it later became incorporated into the work. Because the language still consisted of a continuum of dialects without any universally-accepted standard, they felt free to alter the dialect-forms of the original poem, perhaps destroying stylistic effects intended by the author as they did so.

For their part, medieval authors were well aware of the destruction wrought by the process of copying, but there was little they could do about it. Just before Chaucer's birth, Robert Manning of Bourne in Lincolnshire tells of his experience of the highly-esteemed romance, *Sir Tristrem*, which he ascribes to Thomas of Erceldoun. The poem, he says, has been ruined in transmission, so that it is no longer possible to judge its merit:

> I see in song, in sedgeyng tale
> Of Erceldoun and of Kendale,
> Non þam says as þai þam wroght,
> and in þer sayng it semes noght;
> þat may þou here in Sir Tristrem;
> ouer gestes it has þe steem,
> Ouer alle that is or was,
> if men it sayd as made Thomas;

> But I here it no man say
> þat of som copple som is away;
> So þare fayre sayng here beforn
> is þare trauayle nere forlorn

[I see in song, in tales composed for narration, about Erceldoun and Kendal. But no-one tells [their works] as they were composed, and such recitation makes them seem worthless. You can hear that in the case of *Sir Tristrem*, which has the greatest reputation of any story new or old; or would have if it were recited as it was composed by Thomas. But it is never heard without some part of some couplet missing. So the fine poetry of former times is hardly more than wasted effort.]

Chaucer knew that a similar fate awaited his poetry despite the poetic imprecations he heaped on his scribe, Adam, and he expresses his fears in a famous passage of *Troilus and Criseyde*:

> And for ther is so gret diversite
> In Englissh and in writyng of oure tonge,
> So preye I God that non myswrite the,
> Ne mysmetre for defaute of tonge.   (V 1793–6)

But within decades of his death, scribal copyists had not only marred his metre but confused his poems with those by other authors. At the same time, chance had decreed that none of Chaucer's original manuscripts should survive, so that all our knowledge of Chaucer's writings and his language descend to us through the mediation of these copyists. As a result, the standard editions in which we read Chaucer today do not correspond precisely to any of the surviving manuscripts of his poetry; instead, they are an attempt by scholars to get back to the Chaucerian originals which have vanished. We must consider what this editorial process means to the study of Chaucer's language.

In fact, editors have had to admit that the full restoration of Chaucer's original is impossible: the best that can be done is to produce a version one stage closer to the original than the best existing copy. However, the selection of this 'best manuscript' is not an infallible process and may be fraught with controversy. In modern times, the 'best manuscript' of the *Canterbury Tales* has been variously considered to be either the Ellesmere or the Hengwrt manuscript. Both manuscripts are of London origin, are carefully written, and are of very early date, but recently Hengwrt has found greater favour because it lacks the signs of editorial improvement which are a feature of Ellesmere. It is therefore assumed to be the manuscript closest to Chaucer's original and the best one on which to base an edition.

Having selected the manuscript from which he will edit, the editor then sets about producing a text which can be printed and made understandable to the modern reader, for the manuscript is not laid out like a modern book. A comparison between a passage from the Hengwrt version of the *Clerk's Tale* (plate 1) and a modern edition will illustrate some of the differences:

> Noght fer fro thilke paleys honurable
> Wher as this markys shoop his mariage
> Ther stood a throop of site delitable,
> In which that poure folk of that village
> Hadden hir bestes and hir herbergage
> And of hir labour token hir sustenance
> After that the erthe yaf hem habundance.

(E. 197–203)

Most obviously, the modern printed version has replaced early letter-forms by their modern equivalents, and where the letter þ appears, it has been replaced by *th*. In the manuscript certain words appear in abbreviated form; these are expanded by the editor to *that* and *honurable*. The capitals used by the scribe to emphasise *Markys* and *Throop* do not correspond with modern practice, and so are removed by the editor, and the scribe's punctuation, which is concerned with metre and marks the caesura, gives way to modern grammatical punctuation which distinguishes clauses.

But the decisions which the editor must make are sometimes more substantial than those of spelling and punctuation. His comparison of this passage with other manuscripts tells him that *site delitable* is not the only possible reading which the tradition has handed down. The Cambridge MS Gg 4.27, and a number of others, read *sighte*; MS Corpus Christi 198 has *cite*; one manuscript has *syth*; and yet another has *sigh*. The editor must now decide which of these alternatives to adopt. Taking into account the sense of the line, only *site* and *sighte* seem possible. The sources from which Chaucer adapted the tale offer no help, so that the choice must be made on contextual evidence alone, although no doubt the editor will be swayed by the knowledge that Ellesmere agrees with Hengwrt against Gg. At the beginning of the tale there is reference to 'many another delitable sighte', a reading upon which his manuscripts agree. Is there, then, a repetition of this phrase? Or, on the other hand, did the scribe of Gg not recognise the rather rare Chaucerian word *site*, and, influenced by the phrase occurring earlier, repeat it here? A further piece of evidence may be taken into account: the editor may also know of the similar phrases *places delitables* (F 899) and *place delytous* (RR 489), both of which seem to echo a phrase of Latin rhetoric, *locus amoenus*, in an appropriate descriptive context. On these grounds, he may decide that in the variation *delitable sighte* to *site delitable* in the Clerk's tale, we have an appropriately clerkish piece of Chaucerian wordplay, and that since his most authoritative manuscripts agree, and since the deviant *sighte* can be explained by scribal simplification, he will retain the reading *site delitable*.

The decision he has reached is one of probability rather than certainty, but he may feel reasonably satisfied with it. Later in the same poem, however, the editor's choice becomes more difficult, as will be seen from the second passage (plate 2):

> 'This is thy doghter which thow hast supposed
> To be my wyf, that oother feithfully
> Shal be myn heir as I haue ay supposed.
>
> (E. 1065–1067)

After he has entered modern quotation marks and a comma after *wyf*, there remains the problem of the final word in the passage. The manuscript variants of this are *purposed* and *disposed*. Either of these might be considered better readings than Hengwrt's *supposed*. Yet two other early manuscripts,

Ellesmere and Gg, agree with Hengwrt in reading *supposed*, and this consensus must carry weight. On literary critical grounds, however, *purposed* and *disposed* seem better to suit Walter's autocratic temperament, whereas the repetition of *supposed* is decidedly weak. Furthermore, it might be argued that *supposed* has been written because the scribe's eye has mistakenly transported it from two lines before. There is no doubt that *disposed* is rather rarer than the other two in Chaucer's usage, and also that a very similar use of it is found in line 244 of the tale, and since it is the most satisfactory poetically, it is usually adopted by editors. But, in fact, there is no truly objective means of asserting the right of this reading to be considered as the author's in defiance of the reading of the base manuscript; it is in fact adopted because of a desire to associate the most poetically-satisfying reading with the name of Chaucer.

Let us now take stock of the sources we have for a study of Chaucer's language. In the absence of any manuscripts certainly written by the poet, we have a choice of working from a good modern edition or from the earliest surviving London manuscripts of his poetry. If we were to choose the first option, we ought to be aware that we should be dealing with a text in some sense 'artificial', a text produced by a blend of scholarship and prejudice, but which was never read by any medieval Englishman. Moreover, it would be a text in which punctuation and spelling, and, as we have seen, even the collocations of words, may have been altered by a modern editor. Alterations in punctuation may prejudice our conception of the syntax of the original; changes in the diction would affect our view of vocabulary and phraseology. But if we choose to use manuscripts as sources, although we shall still have no direct access to Chaucer's own language in the narrowest sense of that phrase, at least we shall be dealing with truly medieval sources from a time and place very close to where Chaucer wrote: artefacts from a social and historical situation which we can try to understand. Since it is the purpose of this book to examine Chaucer's language in its contemporary context, the choice of manuscripts as a source is inevitable. In the case of the *Canterbury Tales*, the Hengwrt manuscript has been adopted; for *Troilus and Criseyde*, Corpus

Illustrations 1 and 2: Passages from the Hengwrt version of the *Clerk's Tale*.

Christi College, Cambridge MS 61; and for *Boece*, Cambridge University Library MS Ii 1.38. All three are London manuscripts written within fifteen years of the death of the poet and are considered to contain good texts of his works. As far as possible, examples are taken from them; occasionally, however, examples have been drawn from the Ellesmere manuscript and from the Fairfax manuscript of the minor poems.

1 Chaucer's Grammar

The language in which this book is written is not the direct descendant of that used by Chaucer; indeed, it is derived rather from Caxton and the earliest printers, and they derived their spelling system from that used by the scribes of Chancery who flourished shortly after Chaucer's death. But both the Chancery language and the language of Chaucer were formalisations of the language of London, and were generally similar in type.[1] Chaucer is therefore relatively easy for the modern reader to understand. By comparison, authors of a similar date writing in the north-west Midlands use forms and spellings which make their works scarcely intelligible to us without special study. However, the relative ease with which we can embark upon reading Chaucer is not without its own dangers. Words and phrases may have different meanings and connotations from their familiar modern forms, and (just as insidious) the apparent familiarity of much of the text may encourage us to skip those grammatical constructions which are puzzling, betraying us into literary interpretations dependent upon that incomplete text which is created by our desire to read faster than unrecognised difficulties will properly permit.

What follows in the next few chapters is not an attempt to provide a fully descriptive grammar of Chaucer's language, since for the purposes of interpretation this is unnecessary, but rather it is intended to emphasise some of the ways in which Chaucer's grammar differs from that of Modern English, and to illustrate the significance of these distinct forms and structures.

The Noun

The noun in Chaucer presents few difficulties in interpretation since it is formally and functionally closely parallel to the noun in modern English. As in modern English, inflexional endings are added to the base form to distinguish number, but the complex inflexional system, which in Old English indicated case and gender as well as distinguished weak from strong nouns, has largely disappeared. Occasional traces of a dative inflexional *-e* are found in a few prepositional idioms: *for Gode* (A 3526); *on honde* (B 348); *in lande* (B 4069).[2] But the only inflexional endings commonly surviving are those written *-es* (occasionally *ys* or *is*; and *z* in a few French borrowings) and *-en*. The *-en* inflexion signals plurality, without distinction in case, and is derived from the nominative and accusative plural inflexions of Old English weak nouns. The *-es* inflexion indicates both possession and plurality and in these functions may have been derived separately from the genitive singular and the nominative and accusative plural of strong masculine nouns in Old English.[3]

In the early Middle English period, plurals in *-en* were very common in the south, and indeed, even in Chaucer's time, they remained so in Kent; but overwhelmingly the commonest plural in Chaucer's London language is that in *-es*. Nevertheless, the extension of the *-es* plural to all nouns was still incomplete in the London English of Chaucer's time, and a few words which are found today with *-es* occur in Chaucer with the *-en* inflexion: *eyen*, *yen* 'eyes'; *asshen* 'ashes'. The plural of some words was variable and in the course of transition, so that *doughtren* vies with *doughtres* and *toon* with *toos* in Chaucer manuscripts (see pp. 118–9).

The termination *-es* which had descended from the Old English genitive singular of strong masculine and neuter nouns was used as a marker of possession: *goddes priuetee* (A 3454); *Cristes passioun* (A 3478); *seinte Petres suster* (A 3486). In examples like these the *-es* inflexion is the precursor of, and has the same possessive sense as, the 'apostrophe s' in modern English. In a large number of other examples, however, it marks a shift of grammatical function by which a noun modifies that noun immediately following it, in a way similar to an attributive adjective or noun. In this function, number is often insignificant or ambiguous: *maydens shamefastnesse* (C 55); *wommens conseils* (B 4446); *horses lawe* (*TC* I 223). An alternative to the use of this structure is the use of the periphrasis – probably influenced by French – so that *loue of frendes* (*TC* II 379) exists alongside, and with the same meanings as, *frendes loue* (*TC* III 1591). Although a similar option of variant expression exists in modern English, it cannot be exploited so freely nor in precisely the same expressions as in Chaucer's language. The phrase *sorwes leche* (*TC* II 1066) would be unidiomatic in modern English, and the semantic ambiguity of *loue of frendes* would discourage its use by a modern author.[†]

There is variation too in the expression of genitive groups in Chaucer's language. In Old English, where the *-es* inflexion had been a part of the declensional system of the noun, it necessarily remained bound to the head word in the group. Consequently, we find structures like: *the wyues loue of Bathe* (E 1170); *the Kyng Priamus sone of Troye* (*TC* I 2); *the Grekys hors Synoun* (F 209). This type of genitive continued in use until the time of Shakespeare, but, alongside it, the modern type is also to be found in Chaucer's language: *god of loues seruantȝ* (*TC* I 15). The emergence of the modern type perhaps reflects a tendency to see *-es* no longer as one of a set of inflexions, but rather as a syntactical marker functioning in a way equivalent to the preposition *of* in the partitive construction.

An unfamiliar use of the *-es* inflexion, which also alters the class of a word, is that which, in Old English, converted nouns into adverbs. This function becomes more frequent in Middle English, so that Chaucer has the adverbial expressions: *moste nedes* (A 1290) 'necessarily'; *his thankes* (A 1626) 'with his approval'; *unnethes* (D 394) 'with difficulty'; *hennes* (*TC* III 1425) 'from here': *thennes* (F 326) 'from there'; *amyddes* (A 2009) 'in the middle of'.

Finally, there are certain uses of the noun in which standard modern English would use an inflexion, but where this is lacking in Chaucer. An example above has already shown that Classical names ending in *s* are without inflexion. The same is true of some native nouns: *Kyng Priamus sone* (*TC* I 2); *Phebus wyf* (H 238); *two vers* (B 2801); *hise hors weere goode* (A 74). After numerals and expressions of quantity, the plural of the noun is often identical to the singular: *twenty foot* (A 2607); *twenty wynter* (D 600). In a few formulaic expressions, the possessive also lacks formal marking: *his lady grace* (A 88); *my fader soule* (A 781); *his herte blood* (A 2006); *heuene kyng* (A 3464).

The Adjective

In Old English, adjectives had been very fully inflected, so that their endings changed according to whether the noun which they modified was feminine, masculine, or neuter, singular or plural; or whether it was in the nominative, accusative, genitive, or dative case. Moreover, two entirely different sets of inflexions existed for showing this concord with the noun, and the choice between them depended largely on syntactic environment. The two sets of inflexions are known as the definite (or weak) and the indefinite (or strong) inflexions. Although all traces of case and gender inflexion had disappeared from adjectives in London English by the time of Chaucer, inflexion for definiteness and for plurality is sometimes evident in the form of a final *-e*. The conditions which determine the use of this final *-e* can be stated quite simply, and its use is remarkably stable in good, early manuscripts such as Hengwrt.

Firstly, it must be made clear that these conditions do not apply to adjectives of more than one syllable, which usually have no inflexion; nor do they apply to adjectives whose stem in Old English ended in a vowel; nor to some French-derived monosyllables. Thus, words like *pure, clene, grene, swete,* and *deere* invariably end in *e.* But monosyllabic adjectives whose stem ends in a consonant – for example, *fair, good, old, wys, greet, blak, long, yong, fals,* and *fyn* – are written with an *-e* when they modify a noun in the plural, both attributively and predicatively, and irrespective of whether they occur before or after the noun, thus: *fresshe* floures *white* and *reede* (A 90); Hise nose-thirles *blake* weere and *wyde* (A 557). In the singular, such adjectives clearly exhibit a distinction in usage derived from that of the Old English distinction between definite and indefinite inflexions. Thus, if the adjective is preceded by the definite article *the*, the demonstratives *this*, *that*, or *thilke*, a possessive pronoun, or a possessive genitive noun, or if it modifies a proper noun or some expression of address, then the form with final *-e* is used.[5] Elsewhere, the form lacking the *-e* is employed. A table of examples will make this usage clearer:

DEFINITE	INDEFINITE	PLURAL
This olde man (C 174)	an old man (C 713)	olde bookes (A 1198)
this yonge wyf (A 3233)	a yong wyf (E 1557)	ȝonge wyues (*TC* II 119)
the olde daunce (A 476)	old fissh (E 1418)	faire wyues (A 234)
his longe ladel (A 2020)	a long surcote (A 617)	the nyghtes longe (A 1337)
my longe tale (A 2966)	smal coral (A 158)	smale foweles (A 9)
thy neighbores goode name (I 796)	a fresh knyght (*AA* 34)	fresshe floures (A 90)
O grete god (B 1797)	greet pyne (A 1324)	grete lordes (B 2341)
olde Donegild (B 896)		

Although the pattern of this usage is very stable, there are exceptions to it. Some of these can be explained away: for example, the failure to write *-e* on numerous occasions before a following vowel is undoubtedly due to elision; the use of the *-e* in *false fortune* (B 3859) is because, like *god*, *fortune* is considered a proper noun. There is also some variation before corporate nouns like *folk* or *peple*, where number is perhaps not clear, and, when used substantivally, the phrase *yong ne old* may be regarded as either singular or plural. After such examples have been set aside, there remains about one in a hundred occurrences of these adjectives which does not correspond to the pattern.[6] In almost every case, it will be found that the *-e* has been omitted in conditions which would appear to demand its use. This is a state of affairs which matches the general development of the language of London, where an earlier type of language, proper to the south-east, was gradually being displaced by more northerly influences. Chaucer's grammar was, in this respect, conservative, and matched that of the country areas around the capital.[7] Even before his death, however, loss of final -*e* in adjective inflexion must have been well advanced in the innovating styles which were rapidly to prevail in the city.

One further – rather rare – feature of adjective inflexion requires brief mention. It is the noun-adjective concord which marks plurality by the use of a final -*s*. This usage is derived from French, is usually found with French-derived adjectives, and is mostly associated with technical language or fixed phrases: *places delitables* (F 899); *tables tolletanes* (F 1273).[8]

Pronouns

The forms of Chaucer's personal pronouns differ from those of modern English in some respects:

SUBJECT FORMS	1ST PERSON	2ND PERSON	3RD PERSON
singular	*I* ~ *Ich* ~ *Ik*	*thow* ~ *thou*	*she; he; hit*
plural	*we*	*ye*	*thei* ~ *they*

Variation in the first person pronoun, *I*, is the result of dialectal variation in the *Canterbury Tales*.[9] In the *Reeve's Tale*, Chaucer imitates the speech of northerners, who used the form *Ik*. The southern form, *Ich*, is fairly widespread in Chaucer's writings, but the form *I*, which had been developed originally in unstressed positions within the sentence in Middle English, has become the commonest form in Chaucer's language, and it is used even in positions of emphasis:

> I am thy mortal foo, and it am I
> That loueth so hoote Emelye the brighte. (A 1736–7)

OBJECT AND PREPOSITIONAL FORMS			
singular	*me*	*the(e)*	*hire; him; (h)it*
plural	*us*	*yow* ~ *you*	*hem*

POSSESSIVE FORMS

singular	*my(n); myne*	*thy(n)*	*hire; his*
plural	*oure*	*youre*	*hire ~ thair*

Although the subject form of the pronoun, *thei ~ they* is familiar, the other forms, *hem* and *hire*, are less so. These latter forms are derived from Old English, whereas *they* is of Scandinavian origin. The entire Scandinavian-derived system, in substantially its modern English form, had been adopted into the English of the north-east Midlands from the language of Danish settlers, and is to be found in the *Ormulum* by the early thirteenth century. Chaucer's London English (see Chapter 5) employed only the subject form of this originally-Scandinavian paradigm. The form *thair* occurs once only in the Hengwrt and Corpus manuscripts, where it represents the Norfolk dialect of the Reeve (A 4172). The forms of the possessive, *myn* and *thyn*, are those which are found before a word beginning in a vowel. Like the 'intrusive *r*' in modern English phrases such as 'law and order', the *n* serves here to break the unpleasant hiatus arising from the juxtaposition of vowel sounds in neighbouring syllables. In Chaucer's language, initial *h* is not regarded as a true consonant, but merely as an aspiration, so that words beginning with *h* can be regarded as equivalent to those beginning with a vowel:

> This was *thyn* ooth and *myn* also certeyn;   (A 1139)
> Allas *myn* hertes queene, all as *my* wif.   (A 2775)

Structurally, a number of discrepancies can be found between Chaucer's personal pronoun system and our own. A singular form of the second person, *the; thow; thy(n)*, is to be found, distinguished from the plural. As a possessive, the third-person pronoun does not adequately distinguish between singular and plural, since both the feminine singular 'her' and the plural of all genders 'their' are represented by one form, *hire*. Furthermore, the possessive fails to distinguish in the singular between a masculine and neuter reference: modern English 'his' and 'its' are rendered by the single form *his*, and this can become confusing in sentences where the syntax is loose, and especially where it is possible to assume an antecedent *he* used indefinitely. In the following passage, the *his* in the last line may refer to *tale* in the first line, and be equivalent to modern English 'its'; but it is easy, since the pronoun is so far removed from its antecedent, to assume an indefinite personal reference to the teller of the tale, who has not been explicitly mentioned:

> The knotte why that euery tale is told
> If it be taryed til that lust be cold
> Of hem that han it after herkned yoore,
> The sauour passeth euer lenger the moore
> For fulsomenesse of his prolixitee.   (F 401–5)

Similar ambiguity is common as the result of the uncertain reference of *it*, and it is apparent that, apart from uncertainties in the forms of pronouns, the modern reader must be aware that pronouns can refer to items much further removed in the text than is ordinarily the case in modern English. In the *Legend of Good Women* the following passage occurs:

> Allas, than comth a wilde leonesse
> Out of the woode, withouten more arreste,
> With blody moouthe of strangelynge of a beste,
> To drynken of the welle ther as she sat.
> And whan that Tesbe had espyed that,
> She ryst hire up with a ful drery herte,
> And in a cave with dredful foot she sterte,
> For by the moone she saugh yt wel with-alle.
>   (*LGW* 805–12)

It would be natural to assume that *yt* in the last line is intended to refer to the cave in the line before, but comparison with the source of this passage in Ovid's *Metamorphoses* suggests that it is intended to refer all the way back to the lioness in the first line.

The existence of separate pronouns for second-person singular and plural allows a differentiation in usage which is impossible in modern English, where this system has been reduced to the existence of a single form, *you*, and where *thou* exists only in a few specific registers – such as liturgical language – and in some dialects. In Middle English the plural form is used to address a group of two or more. When addressing a single individual – as in many modern European languages – a choice of singular or plural form is possible, and the contrast between the two forms is no longer one of number, as is shown by the concord of such expressions as *ye ben wys* (E 528), in which the singular form of the adjective is used. The choice between *ye* and *thou* when addressing a single individual is a stylistic rather than a grammatical one, and it has certain social and attitudinal implications.[10] Most obviously, they are concerned with the relative status of the speaker and addressee. If their status or age is acknowledged by both to be distinctly unequal, then the superior may legitimately address the inferior as *thou*, and expect to be answered with the form *ye*. This difference in status is clearly the reason for the usage between Walter and Janicula in the *Clerk's Tale* (E 304–29), and it seems also to be implied in a passage in the *Book of the Duchess* in which the narrator doffs his hood before the Black Knight:

> He was war of me, how y stoode
> Before hym, and did of myn hoode,
> And had ygret hym as best I koude
> Debonayrly and no thyng lowde.
> He sayde, 'I prey *the*, be not wrothe,
> I herde *the* not, to seyn the sothe,
> Ne I saugh *the* not, syr, trewly.'
> 'A, good sir, no fors', quod y,
> 'I am ryght sory yif I have oughte
> Destroubled *yow* out of *your* thoughte.'   (*BD* 515–24)

Such scrupulousness in pronoun address belongs only to polite society; neither the Host in the links between tales nor the churls in the *fabliau* tales necessarily observe it. To idealistic Christians all men are brothers, and so this mark of status is sometimes avoided: in the *Second Nun's Tale*, the *thou*-form is used consistently. *Thou* is used in prayers to God, and voices from Heaven similarly use this form; but prayers addressed by pagans to their gods, or by lovers to Love frequently use *ye*. The courtly gentleman usually calls his lady *ye*, and this is the normal mode of address between husband and wife in polite society. The courtly man, however, addresses male friends as *thou,* the form he also uses when addressing apostrophes to himself. *Ye* has associations of detachment deriving from that remoteness which stems from formal address and discrimination of status; *thou* connotes nearness and intimacy in which such discrimination is forgotten.

Although general hints on the factors governing the choice of *ye* or *thou* can be given, it is important to realise that no unbreakable rules exist. The choice between *ye* and *thou* when addressing a single individual is not a grammatical one, but a stylistic one governed not only by institutionalised forms of social structure, but also by transient emotions and attitudes arising from a relationship. It is notable, for example, that, although Pandarus normally uses a respectful *ye* to Criseyde, when describing her coming old age and ugliness, his distaste is expressed by a switch: 'Go loue; for old, ther wol no wight of *the*' (*TC* II 396). In the *Second Nun's Tale*, Cecilia switches from calling the judge Almachius by the due form, *ye,* to the disparaging *thou* as her scorn for him grows. On the other hand, Troilus's switch from his usual *ye* in addressing Criseyde indicates high emotion and an affirmation of their intimacy: 'I am *thyn* al hool withouten mo' (*TC* IV 1641). In all these examples, the relative social status of the speakers remains unchanged, and the variation in the form of address arises rather from changes in emotional relationships. The nuances implied may therefore be quite subtle, and it is not perhaps very surprising to find that some *Troilus* manuscripts substitute *youres* for *thyn* in the above quotation. Indeed, there are examples of 'switches' which seem to be motivated by nothing more than the demands of rhyme (G 199).

Since the choice of *ye* or *thou* is determined by such complex contextual factors, it is impossible to give a full descriptive account within reasonable limits. However, fig. 1 is intended to provide readers with a device by which they can begin to analyse examples of Chaucer's use of the second-person pronoun: it is a tool which may be refined by practical experience. A preliminary note of explanation is necessary. The diagram is arranged as a flow chart in which the first stage represents the grammatical distinction between singular and plural with reference to the number of addressees. The second stage relates to the speaker and the style he uses. Is he a courtly

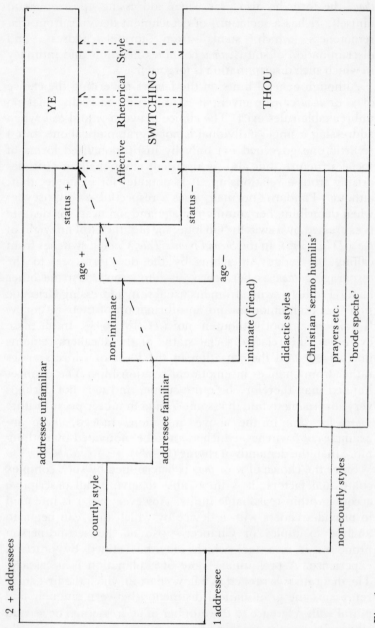

Fig. 1

figure using courtly style to exemplify or promote the ideals of polite society? If not, is he a peasant – a *cherle* – a teacher, a Christian idealist, or a man praying? All are conditions which disregard the pretensions of courtliness. The rest of the diagram is concerned with the addressee. If he is unknown to the speaker, and if his status is not evident, it would clearly be a breach of etiquette to address him as *thou*, since this might imply over-intimacy, patronisation, or the assumption of low social status. If the addressee is known to the speaker, a series of further criteria to do with intimacy, relative age and status comes into play. The choice of pronoun may be made with any one or more of these criteria prominent in the mind of the speaker. The dotted lines represent the path taken when any particular pair of criteria are not of salient importance in a situation; for example, in a formal situation, the degree of intimacy between speaker and addressee may not be important, but rather the relative age and status of the two in the group before which they are appearing. Similarly, if two speakers are of approximately the same age, age itself cannot be the grounds for choice, and the selection of *ye* or *thou* will be according to intimacy and social status.

In any extended conversation, however, as mentioned above, there will be selections of forms which do not correspond to the flow chart, arising from changes in attitude and emotions in the speaker. This 'affective switching', when resulting in *ye*, often connotes detachment, distancing, formality, objectivity, rejection or repudiation. The contrary switch from *ye* to *thou* is perhaps associated with the use of *thou* for intimates, children, or those of lower social status, for it has specific significances related to these distinct uses. It can, for example, be used jokingly and patronisingly (D 432–3); and it can also be used to indicate a sudden *rapprochement* between speakers: a sense of engagement or solidarity, sudden intimacy, cajolery, and even conspiracy. It draws attention to the relationship existing between the speaker and addressee. But these two kinds of meaning are perhaps rather different, since the latter arises from the affective attitude to the relationship, the former from a deliberate rhetorical switch in which a mode of address appropriate to a child is shifted to address an adult. This rhetorical deliberation is the case also with the other kind of meaning in which the form of address appropriate to an inferior is used for an equal, and the result is an insult and a signal of hostility such as that offered by Cecilia to Almachius. A further type of switching is that in which, either in quotation or in parody, momentary switches of style take place, as, for example, when in the midst of an address in the *ye*-form an allusion is made to the wisdom of Solomon, where the didactic style causes a momentary switch to *thou* (E 1485). In the diagram, these three kinds of switching are represented by the vertical arrows.

The use of pronouns reflexively, although it is unlikely to cause great difficulty in understanding, differs somewhat from that of modern English. Forms which are apparently reflexive forms may be used as the subject of a sentence. In a few such cases the verb shows third-person concord even though the subject is apparently first person. The effect is that of an emphatic pronoun:

> This to seye *myself* hath been the whippe   (D 175)

By contrast, the ordinary forms of the pronoun may be used in reflexive constructions:

> This Absolon doun sette *hym* on his knees   (A 3723)

Demonstratives

Chaucer's language uses the demonstratives *that* and *this* (singular) and *tho* and *thise* (plural) together with a contracted phrase, *thilke,* and these present few difficulties of interpretation. But two peculiar usages demand discussion: the first is an idiosyncratic use of *this/thise*; the second is a use of the third-person pronoun in a quasi-demonstrative function. The two uses are best discussed together since they play a similar role in ensuring the cohesion of the text (see Chapter 4). A few examples will serve as illustration:

  (a) Whan that *this* worthy duc, *this* Theseus,
       Hath Creon slayn;   (A 1001–2)

(b) *This* mayde, of which I wol this tale expresse;   (C 105)

(c) Bitwixe Theseus and *hym* Arcite.   (A 1210)

The function of the demonstrative *this* in examples (a) and (b) is an anaphoric one. In (b) it ensures that the expression *this mayde* refers back to the previously-mentioned daughter (C 5) of the knight, Virginius, and to the same expression *this mayde*, in line 30.[11] Turning to line 118 will show that it also forms part of a cohesive chain of references to *this mayde*. Each of the uses of the phrase commences a line, and, more important, marks a division, or a change of direction in the development of the narrative, marking off the elaboration of individual topics. Before line 105, for example, Chaucer completes an elaborate description of the maiden, and tells us 'I moot turne agayn to my matere'. As he turns, he draws our attention to the focus of his interest, and now expands upon her prudence and goodness. In short, the phrase *this mayde* is used to keep the theme clearly before our eyes and hold the text together through a series of digressive topics. A similar technique is used in the *Miller's Tale*, where the structure of the narrative is similarly controlled by the use of *this*, followed, for example, by *clerke*, *carpentere*, and *knave*. It is also commonly used there before personal names: 'This Absolon gan wipe his mouth drye' (A 3730); 'This Nicholas sat ay as stille as stoon' (A 3472). Before a personal name this construction has exactly the same function in relation to the development of narrative as it does before occupational and descriptive terms like *clerke* or *mayde*, but it is often taken by readers of Chaucer to imply some patronising element of familiarity. It is claimed also to be a feature of vivid colloquial narrative. Although it is true that the narrative of the *Miller's Tale* is lively, and that its style is not elevated, it should be remembered that an identical use of *this* with a personal name occurs in works of a notably elevated and artificial style, such as the tales of the Knight and the Physician, so that, although the use of *this* may not conflict with a modern conception of colloquialism and familiarity, it is unlikely that these qualities are inherent in this usage in Chaucer's works.

Example (c), which we have not so far mentioned, illustrates the use of the third-person pronoun in a way closely analogous to that of the demonstrative *this*. It is not used to mark a change in topic, but its anaphoric function is clear in the passage in the *Knight's Tale* in which it occurs. The release of Arcite from prison has been arranged between Theseus and Parotheus; the pairing of the pronoun with the personal name makes its reference unambiguous. In fact, however, it seems somewhat redundant, since there is no great danger of misunderstanding; but the full form of the expression may help to clarify the usage:

> This was the forward, pleynly for t'endite,
> Bitwixe Theseus and *hym* Arcite.

The *forward* is a legal agreement, and the concern to avoid ambiguity is a characteristic of legal style. A contemporary legal document, written in substantially the same language, employs similar devices to clarify the development of the topic. Throughout the *Petition of the Folk of Mercerye* (1386), Sir Nicholas Brembre is referred to as *he Nichol*, *hym Nichol*, *the forsaid Nichol*, *the same Nichol*; the chain of reference distinguishes him from *Nicholas Exton, Mair*.[12] A noteworthy feature of the language of this petition is the way in which Brembre's title is dropped, so that the use of his first name alone seems to imply disparagement. In this context, *he Nichol* may well develop a distancing effect, tinted with revulsion and scorn.

The origin of the use of the demonstrative and the personal pronoun for this cohesive purpose may well be in legal language, but it is not exactly paralleled in the Cordwainers' Petition which accompanies that of the Mercers in the Rolls of Parliament. In this French text, the function is discharged by the phrases *dit*, *le ditz*, *avaunt ditz*, or *lequel*. A closer parallel may be found in Latin pleas, where the common cohesive words are: *dictus*, *supradictus*, *ipse*, and especially *idem*. The two last may perhaps account for the use of the personal pronoun.

The third-person pronoun and the demonstrative are also used in a way which is not primarily cohesive, as in the following examples, where neither Jack Straw nor worldly fools have been previously mentioned:

(d) As doon *thise* fooles that been seculer;   (E 1251)
(e) Certes *he* Jakke Straw and his meynee.   (B 4584)

Here the reference is exophoric; that is to say that it is made to some person, class of persons, or things, which are assumed to be mutually familiar to the author and his reader, but which are not further discussed in the text. With this exophoric reference, only the plural form of the demonstrative occurs (*thise clerkes*, *thise flyes*, *thise loveres*, *thise curatz*). Sometimes it relates an individual to the broader class to which he or she belongs, as with Dorigen in the reference to *thise noble wyues* (F 818). In this way Chaucer casts aspersions without making precise attributions. The demonstrative, when used for exophoric reference, does not precede a personal name, but the third-person pronoun frequently does. The allusion to the peasant leader Jack Straw made in the *Nun's Priest's Tale* has all the familiarity, probably also the implied disparagement, of the modern demonstrative phrase 'that fellow Jack Straw'.

In summary, when used exophorically, both the pronoun and the demonstrative may have a patronising and familiar tone. Although, depending upon context, some of this tone may be extended to the anaphoric use of both, it is not necessarily so in every case, and there are many examples where *this* or *he* followed by a personal name serves a special stylistic or cohesive function, and carries no implication of disparagement.[13]

Relatives

Fourteenth-century English used a range of relatives similar to that of modern English, but differing in certain particulars of their use. Although from Old English onwards there had been a tendency to distinguish between personal and non-personal antecedents in pronoun usage, no distinction was regularly maintained in Chaucer's time, so that *which* frequently follows a personal antecedent:

The knyght cam *which* men wenden had be deed.   (D 2029)

Whos and *whom* are both common as relative pronouns, and these, along with *which*, are commonly preceded by a preposition:

> This Sowdanesse *whom* I thus blame and warye;   (B 372)
> this clerk *whos* rethoryk swete;   (E 32)
> For if a preest be foul *in whom* we truste;   (A 501)
> This duc *of whom* I make mencion;   (A 893)
> Lord *to whom* fortune hath yiuen/Victorie;   (A 915–6)
> this present dignitee/*In which that* I have put yow.
>
> (E 470–1)

Who, however, is not used by Chaucer as a relative, and remains an interrogative and indefinite pronoun, as in Old English.[14]

Perhaps the commonest relative is *that*, and it is, as in modern English, used of both personal and non-personal antecedents, although it is commoner with the former:[15]

> Palamon/*That* serueth yow;   (A 2794–5)
> thilke fyr *that* whilom brende thee.   (A 2403)

Whom, whos, and *which* are often combined with *that*, as in E 471 (above). The forms *the which* and *the which that,* both of which occur in more elaborate poetry, and are especially common in prose, seem to be influenced by the French *liquels*. The parallel is particularly close in cases where these phrases are used in a particularising way in imitation of the anaphoric reference of legal language:

> for *the whiche* resons it were a ful greet peril.   (B 2217)
> pour *lesquelles* choses il seroit grant peril

The idioms *as he that, as he which* both appear to be based upon the French phrase *com cil qui.* Attempts have been made to make Middle English *as* carry an ironic force in expressions like 'As she that hadde hire herte on Troilus/So faste' (*TC* V 953–4). Although tempting from the literary-critical point of view, they are not convincing from what we know of linguistic usage, and it seems that the primary sense of such expressions is a causal one.

Finally, it should be noted that omission of the relative occurs in Middle English in circumstances which would seem unidiomatic in the modern language:

> He sente after a cherl was in the town
> Which that he knew for subtil and for bold.
>
> (C 140–1)

Verbs

Verbs in the Germanic languages can be divided into two great classes: the strong and the weak. In Chaucer's Middle English, as in modern English, these are distinguishable only by the forms of the preterite and the past participle. In the strong verbs, the preterite was formed by a change in the root vowel, and the past participle by the addition of the inflexional ending *e(n)*. Thus, in Chaucer's language we find the following forms:

INFINITIVE	PRETERITE	PAST PARTICIPLE
knowe(n)	*knewe*	*knowe(n)*
take(n)	*toke*	*take(n)*
breke(n)	*broke*	*broke(n)*
stonde(n)	*stoode*	*stonde(n)*
speke(n)	*spake*	*spoke(n)*

Weak verbs form their preterite and past participles by the addition of *(e)d* or *t* as a suffix, usually to the stem of the infinitive, but sometimes to a special preterite form which had arisen by phonetic factors in their prehistoric past, thus:

INFINITIVE	PRETERITE	PAST PARTICIPLE
wedde(n)	*wedded*	*wedded*

but:

seke(n)	*soughte*	*sought*
werke(n)	*wroghte*	*wroght*
wende(n)	*wente*	*went*

Weak verbs, then as now, were the most common class in

terms of total numbers, but some strong verbs were of very frequent occurrence. However, because these strong verbs had long ceased to represent the normal means of forming the preterite and past participles of English verbs, all new coinages, all foreign borrowings of verbs, had been treated as weak since prehistoric times, so that the French borrowings which supplemented Middle English vocabulary are nearly all of the following form:

daunce(n)	*daunced*	*daunced*[16]

The numbers of the weak verbs have been further increased by the tendency of strong verbs to develop weak forms. For example, the originally strong Old English verb *wēpan*, *wēop*, *wōpen* has become the modern weak verb *weep*, *wept*. In Chaucer's time the process with regard to this verb, and to several others like it, was incomplete, so that weak and strong variants are found:

INFINITIVE	PRETERITE	PAST PARTICIPLE
crepe(n)	*crepte*	*crept* ~ *cropen*
wepe(n)	*wepte* ~ *weepe*	*wept* ~ *wepe(n)*, *wope(n)*
helpe(n)	*heelpe*	*holpe(n)*
fare(n)	*ferde*	*fare(n)*
hange(n) ~ *honge(n)*	*he(e)ng* ~ *honged*	*hanged* ~ *honged*

Although it has not been shown in the above lists, the past participles of Chaucer's verbs, both weak and strong, can occur in two forms: with or without the prefix *y-/i-*. This prefix is a phonetically-reduced form of the Old English prefix *ge-* found chiefly in the dialects of the south and west in Middle English. In Chaucer the southern form *ycleped* is found alongside the east Midland *cleped*, and *ycome(n)* alongside *come(n)*.

Infinitive

The infinitive of the verb frequently terminates in *-en*, but forms lacking the final *n* are common, and such forms allow elision with the initial vowel in the syllable following. Phonetic modification of the inflexional ending in verbs whose stem ends in a vowel means that forms of the infinitive occur which end simply in -*n*, rather than -*en*, and with the loss of this -*n*, infinitive forms are found consisting of the base morpheme only, without inflexional ending. The four possible forms of the infinitive can be illustrated by the following examples: *helpen* ~ *helpe*; *don* ~ *do*. The possible forms of the infinitive are multiplied by the fact that each of these four may occur either in isolation (*plain infinitive*) or preceded by the prepositions *to* or *for to*. Earlier, *for to* had had a distinctly purposive sense, but, in Chaucer's writings, this is no longer the case. Both infinitives may be used with purposive sense:

> wolde he take his way/To Thebesward his freendes *for to*
> *preye*;   (A 1482–3)
> ech of yow *to shorte* with oure weye/ . . . shal tellen tales
> tweye.   (A 791–2)

But equally both may lack this significance:

> For vnto a poure ordre *for to yeue*;   (A 225)
> Ther nys namoore *to telle*.   (A 974)

Although the *for to* infinitive is very common in the *General Prologue*, its sense is relatively rarely purposive, and its rarity in contemporary prose from the London area suggests that it may have served an essentially metrical purpose in Chaucer. It is, however, common in his own prose works, so that it may have become for him an habitual mode of expression. It has been shown that purposive sense is most frequently found in its use in adjuncts, and it has also been suggested that the *for to* type serves as a useful clearly-marked form of the infinitive when it is syntactically far removed from the governing verb.[17]

Fluctuation between the plain infinitive and the infinitive marked by *to* results in some unexpected usages in Chaucer's language. As the subject or object of a lexical verb, modern English always uses the *to* infinitive; Chaucer's language may occasionally use the plain form:

> As gret a craft is *kepe* wel as wynne.   (*TC* III 1634)

Both plain and *to* forms are found after auxiliaries, although the distribution is not quite that of modern English. Words which are usually considered lexical verbs may occasionally be found acting as auxiliaries:

I *bidde wisshe* ʒow namore sorwe.   (*TC* II 406)

Here *bidden*, for example, has the quasi-auxiliary meaning 'wish or condescend'.[18] The occurrence of these forms of the infinitive after certain adjectives does not always match modern idiom, and is very variable:

But seyden he was *worthy han* his lyf;   (D 1045)
If swych a man was *worthi to ben* dede;   (*TC* II 1699)
And *worthy for to drawen* to memorie;   (A 3112)
They were *glad* for pees vn to hym *sende*;   (B 3826)
And they were *glade for to fille* his purs.   (D 1348)

Three further uses of the infinitive require mention. Firstly, its use with passive sense, when it may exhibit a distinct form derived from the Old English inflected infinitive:

Remembryng hym his erand was *to doone*.   (*TC* II 72)

However, passive sense may often be intended either by the ordinary form of the infinitive, or by a form with the verb *ben*, as in modern English:

That seruant . . . was demed *for to hange* vpon a tree;
(C 270–1)
. . . worthy *to ben hanged* on the galwes.   (D 658)

The other two infinitive expressions which require special mention are both concerned with verbs of motion. In the first, the infinitive fulfils a function more often discharged by the present participle in modern English. It may be that in such expressions as *he cam ride* 'he came riding' the infinitive originally was felt to have an adverbial function, qualifying the verb *comen*; but in Chaucer's language, and also commonly in the London romances of the generations preceding Chaucer, this expression is used in a way which suggests that *cam* was perceived as an auxiliary, with *ride* as the main verb:

Nece isee who *comth* here *ride*. *(TC* II 1253)[19]

Finally, the omission of the infinitive of verbs of motion should be noted as a common Middle English idiom:

> She wol nat dwelle in house half a day
> But forth she wole er any day be dawed.   (D 352–3)

In examples like this, when the nature and direction of the motion is obvious from the context, finite verbs of motion may also be omitted:

> And took hire leue and hom and held hir stille.
> *(TC* I 126)

Third Person of the Verb

The third person of the verb is perhaps the form most frequently encountered in Chaucer's works. Ordinarily, the third person of the present tense ends in *-eth* in the singular and *-en* in the plural: *he, she, it passeth; they passen.* In the plural, no distinction is made according to person, so that *we* and *you* also take the *-en* ending. As in the infinitive and the past participle, forms lacking the final *n* occur. In verbs whose stem ends in *d* or *t* phonetic modification of the singular *-eth* ending is commonly found, resulting in forms which can seem confusingly like preterite forms to the new reader of Chaucer:

> For euery wight which that to Rome *wente*
> Halt nat o path or alwey o manere.   *(TC* II 36–7)

The words *wente* (to which the scribe has added an unhistorical final *-e*) and *halt* occur also in Chaucer manuscripts in the unassimilated forms *wendeth* and *holdeth*. Other verbs exhibiting such formal variation are: *tit ~ tideth ~ tides; rit ~ rideth; sit ~ sitteth; set ~ setteth; writ ~ writeth; let ~ letteth; smyt ~ smyteth; bynt ~ byndeth; bit ~ biddeth; fynt ~ fyndeth.*

Subjunctive and Imperative

The forms of the third person discussed above are those which occur in the vast majority of Chaucer's sentences, which are in the form of statements of definite facts. However, a second kind of sentence states hypothetical facts, wished-for circumstances, possibilities: it is a kind of sentence in which the speaker's attitude to the action or state described by the verb is as important as the action or state described:

> And thogh that he *weere* worthy, he was wys;   (A 68)
> Be blythe though thow *ryde* vpon a iade;   (B 4002)
> That if gold *ruste* what sholde iren do?   (A 500)
> Euerich a word if it *be* in his charge;   (A 733)
> Telleth youre grief lest that he *come* adoun;   (B 1346)
> Til that she *fynde* som man hir to chepe;   (D 268)
> For which I hope his soule *be* in glorie.   (D 490)

It is apparent that in the above examples the forms of the italicised verbs differ from the third-person forms we have discussed in that they end in -*e* rather than the -*eth* inflexion; and furthermore the second-person singular *thow ryde* is of identical form to the third person instead of having the usual -*est* inflexion. Moreover, instead of *is* and *was*, special forms of the verb 'to be' are used: *be* and *were*. This distinction in form, dependent upon the attitude of the speaker, is traditionally distinguished in grammar as the indicative and subjunctive moods. It is a distinction which has been progressively blurred throughout the history of English, so that in modern spoken English it is rare to hear it observed except in the case of the expression 'if I were you'. Linguistic developments in the generation before Chaucer had obliterated the distinction between indicative and subjunctive in the plural, and, indeed, even in the singular, his usage is not inflexible. In adverbial phrases, a subjunctive form usually follows *if*, *though*, and *lest*, but *til* is often followed by the indicative. In clauses dependent on verbs expressing the thoughts and attitudes of the speaker, the subjunctive is regularly used after *hopen*, but much less regularly after *thinken* and *trowen*.

As well as those sentences which declare facts, and those

which intimate the speaker's attitude to his assertions, we must consider a third kind in which he tries to influence the actions of an addressee by making a request. If the addressee is present to hear the request, the speaker may include himself in it in some such expression as the following:

> What, lat vs heere a masse and go we dyne.   (B 1413)

The first verb is a familiar paraphrase, the second a formulaic use of a subjunctive form. But if the request is addressed to a second person, who is expected to comply with it, a special form of the verb, known as the imperative, is used. The forms of the imperative in Chaucer are quite various. When addressed to two or more recipients, the imperative usually ends in -*eth*, but also very frequently is endingless:

> With long swerd and with mace *fighteth* your fille.
> *Go* now youre wey;   (A 2559–60)
> *Taketh* the moralitee, goode men.   (B 4630)

In addressing a single individual, there is a similar variation between forms in -*eth* and endingless forms, but here a stylistic distinction is found which corresponds to the use of *ye* and *thou* in addressing individuals. The -*eth* inflexion is usually used in the context of *ye*, the endingless form in the context of *thou*:

> Now *telleth ye*, sire monk, if that *ye* konne;   (A 3118)
> And also *thynk* and ther with glade *the*.   (*TC* I 897)

There are, however, exceptions:

> Telle forth youre tale. Spareth for no man
> And techeth vs yonge men of your praktyke.   (D 186–7)

Passive and Impersonal Constructions

English does not possess a passive of the kind found in Latin: there is no special passive inflexion of the verb, but the name 'passive' has traditionally been given to a series of structures in which the verb 'to be' is followed by a past participle. Among these structures a distinction is sometimes made between 'actional passives', which express action (for example, 'the fence was painted by three o'clock'), and 'statal passives', which express states (for example 'the fence was painted bright green'). It is apparent that in the absence of any reference to the agent (the painter) statal passives are not very different from clauses containing an adjectival complement. The effect of many passive expressions, therefore, is to suppress awareness of an agent: the origin of the action or state described becomes vague and indefinite. Precisely this kind of construction and this kind of effect are to be found in Chaucer:

> That in hir coppe ther was no ferthyng seene;　(A 134)
> On which was first writen a crowned A;　(A 161)
> Hir chaar that was with gold wroght and perree.　(B 3550)

In these examples, it is left uncertain who might have seen the *ferthyng*, written the letter A, or worked the gold and pearls; in short, the agent is implied, but indefinite. By contrast, some passive constructions emphasise the role played by an agent:

> Hir names shal not here be told for me.　(*PF* 229)

In modern English, the indefiniteness of the agent which is found in some passive constructions can be duplicated by the use of an indefinite pronoun as subject. This construction can be used both transitively and intransitively:

TRANSITIVE	INTRANSITIVE
John trusts them	John laughs
they are trusted (by John)	—
one trusts them	one laughs

The range of words which may be used as indefinite pronouns is considerable, and they vary considerably both in range of reference and in stylistic associations: some are colloquial, others are literary; some include the speaker and addressee, others specifically do not. The following are commonly used: *a man*; *he*; *people*; *you*; *we*; *they*; *one*. The language of Chaucer's time offered him a similar indefinite pronoun construction as an alternative to the passive, possessing the same advantage of combining indefiniteness of agent with emphasis on the action. This is particularly evident in the veiled threat in the final example:

> But sooth to seyn I noot how *men* hym calle; (A 284)
> Ne though *men* sholde smyten of hire hede; (*TC* III 957)
> . . . litel wyten *folk* what is to ȝerne; (*TC* IV 198)
> If *thow* louest *thyself*, *thow* louest thy wif; (E 1385)
> ȝe knowe ek that in forme of speche is chaunge; (*TC* II 22)
> For if a preest be foul in whom *we* truste; (A 501)
> And, but ye do, certeyn *we* shal yow teche. (D 438)

By far the commonest indefinite pronoun in Chaucer is the word *men*, but *we, thou, ye, he, she*, and *they* are also used indefinitely according to whether the speaker wishes to ally himself, his addressee, or both, with the undefined; or whether he wishes to keep them separate.

Modern English also has a number of expressions in which the subject is not only indefinite, but does not seem to possess any personal reference at all. These often relate to the weather, distance, or time, as in 'it is raining' or 'it is three o'clock', where the word *it* is purely a formal subject empty of reference. They are a type found also in Old and Middle English.[20] A second type with an impersonal and indefinite use of the word *it* are those expressions which signify intellectual or emotional experiences:

> it seems to me that . . .
> it is a pity that . . .
> it says here that . . .

This type too is common in Chaucer, but alongside them is an older type in which the *it*-subject remains unexpressed. The only remains of this in modern English are the archaisms *methinks* 'it seems to me' and *woe is me* 'it is misery to me'. The word *methinks* is derived from the Old English phrase *me þyncð*, in which the subject is left unexpressed, the present-tense verb has third-person concord, and the pronoun is in the dative or accusative case. Such constructions have traditionally been called – without any great accuracy – impersonal constructions. They were very common in Old English, but were reduced in Middle English by the disappearance of the words concerned from the vocabulary; by conversion into structures with the formal subject *it*; and by re-interpretation of the dative or accusative pronoun as a subject form. This tendency to alter the impersonal construction to correspond better with normal subject-verb-object word order was facilitated in the case of the verb *thinken* by confusion of the impersonal *þyncan* with a personal verb *þencan*. Thus Chaucer has:

> Hym thynketh verrailiche that he may se/Noes flood;
> (A 3615–6)
> Thanne is it wisdom, as it thynketh me;   (A 3041)
> As help me god I laughe whan I thynke.   (D 201)

In the first we have the impersonal construction, with the subject unexpressed; in the second, the use of the formal subject *it*; and in the third, the use of *thinken* as an ordinary personal verb with the subject *I*. The verb *listen* 'to be pleased' does not occur with the formal subject *it*, but certain occurrences, especially with personal names, make it clear how easily the name could have been mistaken for the subject and the structure misunderstood:

> What force thogh Theofraste liste lye?   (E 1295)
> God liste to shewe his wonderful miracle.   (B 477)

Nevertheless, many words are used by Chaucer exclusively in impersonal constructions: *bihoven*; *ben looth*; *ben lief*; *neden*, *happen*, *bifallen*; *betyden*; *tyden*; *lakken*. A large number of other verbs are frequently used in impersonal constructions: *deignen*; *availlen*; *gaynen*; *ben*; *dremen*; *metten*; *lyken*; *rekken*; *rewen*; *remembren*; *longen*; *forthinken*; *fallen*; *seemen*; *thursten*; *smerten*; *sitten*; *thurfen*; *wonderen*.[21]

Occasionally, unfamiliar impersonal constructions or the combination of such constructions with assimilated forms of the third person, can present the inexperienced reader with difficult problems, for example in the use of the rare verb *thurfen*:

> Hym thar nat wene wel that yuele dooth;   (A 4320)
> [He need not expect good who does evil;]

or *tyden* with assimilation:

> Hym tit as often harm thereof as prow;   (*TC* I 333)
> [Harm as often befalls him by it as advantage;]

and *sitten*:

> I am a kyng, it sit me noght to lye.   (E 2315)
> ['I am a king, it is not becoming for me to lie.]

Adverbs

Traditionally, children learning modern English grammar have been taught to recognise adverbs by their function of qualifying the verb, and also by their suffix *-ly*. This latter mark of recognition is a very fallible one because, although many adjectives can be converted into adverbs by adding *-ly* to their stem (*quick*; *quickly*), there are many adverbs which are not recognisable in this way (a *fast* car; he drives *fast*). In Middle English, many adverbs are formed by the suffixes *-ly* and *-liche*, but more frequently they are formed by the addition of *-e* to the stem of the adjective. They are then formally indistinguishable from the plural and definite forms of many adjectives, and from the only form of such non-variable adjectives as *clene* and *swete*. This can lead to uncertainty in interpretation. In the following there is a sharp break in sense after *blak*, and the word *hye* is an adverb qualifying the past participle *ywrye* and not a predicative adjective:

> Thurghout the citee by the maister streete
> That sprad was al with blak and wonder *hye*
> Right of the same is the strete ywrye. (A 2902–2904)

Similarly, in a second example from the *Knight's Tale*:

> Ful *hye* upon a chaar of gold stood he.   (A 2138)

In both the above examples, the final *-e* is a clue to the adverbial function of *hye*, for in neither would an inflexional *-e* be correct in the adjective. However, more difficult cases exist:

> Whan set was Theseus ful *ryche and hye*.   (A 2577)

Once again, *riche* and *hye* are adverbs, but they might easily be taken to be adjectives exhibiting definite inflexion when qualifying a proper noun. The major argument against understanding in this way is in the familiarity of the experienced reader with an idiomatic pattern of statal verb qualified by an adverb of place, which also has a strong implication of manner.

2 Time and Tense

It is probable that all languages have some means of time reference; but the range and precision of that reference differ considerably, as do the linguistic devices used to achieve it.[1] Similarly, distinctions between positive and negative statements, and between questions and commands, may be expected in any language; but the speaker of the language who is unfamiliar with the niceties of its means of expressing these distinctions is likely to fail to understand the exact force of a denial or a prohibition. Now, although Chaucer's language is, in outline, similar to modern English, it is to be expected that in such areas there will be discrepancies which coarsen our appreciation of his meaning. In part, this is unavoidable, since meaning in these areas is often closely related to context of situation, and, even more, to patterns of intonation. Indeed, in modern English, a rising tone at the end of a clause is sufficient to turn a statement into a question. Obviously, subtleties of meaning dependent upon variation of sentence stress or intonation will be lost to us, since we must deal only with a written language, but variation in written forms is sufficient in terms of time reference and negation to make a study of Chaucer's usage in these respects valuable from a stylistic point of view.

Traditionally, time reference is considered to be a function of the tenses of the verb, perhaps supported by the use of adverbials, but before discussing these we might begin by introducing a less familiar concept: that of *aspect*, which is also indicated by the choice of verb form.[2] In envisaging an event or an action we often conceive of it either as continuing in progress, or, alternatively, as over and completed. Other relations to the continuum of time are possible. According to how we think of the action, or how we wish to express the relationship, we shall choose a particular form of the verb to represent it. For example:

(a) they are swimming
(b) they swim
(c) fish swim

In all three the present tense of the verb is used, but the expanded form with the verb 'to be' in example (a) indicates that the action of swimming extends over a period of time which includes the present moment. This particular significance would belong to example (b) only in the special language used by sports commentators.[3] Outside such a context, it would be taken to imply a repeated action or habit (*on Saturdays*), or else the statement of an accomplishment true within a rather ill-defined present: they are not actually swimming at the moment. In (c) a rather similar usage expresses a self-evident truth, irrespective of time reference.[4]

Let us consider a further set of examples, which represent a conversation taking place in the vicinity of a table-tennis table:

(a) Do you play table-tennis?
(b) I *have* played (in the past).
(c) We are playing this afternoon; will you join us?

Example (a) uses the simple interrogative form of the present tense. It apparently refers to current accomplishment in the same way as *they swim*. This is confirmed by the answer, which assumes that it is a query about ability rather than frequency. The latter understanding would be implied by the answer 'Yes, but not regularly'. The answer (b) places the action in the past, and it does so by the adoption of two means: firstly by the stress on *have*, and secondly by the use of an adverbial phrase. The adverbial is unambiguous, and, in a modern book, the stress on *have* can be indicated by italics. A similar usage in a Middle English manuscript, however, would not be marked as emphatic, and, without the adverbial, the exact force of such an expression may be lost. In our modern text, with its complicated typography and punctuation, we can attribute quite subtle meanings. The action is felt to be over and complete, but nevertheless the choice of verb form does imply some relevance of the information it carries to the present situation. Such a present relevance would not be carried by the preterite form *I played (in the past)*. The preterite suggests action which used to go on in the past, but which is now over and done with: it might preface a refusal. However, the use of the perfect *have played* is understood to imply a willingness to revive old skills, and example (c) demonstrates this understanding. The expanded form of the present tense is used, but the adverbial *this afternoon* ensures that it is understood with *future* significance. The appended question 'Will you join us?' may at first be taken to be in the future tense, formed by the use of the auxiliary *will*, and indeed it must logically have future reference, but its main significance here is one of modality. Taking their cue from the implication of the choice of perfect rather than preterite in (b), the table-tennis enthusiasts politely enquire after the *wishes* of their acquaintance.

Summing up this short excursion into some of the systems of the modern English verb, it is clear that time reference is a complicated matter, involving not only the simple chronological divisions of present, future, and past, but also many subdivisions within these. Moreover, the different tenses of the verb contain far more information than we are accustomed to think; for example, whether an action in the past has repercussions in the present; whether an action is thought of as habitual, continuing, or completed: such significance is usually called the *aspect* of the verb. Furthermore, whilst the so-called present tense may refer to another time sphere quite different from the one in which it is used, future auxiliaries can be used modally to suggest obligation or desire, to which future time reference may be hardly relevant. Lurking in the usage of what has traditionally been called 'tense' is a complex of *time reference, aspect,* and *modality,* all of which may be clarified and supported by the use of the appropriate adverbials, or by the context in which they are uttered.

In Chaucer's language, as in modern English, only two tenses, the present and the preterite, were distinguished by verb inflexions. Future time is referred to by the use of the present tense, which is made unambiguous by context and by adverbials. Alternatively, a periphrastic form with the auxiliaries *shal* and *wol* followed by an infinitive is used. This form may be used in expressions referring exclusively to future time and in which *wol* and *shal* are interchangeable:

> That er she come it wol neigh euen be; (*TC* V 1137)
> Com doun and I shal telle yow what I mente. (B 4614).

It is often used in predictions of the future, as in the following, where the verb *hopen* means 'expect; believe':

> Oure maunciple, I hope he wol be deed; (A 4029)
> Farewel, my child, I shal thee neuere see; (E 555)

and also in promises:

> My trouthe I plighte: I shal you neuer repreue
> Of no biheeste; (F 1537–8)
> That by my trouthe I wol thee nat biwreye. (C 823).

The equivalence of *shal* and *wol* in this last example is well illustrated by the fact that the Ellesmere MS reads *shal* where Hengwrt has *wol*.

Yet, in some contexts, differences of modality are implied by the choice of *shal* or *wol*, the former implying compulsion, obligation, or inexorability with regard to the action expressed in the infinitive verb, the latter expressing volition, desire, or intention. The presence of such modal colouring is owed to the fact that the two auxiliaries were originally lexical verbs with the senses respectively of owing and of wishing.[5] And indeed both can still be used by Chaucer with their full lexical sense:

> Frende, as I am a trewe knyght
> And by that feythe I shal to God and ȝow
> I hadde it neuere half so hote as now.
> (*TC* III 1648–50)

The sense 'owe' possessed by *shal* in the above passage is the earliest traceable sense of the word, and it is from this that the modal senses of obligation and inexorability have derived. Compare Chaucer's use of *wol* as a lexical verb with the sense 'wish':

> 'Lord,' quod he, 'my willyng
> Is as ye wole; ne ayeins youre likyng
> I wole nothyng, ye be my lord so deere.' (E 319–21)

Between the two extremes of use for purely temporal reference and use as full lexical verbs lie the vast majority of the uses of *shal* and *wol* in Chaucer's writings. They are usually auxiliaries with temporal reference, but nearly always also bearing, according to the context in which they appear, a varying degree of modal significance. Especially in the case of first-person uses, the degree of this modal colouring may be difficult to assess, and the context must be given full consideration. A few examples will show how modal significance may vary; firstly in the case of *shal*:

(a) Of whiche I tolde yow and tellen shal;   (A 1059)
(b) He seyde: 'Syn I shal bigynne the game;   (A 853)
(c) Whoso shal telle a tale after a man.   (A 731)

In example (a) the narrator merely states that he will continue in the future as he has in the past. The form *shal* may have been chosen to rhyme with *wal* in the following line (not quoted). In (b) the Knight's use of *shal* rather than *wol* has to be seen in the light of an obligation placed upon him by the drawing of lots: modal colouring is therefore present. Such modality is obvious in (c), where the compulsion is to tell a tale in a particular manner.

The degree of modal significance varies with the context in the case of *wol* also:

(d) Be murye for the flood wol passe anon;   (A 3578)
(e) For I wol telle forth as I bigan;   (A 1354)
(f) 'By goddes soule,' quod he, 'that wol nat I.
   For I wol speke or ellis go my wey.'   (A 3132–3)

Example (d), of course, can contain no trace of volition, since the subject of the verb is non-personal, *flood*. Example (f), with its oaths, clearly-expressed intentions and desires, and warnings about the consequences of thwarting the speaker's will, has very clear modal significance. Example (e), however, represents a very common Chaucerian type in which modal significance is possibly present but hard to prove from its context.

Wol and *shal* have a number of uses deriving from their distinct senses, and which are peculiar to each: we have space to mention only two of these. Firstly, the predictive use of *wol,* when its subject is non-personal and also of generalised reference, develops into a statement of general truth with vague future implication:

Mordre wol out, that se we day by day.   (B 4242).

Secondly, in some promises, *shal* is used in preference to *wol* perhaps in order to invest the undertaking with a sense of inexorability:

Loue if thee lest, for I loue and ay shal;   (A 1183)
'It shal be doon,' quod Symkyn, 'by my fay.'   (A 4034)

The sense of compulsion associated with *shal* may sometimes be attached to the power of the speaker to influence future events: this is especially true in the utterances of kings and legislators:

'My wyl is this for plat conclusion
Withouten any replicacion

. . . .

That euerich of yow shal goon wher hym leste;
(A 1845–8)'
The cherl shal han his thral; this I awarde.   (C 202)

Anyone may, however, usurp this usage if he feels he has the power to influence the actions of others:

Sire, at o word thow shalt no lenger ryme. (B 2122)

We may close this brief discussion of the auxiliaries *shal* and *wol* by a rather more extended illustration of their use by Chaucer in the course of narrative. In the *Miller's Tale*, when Nicholas predicts impending catastrophe, he seeks the colouring of inevitability associated with *shal*:

> That now a Monday next at quarter-nyght
> Shal falle a reyn and that so wilde and wood
> That half so greet was neuere Nowels flood.
> 'This world', he seyde, 'in lasse than in an hour
> Shal al be dreynt so hidous is the shour'.
>
> (A 3516–20)

His landlord is alarmed at this news, and his thoughts are with his young wife: 'Allas, my wyf./And shal she drenche?' But Nicholas reassures him that the inevitable can be circumvented if, according to the precept of Solomon, he accepts informed advice:

> Werk al by conseil and thow shalt noght rewe.
> And if thow werken wolt by good consayl,
> I vndertake withouten mast or sayl
> Yit shal I saue hir and thee and me.   (A 3530–33)

Here there is an instructive variation between *shal* and *wol*, in which the distinction between inevitability and volitional colouring is very clear. If one is willing to take sound advice, security and salvation are inevitable. Nicholas finishes with the assertion: 'Thy wif shal I wel sauen out of doute' (A 3561); a phrase in which the adverbs *wel* and *out of doute* reinforce the inevitability implicit in *shal*. The auxiliary *wol* would have been quite inappropriate here, since although Nicholas would no doubt have *wished* to save Alisoun for his own reasons, his words are addressed to John, and are crucially aimed at winning his confidence.

Nicholas's rival, Absolon, also employs the auxiliary *shal* in a series of clauses relating to the near future. But here the man to be convinced is himself:

> So mote I thryue, I shal at cokkes crowe
> Ful priuely knokken at his wyndowe

That stant ful lowe vpon his boures wal.
To Alison now wol I tellen al
My loue-longyng. For yit I shal nat mysse
That at the leeste wey I shal hir kisse.
Som manere confort shal I haue parfay.
My mouth hath icched al this longe day.
That is a signe of kissyng at the leeste.   (A 3675–83)

The mixture of the auxiliaries *wol* and *shal* strikingly indicates Absolon's psychological state, in which, confusing wishes and certainties, he seeks to find inevitable prognostications in an itching lip.

Reference to the past is most frequently made in Chaucer's works by forms similar to those in modern English; that is, by the use of the preterite and perfect tenses. Consider the following lines:

Whan that Aueryll with his shoures soote
The droghte of March hath perced to the roote
And bathed euery veyne in swich lycour
Of which vertu engendred is the flour,
Whan Zephirus eek with his sweete breeth
Inspired hath in euery holt and heeth
The tendre croppes, and the yonge sonne
Hath in the ram his half-cours yronne,
And smale foweles maken melodye
(That slepen al the nyght with open iye)
So priketh hem nature in hir corages,
Thanne longen folk to goon on pilgrymages.   (A 1–12)

The opening of the *Canterbury Tales* illustrates one function of the perfect. The initial sentence is a long correlative one constructed around the adverbials *Whan* . . . *Whan* . . . . *Thanne*.[6] All the events and occurrences dependent upon *whan* culminate in those dependent upon *thanne*: that is, the typical natural indicators of the awakening Spring also signal the renewed possibility of travel, and the resultant restlessness communicates itself to men, who desire to depart on the pilgrimage to Canterbury. It is noticeable that most of the verbs dependent on *whan* are in the perfect tense; that dependent on *thanne* uses the present tense to indicate a continuing state of feeling occurring as the result of the earlier perfect verbs. In other words, this opening paragraph employs the perfect in a way similar to the modern English example with which we opened this chapter. It refers to events which are completed before the present of the bird-song and the desire for pilgrimage, but which have a very direct, indeed causal, relationship to that present. The whole has the general truth of common experience, and, setting aside the chronology of causality within it, is therefore timeless. Such a use of the perfect, which is re-iterated in the explanation that the second reason for pilgrimage is that the saint *hath holpen* the pilgrims, is familiar enough to the modern reader, and the switch to the normal narrative preterite (*Bifel that in that sesoun . . .*) is exactly as expected. The alternation between this narrative preterite and the narrator's present tense commentary upon his own function also serves to build up the different spheres of reference of the fiction in a way that seems entirely natural, if not inevitable, to us. But, as he begins to describe the first pilgrim, the Knight, we notice a variation from the kind of usage we would expect:

> A knyght ther was, and that a worthy man,
> That fro the tyme that he first bigan
> To ryden out he loued chiualrye,
> Trouthe and honour, fredom and curteisye.
> Ful worthy was he in his lordes werre
> And therto hadde he ryden, no man ferre. (A 43–8)

From the point of view of the narrator's present, the knight belongs to the past, which he recalls as a reminiscence of the pilgrim band of which he had once formed part.[7] This perspective is achieved by the use of the simple preterite *a knyght ther was*. However, the Knight's initiation into chivalry belonged to the distant past at the time when he embarked on the pilgrimage, even though he still upheld its values. The three time spheres – the narrator's present, the Knight at the time of the pilgrimage, and the Knight's past experience – would be carefully separated by a modern author by the use of the present, preterite, and pluperfect tenses. But Chaucer uses the preterite to refer both to the Knight's career and to his presence among the pilgrims: *first bigan*; *he loved chivalrie*; *ful worthy was he*. The modern usage of the pluperfect occurs only in the last of the lines quoted, but it has the same chronological reference as the preceding preterites. This unmotivated variation between preterite and pluperfect is found throughout the description: 'At Alisaundre he was whan it was wonne' is matched by 'In Gernade at the seege eek hadde he be'. We must conclude, that, although the uses of the preterite, perfect and pluperfect frequently parallel their uses in modern English, Chaucer exploits a flexibility which would seem ungrammatical today.[8] A similar alternation is found between the preterite and the expanded or imperfect form. Thus the reference to the Squire – 'Syngynge he was or floytynge al the day' (A 91) – exhibits an unusual verb form, where we should expect a preterite. Examples where the reverse is found also occur:

> And Palamon, this woful prisoner,
> As was his wone by leue of his gailler
> Was risen and romed in a chambre an heigh.[9]
>
> (A 1063–5)

Variation between the preterite and perfect tense also occurs frequently:

> Togidres han thise thre hir trouthes plyght
> To lyue and dyen ech of hem with oother
> As thogh he were his owene ybore brother.
> And vp they stirte al dronken in this rage
> And forth they goon towardes that village
> Of which the tauerner hadde spoke biforn.
> And many a grisly ooth thanne han they sworn
> And Cristes blessed body they torente:
> Deeth shall be deed if they may hym hente.
>
> (C 702–10)

Some idea of the extent of variation in narrative can be gained by listing the tenses of the verbs describing actions in the above passage. It commences with a perfect (*han . . . plyght*), which is followed by two presents (*vp they stirte*; *goon*), another perfect (*han they sworn*), and culminates in a preterite (*they torente*). All three tenses refer to the same narrative past. An earlier past, consisting of reminiscences of the taverner's words, is alluded to by the use of the pluperfect and an adverbial (*hadde spoke biforn*), and the future events of the story are seen from the perspective of the participants by the use of a future (*shal be deed*) rather than a future-in-the-past. This easy transition through a whole series of tenses is not uncommon in medieval narrative poetry, and indeed such flexibility of expression had obvious formal advantages in the business of versification. But it seems also to contribute something to the vividness of narrative. The use of the perfect tense rather than a preterite may well give a sense of immediacy, since, as we have seen, one purpose of the perfect is to represent an action completed, but with immediate relevance. The use of the present tense to refer to past time is analogous to it, and merits more lengthy discussion.

The most frequent tense used by Chaucer to relate past events is, of course, the preterite. He switches to the present tense when the audience's attention is re-directed from the story to the business of composition, as for example, when the narrator addresses the audience about his conduct of the narration, or when he presents some reflection of timeless relevance, perhaps a proverb or a *sententia* drawn from folk wisdom or written authority. A second occasion when the present tense may be selected is when the author quotes verbatim, with their original time reference, the present-tense words of a character in his story. Such uses of the present tense may seem obvious, and beneath notice, because, for those used to reading modern books, with their apparatus of punctuation and lay-out supporting a stabilised use of tenses, it is hard to believe that these tense switches could cause confusion in the status of a passage of text. But medieval manuscripts do not regularly mark direct speech by punctuation or conventions of lay-out, and where they do, they may use the same paragraph marker ¶ as they elsewhere use for sentential remarks by the author. The distinction between the present tense of character's direct speech and that of authorial general truth may not always be obvious, and indeed it may not have greatly concerned the author that they should be so.

In the *General Prologue*, the Friar is described largely in the preterite; but there are two occasions upon which the discourse moves from the preterite to the present tense. The first occupies lines 225–32, the second, lines 243–9. Both represent opinions held by the Friar; both are continuous with ideas expressed in the preterite; but neither is marked by punctuation nor by introductory formula as direct speech. Formally, there is nothing to prevent us ascribing the following lines to sententious reflections of the narrator:

> For vnto a poure ordre for to yeue
> Is signe that a man is wel yshryue
> . . .
> For many a man so hard is of his herte
> He may nat weepe thogh that he sore smerte.
> Therfore in stede of wepynge and preyeres
> Men moote yeue siluer to poure freres.   (A 225–32)

The universal understanding of this as an echo of the voiced opinion of the Friar himself is an interpretation of the text based upon knowledge of the use of the present tense for direct speech together with the colloquial sound of 'he dorste make auaunt', upon which these opinions seem to depend. Similar considerations make the second passage an echo of the Friar's own words:

> For vnto swich a worthy man as he
> Acorded nat as by his facultee
> To haue with syke lazers aqueyntaunce.
> It is nat honeste, it may noght auaunce
> For to deelen with no swich poraille,
> But al with riche and sellerys of vitaille
> And oueral ther as profit sholde aryse.   (A 243–9)

It is noticeable that this opinion begins and ends with past tenses appropriate to the narrator's report of such views, but that, without any formal indication, it wanders into the present tense, apparently representing the words of this character as they were spoken. Such vagueness about the boundaries of direct and reported speech is characteristic of medieval narrative, where it is found from Old English onwards.[10] It is found again in a passage, which has proved chronically difficult to analyse, at the beginning of the *Merchant's Tale*. The words of Januarie are given, and his speech is apparently closed by the line 'Thus seyde this olde knyght that was so wys' (E 1266). Then follows a long passage of authoritative pronouncements on the subject of marriage, often brought into ironic contradiction, and echoing, perhaps, the material of a debate, yet not organised clearly around two distinct points of view. They might represent chaotic indecision in Januarie, but it is more likely that the use of the present tense here has the function of presenting general truths, *sententiae*, on the subject of marriage. The scribe of Hengwrt seems to have understood it in this way, since he marked the beginning of the passage with a paragraph marker ¶ (line 1267), and both in this manuscript and in Ellesmere, marginal Latin glosses point out the quotations from authorities. It is inevitable, however, that modern criticism, with its presuppositions of dramatic and psychological verisimilitude, should ascribe this passage to the thoughts of the merchant.[11] The problem of distinguishing in Chaucer between the use of the present tense for sentential utterance and for the direct-speech representation of thoughts and previous utterances can present a real difficulty in interpretation, since, as we have seen in the *Pardoner's Tale* and in the description of the Friar, Chaucer is capable of using the present both for the attribution of speeches and thoughts, as well as for sentential utterances. In some genres, as for example in the *Tale of Melibee*, the two purposes become inseparable; in the *Merchant's Tale*, which has some of the trappings of allegorical characterisation, separation is difficult.

The discussion of direct speech and of sentential utterance has not yet exhausted the roll-call of common deviations from the narrative preterite to the present tense, for there remains what is probably the most-discussed device of all, the use of the 'Historic Present'. This title refers to the use of the present tense within narratives of events situated in the past, and one version of it is quite familiar in popular narratives like the following:

> The brake-drum wouldn't come off; so he takes this big hammer and hits it one, and it smashed in two.

This switch from past tenses to the present is very common in Middle English narrative also, but its purpose and effect are in dispute. Of course the purposes and effects of such a switch may be various, and it is unwise to adopt too dogmatic or inflexible a position about it. Two extreme positions would be: on the one hand, that selection of the present is merely a metrical convenience with no other significance; or that, on the other hand, by contrast, the selection of the present tense is a stylistic manoeuvre to give immediacy and vividness to the narrative.[12] These two positions, however, are not necessarily in opposition, since both are good and sufficient reasons for choosing the present tense in individual instances. We shall consider the arguments for metrical convenience first.

As we have already seen, variation between preterite, present, and perfect is found in Chaucerian verse with reference to the same point in time. Indeed, the scribes of Chaucer manuscripts could be very cavalier in their approach to copying tense forms. The scribe of MS Gg 4.27 freely varied the preterite with the present in his re-copying.[13] This suggests that he saw no important stylistic function in their choice. It is even possible that to some scribes the -*eth* of the present and the -*ed* of the preterite of weak verbs represented no more than alternative spellings. This evidence of phonological and morphological interchangeability both lessens the likelihood that the historic present was an important stylistic device, and makes the interpretation of the data hazardous. Furthermore, it has been pointed out that, like the fluctuation between preterite, perfect, and pluperfect, Chaucer's use of the historic present is relatively rare in prose, whereas in verse its occurrence is especially common in strong verbs, where the switch from preterite (*he came*) to present (*he cometh*) constitutes a change from a monosyllable to a disyllabic form. Conversely, weak verbs which may be metrically too long in the preterite (*they assenteden*), may have shorter present tense forms (*they assenten*).

Variation in the forms of grammar, as we have already seen, and shall see again in Chapter 5, is a characteristic of Chaucer's language, and there is no doubt that he exploits it for metrical purposes, so that the claim that Chaucer's use of the present tense in past contexts is metrically-based coincides with his practice with other grammatical forms. We have noted the use of a periphrastic perfect tense with *have* and *be,* and we may supplement these by examining two other periphrases, those with *do* and *gan.* The former is relatively uncommon, the latter frequent. In examples like the following, it is clear that the *gan*-periphrasis is semantically equivalent to a preterite, and that the reason for its use must be metrical:

> This Palamon gan knytte his browes tweye.   (A 1128)

The periphrasis also has a second common function in versification, and this is evident in the following, where its use facilitates the rhyme:

> Til that the belle of laudees gan to rynge
> And freres in the chauncel gonne synge.   (A 3655–6)

Indeed, investigation has shown that most uses of the *gan*-periphrasis serve to bring its dependent infinitive into rhyme position.[14] There is no doubt, therefore, that its use as an alternative to the preterite may serve the purposes of versification. However, its use may also have semantic implications. In the above quotation *gan to rynge* has a strong sense of 'commencement'; of the action of ringing actually beginning. The verb phrase has ingressive aspect. Compare it with the following:

> But al that he myghte of his frendes hente
> On bookes and on lernynge he it spente,
> And bisily gan for the soules preye
> Of hem that yaf hym wherwith to scoleye.   (A 299–302)

Obviously the time reference is equivalent to that of the preterite, but aspectual significance is different. In translation, the sense might be rendered as 'he applied himself to praying for the souls . . .'. In other words the phrase suggests leaving one action and turning to another. It seems also to have some suggestion of habit. Thus, the possible aspectual significances of the *gan*-periphrasis are numerous, including ingressive, mutative, and iterative; and here it may be semantically distinct from the choice of the simple preterite. That ingressive aspect was sometimes understood is plain from an example in the *General Prologue*, where Hengwrt reads 'day bigan to sprynge' (A 822), but Ellesmere substitutes the periphrasis, clearly demonstrating that it was capable of carrying the ingressive force of the lexical verb *biginnen*. There is, therefore, no room for doubt, that, although the *gan*-periphrasis can be a mere convenience in versification, it also frequently signifies that the action of the verb which it governs is thought of as commencing, that the actor is turning from some other occupation to commence it, or that, according to the meaning of the verb, the action will be continued or repetitive. Similarly, the auxiliary *do*, as well as serving as a metrical convenience, acts also as a causal auxiliary, like *let* and *maken*:

> Thanne wolde he seye: 'Freend, I shal for thy sake
> Do stryke hir out of oure lettres blake.'[15]   (D 1363–4)

The discussion so far leaves no doubt that the choice of particular tense forms and of periphrases may be motivated in any given instance by the needs of versification; but it is equally clear that aspectual differences may make them semantically distinct. It is therefore reasonable to acknowledge that the choice of historic present in preference to the preterite may also have a distinct stylistic effect of this kind. Let us consider the use of the verb *riden* in a passage from the *Knight's Tale*. In this verb, the third-person singular, both preterite and present tenses, are monosyllables. In line 964, Theseus's punitive expedition to Thebes commences. It begins with a historic present, for the choice of historic present frequently coincides with the initiation of a new topic; but this is immediately followed by the verb *riden* in the preterite:

> And right-anoon withouten moore abood
> His baner he desplayeth and forth rood
> To Thebesward.   (A 965–7)

The choice of preterite is obviously dictated by the rhyme. A few lines later, however, the final clause of line 966 is nearly repeated, with the verb *riden* in the middle of the line:

And forth he ryt. Ther nys namoore to telle.   (A 974)

Here neither rhyme nor metre necessitates the choice of historic present. Rather, it looks forward to the next topic, which is an evocation of the splendour of Theseus by the description of his banner as he leaves on his mission. This amplification upon the basic narrative commences in the present tense:

> The rede statue of Mars with spere and targe
> So shyneth in his white baner large
> That alle the feeldes glitren vp and doun;
> And by his baner born was his penoun
> Of gold ful ryche, in which ther was ybete
> The mynotaur which that he wan in Crete.
>
> (A 975–80)

This passage is marked as worthy of note by the scribe's use of the paragraph marker ¶, and it is summed up by a further use of the present tense in a line which advertises the rhetorical craft of the whole:

> Thus ryt this duc, thus ryt this conquerour,
> And in his oost of chiualrye the flour.   (A 981–2)

It seems unlikely that the choice of the present tense in line 981 is anything other than a deliberate device. The adverb *thus* is clearly demonstrative, and refers back to the carefully-crafted picture in the preceding passage, which was itself introduced by the present tense verb *ryt* and the word *so* with a similarly deictic function. In such examples, it is difficult not to believe that the choice of the historic present is concerned with the creation of a vivid picture, an attempt to shorten the distance between the events of the narrative and the audience who are asked to observe them. The present tense, supported by the use of deictic adverbs, is an endeavour to present events as though they were actually occurring before the eyes of the audience.

Indeed, the historic present is often used in series in this way, binding together in a sequence verbs which are already semantically related, and which are then combined into a passage amplifying emotion, ceremony, or violent action. Consider, for example:

> How greet a sorwe suffreth now Arcite.
> The deeth he feeleth thurgh his herte smyte.
> He wepeth, wayleth, cryeth pitously.
> To sleen hymself he wayteth pryuely.
> He seyde: 'Allas the day that I was born.'

(A 1219–23)

Once more the power of the present tense to actualise events is supported by the use of the adverb *now*, and indeed such an attempt to alter the time perspective is evident in most of the longer set-piece uses of the historic present in the *Knight's Tale*: 'Who looketh lightly now but Palamon?' (A 1871 ff.); 'Now ryngen trompes loude and clarioun' (A 2600 ff.). In the medical description of the death of Arcite, the Ellesmere MS has the same device of an adverb and a present tense verb: 'Nature hath now no dominacioun' (A 2758).

The artful use of the possible variation in narrative tenses to control the perspective of the audience upon the events of his story is well-illustrated by other passages from the *Knight's Tale*:

> In derknesse and horrible and strong prison
> This seuen yeer hath seten Palamon
> Forpyned, what for wo and for distresse.
> Who feeleth double soor and heuynesse
> But Palamon, that loue destreyneth so,
> That wood out of his wit he gooth for wo.

(A 1451–6)

The perfect, *hath seten*, indicates a state of affairs commenced in the past but with continuing relevance to that present which is indicated by the present tense verbs describing Palamon's emotions. The adverbial stating the length of continuity from the past, *this seuen yeer*, is of a form in which the demonstrative emphasises the unity of the audience's and Palamon's present. It is equivalent to the modern English phrase 'these last seven years'. Such a combination of tenses and adverbials can hardly result from anything else than a deliberate manipulation of chronological perspective; it cannot be claimed to be required by versification. What seems to be a coherent attempt by the author to bring his audience into closer association with his characters has its clearest manifestation in the use of the present tense in a passage in which the narrator himself directly addresses the audience with a *demande d'amour*:

> Yow loueris, axe I now this question:
> Who hath the worse, Arcite or Palamon?
> That oon may seen his lady day by day,
> But in prison moot he dwelle alway.
> That oother where hym list may ride or go,
> But seen his lady shal he neuere mo.   (A 1347–52)

The purpose of the present tense is here quite easy to identify. It is not so much a historic present as that present which refers to ideas outside time. It removes Palamon and Arcite from their narrative context, and bestows upon them an exemplary function. They become, instead of characters in a story, a problem cast in terms of the love ideals which supposedly inspire the audience, so that, instead of telescoping time, the present tense here serves to state the unity of the experience of love, regardless of time. As in the case of the Pardoner, the use of the present tense is related to a tendency, noted by critics, for Chaucer's characters to take on symbolic, or representative, significance.

Such examples from the *Knight's Tale,* in which the historic present is used for deliberately creative effect, often in passages which are rhetorically wrought, or, at least, contrived with an awareness of stylistic function, prove that the choice of the present tense with past reference *may* have a distinct significance from the preterite in such uses; but they do not prove that *all* uses of the historic present have this significance. Many present tense verbs are undoubtedly chosen for the sake of versification. There is certainly a significant variation between individual verbs: for example, *gooth* appears very commonly as a historic present whereas *bifel* is nearly always a preterite.

In the *fabliau* narrative of the Miller's and Reeve's tales sequences of present tense verbs are common, but are usually less obviously the product of artifice than in the *Knight's Tale*. Yet one still finds set-piece amplifications in which the present tense is used to give a sense of vivid immediacy. The narrator makes a general proposition on the power of the *imaginacioun*, and immediately illustrates it by creating the images present in the old carpenter's mind, and their effects upon him, expressed in the present tense:

> This sely carpenter bigynneth quake.
> Hym thynketh verrailiche that he may se
> Noes flood come walwyng as the see
> To drenchen Alison, his hony deere.
> He wepeth, waileth, maketh sory cheere.
> He siketh with ful many a sory swogh.
> And gooth and geteth hym a knedyng-trogh.

> (A 3614–20)

The immediacy of this passage is a comic one, and it gains in comic effect by the fact that it is obviously contrived as an echo of the similar passage in the *Knight's Tale* (A 1219 ff.). It is therefore reasonable to assume that once more, in a *fabliau* setting, we have an artful use of the present tense.

A summary of the potential subtleties of verbal significance in Chaucer's language is scarcely possible, but they are clearly of great importance both in the creation of character and in the management of narrative. Important as it is to recognise this potential subtlety, it is equally important to recognise the fact that it is *potential*. Not every use of the auxiliary *wol* exploits its modality, nor is every use of the perfect or present tense with past reference a triumph of art. Satisfactory interpretation of Chaucer's poetry springs from an awareness of the possibilities of his language together with literary sensitivity and common sense in reading.

3 Negation

In discussing negation we should first of all be aware that we are dealing with a feature of language meaning, with a logical category. Like time reference or modality, it may be indicated by the formal devices of language in a variety of ways, and not merely by the use of a few words beginning with *n*. Indeed, although the words *no*, *never*, and *nobody* are immediately recognisable as bearers of negative force, negation can also be traced in such words as *deny*, *refuse,* and *reject*. In modern English this is possible semantically, by invoking paraphrase, but also grammatically by demonstrating the co-occurrence with them of certain characteristic forms. Assertions (imperative and declarative statements) are followed in some cases by forms distinct from those following non-assertions (questions and negatives).[1] Thus the assertions:

Give him *some* pencils.
There are *some* pencils.

are matched by the non-assertions:

Are there *any* red pencils?
There aren't *any* red pencils.

The variation between *some* and *any* corresponds to specific syntactical environments, and they are known respectively as assertive and non-assertive forms. If we consider the verbs *refuse* and *reject*, we find that they require non-assertive forms:

Reject any broken pencils.
He refused any other pencils.

We must assume that the non-assertive forms are selected because of some sense of negation inherent in these verbs.

In modern English, then, negation may be implicit in lexical meaning; it may be indicated by the use of a negating particle, like *-n't* or, alternatively, by a special structure with an auxiliary (*I know*; *I don't know*), and, in the spoken language, by related modifications of the intonation pattern of the clause. All these devices may receive support in their task of signalling the nature of the clause by the selection of non-assertive forms. Taken together, such devices render the status of the clause clear and unambiguous. In Chaucerian Middle English, however, these non-assertive forms are not found. Negative is often distinguished from positive in statements, questions, and commands by the repetition of negating particles, adjectives, or adverbs; that is, by what later grammarians stigmatised as 'double negatives', and what still-later ones restored to respectability by the use of the phrase 'negative concord'.[2] If we consider this duplication of negators from the point of view of the addressee of an utterance, this apparently redundant repetition can be seen as 'negative support', since each negating item is mutually supportive of the others in clarifying the total negative character of the clause.

In interpreting the significance of negation, three major features of its use demand our attention: its emphasis or *intensity* (which is a psychological as well as a grammatical and phonological question); its extent or *scope* (the extent of the clause or sentence which is understood to be included within the negation); and the direction or *focus* of attention within that scope (that is, which item in particular is considered to receive the force of negation). Expressed less formally, in terms of our needs in interpreting Chaucer's poetry, we must know how firmly his characters make denials, to what extent of their utterance that denial is meant to refer, and whether any particular item is singled out for emphasis. All these are potentially confusing to the modern reader of Middle English, and since focus is heavily dependent upon intonation, this, at least, will often remain speculative.

We may distinguish two basic types of clause negation in Chaucerian English, and these may differ in their scope. Both are what prescriptive grammarians would condemn as 'double negatives', so that it is perhaps worth stating at once that the repetition of negatives in Middle English, just as in non-standard Modern English, is not intended to imply a positive statement; nor does it necessarily imply any special intensity of negation. The first structure is of the type *ne + Verb + no + Complement*. When the word acting as complement begins in a vowel, or with initial *h*, the form *noon* is substituted for *no* (cf. *my*; *myn*, p. 16). The second common type of negative pattern has the structure *ne + Verb + nat ∼ noght*. The variation between *nat* and *noght* is a feature of the London language of the period, in which the more northerly form *nat* was gradually replacing the earlier *noght*. The various types may be illustrated by the following examples:

But wedded men *ne* knowe *no* mesure;   (E 622)
O Donegild, I *ne* haue *noon* Englissh digne;   (B 778)
Hise hors weere goode, but he *ne* was *nat* gay;   (A 74)
Ne studieth *noght*. Ley hond to, euery man.   (A 841)

Double negation of these kinds is common enough to be regarded as normal in Chaucer's language, but it is evident that single negation is also very common. The structure *ne . . . nat ∼ noght*, in particular, is frequent in formal style, but even in the formal prose of *Boece* and in the tales of *Melibee* and the Parson single negation is also quite usual. This single negation may, for the sake of description, be considered to involve the deletion of the element *ne* in the above patterns; and such single negation is especially common in informal styles.[3] More rarely, single negation results from the deletion of the forms *no ∼ noon* or *nat ∼ noght*:

He saw *nat* that;   (A 3461)
Ne was ther swich another pardoner;   (A693)
'It were to thee,' quod he, '*no* greet honour.'   (A 1129)

Although double negatives rarely present serious difficulties in interpretation, and the scope of the negation which they mark unambiguously covers the entire predicate of the clause, certain problems may arise in regard to these single forms. In the first two examples above it is evident that the scope of negation is the entire predicate of the clause; in the last example, however, this is less certain. What exactly is it that Palamon wishes to say? Does negation extend over the clause, or it it focussed upon the words following the negative, upon *greet honour*? In other words, should a modern English version read 'it isn't very honourable' or 'it is no great honour'? If the latter were the case, the irony of Palamon's remark would be more pointed. However, lacking the guidance of pronunciation, the rendering of the Middle English is far from certain.

We may turn to etymology for guidance and discover that whereas *noght* is derived from an adverbial group *no . . . wiht* (that is, 'no . . . thing'), the negator *no* is not an adverb, but is rather a negative form of the determiner *an*, which might therefore be expected to be closely associated with the head of the noun group. In some uses a sense corresponding with this origin is quite clear:

> For half so boldely kan ther no man
> Swere and lye as a womman kan.   (D 227–8)
> I am a gentil womman and no wenche.   (E 2202)

Here the semantic oppositions between *gentil womman* and *wenche*, and between *man* and *womman*, are paralleled by the alternation between *a* and *no*. The rhetorical structure shows the scope of negation to be restricted to the word following the negator. A similar restriction is evident when the negative determiner forms part of a group acting as the subject of a clause:

> No man hateth his flessh, but in his lyf
> He fostreth it.   (E 1386)

In such examples, the restriction of the negative scope is clear, but some hesitation may again be experienced in determining the precise significance of the following:

> Ther wolde I chide and do hem no plesaunce.   (D. 408)

Is the scope of negation in this example coincident with the entire second clause, indicating that the Wife would show no solicitude for her hapless husbands? Or is negation directed specifically upon *plesaunce*, suggesting that she refuses particular acts of kindness? In view of the general tenor of the Wife's self-revelations, it would be reasonable to suppose that she is referring euphemistically to the sexual tyranny which she exercises over her husbands, and the immediate context would support such an interpretation. But, historically, the phrase *don plesaunce* is an inseparable idiom, so that it is probable that negation is felt to extend throughout the clause. In examples such as these, we must admit the possibility of ambiguity about the scope of negation in Chaucer's language. It is an ambiguity which might have been cleared up by the stresses and intonation of spoken language, but once committed to writing would have been almost as imponderable to Chaucer's first audience as to us.

This potential ambiguity resulting from the flexibility in the use of negatives in Chaucer's language is neatly illustrated by the variation between the Ellesmere and Hengwrt manuscripts in their renderings of the *General Prologue*. On five occasions, variation between the manuscripts is that between single and double negation. On another occasion, the scribes treat negation by *none* and by *noght* as though they were equivalent: thus in line 178 Hengwrt has *hunterys been none holy men*, but Ellesmere reads *hunters beth nat hooly men*. In the *Knight's Tale*, (A 2322), variation is found which closely relates to our problem with the phrase *do plesaunce*. Hengwrt reads:

And if so be thow wolt noght do me grace

where Ellesmere has:

And if so be thou wolt do me no grace.

In the first example no difficulty arises, since *noght* clearly negates the whole clause; but in the latter case some uncertainty is possible as to whether *no* is taken to act adverbially upon the entire verbal idiom *do grace* or whether it is a determiner of the noun *grace*. The former is probably the correct answer, but whether this is true or not, it is apparent that scribes copying Chaucer's poetry a few years after its composition saw no consistent distinction between these two types of negation. In their usage, *no ~ noon* fluctuated between adverbial use and use as a determiner, and hence was various in negative scope. Indeed, this discussion of the problem of negative scope in Chaucer's language began with a query about the scope of negation in the line 'It were to thee quod he no greet honour', which is the form of the line in the Hengwrt manuscript. In Ellesmere, however, this problem would not have arisen, since in that manuscript the line reads 'It nere quod he to thee no greet honour'. Here the double negative indicates unambiguously that the scope of negation includes the entire clause. It may well be that in writing Hengwrt the scribe thought that his usage there fulfilled an identical function.[4]

We may briefly conclude that double negation unambiguously includes the entire clause within its scope, but that with single negation there is often some uncertainty. This is especially so in the use of *no*, but is found also with *noght* in examples like the following:

He was a sheepherde and noght a mercenarye.

(A 514)

More precise focus and limitation of scope may be signalled by rhetorical structures, but in cases where these are not evident, and in the absence of the intonation patterns of speech, ambiguity may result. This uncertainty is represented by scribal variation in rendering negation when copying the *Canterbury Tales* into various manuscripts.[5]

The example by which we began and ended our discussion of negative scope referred to the distinct forms *were* and *nere* in the Hengwrt and Ellesmere manuscripts, so that an explanation of this latter negative form, and of others like it, seems desirable. Neither negation nor interrogatives in Middle English require the use of the auxiliary *do*, so that there is no parallel to modern English *don't*; but other auxiliaries and some common lexical verbs have contracted negative forms. In the well-known line from *Troilus and Criseyde*, Chaucer protests his ignorance of the truth of popular opinion rather than dissociates himself from it, since the word *not* is here the negative preterite form of the verb *witen* 'to know', and not a form of the adverb *noght*:

> Men seyen I not that she ȝaf hym hire herte.
>
> (*TC* V 1050)

Other verbs with forms in which a preceding *ne* has coalesced with the stem of the verb are: *ben, wol, have,* and *wiste.*[6] The forms encountered in the Hengwrt and Corpus manuscripts are:

'not to be'	'not to have'	'not to wish' (will not)	'not to know'
I nam			
thow nart		*thow nilt*	*nost(ow)*
he nys	*he nath*	*he nyl*	*he niste*
he nas	*he nadde*	*he nolde*	*he not*
it nere			

These contracted forms negate the entire predicate of the clause in which they are found. But the degree to which contracted forms of this kind receive negative support, thus forming double negatives, varies considerably. The word *nam*, for example, rarely occurs unless supported later in the clause by *noght* or *no*, or some other negator. *Nas, nys, nyl, nolde,* and *nost*, all of which are in common use, are also most commonly supported.

The relationship of negative support to intensity of negation is an uncertain one, since approaching the question purely from the point of view of the co-occurrence of negating forms, it is practically impossible to distinguish the demands of clarity from emphasis in negation. As we have seen, by contrast with single negation by *no* or *noght*, the constructions with a preceding *ne* unambiguously distinguish the scope of negation in the clause. Negative support for contracted verbs is therefore unnecessary to mark scope, yet might serve the ends of communicative clarity by confirming the negative character of a verb which occurs at the beginning of an utterance, and which therefore may not have been clearly heard. Phonetic and communicative considerations of this kind have encouraged some scholars to see emphasis as directly related to phonetic 'weight', so that *noght* might be regarded as a more emphatic form than *nat*. Although it is true that such forms may be more easily noticed by the hearer, and they may serve communicative clarity better on that account, it could hardly be claimed that the variation between *nat* and *noght* is one of negative intensity. When analysing written forms, however, we may legitimately suspect intensity of negation in those examples where negators are multiplied or more elaborate lexical negators are used, in contexts where there is evident vehemence of feeling, and in circumstances where we can reasonably posit a stressed form. Intensified negation may arise from the selection of constructions which use negating phrases rather than particles; for example:

> That noon of vs ne speke noght a word
> Ne clepe ne crye, but been in his prayere.
>
> (A 3586–7)

Here, *noon of vs* and *noght a* could equally well – although unmetrically – have been omitted and replaced respectively by the simple pronoun *we* and the adjective *no*. The contrast with these simple forms suggests that emphatic forms have been chosen here. The use of multiple negation is, however, the commonest means of lending emphasis, and a good example of this is also to be found in the *Miller's Tale* in which the negators are reinforced by a series of asseverations. The entire context in fact is exhortatory, as Nicholas tries to persuade his landlord of the danger of a second deluge, and John, for his part, naïvely asserts that he is a man worthy to be trusted with such grave confidences:

> 'Nay, Crist forbede it for his holy blood',
> Quod tho this sely man, 'I nam no labbe.
> And thogh I seye, I nam nat lief to gabbe.
> Sey what thow wolt, I shal it neuere telle
> To child ne wyf by hym that harwed helle.'
>
> (A 3508–12)

In this passage the force of negation derives from various other sources in addition to the repeated negators: from the context of appeals to Christ, from the implied inexorability of 'never telling' implicit in the choice of the modal *shal*, and also from the selection of the adverb *neuere* itself. In the course of the development of Middle English, as the form *noght* lost emphasis, it tended to be replaced in emphatic use by other adverbial phrases such as *no thing* and *no wight*; and *nowher*, *neuere*, and *namore* were also used without specific place and time reference for this purpose. A few examples will illustrate the usage:

> Seend me *namoore* vnto *noon* hethenesse;   (B 1112)
> *Nat* for youre boost he wol hym *nothyng* hyde   (C 764)
> ('He certainly won't want to hide [himself] on account
>   of your bragging)
> And therfore he of ful auisement
> *Nolde neuere* write in *noon* of his sermons
> Of swiche vnkynde abhominacions.   (B 86–8)
> She preyde hym eek he sholde *by no weye*
> Vnto hir fader *no* word of hir seye;   (B 1084–5)
> I conferme þat hap *nis ryght naught in no wise.*
>
> (*Bo* V p.1, 35)

The *General Prologue* is full of descriptions of characters who are unsurpassed of their kind, and it is full of emphatic negation used to assert the status of these *non-pareils*:

> So greet a purchasour was *nowher noon*;   (A 318)
> A bettre envyned man was *neuere noon*.
> Withouten bake mete was *neuere* his hous;   (A 342–3)
> Ne *neuere* yet *no* vileynye he sayde
> In al his lyf vnto *no manere* wight;   (A 70–1)
> In al this world *ne* was ther *noon* hym lyk.   (A 412)

Emphasis in this last quotation arises largely from the position of stress occupied by the word *noon*, but also from the adverbial, *in al this world*, which depends upon it. The form *noon* is here a contracted form equivalent to modern English 'no-one'. Other phrases with similar function are: *no man*, *no wight*, *no thing*.

Multiple negation is often used to impart that vehemence and gravity which the rhetorical tradition associated with 'high style'. It has already been mentioned that double negation is especially common in formal prose, but we also find this kind of emphatic negation in sober and weighty statements in verse, such as this solemn undertaking of Griselda in the *Clerk's Tale*:

> And heere I swere that *neuere* willyngly
> *In werk ne thoght* I *nel* yow disobeye
> For to be deed, thogh me were looth to deye.
>
> (E 362–4)

The dignity of her declaration derives in no small measure from its accumulation of emphatic negatives.

To summarise, then, although double negation in itself does not constitute emphasis, multiple negation may add intensity. This is particularly so if the negative support is in the form of a time or place adverbial, like *neuere* or *nowher*, whose time or place significance is eclipsed by its role as intensifier. The selection of such forms, or of other negating phrases in preference to simple *noght* or *no*, may also be considered to be in some degree emphatic. But intensity of negation may also arise from psychological factors, such as assertiveness, which may be reflected in style by the use of asseverations and oaths, or by the particular choice of modals. Finally, we may assume that multiple negations in passages of more informal or colloquial style are more certain to indicate intense negation than similar usage would do if found in literary prose. The emphatic nature of Griselda's words, discussed above, stands out more obviously because of the general lack of assertive stylistic devices in the *Clerk's Tale*.

As we have seen, the particle *ne* is used in Chaucer's language to mark the negation of the clause, either alone or with negative support, but it has already appeared in certain of our examples with another function. In the last quotation, in the phrase *in werk ne thoght*, *ne* obviously acts as a conjunction equivalent to the modern English 'nor'. In this role, it serves to link together the elements of a negative clause:

And Salomon seith: Neuere in thy lyf to thy wyf *ne* to thy
child *ne* to thy freend ne yif no power ouer thyself.

(B 2251

Or it may join a negative clause to a preceding positive one, or
a series of negative clauses to each other:

> Chaste goddesse, wel wostow that I
> Desire to been a mayden al my lyf.
> *Ne* neuere wol I be no loue ne wyf.   (A 2304–6)

> *Ne* his desire *ne* wherfore he stood thus
> He *neither* cher made *ne* worde tolde.   (*TC* I 311–12)

The famous rhetorical *occupatio* in the *Knight's Tale*, (A 2925
ff.) extends to a list of seventeen such *ne*'s, used to itemise
those things which the poet is *not* going to tell us. What is the
semantic function of *ne* in lists of this kind? If we were to re-
write such a list in the positive, this becomes clearer: in many
cases *ne* would be replaced by *and*, in others, by *or*.[7] In other
words, *ne* may serve to signal either an additive relationship
between the items of the list, or, often with *neither*, an
alternative one. In the *occupatio* from the *Knight's Tale*, which is
too lengthy to quote, the function of *ne* is clearly additive, since
all the items of the list combine to make a full picture of the
preparations for Arcite's funeral. The various items are not
related as options. In the instructions of God to the four winds,
quoted in the *Man of Law's Tale* from *Revelations*, the list is,
however, conceived of as one of alternatives:

> Anoyeth *neither* see *ne* land *ne* tree.   (B 494)

A similar itemised list of alternatives is found in the *Book of the
Duchess*, where Chaucer is eager to give sensuous actuality to
the golden colour of Blanche's hair:

> For euery heer on hir hede,
> Soth to seyn hit was not rede
> *Ne nouther* yelowe, *ne* broune hyt was.   (*BD* 855–7)

In its conjunctive use, then, within the scope of a negative, *ne* can be seen to work either as a cumulative device, or as the creator of a field from which choices may be made.

Occasionally, we find items within the scope of a negator linked not by *ne* but by *or* or by *and*. The second commandment, quoted by the Pardoner, is an example:

> Take nat my name in ydel *or* amys.   (C 642)

The use of *or* rather than *ne* here seems due to the translators' habit of stating alternative renderings: the Latin of the Vulgate (*in vanum*) may be rendered either by the phrase *in ydel* or by *amys*. Both fall as alternatives within the scope of the negation signalled by *nat*, and they are not distinguished as separately negated items in a list. It is possible that the use of such positive forms within the scope of a single negative indicates that Chaucer felt a particular conceptual affinity to exist between items so joined. A similar association between duchesses and queens in the *Knight's Tale*, and penitents and ghosts in the words of the Host to the Monk is represented by a positive form of the conjunction:

> For certes, lord, ther is noon of vs alle
> That she ne hath been a duchesse *or* a queene;
>
>   (A 922–3)
>
> Thou art not lyk a penaunt *or* a goost.   (B 3124)

Such examples, because the selection of *or* is governed by the requirements of metre, are however less satisfactory than the following, from *Troilus and Criseyde*, in which the alternatives are clearly perceived as complementary parts of the *love* to which they are in apposition:

> Was nevere man nor womman yit bigete
> That was unapt to suffren loves hete
> Celestial *or* elles love of kynde.   (I 977–9)

Chaucer's portrait of the Parson in the *General Prologue* is wrought in negatives, and indeed largely in a series of negative correlations based upon the adversative structure *noght . . . but*, which is comparable with the very frequent *ne . . . ac* structure found in Old and early Middle English. In the following account of the Parson's pastoral virtue, the scope of negation is marked by the use of the words *noght . . . but*, and the intervening clauses are co-ordinated by the use of *and* and *or*. The negative *ne* might well have been expected, since, without it, the intervening clauses may appear to have positive force:

> He sette *noght* his benefice to hyre
> And leet his sheep encombred in the myre
> And ran to Londoun vnto seint Poules
> To seeken hym a chauntrye for soules
> Or with a breetherede to been withhoolde,
> *But* dwelte at hoom and kepte wel his foolde.
>
> (A 507–12)

Apparently Chaucer wished to connect this series of events more intimately than would have been implied by the use of *ne*, with its separating and itemising tendency. Desertion of his flock by the shepherd immediately entails disaster for his sheep, and this direct causation would have been lost by the use of *ne*. Furthermore, having established a sequence of inevitable events by the inclusion of them additively within the scope of a single negative, he completed the sequence by a clearly alternative ending to the history by introducing *or*. *Ne*, which would have separated the items as separated negations, and which is ambiguous with regard to addition or alternative, could not have been used to achieve this conceptual strategy.

So far, we have discussed negation very largely as it is represented in syntax, but it may also be expressed lexically. The concept of being free from guilt, for example, can be expressed syntactically:

> of whiche that thow were neuere gilty;   (I 1019; El.)

or it may be expressed lexically:

> Withouten gilt this Nero hath hem slayn;   (B 4563)
> If I be giltlees of this felonye.   (B 643)

Even more common than the suffix *-lees* is the use of the prefix *un-*, which performs the function of negating adverbs, adjectives, and participles: *unnethes, unable, unapt, uncertain, unkonnynge, unfamous, unburyed, undeserved,* and, sure enough, *ungiltif.* The Prioress's ignorance of French is revealed by lexical rather than syntactical devices of negation:

> For Frenssh of Parys was to hire vnknowe. (A 126)

The *un-* prefix is used also with verbs and nouns, but in this use the modification in sense which follows is often more complicated than simple negation. In a process verb, the *un-* prefix may indicate not negation but reversal of the process, so that *unclose,* for example, means 'open', but may have connotations beyond what would be evident in the use of the verb 'to open'.[8] Nouns too may develop more complex associations when compounded with *un-.* The word *hap,* which means 'chance', develops pejorative connotations, so that the semantic relationship between *hap* and *unhap* is very much that between modern 'chance' and 'mischance'.

The negating element is obvious in words like *unapt, rewthelees,* and *displesance,* but a very few words exist which seem to have a negative component in their sense even though this is not obvious in their form. In formal prose, the words *denye* and *doute* are sometimes followed by a negating particle in the dependent clause:

> But . . . may any man denye þat al þat is ryght *nis* good, and also þe contrarie, þat al þat is wrong is wikke?
> (*Bo* IV p.4, 136–8)

> no man douteth þat they *ne* be more derworthe to the than thyn owene lif. (*Bo* II p.4, 49–51)

In the examples above, the sense of the clauses dependent upon *denye* and *doute* is positive. The italicised negators are simply a formal recognition of a negative component in the sense of the governing verb, and their appearance is analogous to that of non-assertive forms in modern English:

He said that he had *some* part in it
He denied that he had *any* part in it.

The discussion of words with negative affixes or negative components in their meanings has altered the level at which negation has been discussed from the general rule towards the particular example, so that it would now seem justifiable to close with a brief discussion of a few individual negative idioms whose use may be problematic.

It is no nay means simply that there can be no denial; that the answer to a preceding assertion cannot be 'nay!' The phrase is common in romances, and its bathetic use in *Thopas* (B 1956) may reflect Chaucer's opinion of its lack of sophistication.

noskynnes This is to be translated 'do no labour of any kind':

> They these ben that wolden honour
> Haue, and do noskynnes labour,
> Ne doo no good.   (*HF* 1793–5)

The phrase is descended from, and preserves the inflexion of, the Old English *nanes cynnes*.

I nam but deed. It is not uncommon to find this phrase incorrectly rendered into modern English as 'I am only dead', perhaps with the added suggestion of irony, for some scholars maintain that Middle English *ne . . . but* is derived from Old French *ne . . . que*.[9] Indeed, in some cases, *ne . . . but* translates very well into modern English as 'only', although the fact that *ne . . . que* has the same modern English translation does not prove the French origin of the Middle English phrase:

> It nys but wast to burye hym preciously;   (D 500)
> That I ne sholde wedded be but ones.   (D 13)

However, let us consider a few related phrases: the following, from the *Knight's Tale*, would be best rendered by 'no more than' or 'nothing other than':

> This world nys but a thurghfare ful of wo.   (A 2847)

The word *but* often has the sense 'except' in Middle English:

> He wolde han fled but that the fox anon
> Seyde . . .   (B 4473–4)

In *Troilus and Criseyde*, the following passage is found:

> He was so fallen in despeir that day
> That outrely he shope hym forto deye;
> For right thus was his argument alway:
> He seyde he nas but lorn weylaway
> For al that comth comth by necessitee
> Thus to be lorn it is my destinee.   (IV 954–9)

This last passage illustrates well the implication of inexorability which is proper to the expression *nam but*: it is found in every occurrence. Consider also the following:

> I nam but deed but if that I kan seyn
> What thyng it is that wommen moost desire;
>   (D 1006–7)

> Syn that I may nat seen yow, Emelie,
> I nam but deed. Ther nys no remedie.   (A 1273–4)

We are now perhaps in a position to explain the significance of the idiom *I nam but deed*. Firstly, we must consider it a use of the present tense in a function subsidiary to its role of reference to the future; that is, in the function of expressing determinism and inevitability.[10] Consider, for example:

> 'For I am deed if that this thyng be kyd'.   (E 1943)

Secondly, we must be aware of the sense 'other than, except' which is often borne by *but*. The sense of the idiom can then be seen to be 'I shall not be other than dead'; in other words, death is inescapable.

In the Fairfax version of the *Book of the Duchess*, the ghost of Ceix appears to his wife and utters the following words:

Awake, let be your sorwful lyfe,
For in your sorwe there lyth no rede;
For certes swete I am but dede.
Ye shul me never on lyve yse. (*BD* 202–5)

As they stand, these words seem to mean something like 'Cheer up, I'm only dead; it could be worse'. But such irony seems contextually inappropriate. Should *am but* be understood in the same way as *nam but*, or have all manuscripts perpetuated a scribal error? Editors have assumed the latter to be the case, so that in the editions of the poem read by modern students the familiar form of the idiom has been silently restored, and these lines have been invested with the sober significance: 'I am quite dead. You will never see me again. The position is irremediable; therefore cease this fruitless grieving'. Thus the omission or editorial restoration of a single letter can radically alter the literary meaning of a text and conceal evidence of possible linguistic variation.

In the course of the last three chapters, two important general points about Chaucer's grammar have slowly emerged. Firstly, that the meaning to be derived from his language does not derive simply from the formal contrasts between words seen as isolated items, but much more from their inter-relation within the context in which they occur: time reference depends not only on the tense of the verb, but upon the adverbials which go with it; modality may be connected with intensity of negation; the idioms with *this* and *he* depend for their exact shade of meaning upon the context in which they occur. Secondly, it has been evident that considerable formal variation exists in Chaucer's grammar, from the variant forms of the third-person verbal inflexions to the alternative of single or double negation.

An expansion of these two observations about Chaucer's language, when considered in a broader context, constitutes the second part of this book; but first we must consider the interaction of linguistic items and non-linguistic context in the creation of connected and meaningful text.

4 Textual Coherence

Language is an abstraction which we encounter in two distinct physical realisations: that is, either as a string of spoken sounds, or as a sequence of marks upon a page. Although we rarely stop to consider whether these two are identical reflections of each other,[1] there are few of us who would write an expression like 'When he saw us, he went: "Oh no!"' unless we were deliberately imitating speech.[2] Evidently, therefore, there is a distinction between written and spoken language on the level of phraseology at least. Furthermore, we have seen in the last chapter how ambiguity in the scope of negation occurs in written language, but might have been clarified by stress in the spoken language of the day. There are, indeed, important differences both in the forms and working of the two realisations of language.

To some extent, spoken and written languages fulfil different cultural roles, since the latter has a permanency denied to the former. Its permanency gives it both greater institutional usefulness and higher cultural esteem. It has more serious legal implications, and was until recently the only means of making official records. Given such purposes, and such administrative importance, it is essential that written language should possess the means of stating its content with clarity. And in this respect its permanence is something of a mixed blessing, for although it enables a reader to work over a passage repeatedly and tease out meaning, by the same token it enables him to see ambiguity where it was never intended. Spoken language, on the other hand, does not normally encourage such scrutiny, but it has the great advantage of being related to a situation of utterance, of using intonation and stress patterns, and of constantly being revised to take account of the reactions of the addressee. Repetition and paraphrase are characteristics of spoken communication. Given such variation in the potential of the medium, written and spoken languages naturally tend to seek clarity by different routes: the former by syntactical organisation and the latter by rhetorical arts.

A further basic distinction between written and spoken forms of language, and one of which we are not ordinarily conscious, is that of how the symbols constituting each form are distributed. Although the sounds of spoken language may merge into continuity for long periods, written language is obviously divided upon the page into distinct graphs which cluster together in small groups, after which a space is conventionally left. These groups are words, and their invariability from one occurrence to another is, in the modern spelling system, such that we often overlook the fact that they do not represent distinct units of the spoken language, if that is assessed in terms of the continuity of the sounds of speech. They are, in fact, the basic, conventionally-accepted units of a technique for rendering the abstraction 'language' in written form. There is nothing God-given about the spellings or the boundaries of words, and this is evident both in medieval spellings and in uncertainty about word-boundaries: *þin aunt* occurs beside *þy naunt*, *the othir* beside *tothir*, and *at the fulle* beside *atte fulle*. The present stability of orthographic words is the product of custom in society and not divine dispensation.

In attempting to describe the structure of languages, the definition of 'word' often presents difficulties to linguists.[3] The various possible means of definition – semantic, phonetic or grammatical – do not correspond with all that orthography treats as words. Nevertheless, it is true that what we conventionally write as a single word often acts as a basic unit of grammatical structure, as well as being the index of meanings in the dictionary, so that it is not surprising that the orthographic word has a powerful psychological reality for us, and has become deeply entrenched in our ways of perceiving language.[4] Words, words, words is how we think of speech; yet our words, with which we are so familiar, are essentially units of the written representation of language. To a considerable extent they are an ordering placed upon language by the needs of writing. However, a written text, by definition, is not merely a list of words. Indeed the very etymology of the word 'text' shows it to be a dead metaphor drawn from an analogy between the continuous threads of sense and the yarn in weaving.[5] Although the isolation of individual words by leaving spaces between them is of primary – but rarely recognised – importance in identifying the units, it is from the relationships between these isolated units that text is formed. These relationships are of various kinds, and the most important is the syntactic structure of the language which underlies the pattern of words upon the page. According to the syntactic structure the words on the page are unconsciously assigned by the reader to their appropriate grammatical and lexical function. Now, although the rules of syntax direct the competent reader to relate words, phrases, and clauses together to create sentences, the relationships which exist in the text beyond the extent of the sentence are usually considered to lie outside the reach of syntactical analysis. Rather, they rely on a number of semantic devices which have come to be known as 'cohesive' devices. The characteristic which their use confers upon a connected passage is known as 'cohesion'. It is its cohesion which distinguishes a connected text from a mere list of sentences.

Cohesion is achieved by a wide variety of means, ranging from the use of obvious conjunctions like *and*, which are easily specified in linguistic description, to much more uncertain subjective connections, which may be perceived to exist even between lists of sentences deliberately jumbled together at random. All the resources available to the determined reader for creating connected text from incoherent sentence lists are not acceptable to the linguist, who is concerned with the ordinary linguistic means of textual continuity. His descriptions must possess considerable generality. Nevertheless, in describing the literary use of language, we must be aware of the widest range of connective devices; hence I have preferred to refer to text connectivity, not by the technical term 'cohesion', but by the more informal one 'coherence'.[6] My discussion will include the main devices ascribed by linguistic description to cohesion, but will also include other devices and effects of coherence which may be restricted to literary language, and even perhaps to verse, and which may arise relatively infrequently.

The devices of cohesion within a text can be divided into four main types: conjunction, substitution, ellipsis, and reference. The first of these, *conjunction*, refers to a logical process and not, as we might suppose, to an item of grammar. Indeed it is a process which operates at all levels of grammar: between words and phrases, as well as across sentence boundaries. In the phrase 'red and white roses' a conjunctive process is going on, and this is signified by the word 'and'. Precisely what items are being conjoined in this expression is ambiguous. The same process of conjunction is found operating between clauses and phrases in the following: 'he went to sleep *and* dreamed of golden hills *and* unicorns'. If, against all the precepts of prescriptive grammar, one begins a sentence with 'and', the presence of that word indicates, in just the same way, that that sentence is to be added to the one before. Now, 'and', 'but', 'yet', 'however', or 'also' are what would traditionally have been described as conjuctions. But we should not forget that cohesion, although it may depend upon elements of grammatical structure, is primarily concerned with meaning. What were traditionally called *adverbs* may also perform a conjunctive function: *William was ill. Thomas was too.* Here the adverb 'too' serves to link the separate statements together, and so, in terms of the cohesion of the text in which it occurs, its role is one of additive conjunction. As well as additive conjunctions, we find those which express a causal relationship between the units which they join:

he couldn't get there *because* the buses weren't running.

or an adversative one:

he ran quickly *but* he came in third.

or a temporal one:

he stayed to tea, *then* he went home.

A common device of conjunction, especially in medieval texts, is the correlative, which is frequently of a temporal kind (*when . . . then . . . then*).

Substitution operates as a device of cohesion by the use of certain pro-forms which can operate in a sentence instead of repeating a particular word or phrase mentioned earlier in the text. 'So' and 'thus' are frequently used for this purpose:

William was ill; so was Thomas.

The pro-form *do* is equally common in modern English:

He comes here often. Do you?

Ellipsis is, in effect, a sub-division of substitution, since it can be considered as substitution by zero:

Fred was first, John second.

Compare the following examples:

(a) Will you have the red or the white wine? The red, I think.
(b) Will you have the red or the white wine? The red one, I think.

Example (a) is an example of ellipsis, since the word 'wine' is omitted and replaced by zero. Example (b) is an example of substitution by the pro-form *one*. In ellipsis, the attention of the reader is drawn to the cohesive function by an anomaly in ordinary grammar. The expression *John second* omits a verb, and therefore does not conform to ordinary clause structure. *The red, I think* is odd because it appears to alter the usual clause structure from Subject-Verb-Object to Object-Subject-Verb, and also to employ an adjective as a substantive. In substitution, the attention of the reader is caught by the use of a special pro-form. By these different means, both signal that the particular piece of text in which these peculiarities occur can only be understood by reference to something earlier in the text. Indeed, a useful rule of thumb by which a native speaker can ascertain whether any item is functioning cohesively is to ask himself whether it is a form which could ordinarily occur in isolation. The phrase 'so was Thomas', for example, could never be an utterance complete in itself, since 'so' presupposes earlier text to which it must refer.

The fourth major device of cohesion, *reference*, also uses characteristic forms to refer to items elsewhere in the text: most commonly definite articles, demonstratives, and personal pronouns.[7] In the answer 'the red one', quoted above, the certainty that previous information has been given arises not only from the use of the pro-form *one*, but also from the use of the definite article, *the*, which implies reference to some specific thing previously identified in the text. Of course, it is frequently the case that a text begins with the definite article, so that it is apparent that the definite article need not always function cohesively; nevertheless it always refers to something. For example, as an opening remark, 'The government's done it again!' might possibly be the continuation, after a long gap, of an earlier discussion in which the particular government, and the speaker's attitude to it, had been made clear; but it is perhaps more likely to be a reference, unprepared for, but understood in a particular political situation. Reference, then, may be reference either back or forth within the text, referring to things already mentioned, or to things about to be discussed (*endophoric reference*), or, alternatively, it may be reference outside the text to a political, cultural or other set of circumstances, or to features of the immediate physical situation (*exophoric reference*).

That cat did this. It's a pest.

In the above example, the demonstratives *that* and *this* refer exophorically to a mutually understood context, and to the immediate situation, respectively. The pronoun *it* refers endophorically to the word *cat*, which has appeared in the earlier sentence. Commonly, the function of third-person pronouns is one of endophoric reference, and this type of reference is divided into two types, by which names we shall henceforth call it. The type exhibited in the above example, in which the pronoun refers back to, or repeats the reference of, something mentioned earlier, is known as *anaphoric* reference.

The second type, which refers forward to something which will be elaborated upon, is known as *cataphoric* reference:

> This is it! They've closed it down now.

Here *this* and *it* in the first sentence have cataphoric reference to the whole of the following sentence. In that sentence *they* and *it* have exophoric reference to some mutually-familiar situation.

Naturally, in written language, exophoric reference is unusual, at least with respect to an immediate situation, and the use of the third-person pronoun for exophoric reference – except for an indefinite *they* – is rather rare.[8] However, use of the third-person pronoun exophorically for special stylistic effects can be found, as an example from the *Knight's Tale* demonstrates:

> Ther seen men / who kan Iuste / and who kan ryde
> Ther shyueren shaftes / vpon sheeldes thikke
> He feeleth / thurgh the herte spoon the prykke
> Vp spryngeth speres / twenty foot on highte
> Out goon the swerdes / as the siluer brighte
> The helmes they tohewen / and to shrede
> Out brest the blood / with sterne stremys rede
> With myghty maces / the bones they tobreste
> He thurgh the thikkest / of the throng gan threste
> Ther stomblen steedes stronge / and doun gooth al
> He rolleth vnder foot / as dooth a bal
> He foyneth on his feet / with his tronchoun
> And he hym hurteth / with his hors adoun
> He thurgh the body is hurt / and sithen ytake
> Maugree his heed / and broght vnto the stake.[9]

> (A 2604–18)

In this passage the anaphoric reference of the third-person singular pronoun, *he/his*, does not extend beyond each clause in which it occurs. That is to say, that, although the *his* repeated in line 2615 refers back to the *he* at the beginning of that line, it has no relevance to the *he* in any of the other lines. The use of the pronoun is largely exophoric, referring to a series of events which, it is pretended, are unfolding before the eyes: events which are given vitality by the selection of the present tense for the commentary, and organised into a list both by their incompatibility and by the repetition of *he* as the initial item of the verse line. The whole is given additional vigour by the alliterative verse rhythms.[10] A similar scene is described by the author of a romance written in London two or three generations before Chaucer, *Kyng Alisaunder*. He uses more anaphora, eschews the historic present, and restricts his material to the unsophisticated rhythms of the four-stress line:

Many dou3tty 3onge kni3th	
þat ilk day assayed his mi3th;	
Vche on oþere, wiþ grete mayn	*force*
Tobrusten her launces in þe playn	*shattered*
Summe hadden perced þe þarmes	*intestines*
þorou3 þe shelde and her armes	*armour*
Somme þe þrote summe þe hertes	
Hadde perced and storuen certes	*died*
After launces swerdes þai drowe	*drew*
And many kni3ttes oþer slow3e	*slew*
Many þere weren þat yuel sped	*fared badly*
For þai laiden heuedes to wed	*forfeited their heads*
Summe armes and hondes loren	*lost*
And summe legges wiþ þe sporen	*spurs*
Many kni3th in litel stounde	*space of time*
Lagh3tte þere dedly wounde.	*sustained*
	(931–46)

The result is a very much more pedestrian description of battle. The *Kyng Alisaunder* excerpt, although grammatically loosely structured, is nevertheless made quite cohesive by the use of anaphoric reference (*many dou3tty 3onge kni3th . . . his . . . her*) and substitution (*vche . . . oþere . . . summe . . . many*). The Chaucerian excerpt, however, is notably dislocated, and it gains its coherence not from the linguistic devices of cohesion so much as by exophoric reference to an imagined situation. This kind of unity in a text, brought about by persistent reference to a fictional situation created by the text itself, falls outside the bounds of what Halliday would describe as 'cohesion'. The limitation of the term cohesion to refer to textual integrity based purely on endophoric (anaphoric and cataphoric) criteria may be valid for orderly linguistic description, but an approach which disregards the internal continuity lent to a passage by persistent and integrated exophoric reference is too restrictive for an interpretative approach to Chaucer's language, such as that adopted in this book. Within the notion of the coherence of the text, then, we should include that unity drawn from reference outside the language to an individual situation, circumstance, or event. This type of reference, which may be implicit in pronouns, demonstratives, and even certain uses of the present tense, has been called by some linguists *deixis*, a term we used in discussing tense and demonstratives in Chapter 2.[11] *Deixis*, which can be considered a special case of exophoric reference, is the situation-referring and creating function of language, and in literary texts it is capable of creating its own unity. Indeed, the standard descriptions of cohesion tacitly admit the relationship between unity of situation and continuity of text, since it is admitted that cohesion may depend upon lexical items.[12] For example, repetition of the same word (*kniȝth*) or of synonyms or near-synonyms (*steede . . . hors* in passage 1) may function cohesively. Hyponymic sets too (*body . . . heed . . . bones . . . foot . . . blood*) may have the same effect.[13] However, the co-occurrence of forms from the same lexical set, often semantically-related, is characteristic of the description of familiar scenes, or the discussion of well-known topics. Lexical sets, furthermore, are created, and recognised for what they are, primarily as the result of their frequent collocation in use referring to such familiar topics or situations.[14] Therefore, although it is no doubt proper for the synchronic linguist to discover the unity of the text through noting the co-occurrence of lexical items, for the scholar concerned with the interpretation of historical traditions of literature, there is no reason why he should not recognise, from his experience of the literary tradition, the unity of any particular scene which is reflected in the connectivity of the text. For him, the insights of the linguist on strictly linguistic cohesion will be a matter of the validation of his perceptions by another method, rather than a new discovery. In the piece from *Kyng Alisaunder*, for example, the coherence of the scene will depend in part upon its linguistic cohesion, but it will depend also upon the recognisable structure of narrative events, which follow an established pattern for the *motif* of battle in romances: swords follow the clash with lances, details of wounds are given, and the *summe . . . many* formula is used.[15]

Finally, it can be argued that, not only in literary language, the coherence of an artfully-created text is marked by the repetition within it of patterns of expression. These patterns arise from the repetition of grammatical structures in concert with repetition of metrical, semantic, or phonetic items or patterns.[16] A simple example is found in the Chaucer passage quoted above, where repetition of unusual grammatical structure, semantic resemblance, and similar metrical patterns help to unite the text:

> Vp spryngeth speres / twenty foot on highte
> Out goon the swerdes / as the siluer brighte
>
> Out brest the blood / with sterne stremys rede
>
> He thurgh the thikkest / of the throng gan threste
>
> He rolleth vnder foot / as dooth a bal
> He foyneth on his feet / with his tronchoun
>
> He thurgh the body is hurt / and sithen ytake.

Similar patterning devices are used to order a complex sentence found later in the *Knight's Tale*:

> ¶ I haue heer / with my cosyn Palamon
> Had stryf and rancour / many a day gon
> For loue of yow / and for my Ialousye
> And Iuppiter / so wys my soule gye
> To speken / of a seruaunt proprely
> With circumstaunces alle / trewely
> That is to seyn / trouthe / honour / knyghthede
> Wisdom / humblesse / estaat / and heigh kynrede
> Fredom / and al / that longeth to that art/

> So Iuppiter / haue of my soule part /
> As in this world / right now ne knowe I non
> So worthy to been loued / as Palamon
> That serueth yow / and wol doon al his lyf.
>
> (A 2783–95)

In Robinson's edition this passage is heavily punctuated. A stop after *Ialousye* divides it into two sentences; and commas at the ends of lines 2786, 2787, 2792, as well as after *Fredom* and *yow* in the last line, distinguish the clauses. Lines 2789–91 are set apart by dashes, and the items within the list separated by commas. Punctuation in the Hengwrt manuscript, although quite full for a medieval manuscript, is still relatively light. The change of topic from complaint to commendation is indicated by a paragraph marker, and the verse caesura is throughout marked by an oblique stroke. The interpolated list of a lover's virtues is itemised by this same oblique, and a short oblique is added to the letter *t* at the end of lines 2791–2, presumably in order to mark off the asseveration addressed to Jupiter. This punctuation is undoubtedly useful in distinguishing the status of the passage as a continuous speech by Arcite, and it also gives some aid in relating the parts to the whole, but understanding is more essentially dependent upon the recognition of syntactic patterns and idioms – for example, that *so wys* and *so* are adverbials qualifying the subjunctives *gye* and *haue* respectively – and upon the knowledge of lexical sets – that *properly* and *circumstaunces* are words associated with rhetorical description and introduce the list of lover's qualities, which are the *circumstantiae* of Latin theory.[17] The cataphoric phrase *that is to seyen* serves effectively to introduce this list, and to make the connection with proper and full description mentioned earlier. Lexical repetition of *seruaunt, serueth* helps to unite the passage, linking the ideal lover to the real Palamon, and a similar unifying function is served by the near-repetition of lines 2786 and 2792, which bridge the digression on the qualities of a lover.

In Chaucerian English, then, where manuscript punctuation is more rudimentary than in modern English, and does not consistently indicate grammatical relationships or logical function, we may expect to find that verbal patterning will play an important role, both in uniting text and in demonstrating the logical relation of the parts. The resources of written language in achieving communicative clarity are today much greater and more subtle than those available to Chaucer. Moreover, language is more standardised, and the author can expect the printer to reproduce his text complete with its original punctuation. Chaucer, however, could not expect such accuracy, even if the devices had been available; he was therefore compelled to employ devices of verbal patterning in his text which strike us as rhetorical. Indeed, in that they are primarily means of ordering oral discourse, they *are* rhetorical. Such patterning confers upon spoken language two features which are more typical of written language: a capacity for ordered discussion, and a mnemonic function. Although patterning devices were commonly used in literature primarily intended for oral performance, and this may partly explain their origin in Chaucer, it is by no means the only reason for their use.[18] They are also inevitable as a supplement to uncertain punctuation in written language, and will help to preserve the sense of a text in the face of scribal abandonment of even rudimentary punctuation in the course of re-copying. From the historical point of view, it must be acknowledged that their use could become habitual in some styles, regardless of whether the text was intended to be read aloud or not. In order to illustrate the techniques of coherence employed by Chaucer, there is no better way than to examine in detail some passages of his work with only the original manuscript punctuation as our guide. The first to be considered is a piece of translated prose, which is a conspicuously literary effort, unlikely to have been intended for reading aloud before any but the smallest audience. Indeed, the *Tale of Melibee* has been identified as an example of Chaucer's proficiency at writing in a particular learned style which gained popularity during his lifetime and flourished in English in the fifteenth century.[19]

¶ Whanne Dame Prudence / hadde herd the answeres of thise men ⌒ she bad hem go agayn priuely / and she retourned / to hir lord Melibe / and tolde hym / how she fand his Aduersaries ful repentant / knowlichynge ful
5 lowely / hir synnes and trespas / and how they weren

redy / to suffren al peyne / requerynge / and prayynge
hym / of mercy and pitee ¶ Thanne seyde Melibe ◁ he is
wel worthy / to haue pardoun and foryifnesse of his
synne / that excuseth nat his synne / but knowelicheth
10   and repenteth hym / axinge Indulgence ◁ For Senek
seith ◁ There is the remissioun and foryifnesse / where
as the confessioun is / for confessioun / is neighebore to
Innocence ◁ And he seith / in another place [that he]
that hath shame of his synne and knowelicheth it ◁ [is
15   worthy remissioun] And therfore / I assente and
conferme me to haue pees ∽ but it is good / that we do
it nat with outen thassent / and wil / of oure freendes
¶ Thanne was Prudence / right glad and ioyeful / and
seyde ◁ Certes sire quod she / ye han wel and goodly
20   answerd / for right as by the conseil / assent / and
help / of youre frendes / ye han ben stired / to venge
yow / and make werre ∽ right so / with outen hire
conseil / shul ye nat acorde yow / ne haue pees with
youre Aduersaries ◁ for the lawe seith ◁ Ther nys
25   nothyng so good / by wey of kynde / as a thyng / to been
vnbounde / by hym that it was ybounde ◁ And thanne
Dame Prudence / with outen delay / or taryynge / sente
anon messages / for hir kyn / and for hire olde
freendes / whiche that were trewe and wise / and tolde
30   hem by ordre / in the presence of Melibe / al this
matere / as it is aboue expressed and declared / and
preyde hem / that they wolde yeuen hir auys and
conseil / what best were to do / in this nede ◁ And whan
Melibees freendes / hadde taken hire auys and deliber-
35   acioun of the forseyde matere / and hadden examyned
it / by greet bisynesse and greet diligence ∽ they
yaue ful conseil / for to haue pees and reste / and that
Melibe / sholde receyue with good herte / hise Aduersaries / to foryifnesse and mercy.[20]

(B 2959–80)

The scribal punctuation of this passage is rather more
elaborate than usual, and indeed is quite helpful to its
interpretation. The mark ◁ is placed where, at first, it seems
to distinguish speech from narrative. However, it does not

function in the way modern quotation marks would, since it is not restricted to direct speech: both the utterances of the characters, and the opinions of past authorities are marked in the same way. The fact is that this mark is used to indicate *sententiae*, wise sayings which have bearing on the situation described in the narrative. We have already met some uncertainty about this distinction when discussing the use of the present tense in Chapter 2.[21] Here, in this passage, punctuation proclaims that, in the eyes of the scribe, we should not look for the interaction of characters. The speeches are perceived not as dramatically appropriate utterances, so much as pieces of proverbial wisdom. Indeed the final sentence, which is marked out by the use of the ◁ symbol, is simply indirect speech subsumed in narrative, but it merits the use of this symbol simply because it represents a judgement (the *sententia*) of Melibee's friends on the matter under discussion.

Formal changes of speaker, or of the narrative focus upon one or the other protagonist, are marked by the use of the paragraph marker ¶ (thus ¶ –Prudence; ¶ –Melibe; ¶ –Prudence). Oblique strokes are employed to divide the text into sense-groups, and a ligature ᴔ indicates where the sense of one clause is dependent upon what has gone before, as, for example, in correlative or adversative relationships (2, 16, 22, 36).

Scribal punctuation, then, serves to identify some of the elements involved in making up a continuous text, but offers only scant help in recognising the connection between those elements. It is therefore incumbent upon the medieval author to construct his text in such a way that its coherence emerges from its arrangement, and this is particularly difficult in the case of prose. In this case our text is divisible, for the sake of discussion, into sections which begin with the temporal conjunctions *whanne* or *thanne*, followed by a proper name, creating a correlated series. Together with the inconsistent use of paragraph markers, these repetitive introductions form the cohesive framework of the text (lines 1, 7, 18, 26, 33). Within this *whanne . . . thanne* framework, which is that used also for the beginning of the *General Prologue*,[22] clause connections are usually simple. The additive conjuncts *and*, the adversative *but*, manner conjunct *how*, and a rather loose use of the causal *for* are found. Ellipsis is rare, and indeed more or less limited to the suppression of the subject in such examples as *and tolde hym* (l.3). The present participle is used sparingly, as in *requerynge and prayynge* (l.6) to create an adjectival clause where modern English would prefer co-ordination. *Which that* and *that* occur as relatives. In lines 7–9 (*he . . . that*) and 13 there are cataphoric uses of the pronoun, but generally pronoun usage is anaphoric, and it is by anaphoric reference, and by simple additive conjunction, that continuity is maintained within the five divisions linked by the *whanne . . . thanne* structure. The clarity of pronoun reference is carefully maintained by the frequent use of the two proper names *Melibee* and *Prudence*, and by the lexical repetition in references to the other important protagonists, *youre Aduersaries*, and *youre freendes*. Lexical cohesion is achieved by the device of variation within the doublets used to refer to the most important ideas in the passage, and also by the choice of and repetition of words clustering in sense round these few important ideas, such as penitence, confession, offence, and forgiveness.[23] Some of this repetition can be seen from the following table:

ful repentant / knowelichynge	(4)	Indulgence	(10)
knowelicheth and repenteth	(9–10)	synnes and trespas	(5)
confessioun . . . confessioun	(12)	synne . . . synne	(9)
knowelicheth	(14)	Innocence	(13)
mercy and pitee	(7)	synne	(14)
pardoun and foryifnesse	(8)	pees	(16)
remissioun and foryifnesse	(11)	acorde . . . pees	(23)
remissioun	(15)	pees and reste	(37)
foryifnesse and mercy	(39)		

The further management of lexical cohesion is evident in the sequence *mercy* and *pitee* (l.7), followed by the semantically-related *pardoun and foryifnesse* in the next line. Following these two phrases, continuity is maintained, together with variation, when *foryifnesse* is linked with *remissioun*, and the passage is completed with the re-appearance of the word *mercy*, when the forgiveness, which had been sought in the opening lines, is finally granted: *foryifnesse and mercy*. If it could be disputed that we have here the artful deployment of lexical resources to produce a coherent argument, doubts may be resolved by considering the expression of the important theme of taking counsel of allies before making political decisions. At line 17 it is suggested that *thassent and wil* of friends be consulted. This echoes the personal assent of Melibee in the previous line. The phrase is repeated in variant form in line 20, *the conseil / assent / and help*, and as *conseil* (l.23). In line 32, this latter is expanded to *auys and conseil*, before evolving in line 34 into *auys and deliberacioun*. This particular cohesive chain culminates with the statement that Melibee's friends 'yaue ful *conseil /* for to haue *pees and reste /* and that Melibe / sholde receyue with good herte his *Aduersaries /* to *foryifnesse and mercy*'. From the words italicised in this quotation, it will be seen how satisfactory is the final sentence as a summation of the passage as a whole, since contained within it are the culminations of almost all the lexical ties which have helped to give coherence to the passage.

It is clear that, although *Melibee* is a consciously literary work, the most striking feature of the coherence of this passage is not its syntactic complexity, but lexical and semantic repetition, arranged within a simple rhetorical strategy based upon the *whanne . . . thanne* device, and further elaborated by minor correlative patterns like *ther is remissioun . . . where as confessioun is* and *right as by conseil . . . right so*. This is studied literary language; but the principles of its organisation are quite different from those of a piece of modern prose. Let us, therefore, consider a second piece of prose in the same manuscript, a passage from the *Parson's Tale*, in which the scribe has used similar devices of punctuation as in the *Tale of Melibee*. Is it, too, ordered by similar devices of coherence?

¶ Now as for to speke of goodes of nature / god woot / that som tyme we han hem in nature / as muche to oure damage / as to oure profit ¶ As for to speke of heele of body / certes it passeth ful lightly / and
5   eek / it is ful ofte enchesoun / of the siknesse of the soule / for god woot / the flessh is a ful greet enemy to the soule / and therfore / the moore that the body is hool / the moore be we in peril to falle ◁ Eke / for to pryde hym in hys strengthe of body / it is an heigh
10 folye / for   certes / the   flessh   coueiteth   agayn   the

spirit / and ay the moore strong that the flessh is / the
sorier may the soule be / and ouer al this / Strengthe of
body and worldly hardynesse / causeth ful ofte many
man / to peril and meschaunce ◁ Eke / for to pryde hym
15   of his genterye / is ful gret folie / for ofte tyme / the
genterie of the body / bynymeth the genterie of the
soule / and eek / we ben alle / of o fader and o
moder / and alle we ben of o nature roten / and corrupt / bothe riche and pouere / for sothe / o manere gen-
20   tilrye / is for to preise / that apparayleth mannes corage
with vertues / and moralitees / and maketh hym cristes
child / for truste wel / that ouer what man that synne
hath maistrye / he is verray cherl to synne ¶ Now / ben
ther general signes of gentilnesse / as eschewynge of
25   vice / or rybaudye and seruage of synne / in word /
in   werk   and   contenaunce   /   and   vsynge
vertu / curteisye / and clennesse / and to be liberal / that
is to seyn / large by mesure / for thilke that passeth
mesure / is foly and synne ◁ Another is / to remembre
30   hym of bounte / that he of oother folk hath receyued ◁
Another   is / to   ben   benygne / to   hise   goode
subgetz / wher fore as seith Senek / ther is no thyng
moore couenable to a man of heigh estat / than
debonairetee and pitee / and therfore thise flyes / that
35   men clepe bees / whan they maken hire kyng / they
chesen oon that hath no prikke / wher with he may
stynge ◁ Another is / a man to haue a noble herte and a
diligent / to attayne to hye vertuouse thynges.

(I 457–69)

It is at once evident that in this passage, too, the grammatical
devices of cohesion are relatively simple and explicit. The
anaphoric use of third-person pronouns links clauses, but a
similar use of the definite article is absent. Additive
conjunction is common, by the use of the words *and*, *eke*, and
and ouer al this; temporal conjunction is found with the word
whan (l.35). Adversatives are absent, but, by comparison with
the *Tale of Melibee,* the number of causal and result connectives
is very high: *for*, *and therfore*, *wher fore*. This concern with causal
relations is reflected at the lexical level by the use of the words

causeth and *maketh*. Ellipsis is not employed as a cohesive device, but substitution is evident in the repeated use of *another* (29, 31, 37). Lexical cohesion is evident in repetition of a few words from a few restricted lexical sets: *body, flessh, soule, spirit, corage; genterie, gentilrye, gentilesse, cherl, seruage;* and *vertues, moralitees, synne, vice, rybaudye*. A hyponymic grouping of specific virtues also occurs. But the most striking feature of these lexical sets is that they are arranged within the passage into antithetical groups. Indeed, whereas grammatical cohesion is simple and merely links clauses serially together, it is antithesis, a feature of rhetorical organisation, which binds together the overt listing of items in the passage.

The passage concerns the traditional subject matter of the goods of nature, which are the benefits bestowed by heredity or circumstances of birth.[24] They have already been distinguished into those of the soul and those of the body before the excerpt begins, and the goods of the body have been listed as: *heele of body, strengthe, delyuernesse* (agility), *beautee, genterie, franchise*. Of these, Chaucer, or his source, selected only the first, second, and *genterie* for further discussion. As the particular benefits which together constitute the physical goods of nature, we might have expected these three to be arranged as sub-headings within the discussion of this topic, since this is the method adopted when *genterie* itself is discussed. There the major topic is marked by a paragraph marker and the sub-headings by the ◁ symbol. The logical organisation of this passage on these lines would, therefore, be as follows:

A three-level hierarchy of this kind is, however, beyond the capacity of our putative system of punctuation, which can only mark major topics and their immediate constituents. But this problem does not arise, for Chaucer does not choose to arrange the passage in this way, and his discussion of *genterie* looms disproportionately large in it. Let us consider what logic may lie behind the scribe's punctuation. First, he introduces the important topic of the *goodes of nature* with a paragraph mark, then follows that with a second paragraph mark to introduce the discussion of physical well-being (*heele of body*). Subsequently, *strengthe* and *genterie*, which are equal constituents of *goodes of nature* along with *heele*, are both preceded by the subsidiary mark ◁ . Now it may be that the scribe thought that the switch from the general mention of the *goodes of nature* to their particular parts constituted a sufficiently new beginning to justify the use of a paragraph mark, but it is equally likely that the distribution of his punctuation was guided by the overt layout of the text, evident to him in the author's use of verbal repetition. The pattern is as follows:

¶ *Now as for to speke of goodes of nature*
  ¶ *As for to speke of heele of body*
                    ◁ *Eke for to pryde hym in . . . strengthe*
                    ◁ *Eke for to pryde hym of . . . genterye*

  ¶ *Now ben ther . . . signes of gentilnes*
                    ◁ *Another is*
                    ◁ *Another is*
                    ◁ *Another is*

Punctuation evidently follows an inherent lexical organisation of the text, which itself diverges from the logical hierarchy outlined above. If the punctuation is indeed of scribal origin, we must assume, that, rather than impose the obvious logical organisation upon the passage, the scribe looked to the rhetorical cues left by its author for the principle of its coherence.

The development of the sense of this passage is less by continuously connected argument than by persistent implication extending from one section to another, dependent upon a continuously developed set of oppositions and implicit equations between the body and the soul, sin and virtue, social debasement and elevation. This is apparent in the lexical fields mentioned earlier, but it is rhetorically developed in the actual employment of the words there mentioned. In lines 4–6, *heele of body* is brought into opposition with *siknesse of the soule*; and the antithesis is enforced by a meta-phor of the enmity between body and soul, and the use of a correlative: 'the moore that the body is hool / the moore be we in peril to falle'. A parallel structure, with different wording, is used of bodily strength: 'the flessh coueiteth agayn the spirit / and ay the moore strong that the flessh is / the sorier may the soule be'. Both discussions also close on the word *peril*. The discussions of physical health and strength, then, are matched together by rhetorical structure and parallelism of content, and it is the metaphor of the body's threat to the soul which opens the discussion of *genterie,* where it is used to introduce the important notion of antithesis within the concept of nobility itself; that between spiritual and corporeal. This revelation ends with the traditional paradox that *synne* may make a churl out of a nobleman. The passage then closes with a simple listing of the virtues constituting spiritual nobility. Once again, as in the prose passage from *Melibee,* the coherence of Chaucer's prose is seen to be achieved largely by the use of rhetorical devices, by verbal and structural repetition, and especially by alternative ways of linguistically expressing traditional patterns of thought: the passage derives its coherence essentially from the familiar antithesis between the body and the soul, and from a series of oppositions subsidiary to this.

Since we have considered two prose passages, it seems right, for our final example, to examine a passage of verse. This is an example of narrative verse style, used in a plain unelaborated way for an exemplum in the *Nun's Priest's Tale*:

> ¶ And certes / in the same book I rede
> Right / in the nexte Chapitre / after this
> I gabbe nat / so haue I Ioye or blys
> Two men / that wolde han passed ouer see
> 5   For certeyn cause / in to a fer contree
> If that the wynd / ne hadde ben contrarie
> That made hem / in a Citee for to tarie
> That stood ful myrie / vp on an hauen syde
> But on a day / agayn the euen tyde
> 10   The wynd gan chaunge / and blew right as hem leste
> Iolif and glad / they wenten vn to reste

And casten hem / ful erly for to sayle
But herkneth / to that o man / fil a gret meruaille
¶ That oon of hem / in slepyng / as he lay
15   Hym mette a wonder dreem / agayn the day
Hym thoughte / a man stood / by his beddes syde
And hym comanded / that he sholde abyde
And seyde hym thus / if thow tomorwe wende
Thow shalt be dreynt / my tale is at an ende
20   ¶ He wook / and tolde his felawe what he mette
And preyde hym / his viage to lette
As for that day / he preyde hym to byde
¶ His felawe / that lay / by his beddes syde
Gan for to laughe / and scorned hym ful faste
25   No dreem quod he / may so myn herte agaste
That I wol lette / for to do my thynges
I sette nat a straw / by thy dremynges
For sweuenes ben / but vanytees and Iapes
Men dreme alday / of Owles / or of Apes
30   And of many a maze / ther with al
Men dreme of thyng / that neuere was ne shal
But sith I see / that thow wolt here abyde
And thus forslewthen / wilfully thy tyde
God woot it reweth me / and haue good day
35   And thus / he took his leue / and wente way
But er that he / hadde half his cours yseyled
Noot I nat why / ne what meschaunce it eyled
But casuelly / the shippes botme rente
And ship and man / vnder the water wente
40   In sighte of othere shippes / it bisyde
That with hem seyled / at the same tyde
And therfore / faire Pertelote so deere
By swich ensamples olde / maystow leere
That no man / sholde ben to recchelees
45   Of dremes / for I sey thee doutelees
That many a dreem / ful soore is for to drede.

(B 4254–99)

Scribal punctuation in this narrative verse is light, and its purpose is not always easy to understand. The oblique stroke marks the caesura in the verse-line, but the paragraph mark does not seem to be used consistently. It indicates the commencement of this *exemplum*, and various shifts in narrative focus, but it is entirely lacking in the latter part of the passage; even at line 42, where its use might have been expected to mark the *moralitee*. The symbol ⊿, which was used to mark *sententiae* in the prose passages, is absent here, and the simple, non-sententious, direct speech is undifferentiated from the narrative by punctuation.

Perhaps surprisingly, the coherence of this passage, although it is in verse, relies less upon verbal and rhetorical devices than either of the prose passages we have discussed. The difference lies not so much in the dichotomy between verse and prose as that between narrative and exposition, or indeed, in the *Parson's Tale*, between narrative and exhortation. Paradoxically, then, coherence in the passage from the *Nun's Priest's Tale*, depends upon those devices of cohesion which we are accustomed to consider prosaic. The syntax of the passage is simple, and largely co-ordinate, using the additive conjunction, *and*, and the adversative, *but*. There are relative clauses, introduced by *that*, and causal conjunctions also occur: *and therefore* (l.42); *but sith* (l.32). Two clauses are introduced by the conditional, *if*. The adverb, *thus*, is used cataphorically in line 18 as a device to introduce the speech of the dream-visitor, and substitution occurs in *that oon* (l.14), but the cohesion of the passage depends essentially upon anaphoric reference by the use of pronouns. The chain of reference is carefully maintained throughout the passage, beginning with the first mention of the two companions as *two men* in line 4. Until line 12, the reference is maintained by the use of the pronouns *hem* and *they*. Their fates then become distinct, and a demonstrative preserves the referential tie in the expression *that o man* (l.13). He now becomes the focus of narrative interest as his dream is recounted. *That oon of hem* is now the principal protagonist, and the referential links are consequently carried on by the use of the pronouns *he*, *his*, *hym* until, in line 20, *his felawe* is re-introduced. Until the beginning of the final section marked by the scribe, in line 23, the third-person pronouns refer both to *that o man* and *his felawe*, the proper references being kept separate by the former acting as subject of the sentence, the latter as object. At line 23, however, *his felawe* takes the initiative in the action, and the grammatical roles of the pronouns (in relation to their reference) are reversed: *he* now means *his felawe*, whose speech is now interpolated. This speech is noticeably more rhetorical than the narrative in which it is set. Notice, for example, the repeated *men dreme*, the alliteration of *many a maze*, the somewhat more complex syntax, and the ellipsis in *neure was ne shal*.

The closing lines of the passage, like its opening two lines, relate the passage as a whole to the wider context, in which it functions as an exemplum demonstrating the importance of dreams. The cohesive devices here are also anaphoric and conjunctive: *the same book* (1.1); *the nexte chapitre* (1.2); *after this* (1.2); *swich ensamples* (1.43). The most striking feature, however, which both delimits the passage as complete in itself, and also, by the traditional form of its expression, marks it as an illustrative example relevant to the argument of its more general context, is the use of the line which immediately precedes the excerpt quoted, and which is echoed in its final line:

Heere may men sen / that dremes ben to drede.

The phrasing of this line, which is the culmination of an earlier exemplum supporting this argument, is precisely the phrasing commonly used by preachers to press home the force of their anecdotes.[25] Even disregarding its internal coherence, therefore, the contemporary audience, familiar with the devices of preaching, would recognise its extent and purpose from the use of these words. Lexically, the passage is cohesive, it is true, since words are repeated from two distinct conceptual fields – *see, tyde, hauen, sayle, shippe* and *slepyng, dreem, mette, beddes syde, woke, sweuenes, dreme* – but there is nothing to indicate the deliberate and artful use of lexical ties by the author.

The devices by which coherence is bestowed upon this little anecdote may seem so obvious, and even inevitable, that it should be unnecessary to analyse them. But we should remember that this is Chaucerian English, modern as the devices may seem, and that earlier authors did not always exhibit the same skill in managing the cohesive chains of pronoun reference, nor indeed, in the absence of punctuation, were they so adept at singling out direct speech from narrative by other devices: *seyde hym thus . . . my tale is at an ende*; *quod he . . . haue good day / And thus he took his leue.* Nor were they necessarily so skilled at blending indirect speech with narrative as Chaucer was when he so wished (ll.20–22). These are skills which cast light on the ambiguity of the direct speech in the *General Prologue,* discussed in Chapter 2, reassuring us that it is not merely the product of medieval stylistic naïveté. The truth is that the plain, and, to us, prosaic narrative verse, and the rhetorical and artifical prose with its more complex manuscript punctuation, are equally the product of artistic skills, but of very different stylistic aspirations.

PART TWO
Variation, Context, and Style

Preliminary Note

By comparison with other medieval English authors, Chaucer is notable for the variety in dialect and in levels of speech which his language contains. Some of this variety, such as his use of the Northern dialect in the *Reeve's Tale*, is in pursuit of particular literary effects; but much of it, although potentially useful for versification, is to be found in his works simply as the result of its prior existence in the contemporary language of London. Fourteenth-century London English, which was Chaucer's native language, had been made various, as we shall see in the opening chapter of Part Two, by the immigration of dialect speakers from the countryside; but variety also arose in its vocabulary from the influence of French and Latin. In the case of Chaucer himself, the Italian language can also be added to these more general sources of foreign influence.

At the end of his *Compleynt of Venus*, Chaucer tells his audience that he has painstakingly translated the work, in so far as is possible, from the French of Granson, whom he considers to be pre-eminent among French poets. That his audience should have been expected to be familiar with the reputation of a French author and to appreciate the difficulties of translating his verse into uneloquent English may seem surprising. But reference is made also in the *Parson's Tale* to a 'newe Frenshe song' with which the audience are likewise expected to be familiar: indeed, Chaucer uses its title (*I'ay tout perdu mon temps et mon labour*) again as a refrain for his lyric on Fortune.

It is nearly as surprising to the modern reader to find Chaucer accompanied on his pilgrimage to Canterbury by fellow-pilgrims who seem to be linguists. The Prioress speaks

French *faire and fetisly*. The Pardoner has recourse to Latin in his preaching. The Summoner will speak nothing else but Latin when he's drunk. However, this limits his conversation, since he seems not to be very familiar with the language. A better scholar, the clairvoyant clerk in the *Franklin's Tale*, can greet his visitors civilly in Latin.

None of this prowess at foreign languages would have seemed particularly surprising to the medieval reader; indeed, the only cause for comment would have been the Summoner's apparent weakness in Latin, and the Prioress's limitation to the French of Stratford-at-the-Bowe. But to the medieval reader these languages would not have seemed so essentially foreign as they do to us. Both had been used in England for hundreds of years in their appropriate contexts, and both formed part of the rich complex of linguistic options open to Englishmen; for the linguistic history of medieval England is also a chapter in the histories of Norse, French, and Latin, as well as of English.

Norse, the language of the Danish and Norwegian settlers, who from the middle of the ninth century had occupied a large part of Northern and Eastern England, had never been a written language in England, and by Chaucer's time had been forgotten, surviving only as dialectal peculiarities in areas of heavy Norse settlement. Latin, from the age of Bede onwards, had been the language of scholarship, of the Church, and of the most solemn matters of state, and continued to be so throughout Chaucer's lifetime. But it is the history of French in England which most affected Chaucer's language and poetry, and so it is to French that we must pay closest attention.

The French language is relevant to that of Chaucer in two distinct ways: historically, as the agency by whose presence in England after 1066 certain changes in English spelling, sounds, and vocabulary had come about; and contemporaneously, as a stylistic choice with characteristic values and associations at the time when Chaucer wrote. It is apparent that for the purposes of understanding Chaucer's poetry it is this second kind of French influence which most interests us. But, in order to understand the stylistic values in which French and French-derived words and phrases participate, we must first know something of the prior history of their use in England.

Following the Norman Conquest, the Norman dialect of French survived in England as a mother tongue for perhaps two generations. By the end of the twelfth century, although literature in Anglo-Norman flourished, its writers were well aware that their language had deviated from the kind of French found on the Continent. Long before the Prioress's French of Stratford, the sneer of 'Marlborough French' had been used, and carried with it the implication of a social rebuff. Because the aristocracy of early medieval England was an almost exclusively Norman one, the contamination of their French by contact with peasant English could be regarded as tantamount to social disparagement. Indeed in an Anglo-Norman romance of about 1175, the hero taunts his antagonists with the suggestion that, when drunk, they will forget themselves and lapse into the English oath *witegod*. English is the language of the peasants, the *vilains*, who do not understand the customs of courtly society. The author of the *Vie de St. Clement* (c.1200) does not mince his words:

> De si escrive en purpos ai
> Que clerc e lai qui l'orrunt
> Bien entendre le porrunt,
> Si si vilains del tut ne seient
> Que puint de rumanz apris n'aient.

[I intend to write so that both clerks and laymen who hear it may understand it well, even if the peasantry cannot grasp it at all because they have learned no French.]

But this quotation is significant in two ways: firstly in its assumption of a social division between those who know French and those who do not; and secondly in the implication that the proficiency of the former group may be through learning rather than the assimilation of a native tongue. This admission is the precursor of the earliest French grammars written in England and of the hiring of teachers of French; the means by which the thirteenth-century gentry sought to keep its linguistic distance from the peasantry.

By Chaucer's time, the French language had lost none of its social and cultural prestige, although it had lost many of its practitioners. The use of French was in decline, but good correct Parisian French was the more valued. French literature was still esteemed and read in aristocratic circles, and indeed more than one of Chaucer's acquaintances wrote poetry in that language. But outside the royal court, in less urbane circles, the ability to write French could be very poor, even among noblemen. Traditionally, letters exchanged between members of the aristocracy had been written in French, but in 1400 the young Earl of March was forced to apologise 'that I write my letters in Englische, fore that ys mare clere to myne understanding than Latyne or Fraunche'.

In failing to write his letters in French, the Earl was breaking only one of the customary uses of written French which had grown up alongside the urbane French of the royal court. For, in an increasingly debased form, French was used as the language of legal cases and records, of Parliamentary business, and of secular administration. Wills and inventories were also often written in French; so that, as the language of the majority of legal and administrative transactions, undoubtedly the greatest use of French in England in Chaucer's time was its use as a technical language. As such, in the wider world outside the royal court, French had become ossified and formulaic. Even as early as 1225 it had begun to replace Latin in monumental inscriptions: although not yet a dead language, its colloquial use was sufficiently removed from most of the people for it to be accepted as a language suitable for the commemoration of the dead.

The history of the use of French in England, then, had ensured that whilst on the one hand it was associated with great social prestige and cultural refinement, on the other it might be regarded as a kind of 'officialese'. Good French – and for that matter adoptions from Italian – may still be taken as a sign of refinement, but it is apparent that for stylistic purposes we cannot treat this French as equivalent to the formulae of officialdom. The French used in England was itself various, and, indeed, outside purely French contexts, had become, over a period of some hundreds of years, incorporated into the English expression system. The process of adoption of French from technical spheres was at its fastest during Chaucer's lifetime, when English was encroaching on those traditional registers where French had previously predominated. Once accepted into the expression system of English, French words were no longer recognised as foreign: the French noun *joie*, for example, forms the base of the Middle English verb *joyen* and the phrase *faire joie* is half-translated into the English *maken joye*. The clause *I . . . me recomaunde vnto ʒoure noble grace*, although employing three words of French origin, and also a French reflexive construction, is likely to have been perceived rather as a gracious epistolary formula than as an adoption from French. This is perhaps borne out by the fact that the scribe of the Corpus manuscript of *Troilus and Criseyde*, in which it appears, closed the letter in the text with another epistolary formula of more obvious French form, *le vostre T*.

It is apparent from this discussion that in discovering the effectiveness of Chaucer's vocabulary for poetic use, we should not be interested in the variety bestowed by etymological origins so much as the variety of stylistic values which the history of their use has imposed upon words. Although etymological origins carry with them certain stylistic presuppositions – for example, that Norse words are for the ordinary, everyday concerns, French to do with cultural refinement, and Latin to do with scholarship – we must be ready to make finer distinctions based upon register, that is, upon area of use. This kind of stylistic differentiation, based upon the contemporary use of language rather than its etymological origins will form the subject of the following chapters.

5   Linguistic Diversity

> And for ther is so gret diversite
> In Englissh and in writyng of oure tonge,
> So prey I God that non myswrite the,
> Ne the mysmetre for defaute of tonge.
> (*TC* V. 1794–6; Robinson's text)

The lines from *Troilus and Criseyde* quoted above are frequently cited as a rueful reflection on the manuscript tradition of Chaucer's works; but they also state an important fact about his language as the medium for verse writing: its *diversite*, its variousness.

What Chaucer meant by his use of this word was that in his time *Englissh* was really a collective term representing a number of distinct dialects. There was no universally-accepted standard for writing English as such, merely a set of conventions for writing each scribe's local dialect. The major dialect divisions distinguished by modern scholars are shown in the map on page xvi. This map, however, greatly simplifies the true circumstances, since experience and common sense alone can tell us that dialect boundaries are never so clear-cut. In reality, the transition from one dialect to another forms a continuum of subtle distinctions in pronunciation, grammar, and vocabulary, which to some extent were reflected in the language written by each local scribe.[1] The resulting variety was increased in written texts by the habit of 'translating' – or often partially translating – a text as it was re-copied in any dialect area different from that in which it originated. Inevitably, such dialect translation would tend to destroy the rhymes and rhythms of the original, and indeed even the very sense may suffer.

Re-copying had the further effect of producing in the completed text a great diversity of linguistic forms, and, because these are features of more than one of the traditional dialect areas, the resulting language is often called a 'mixed dialect'.[2] There is, however, another kind of dialect mixture which is often known by the same phrase, but which is really quite different in that it does not arise as part of the copying history of a text: this is the case in which a scribe feels free to use dialect forms from more than one area as part of his own individual linguistic skills. The reasons why such diversity should arise in the language of an individual can be many. It may be that he has migrated from one area to another, learned new forms, but also retained his old ones; it may be that certain spellings which he has encountered in his professional life as a scribe have achieved a wide degree of currency, so that he adds them to his native ones; or, indeed, it may be that he comes from some dialectal border area where variety of certain forms is a fact of his everyday language.

The geographical position of London – as a glance at the map of Middle English dialects will show – ensured that the language spoken there possessed linguistic forms which were dialectally at home in both the south-east and in the east Midlands. Indeed, the very earliest texts of London Middle English show it to be a 'mixed dialect' in the second sense of the term. In their copying, London scribes wrote a diversity of dialect forms. Compare the following:

WS STANDARD	LONDON DOCUMENTS	
stræt	*strate ~ strete*	street
brycg	*bregge ~ brugge*	
	~ brigge	bridge
eald	*eld ~ old*	old
menn	*man ~ men*	men
isern ~ iren	*yse(n) ~ yren*	iron

In the left-hand column are the spellings found in standardised West Saxon writings of the last century before the Conquest. The centre column illustrates the variety of spelling for the same words found in thirteenth-century London documents, where considerable variation is apparent. If we were to explain this diversity in terms of the Middle English dialectal area to which each of the spellings is proper, it would have to be in this way: *bregge* is a spelling found in the south-east; *brugge* is west Midland and south-western; *brigge* – from which the modern form descends – is east Midland. Similarly, the familiar form *old* is east Midland, and *eld* is found in southern, south-eastern, and south-western dialect areas. The form *yse* is much more restricted in its distribution, since it is found only in London and adjoining areas of the south-east.[3] The forms *man* and *strate* are found only in London and a few of the extreme south-east Midland counties.[4] Elsewhere in Middle English, *men* and *strete* were used. Although each of these forms can be attributed to a distinct dialectal area, their *combination* in a manuscript has been claimed to indicate its London origin.[5]

But to say that London texts from the earliest Middle English times contain a 'mixed dialect' is only part of the story which leads to Chaucer and the manuscripts of his poetry. The variation in the forms of the word 'bridge' is paralleled by forms like those for 'hill' (*hell ~ hull ~ hill*) and the place-name, Cripplegate   (*Crepelgate ~ Crupelgate ~ Cripelgate*),   implying a certain regularity in the variation $e \sim u \sim i$. However, in the case of 'hill' this is true of only the very earliest texts, for spellings with *e* disappeared early. Spellings of Cripplegate with an *e* survived until much later, before they too disappeared. In short the history of these words forms part of a pattern of chronological development throughout the Middle English period in which *e* and *u* spellings gradually decline in frequency as there is a proportionate increase in *i* spellings. Expressed in dialectal terms, what happens is that the originally East Saxon London language, which has much in common with the dialects of the south and south-east, is gradually infiltrated by dialect features proper to the east Midlands and the north. This process continued into the fourteenth century and indeed throughout Chaucer's lifetime, so that ultimately the whole character of London English was to change, and the fifteenth-century language upon which the modern written language is based was a language of a central east Midland type.[6]

The reasons for this progressive change are to be sought not so much in the geographical position as in the social history of the capital. Even in Anglo-Saxon times, long before the Conquest, London had seemed to Bede 'a trading centre for many nations who visit it by land and sea'.[7] Its growth and importance as a mercantile centre increased after the Conquest, so that it became a magnet with the power to draw immigrants from the surrounding rural areas. By 1377, despite the fact that wealthy merchants could still hunt outside its walls, the city could boast a population of 40,000; considerably larger than that of the next largest cities – York and Bristol – put together.[8] If at first the need had been for craftsmen from the surrounding counties, the growing complexity of commerce and administration in the fourteenth century demanded the skills of literate men, of clerks, merchants and lawyers. Langland and Chaucer both deplore the tendency for village priests to desert their parishes and seek more lucrative employment in London; yet Langland himself was an immigrant from the west Midlands, and although Chaucer had been born in the city, his family had first entered the wine trade in Ipswich, and only later moved to London to contribute to its success there.

The immigration of literate men would naturally have a direct – but not necessarily lasting – influence on the written language of London texts and documents, but we must assume that the spoken language too was affected. The immigrants came seeking material success, and were associated with it. A feature of the behaviour of successful merchants served to strengthen this associative bond between success and recent immigration. Chambers and Daunt remark in a footnote upon the difficulty of tracing the genealogies of London families for more than three generations.[9] The reason for this is that the incomers either rapidly achieved success, became rich, and withdrew to lands usually close to their place of origin, or else they failed, and quickly sank into the anonymous mass of the population. If this is a true estimate of the situation it means that the prominence of any successful group within the city would be quite closely related to its recent arrival there, and that as a result the successful commercial and professional classes must normally contain a substantial proportion of

1270 – 1299

Map 2

1300 – 1329

Map 3

0 20 40
miles

Map 4

Maps 2, 3 and 4: Medieval Immigration into London, 1270–1359
(Northern counties only).

people whose linguistic habits distinguished them as much as
their obvious affluence.

Throughout the fourteenth century, then, the ranks of the
successful in London were constantly being replenished by
immigrants whose speech and writing proclaimed their
Midland or northern origin. Studies of names of a form like
John of Northampton, which indicate their places of origin,
show that in the early part of the century a substantial
proportion of this immigration was from East Anglia. As this
declined, it was supplemented from about 1350 by an influx
from the counties of Northamptonshire, Bedfordshire,

Huntingdon, and a growing number from Lincolnshire. Although there may well have been some conservative reaction against them as *parvenus*, it was inevitable that, whether by the social prestige which eventually attaches to material success, or simply by weight of numbers, their east Midland dialect gradually became the language of London.[10]

Chaucer, then, was born into a linguistic community which was not only marked by its *diversite* in terms of dialect forms, but which was undergoing rapid change as the result of immigration. All this is evident in fourteenth-century London manuscripts. But to what extent did this diversity extend to acceptable forms of the spoken language in Chaucer's circle? After all, from the point of view of the versifier in modern English, there is little to be gained from the choice of the two spellings *jail* and *gaol* because both rhyme with *nail*. It is important, therefore, that we should know whether pronunciation as well as spelling variants were available for Chaucer's use in versification.

Let us recall two of the variant spellings found in thirteenth-century London documents: *yse(n) ~ yren* and *man ~ men*. These two variations live on in the texts of London romances written down within two decades of Chaucer's birth, in both *Kyng Alisaunder* and in *Of Arthour and of Merlin*.[11] Their use in these two romances casts valuable light upon the linguistic situation of Chaucer and the manuscripts of his poetry. In the Laud manuscript of the former romance, rhymes upon *fen* (ll.4081–2) and *ken* (ll.4669–70) – the south-eastern form of the word *kin* – prove the existence of the plural *men* in the language of the original. Rhymes on *ten* (ll.1563–4) and *hem* (ll.389–90) prove the existence of this same form in the original language of *Arthur and Merlin*. But both romances also have rhymes which demonstrate the existence of the older London pronunciation, *man*, for the plural. The proof of this can be made by pointing to the repeated rhyme in *Arthur and Merlin* between *woman* (singular) and *men* (plural). The existence of this rhyme shows that despite the spelling the singular and plural could be pronounced identically in the poet's language. Was the rhyme on *men*, *man*, or *mon*? There is no Middle English evidence of a singular *men* or of a plural *mon*; therefore it appears that the rhyme must have been on *man*. This is confirmed by a series of rhymes and assonances in the two romances which point in the same direction: *can, wan, cam, nam, Ban* (proper name), and *Rokeingham*. In brief, in the language of these romances a variation of pronunciation is exploited for the purposes of rhyme.[12] The copyists, however, sometimes spoil the impression of good rhymes by substituting the later spelling *men* in instances where rhyme requires the pronunciation *man*.

It is evident from what has been said above that although two variants, *man* and *men*, existed in the language of the authors of the romances, they were not of strictly equivalent status: *man* is the older form which is destined to be ousted by the form *men* which had been brought into London by immigration. The innovating form tended to replace the older when the poems were copied into their existing manuscripts. This process is even more clearly apparent in the case of the variation *yse(n)* ~ *yren*. Here the copyists have used the innovating form *yren* within the line, except in a few poetic formulae in *Arthur and Merlin* – *ysen hatte* 'iron helm' (l.7114) and *ysen cheld* 'cold steel' (l.8829) – but have sometimes preserved the older form in rhyme: on *wise* (l.5140) and *marchaundise* (l.7064) in *Kyng Alisaunder*.

The case of the three forms of the present participle found in *Arthur and Merlin* is a combination of the circumstances found in the two examples just discussed. Rhyme analysis shows the original language of the poem to have had alternative forms of the present participle: *-inde* and *-ing* – *rideinde* rhymes on *bihinde* (ll.7163–4) and *þat rideing* on *biteing* (ll.3356–7). These are both southern or south-western variants. In copying, however, the scribe has substituted the northern and north-Midland *-ande*, but he has done so only within the line, so as to preserve the original rhymes.[13]

The diversity of the language evident in the Auchinleck manuscript of *Arthur and Merlin* and the Laud manuscript of *Kyng Alisaunder* illustrates for us two important facts to preface a discussion of variation in Chaucer. Firstly, that variation in pronunciation had long existed in the London language in the spoken as well as written mode, and that it had equally long been exploited by poets for rhyming purposes. Secondly, that the variation in the London language was a dynamic and not a static one: established variants were constantly being replaced by new forms, generally of Midland origin, and this process of replacement became enshrined in the copying history of London texts.

At this point it is as well to recall that we know Chaucer's language only from the evidence supplied by the early copyists of his poetry. In the prevailing linguistic circumstances we must presuppose that their manuscripts, made in the first decade or so after Chaucer's death, will contain more Midland and northern forms than he actually wrote. Some manuscripts of *Troilus and Criseyde*, for example, contain the form *them* where Corpus has *hem*, and it is probable that this latter is what Chaucer wrote.[14] The famous northern forms in the *Reeve's Tale* are more numerous in the Ellesmere manuscript than in Hengwrt, and, more significantly, the entire manuscript has a slightly increased number of northerly variants. Given a perceptible drift in the London language which ultimately changed its dialectal constitution, it will obviously be necessary when discussing the use Chaucer made of variation to distinguish, as far as possible, between the usage of the poet and the changes imposed by the copyists. Failure to do so may cause errors to arise by confusing the products of the contemporary linguistic situation with literary creativity. For example, if we examine Robinson's edition of Chaucer's works, it quickly becomes evident that it contains a peculiar distribution of the variants *yeve ~ yive* and *yit ~ yet*. Generally, *yive* and *yit* are employed as rhymes whereas *yeve* and *yet* are found in the line. It would be an easy assumption – and indeed one made by some early scholars – that Chaucer reserved certain forms for rhyme.[15] It might, furthermore, be tempting to claim poetic manipulation of these variants, as in these lines from the *Knight's Tale*, where it might seem that avoidance of exact repetition enhances the poetic effect:

> For I moot wepe and wayle, whil I lyve,
> With al the wo that prison may me yive,
> And eek with peyne that love me yeveth also.
>
> (A 1295–7; Robinson's text)

But such literary appreciation of Chaucer would be in vain, for in the Hengwrt manuscript line 1296 reads *yeue*, and is obviously a scribal modernisation of the original form rhyming on *lyue*. By the same token, it is probable that *yeveth* in line 1297 replaces an original *yiveth* in Chaucer's own language. This cannot be proved, but the probability arises from our knowledge of the general development of London English at this time and from the fact that, although Ellesmere carefully preserves the spelling in rhyme, both manuscripts use the innovatory *e*- spelling in the line, where rhyme is not affected. The analogy with the distribution of *yse(n)* ~ *yren* and the participles *-inde* and *-ande* in *Arthur and Merlin* is obvious.

The characteristics of the London language, and the conduct of scribes were repeatedly commented upon by Chaucer. The state of the language presented him with difficulties in composition, in particular in finding rhymes, and, at the same time, he feared the destruction of his efforts at the hands of the scribes. Yet matters could have been a great deal worse, for the language of London offered a unique range of grammatical and phonological variants which were potentially of great value to the versifier. The perennial struggle of the poet with his language is that of manipulating language so that he can, at one and the same time, communicate his complex meanings (without too many inappropriate ones) to an audience, whilst still observing the formal and metrical constraints he has voluntarily placed upon himself by his decision to write in verse. The verse line emerges from an interaction between the poet's intended meaning, the formal requirements of the structure of language, and those of the verse form he has chosen. None of these is absolute and fixed at the moment of creation, and the poet may decide to compromise any one of them in order to realise more fully his intentions for the others. However, it is normally the case – and from Chaucer's words in Book V of *Troilus and Criseyde* (see p. 108) we must assume that it was true for him – that meaning and verse form (which includes rhyme and metre) are more sacrosanct than observance of the typical syntactical structures of everyday speech. Now it is evident that, if the everyday language of a poet admits many variants in sound and structure, the achievement of his ends with regard to meaning and versification will be more easily accomplished. Variant grammatical patterns, such as those already seen in Chapters

1, 2 and 3, and flexibility in clause structure, will enable rhythmical patterns to be maintained with greater ease, without at the same time distorting the structure of ordinary language to the extent that meaning is threatened. The line, too, can be more easily re-cast to facilitate a rhyme, and, if rhymes are few, a selection of phonetically variant forms of a word will prove a great convenience. Thus, despite Chaucer's complaints about the 'skarsete of rhyme' in English, and his tendency to remedy it by the extensive use of French-derived rhyming pairs – as well as exploiting the variable stress of such borrowings – yet the London language greatly compensated him by the metrical possibilities which its variant forms offered him.

The fact that spoken variants – as distinct from those appearing in manuscripts as the result of re-copying – were available in the London language, and that they had been exploited by London poets of the generations before Chaucer, does not mean that he always employed these variants in consistent ways, or even that his own use of them inevitably implies a consciously artistic purpose. On some occasions, Chaucer must simply have used variants as a reflection of the everyday language of people around him.[16] The variant forms of the third-person plural of the verb 'to be' (*ben* ∼ *ar(e)* ∼ *arn*) all occur in the Hengwrt manuscript. Although of east Midland origin, *ben* is undoubtedly a form used by Chaucer, since it occurs in rhyme. The more northerly *ar-* forms are certainly used creatively in the *Reeve's Tale* as part of the speech of northern clerks, but they are also randomly scattered through his works. It is possible that they are of scribal origin, but it is more likely that both *ben* and *ar-* were forms used by Chaucer. Certain nouns, too, exhibit variation between *-(e)s* and *-(e)n* as their plural inflexion. Although the *-(e)n* plural is usually considered that common in the south and in early London, it was also widespread in the east Midlands as the plural of nouns whose stem ended in a vowel.[17] Hence we should not regard this variation as a simply southern-northern one in Chaucer's language. The proportion of the two forms varies between Chaucer manuscripts, but in Hengwrt is the following:

doughtren	4	*doghtres*	4
hosen	3	*hoses*	4
(typ)toon	2	*toos*	2
fleen	1	*flyes*	2
sustren	1	*sustres*	2
shoon	1	*shoes*	3
been	1	*bees*	4
foon	1	*foos*	7

Strangely, given the alleged paucity of English rhyme,[18] this type of variation is rarely used as a rhyming convenience: only the variants *toon ~ toos* are used for this purpose. In discussing Chaucer's use of variation, therefore, we should not exaggerate his exploitation of it, especially in rhymes. But the irony is that it is only in rhymes that we possess any method of distinguishing with absolute certainty which examples of variation are truly Chaucer's and which are the product of scribal re-copying after his death. Having sounded this warning, we may now go on to consider some examples of variation which were undoubtedly used by Chaucer: firstly those with metrical value, and secondly those used in rhyme.

The grammatical variation found in Middle English at all levels of description, from the variety available in clause structure to the alternative forms of inflexions, could prove very useful in versification, but might prove a liability to the transmission of that verse. Let us take as an example some of the variant forms of negation discussed in Chapter 3. In line 2322 of the *Knight's Tale*, the Hengwrt and Ellesmere manuscripts employ variant forms of negation. We have already decided (pp. 63–4) that this variation scarecely affects the meaning of the two lines, but nevertheless the choice between the two negators affects the way in which the lines scan:

Hg   And íf so bé thow wólt nóght do me gráce;
El   And if so be thou wolt do me no grace.

The Hengwrt line scans easily as an iambic pentameter with inversion in the fourth foot; the scansion of Ellesmere is very much less certain. The line might naturally be read with stress on *thou*, *no*, and *grace*, but although this would make good sense in a context which couples *thou* and *destynee*:

> And if so be thou wolt do me no grace
> And if my destynee be shapen so
> That I shal nedes haue oon of hem two   (A 2322–4)

the scansion would be extremely irregular. Any attempt to read the line as a regular iambic pentameter leads to the option of stressing either *do* or *me*, neither of which is satisfactory. The verb *do* is an auxiliary in a fixed phrase, and cannot sensibly be stressed; *me* can only receive emphasis when there is a possible contrast with some third party. There is no such contrast: Emelye has just asked for a favour from the goddess Diana (*thy grace*) and outlined what it is. She then raises the alternative, which in Hengwrt reads:

> And if so be thow wolt noght do me grace
> Or if my destynee be shape so
> That I shal nedes haue oon of hem two.

Here the emphases fall suitably upon the willingness of the goddess to grant the favour sought, and upon the alternative dictate of destiny. This maintains the essential topic of the passage as the interplay and frustration of wills; the coherence of this topic arising from the distribution of stresses determined by the choice of negator. It is not too much to say that the sense of the passage depends, through the metre, on the choice of negator. A similar example is to be found in the Wife's *Prologue*, where Hengwrt uses the contraction of the negator *ne* with the pronoun *I*, but Ellesmere has the uncontracted form:

Hg   Ny wólde nát of hým corrécted bé;
El   Ne Í wolde nát of hým corrécted bé.   (D 661)

The scansion suggested by Ellesmere detracts from the scornful emphasis on *hym* by matching it with stress on *I*. The result distracts attention from the Wife's onslaught upon her hapless husband by the implied comparison found in emphatic uses of the first-person pronoun.

The variation between single and double negation can also lead to discrepancies in scansion between manuscripts, as in a famous line from the description of the Knight:

Hg   Hise hórs weere goóde but hé ne wás nat gáy;
El   His hors weren goode but he was nat gay.   (A 74)

The line scans well in Hengwrt, where the stresses fall appropriately to maintain the importance of the contrast between the excellence of the Knight's equipment and the shabbiness of his own appearance. Scanning the Ellesmere line, however, is a much more uncertain business, which may bring this contrast into jeopardy. In such examples, scribal exercise of grammatical options has resulted in damage to both metre and sense. Similar effects often result from the variation found in the second-person plural form of the imperative, as in the following example from the *Shipman's Tale*:

> Allas, my nece, god forbede
> That ye for any sorwe or any drede
> Fordo your self. But telleth me youre grief.
> Parauenture I may in youre meschief
> Conseille or helpe, and therfore telleth me
> Al youre anoy for it shal been secree.   (B 1315–20)

The above passage is from the Hengwrt manuscript; in Ellesmere, line 1317 reads:

> Fordo youre self but tel me of youre grief.

The use of the monosyllabic form of the imperative, *tel*, and the compensating *of*, introduce ambiguity into the scansion. Does the line now have inversion in the fourth foot, or is it, like Hengwrt, a regular iambic pentameter? If the latter is the case, the pronoun *me* loses its stress. A glance at the context, in which the monk is so insistently offering himself as confidant, is enough to convince us of the need to retain the stress on *me*. Here, then, the variation exercised between copies results not so much in loss of meaning and metre, but a trap for the inattentive reader: Hengwrt is unambiguous, Ellesmere requires care.

The diversity of which Chaucer complained could evidently be destructive, even when a text was being copied by a relatively careful scribe, but we should not forget that it was this very diversity which had also offered to Chaucer the variant forms of expression which had enabled him to construct the lines in the first place. We must now consider some examples of Chaucer's creative exploitation of such variation, and we may begin by considering the forms of the infinitive.

As we saw in Chapter 1, the Chaucerian infinitive was extremely various. All forms of the infinitive could occur either with or without a final *n*. The plain infinitive (that is, without a preceding preposition) is the commonest form following an auxiliary, but in other infinitive uses the prepositions *to* and *for to* may precede the verb. We may consider some uses of these prepositional types in the *Knight's Tale*. At line 985, the narrator expresses his intention of dealing cursorily with his material: 'But shortly for to speken of this thyng'. The line is the normal decasyllabic line of the poem; but it is so only because Chaucer selected this particular form of the infinitive. A form without final *n* would have resulted in the elision of final -*e* before the following *o*, and the consequent loss of a syllable. A few lines later, the restless narrator expresses a similar sentiment again. Had he so wished, Chaucer could have made him use the same expression, but not without a certain uncolloquial awkwardness: a mechanistic association which would threaten the persona of the narrator as an autonomous literary creation. A variant expression is therefore used, and, in order to adapt it to the metrical requirements, a different form of the infinitive is found: 'But shortly for to telle is myn entente' (1.1000). The rhythm of the lines is similar, but elision, resulting from the use of an *n*-less infinitive, preserves the proper syllable count in the line.

The phrase *shortly for to telle* is interesting, since, with *soothly for to telle/seye*, it appears to represent a Chaucerian idiom which is subject to significant variation. In these phrases, after the adverb formed with -*ly*, the *for to* infinitive is almost always chosen. However, after the monosyllabic noun *sooth*, the form *to telle* is the commoner.

Right as the Friday soothly for to telle;   (A 1534)
From which it is diryued sooth to telle.   (A 3038)

The reason for this is obviously metrical: both the phrases, in the forms quoted, are metrically regular. This general rule about the usage of these phrases is not absolute, but there are usually clear metrical reasons for breaking it, as in the following:

And shortly to concluden, swich a place;   (A 1895)
To tellen shortly the conclusioun.   (G 394)

This feature of his usage is not present in Chaucer's prose, so that we may assume that it developed as a metrical convenience. Nevertheless, it would be a mistake to view this too mechanically, to see Chaucer selecting one or other variant, as a computer might, when the serial development of the line came to the moment of decision. He seems, rather, to have carried with him two variant infinitive formulae (*adverb in -ly* + *for to infinitive* and *noun* + *to infinitive*), neither of which are to be considered as invariant 'block language'. Indeed, the use of the adverb can trigger the *for to* infinitive even when the two are widely separated:

But shortly forth this matere for to chace.   (E 341)

Nevertheless, they seem to be poetic schemata, and we should expect conscious modification only where the established pattern of their usage is broken, as in the following example, where the use of the *for to* form would have upset the rhythm:

That whan that oon was deed soothly to telle.   (A 1199)

The past participle also offered considerable variation to Chaucer. It exists in two forms: that of weak verbs ending in *-ed* or *-t,* and that of strong verbs in *-(e)n*, or, after the loss of *n,* in *e* alone. Both the strong and weak forms may also be marked by the use of the prefix *y-*. The dialectal affinities of these various forms to be found in the language of London can be shown by a diagram. Here Southern English (SE) is understood to include the thirteenth-century London language:

	STRONG	WEAK
East Midlands	*comen*	*clept, nempned*
Southern English	*ycome*	*yclept, inempned*
Chaucer	*come(n)*	*clept, nempned*
	ycome(n)	*yclept, ynempned*

There is no purpose in illustrating at length the use of the variant inflexional forms of the strong past participle, since the presence or absence of *n* operates metrically in exactly the same way as in the infinitive. But the use of the prefix deserves comment. The rhythm of the following two lines depends upon the selection of particular forms of the past participle, in company with an equally careful choice of the infinitive form in the first line:

> Neyther to been yburyed nor ybrent;   (A 946)
> For which thow art ybounden as a knyght.   (A 1149)

The importance for the metre of the forms used is best illustrated by imagining the first of these lines re-written by a northern scribe, when *been* would lose its final *n*, and the participles would lose their prefixes. If a Kentish scribe were to re-write the second line, the participle *ybounden* would lose its *n*, and would consequently be elided with the following *as*, once again ruining the metre. Finally, it might be noticed that very frequently both infinitive and past participle occur at the end of the line, and indeed often rhyme together. This was a possible rhyme-technique in the east Midlands, but in southern Middle English, where the past participle lacked final *-n*, such rhymes would have been impossible. In the following couplet, which demonstrates the dialectally-mixed nature of Chaucer's language, neither east Midland (*yeuen*) nor southern (*iyiue*) could have provided this rhyme:

> She seyde: 'Lord, to whom fortune hath yiuen
> Victorie and as a conquerour to lyuen.   (A 915–16)

The third person singular, present tense of the verb in Chaucer is ordinarily in -*eth*, but also fairly commonly in -*t*. This latter ending is found with verbs whose stem ends in a *t* or *d*. In the east Midlands, however, even such verbs would normally preserve the full -*eth* ending, as did their antecedent forms in Anglian Old English. In Old English, in the Saxon dialects, the *e* was syncopated, and the remaining þ became assimilated to the *t* or *d* of the stem. Since the dialect of Essex was the foundation of the earliest London language, these assimilated forms were found also in early London. By Chaucer's time, however, the familiar variation between early London and innovatory Midland forms had appeared, resulting in a series of variants: *fint* ∼ *findeth*; *bint* ∼ *bindeth*; *rit* ∼ *rideth*. We have already discussed these, along with line 981 of the *Knight's Tale*, when discussing grammar and the uses of the historic present. It is, however, perhaps worth emphasising that such a line as:

> Thus ryt this duc thus ryt this conquerour

would have been impossible for a poet of the east Midlands, since it depends upon the use of the originally Saxon form of the third person. Line 1691, which is equally a Chaucerian line, would, however, have seemed natural to such a Midland poet:

> And to the launde he rideth hym ful right.

Chaucer is, once again, able to exploit an originally dialectal variation, present as the result of London's social history, to write lines which would have been denied to a provincial poet.

If Chaucer was concerned at the effects of grammatical variation upon the metre of his *Troilus* when it fell into the hands of the copyists, in the act of composition he claims to have been tormented by a paucity of rhymes in English. These remarks about rhyme and metre are worth our attention, since they imply a concern with achieving a certain standard in these respects, presumably to be understood as regularity of metre and purity of rhyme. Although this is an automatic assumption for us, since our traditional attitude to rhyme is that it should be exact, it is by no means obvious that Chaucer should have shared this perspective. Indeed, in the London romances copied a decade before his birth, half-rhymes and assonantal rhymes seem to have been common.[19] Whether they were fully accepted, or regarded as makeshift devices for a difficult linguistic situation, it is impossible to tell. It may well be, however, that Chaucer's concern with rhyme represented his conception of one feature in which his poetry differed from and was superior to that poetry which had preceded him. The value placed on exact rhyme is suggested by the attention paid to spelling in some Chaucer manuscripts. In cases where variant spellings for a particular single sound exist, the possibility of matching the spellings in rhyme is nearly always exercised: thus *gras* rhymes with *pas*, but *grace* with *space*. The spelling parallelism is apparently meant to complement the audible rhyme. Now eye-rhyme of this kind is also found in earlier London works such as the romances of the *Kyng Alisaunder* group, but it is found much less consistently than in Chaucer manuscripts. In the former group as many as one in five exact rhymes lack matching spellings, whereas in the Hengwrt and Ellesmere manuscripts the figure is closer to one in twenty.[20] However, not all Chaucer manuscripts are so careful as these two, and indeed the scribe altered his methods slightly between copying them, but it is evident that Chaucer copyists were more aware of the importance of exact rhymes than those of two generations before, and it may be that Chaucer himself emphasised his interest in rhyme by using parallel spellings.

The implication of all this is that Chaucer, wherever possible, strove to use exact rhyme, and the phonological variants present in London English should have been of value to him in this. And indeed they were, but the extent to which they were is worth considering. The variation between *i* and *e* as the descendants of the West Saxon *y*, although used in many rhymes, is by no means fully exploited. The following words, for example, are used only in their south-eastern forms: *shette*, *berien*, *dent*, *melle*, *sherte*, *steren*. Others are used only in their east Midland form: *hille*, *clifte*, *mirthe*, *birthe*, *wirchen*, *wirdes*, *hirdes*, *kinde*.[21] The reason for Chaucer's failure to use the first word in each list may be obvious: indeed all except the earliest London documents avoid the form *helle*, although it was used in its plural form by the Kentishman, Gower. But unintentional comic effects by the inappropriate invocation of taboo subjects do not account for Chaucer's failure to exploit the variation theoretically available in other forms.[22] It is possible that his choice of variant was in fact dictated by associations of the particular forms – possibly associations of provinciality – which we can no longer recognise.

In his earlier works, such as the *Book of the Duchess* and the *House of Fame*, Chaucer uses rhyme-forms which he later abandons: *elles: it telles* (*BD* 73); *al that fallys: hallys* (BD 257); *ellis: the booke tellis* (*HF* 426); *thou . . . bringes: tydynges* (*HF* 1908). The verbal inflexions, variously spelt *-es*, *-is*, and *-ys* by the scribe of the Fairfax MS, are usually considered to be northern forms sought by the youthful Chaucer to eke out a scarcity of rhyme. This northern inflexion is used later by Chaucer in the *Reeve's Tale* to add local colour to the speech of the students. But it is odd that Chaucer should have been driven to use rhyme forms from an outlandish dialect when the very rarity of them in his work as a whole suggests that he preferred to avoid them. The truth of the matter may perhaps be that the use of second and third-person singular forms in *-s* was not considered by Chaucer as exotically northern, but rather that they were variants in London speech to be heard around him. These inflexional forms are in fact common in the Auchinleck romances, copied in the decade before Chaucer's birth, and indeed they occur there in rhyme.[23] Whatever the origin of these early London *-s* inflexions, Chaucer renounced them in his later works, and indeed such forms were among those proscribed by the reviser of the manuscript of the *Mirror*.[24] The use of similar forms in the context of an imitation of northern speech in the *Reeve's Tale* is an entirely different matter. The *-s* rhymes in the early poems may belong rather to a group of linguistic usages, such as pronunciations of the word 'street' with a long *a*, the form *yse*, or the plural *man*, which had vanished or were in the process of vanishing from upper-class speech when Chaucer began his literary career. Occasionally a development of this sort can be recognised within Chaucer's output: for example, the Midland form *knitte* gradually replaces the earlier London form *knette* as we proceed through the chronology of Chaucer's works. From this it is apparent that a phonological treatment of variants in Chaucer's language would be a difficult and major project, since variation must be studied at the level of individual words. In Gilliéron's famous phrase 'each word has its own history'. That history is rarely recoverable and its effects may be inconsistent and enigmatic. We can, however, as an example of the exploitation of variants in rhyme, provide a list dependent upon the variation we have discussed above between Midlands *i*, south-eastern *e*, and west Midlands *u*:

myrie ~ *mury* ~ *mery*	*synne* ~ *senne*
fille ~ *felle*	*thynne* ~ *thenne*
knitte ~ *knette*	*stynt* ~ *stente*
fyr ~ *feere*	*thynke* ~ *thenche*
liste ~ *leste*	*kille* ~ *quelle*
kisse ~ *kesse*	*triste* ~ *truste*
kyn ~ *ken*	*abye* ~ *abeye* ~ *abegge*

Of these variants used in rhyme, only six are extensively used for this purpose: *mury* ~ *mery*; *knitte* ~ *knette*; *fyr* ~ *feere*; *liste* ~ *leste*; *kisse* ~ *kesse*; *triste* ~ *truste*.

Only in the case of a few words can we suggest reasons why Chaucer might have avoided exploiting variation in rhyme, but it is certain that the variability and flexibility of grammar and syntax was an aid to him in this. Another aspect of this question, which we have not previously considered, is to do with the effect of verse form. It is noticeable, for instance, that Chaucer is compelled to seek unusual rhyming variants more often in poems like the *Parliament of Fowls* or *Troilus and Criseyde*, where the stanza form requires more than a pair of rhyming words. Thus in *Mars*, we find the rhyme scheme *besette*: *hette*: *lette*: *knette*, and in *Parliament of Fowls*, *tercelet*: *lette*: *knette*, both dependent upon the south-eastern *knette*. A few other examples will suffice to give an idea of Chaucer's creative use of variants: in *Troilus and Criseyde* (III 978) he selects the uncommon south-eastern variant *feere* to complete rhymes with *heere* and *deere*. In the same book, at line 510, the unique use of the form *fulfelle* occurs to achieve a rhyme on *telle*, and the sole use of south-eastern *ken* furnishes a rhyme on *ten* in *Book of the*

Duchess (438). The commonest form of the preterite of the verb 'to kiss' is the Midland one *kiste*, but a south-eastern form, *keste*, is employed to rhyme with *reste* and *leste* at *Troilus and Criseyde* (III 1129).

Poems like these, which require multiple rhymes, place demands upon the poet and his language which perhaps justify Chaucer's exasperation about the scarcity of rhyme encountered in English. But many of the Canterbury tales, and both the *Book of the Duchess* and *House of Fame* are written in couplets, and here the pressures cannot have been so great. Moreover, couplets had been the form of the earlier London romances, so that it is possible that tradition had rhymes to suggest to Chaucer when writing in this form. The romance tradition often used highly predictable rhymes, and indeed there is some evidence to show that Chaucer was not above lightening his load by employing formulaic rhyme schemes. Some of these are identical to those of the romance writers, others are apparently personal habits of rhyming. Just as he developed grammatical and metrical formulae, such as *sooth to seye* and *soothly for to seye*, so he also had a number of preferred couplet rhymes. The word *fulfille* occurs ten times in rhyme in Chaucer's works, and on seven occasions the rhyme is upon *wille*. The form *fille* rhymes on *wille* in four out of five occurrences in rhyme. Similarly the word *(for)yiue(n)*, which occurs in rhyme twenty-five times, rhymes on *liue(n)* on twenty of these occasions. Its only other rhymes are on *yshryue* and *dryuen*.

Further analysis would show that over a large number of common words Chaucer has rather a restricted range of habitual rhymes. However, accepting the existence of such habitual rhyming, we must acknowledge that he frequently extends his range beyond these, and also beyond the abilities of the earlier authors of romance. A comparison between Chaucer's practice and that of two early London romances, *Arthur and Merlin* and *Kyng Alisaunder*, is instructive in this respect. There are more than ninety occurrences of the word *knight* in rhyme in Chaucer's works. Of these, rhymes on *might* account for 32, on *wight* for 22, *night* (9), *right* (8), *bright* (5). A whole range of others occur on three occasions or less: *flyght*, *alight*, *hight*, *bihight*, *sight*, *to-night*, *aright*, *light*, *upright*, *(y)plight*, *twight*, and *fourtenyght*. Fig. 2 illustrates the relationship of Chaucer's practice to that of the romances:

Fig. 2

Kyng Alisaunder

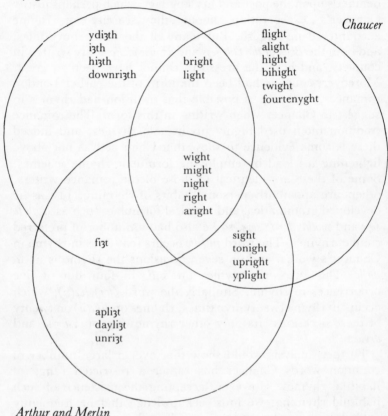

Chaucer

ydiȝth
iȝth
hiȝth
downriȝth

bright
light

flight
alight
hight
bihight
twight
fourtenyght

wight
might
night
right
aright

fiȝt

sight
tonight
upright
yplight

apliȝt
dayliȝt
unriȝt

Arthur and Merlin

In descending order of frequency, the commonest rhymes in *Kyng Alisaunder* are: *wi*ȝ*th*; *fi*ȝ*th*; *ri*ȝ*th/mi*ȝ*th*. In *Arthur and Merlin*, they are: *fi*ȝ*t*; *ri*ȝ*t*; *wi*ȝ*t*. It is at once apparent that the central core of Chaucer's rhyming on *knight* is not only habitual but traditional. His commonest rhymes – with the exception of *night* – are the commonest rhymes of the romances also, and he shares all his commonest rhymes with both the romances. The exception, the adjective *bright*, which he shares only with *Kyng Alisaunder*, is nevertheless used in a traditional way, for it occurs in Chaucer only in the phrase *lady bright*, itself a formulaic one of popular romance.

Although it must be admitted that Chaucer's rhyming practice in this case depends heavily upon romance tradition, two special features are notable. Firstly, his individual rhyming has a rather wider range than that of the authors of romance, and secondly he totally omits what is perhaps the commonest rhyming pair in the entire romance tradition, the rhyme between *knight* and *fight*. Although this omission may be in part dependent upon Chaucer's subject matter, one is nevertheless tempted to assume that its complete absence may owe something to his perception of it as a hackneyed rhyme.

In the complicated balancing act which the poet has to maintain between rhyme, metre, and meaning, there is no doubt that Chaucer placed most emphasis upon meaning. Yet it is difficult to make general statements about his inconsistent practice. Although he was content to leave some rhymes imperfect, and some of his lines defy regular analysis, there are contradictory signs that he was concerned about purity of rhyme and regularity of metre. Although he was often content to employ familiar and traditional rhymes, there is also evidence of resourcefulness in seeking unusual rhymes, as well as of avoiding rhymes which might have proved unacceptable to his audience. Among variants, the evidence is that a choice was made not according to any generalised dialectal criteria, but rather according to the individual associations of each word or its form. The selection of variants in rhyme, then, depended on their availability in London speech, their acceptability in terms of their social or other associations, and upon the pressure of rhyming needs. Rather than exploit variants in pronunciation to their extreme limits, Chaucer, on the whole, preferred to capitalise on the amount of variation possible both in syntactical structure and in the morphology of words. Variety in the means of expression helped not only in preserving a great degree of metrical regularity, but also in avoiding excessive flamboyance in rhyming technique. For a narrative poet, the London language offered variant forms in just those places where they could be most useful. The preterite and the present tenses were largely interchangeable in narrative, and the third-person singular of the latter had monosyllabic or disyllabic forms. Contracted negatives like *nolde*, *noot*, *nere* also provided monosyllabic or reduced alternatives to their fuller expression, as did assimilations like *atte laste*, and elisions like *th'effect*. Variation in the infinitive meant that compound tenses too were capable of presenting various metrical shapes, and the past tense was variable in the third-person plural, not only as a result of the various forms of the past participle, but also because of the variation *han~have* found in the auxiliary. Although strictly outside the purview of the diversity of English, Chaucer's familiarity with French added other variation in the forms of words whose variable stressing (either original French stressing or modified English) also served to reduce the necessity of using stigmatised English variants.

In conclusion, then, we can say that, just as London provided Chaucer with an audience for sophisticated poetry in English, so it also furnished him with the medium in which to compose it. The unique linguistic mixture of fourteenth-century London, with its range of variant English forms, its tradition of the exploitation of such variants in literature, and the subordination of language and literature to a higher culture, represented by French, all combined to give Chaucer the historical moment and the material from which to weave original poetry. He did this by blending the English and French traditions he found, and by making an individual language amalgamated from a selection of variants found in London English, made elegant by borrowings from French. This latter aspect, which is best illustrated by an examination of his vocabulary, will be considered in the next chapter.

6   Chaucer's Vocabulary

The mere size of an author's vocabulary is likely to tell us very little of value in assessing or understanding his work. Nevertheless, it is a statistic which has a perennial fascination. Scholars of the last generation repeatedly computed it for various authors, and their results are certain of incorporation into any student's lecture notes. In fact, of course, precise comparative statistics are not usually available because the size of an author's vocabulary depends essentially on the definition of 'word' adopted by the statistician. For example, do the three Chaucerian forms *syngen, syngynge,* and *song* represent three separate items of his vocabulary, or are they merely the differing grammatical representatives of a single item? A decision of this kind will, when repeated hundreds of times, greatly influence the final tally. Are proper nouns and variant spellings also to be included? Gower's vocabulary, estimated at a remarkably precise 6006 items, falls drastically to 4648 when variants and proper names are excluded.[1] Acknowleding such uncertainties, it has been estimated that Chaucer's vocabulary is approximately twice that of Gower, that it equals that of the Authorised Version of the Bible, but is only one-third of that wielded by Shakespeare.[2] The naïve assumption that literary greatness goes hand in hand with an extensive vocabulary is fostered by the fact that it is largely prominent authors who are selected for investigation; but it is probable that a count of Lydgate's words would show him to be Chaucer's equal in copiousness, even though his critical reputation is much more modest. Certainly the extent of the corpus of an author's works as well as the variety of his subject matter have a more direct effect on vocabulary size than any abstract notion of literary quality.

Nevertheless, concern among Englishmen to expand their vocabulary is not new. Even in Old English an extensive vocabulary was valued and referred to as a treasury to be unlocked in speech.[3] Indeed, the adroit use of an extensive vocabulary, which is implied by the word 'eloquence', has been considered to be indicative of wisdom from Classical times, through the Middle Ages, into the Renaissance; and may be traced today in the assumed desirability of the promise of *The Reader's Digest* to 'increase your word power'. In the later Middle Ages the cultivated man, the man who knew *curtesie*, may be described as *wel-seyinge* and *full of wordes*, and although this linguistic adroitness may be morally ambiguous it was a possession to be prized by all men of the world.[4]

The co-existence of French and English as the twin vernacular languages of England after the Conquest was a very unequal one. Since the ideals of social behaviour were drawn from France, so the French language was associated with social elevation, and French words and phrases were thought to give elegance to English expression. For Chaucer, living on the fringes of the court, and involved in legal and administrative work, the pressures encouraging him to exploit the resources of that language would have been considerable. It may be that the adoption of French words or phrases was occasionally a communicative necessity for him, but much more often it would be truer to see that adoption as socially-motivated.[5] A poet was judged by his art, but equally he was judged by the social acceptability of his verse, by his own *curtesie* reflected in it; and this imposed the need to employ a French-influenced vocabulary. Even among the London romances of the generations before Chaucer we find aspirations to literary seriousness and social acceptance, and a liberal sprinkling of the text with French phrases like: *ioe vus di*; *gramercy*; *Dieu me saut*; *fiȝ a putain*; *a male eys*; *Ore tost a ly a ly*; *Jeo crey ben*.[6] In Chaucerian manuscripts, too, such phrases are used, and tend to perplex the modern editor, who must decide whether to italicise as foreign quotations such phrases as: *ma foy*, *madame*, *paramour*, *parchance*, *temps*.[7]

This dilemma represents an important distinction to be made in Chaucer's vocabulary. But it also raises the further problem of whether it is a distinction which can in fact be made with any confidence, for it is apparent that a simple etymological distinction between words of French and English origin would be a misrepresentation of the way in which Chaucer's compatriots would perceive their language. At the least, we must distinguish between established French borrowings, which have become incorporated into the common core of the language, and those which are new and are still felt as foreign. Statistical statements to the effect that Chaucer's vocabulary contains 51.8 per cent of Romance loan words are of little use in assessing Chaucerian style, and indeed simply ignore the crucial factor of the contemporary perception of the status of the words.[8]

In fact, we can be fairly confident that early Anglo-Norman borrowings, which are often distinguishable by their forms, like *castel*, *prisoun*, *daunce*, *werre* 'war', would attract no attention in an English context; neither would phrases like *have mercy* or even *grant mercy*. Such words and phrases had become part of the everyday expression of English through long and frequent usage. A lesson may be learnt from the *Parson's Tale* (869), where, speaking of the Latin *fructus*, Chaucer tells us that the English word is *fruyt*. Similarly, in the *Second Nun's Tale*, we are told that the Greek *leos* is *peple* in English.[9] Etymologically, of course, both *fruyt* and *peple* are French borrowings which had become established in English usage. Clearly, as students of language, we must be wary of imposing our own linguistic insights upon the actual users of the languages we study. No doubt, if questioned, Chaucer might have assented that both words were also French, but their familiarity in English contexts made them a part of English usage for him and his audience. It is evident from this, that, in assessing Chaucer's vocabulary, degree of familiarity and frequency of use are more important than etymological origins, and we may well find that Chaucer and his contemporaries included much within their competence which we should be ready to consider foreign, and which an editor might therefore italicise.

The co-existence of two languages in the everyday life of Chaucer's circle would inevitably lead to a certain 'fuzziness' in the demarcation between their two language skills. English was regarded as shifting and various, and the extent of its resources was uncertain; French was often written, at least in technical fields, with a phrasing and syntax owing much to English, whereas English had long ago adopted many of the phrasal idioms of French.[10] In the minds of men with bilingual competence, the boundaries of the languages would be particularly ill-defined, and the elevation of English style, for them, would most naturally be achieved by the importation into it of the words and expressions of prestigious French. If words were meant to be noticed, they must be unusual or technical, and it is in these words, meant largely for display purposes, that we can most easily be certain of deliberately new borrowings.

There is little doubt that the ability to use complicated words of Latin, French or even Italian origin was considered by Chaucer, his contemporaries, and more notoriously his fifteenth-century successors, to add dignity and ceremony to literary composition. Neologisms had been sanctioned for such a purpose by early writers on poetics, and indeed Horace himself had allowed their sparing use, declaring that they would find acceptance if drawn from a Greek source.[11] Although Chaucer expresses no awareness of this as a deliberate literary technique, his practice is culturally analogous to that suggested by Horace: for him, the Romance languages occupied the prestigious role filled for Horace by Greek, and with differing degrees of evident consciousness, he introduced many new words into his poetry.

A word of warning is perhaps necessary here: in order to avoid an excessively simplified interpretation of the phrase 'new word', it must be emphasised that this phrase must be constructed as meaning 'new to, or rare in, contemporary written English'. It is impossible to determine how long words have had currency in speech, but, repeatedly, Chaucer seems to have acknowledged that such words would not have been familiar to his audience, and offers a gloss rather in the manner in which earlier English writers in the thirteenth century had glossed words which later became common:

> And but if Calkas lede us with ambages,
> That is to seyn with double wordes slye,

Swich as men clepen a word with two wisages,
3e shal wel knowen that I naught ne lie.

(*TC* V 897–900)

The word *ambages* in the above quotation is here first recorded
in English, and it is not again recorded until the sixteenth
century. Chaucer's immediate source must have been *Il
Filostrato* (VI, 17, 3), but it is hardly likely that it would have
been borrowed so readily had conditions not been receptive.
The word occurs in medieval Latin also, both in the
encyclopaedia of Isidore of Seville and in a thirteenth-century
dictionary where it is understood to mean a complicated
expression of uncertain significance.[12] In contemporary French
it meant 'circuitous or deceitful speech', and Chaucer indeed
seems to associate it with deliberate ambiguity.

Ambiguity is of particular interest to Chaucer, and both
Gower and he refer to 'double wordes' which form part of the
irresponsible use of rhetoric. The narrator in *Troilus and
Criseyde* commends Pandarus to Janus, the two-faced god,
when he sets out to practise the arts of persuasion on his niece
in Book II. A similar concern with deliberate ambiguity is the
occasion of the introduction of a second new word rather
earlier in *Troilus and Criseyde*:

. . . and beren hym on honde
He hath nat wel the goddes understonde;
For goddes speken in amphibologies
And for a sooth they tellen twenty lyes.

(IV 1404–7; Robinson's text)

The consistency of Chaucer's attitude to the pagan deities can
be gauged by his treatment of their pronouncements elsewhere
in his works; in, for example, the *Merchant's Tale*, and more
especially, in the *Knight's Tale*. The ironic promise of Mercury
to Arcite that at Athens he will find an end to his sorrows is an
excellent example of a divine *amphibology*. Perhaps for the very
reason that his attitude to the casuistry of the gods is so
consistent, Chaucer does not explain the meaning of
amphibology, but contents himself with the simple statement of
the god's deceit. Whatever the reason, the word itself is here

recorded in English for the first time. As with the previous word, and with other such technical words, it is impossible to be sure whether Chaucer first encountered it in French or Latin. This word occurs in the advanced Latin grammar of Alexander of Villa Dei, but, because of the linguistic history of English education and scholarship, even direct borrowing from Latin could result in a word adopting a French appearance. At any rate, Chaucer's use of the word matches very well the sense given by Alexander's *Doctrinale*, which is that of a construction from which two distinct senses might be derived.[13] The rhetorical tradition, in which these words were discussed in relation to the interpretation of legal documents, may point to the kind of milieu in which Chaucer became familiar both with the concept of interpretative ambiguity and also the words by which to denote it. There is historical evidence to suggest that he was familiar with many men who had had legal training. Hence, although *ambages* is borrowed from Italian at a particular point in a translation of *Il Filostrato*, *amphibologies* is a Chaucerian addition to that text, springing from a prior familiarity with the concept involved.[14] The idea of verbal 'newness' must be treated with caution.

The sources of the word *urne* are also uncertain:

> The poudre in which myn herte ybrend shal torne
> That preye I the thow take and it conserue
> In a vessell that men clepeth an vrne
> Of gold . . .   (*TC* V 309–12)

Chaucer seems to have felt it necessary to explain the sense of the word *urne* and its meaning in Trojan funeral customs. It seems, indeed, to have been a rare word, for although Lydgate seized upon the phrase *urne of gold*, according to the *OED* the word did not gain general currency until the mid-seventeenth century. In this same conceptual area, however, Lydgate certainly knew the word *palestral* (athletic) and uses both the noun *palestre* and the adjective *funeral* repeatedly in his *Troy Book*. Both are words first recorded in Chaucer, which seem to have been adopted from his sources in Boccaccio, but which may have been previously known to him from French or Latin sources. It is indeed a marked feature of both Chaucer and

Gower, as well as of their follower, Lydgate, that they sought both the inspiration for their stories and the elevation of their styles by recourse to classical sources, direct or otherwise; and it is significant that in the Middle English period they are among the very few recorded users of classical-mythological words like *nymphe, amadriad,* and *faun.*[15] All three offer their own explanations of the meaning of this last word, demonstrating their conscious awareness of introducing new classical material and linguistic elevation into English; and indeed, of their efforts to join themselves, writing in English as they were, to the great tradition of western literature.

If Chaucer was ready to import new French, Latin and Italian loan words in order to lend grandeur to his diction and proclaim his erudition, he was also ready to employ words of a far less estimable kind in the cause of stylistic propriety; and he makes it very clear that in using them stylistic propriety alone is his motive.[16] They are words of an outlandish dialect, as in the *Reeve's Tale,* or words which have become old-fashioned, and would consequently have been shunned by a practitioner of courtly literature except for a specific stylistic purpose. Outstanding among this latter group is the word *hende* 'gentle, polite, courteous', for in the case of this word it may seem that a restriction in its usage developed in the course of his poetic career. If Fragment A of the *Romaunt of the Rose* is truly Chaucer's work, the two uses of *hende* to be found there are the only uses of the word in an undeniably courtly context and as a term of unqualified praise. Notoriously, it is used as a fixed epithet for Nicholas, the knowing clerk of the *Miller's Tale.* Nicholas's range of skills include astrology, singing, weather-forecasting, and those of *deerne loue,* but we might hesitate to call him kind and courteous. Indeed, he is courteous only to the extent that it will advance his cause as a lover; his rival Absolon, on the other hand, goes through all the procedures of courteous wooing, but fares less well. If *hende* is glossed here in the sense of 'knowing' (*MED,* 3a) rather than 'courteous' we shall have a better idea of its general significance for Chaucer. Even in the two uses in the *Romaunt,* it translates French phrases which imply skill and knowledge of the external forms of courtliness, and, furthermore, Chaucer uses the word outside that work almost exclusively to refer to clerks, and in the context of love: to Nicholas and to 'This joly clerk, Jankyn, that was so hende' in the *Wife of Bath's Tale* (628). In the French *fabliaux*, and in the popular lyrics, clerks are notorious for their knowledge of *deerne loue*, so that it begins to appear that Chaucer's usage has been affected by this fact.[17] The only example of its use outside this context in the later works is in the Host's exhortation to the Friar to be 'hende and curteys' (D 1286), which is a call for courtesy and consideration made in the bluff and direct way typical of Harry Baily. Evidently the word *hende* has become for Chaucer, and probably also for Gower, a word not to be used seriously in elevated discourse, nor by people of high rank, nor by those whose urbanity is meant to attract our admiration. It seems instead to represent a kind of *savoir faire*, an astuteness in social relationships, fallen below the level of the socially elect. In the usage of Harry Baily, it may have associations of would-be gentility, of social aspirations which had become dated, and therefore scorned. That the word had become *déclassé* is suggested by the fact that it is so only in the limited circle of courtly London poets; provincial authors still used it widely and unblushingly in romances and in lyrics, and it had been common enough in London romances of the generation before Chaucer. Clearly, it had not disappeared from London speech, but its days were numbered as the result of its rejection by the language of courtesy.

The case of *hende* is matched by a number of other words which show a curiously restricted distribution in Chaucer's works, mostly limited to what appears to be deliberate literary parody in the *Miller's Tale* and *Sir Thopas* (see p. 197). *Hende* and most of the others are of Old English derivation, but etymology is no sure guide to whether a word will be regarded by Chaucer as *demodé* and *declassé*. Indeed, some of the French-derived personal names which had been adopted by the peasantry in the previous century were equally lacking in elevation. *Robyn, Perkyn, Alisoun, Jille, Jankyn*, and perhaps also *Roger*, are the names of characters within the *fabliau* tradition, and would be improbable as the names of courtly characters. *Jankyn* is as much to be associated with clerks as *hende*, and a likely name for the clerk's mistress is *Alisoun*. Certain French-derived words used in the *Romaunt of the Rose* have also undergone a social debacle parallel to that of *hende*. The word *drurye*, for example, used in the *Romaunt of the Rose* (844) to mean 'affection', is a word common in Old French romance, where it can signify not only love between the sexes, but also companionship between knights. But already in the twelfth-century Norman of Béroul it could be associated with a pejorative view of sexual love.[18] In Middle English its connotations are not necessarily bad, but it refers overwhelmingly to love between the sexes and is susceptible to morally hostile interpretation. Its frequency in popular romance encourages Chaucer to use it in the compound *loue-drurye* in *Sir Thopas*, but he uses it nowhere else. It is evidently a part of that diction which he judged to have fallen into disrepute.

Similarly, the words *fetys* and *tretys* show a peculiar distribution in the Chaucer corpus. Outside the *Romaunt*, the latter is used only in the *General Prologue* description of the Prioress. The former, and the adverb *fetisly*, are used repeatedly in the *Romaunt* as approving epithets of the courtly personifications found there. Outside the *Romaunt*, they are words of the *fabliau* tales: Nicholas's chamber is *fetysly ydight* (A 3205); Absolon's hose (A 3319) and Perkyn's hair (A 4369) attract the same epithet, as does the Summoner's writing instrument, his *poyntel* (B 1742). In the *General Prologue* the word describes the Merchant's boots, and Prioress's cloak, and, in a strikingly unusual collocation, her speech. Here, in the description of the Prioress it forms one of a group of related words and expressions which serve to associate her with the heroines of romance and the prescriptions of courtesy books. The word *coy*, also, as Lowes and others have pointed out, except for a couple of references to men as 'coy as a mayde', is used outside the *Romaunt of the Rose* only of the Prioress.[19] Now the picture of the Prioress given in the *General Prologue* is rather more acerbic than is usually allowed. She is not described with admiration or sentiment as the epitome of old-world courtesy, but rather the description focuses upon her strivings to achieve the doubtful distinction of a rather dated ideal of behaviour. Her efforts to imitate what she perceives of the behaviour of the court; her manners learnt from courtesy books; her use of French whose associations are aristocratic but whose pronunciation is dire; these are the aspects which are stressed. They are compounded by misplaced *pitee*, substituting sentimentality for small animals for charity towards mankind.

If Chaucer sees the Prioress as a social aspirant of *bourgeoise* origin who has an imperfect grasp of the ideals with which she would like to be associated, and whose moral sense is dubious, then his choice of inappropriate and outdated courtly language to describe her may seem to reflect his view.

Alongside the language of popular poetry used in the *Miller's Tale*, most of which is of Old English derivation, there is, then, a section of Chaucer's vocabulary consisting of French-derived words once used in courtly contexts, but since declined into socially-ironic use.[20] Such words can often be recognised by their occurrence in courtly contexts in the *Romaunt of the Rose* and their subsequent restriction to *fabliau* tales, their use for reference to low characters, or their exploitation for literary parody, as in *Sir Thopas*. Into this category must fall *tretys*, *fetys*, *coy*, and *gent*. Such words, which seem to have been destined to evoke a smile from Chaucer's original audience, had become intrinsically ironic and should be kept separate from other high-sounding French-derived terms which may be used ironically, but which may also be used without trace of irony throughout Chaucer's works. Thus, the word *facounde*, which is laden with irony and social scorn in describing the *facounde gent* 'elegant speech' (*PF* 558) of the humble goose, can be used seriously and admiringly to denote the eloquence of idealised ladies in the *Book of the Duchess* and *Physician's Tale*. So too, the French phrase *par compaignye* and the borrowing *melodye*, both of which would not have been out of place in a more elevated context, can be used with comic irony to describe the unified snoring of Simkin and his well-born wife in the *Reeve's Tale*.

Ideally, in assessing Chaucer's lexical resources, we should consider not only the use and status of individual words, but also those of the individual senses which a word may possess. Very frequently the stylistic effect of a word is due to the particular sense realised in context rather than to the mere existence of the word-form itself. We may take as an example the use of the word *reuelour* in the *Wife of Bath's Prologue*, where, rather surprisingly, it is the subject of contextual glossing, as though it were a neologism like those discussed above:

> My ferthe housbonde was a reuelour;
> This is to seyn, he hadde a paramour.   (D 453–4)

Although the noun *reuelour* is first recorded in Chaucer, it cannot have been too opaque to his audience since the associated verb had been in use since the thirteenth century. The necessity of explaining the form *reuelour* perhaps arises not so much from the need to give it a meaning, but rather to specify among a range of possible meanings. A *reuelour* may seem to be a man who enjoys himself and is sociable. How then does he belong to the Wife's rogues' gallery? The simple statement given of the nature of her husband is felt to be incomplete, and, in the context of the misdemeanours of her other husbands, cries out for further qualification; and, indeed, the morally ambiguous attitude to pleasure shown by most serious medieval authors might have warned us that the word may have potentially bad connotations. The explanation given is that the husband was a womaniser, like Perkyn Revelour in the *Cook's Tale*, who we are told was 'ful of loue and paramour'. The sense of sexual promiscuity which Chaucer specifies in his use of *reuelour*, although not originally a necessary implication of the word, is yet present in many of the later Middle English uses of the noun.

   The fact that most words have more than one sense can also be exploited by Chaucer for characterisation through direct speech. For example, the word *cors*, which is widely used in Middle English to mean 'body' – and on a famous occasion in *Sir Gawain and the Green Knight* is used in imitation of a French idiom to function as an equivalent of the pronoun *me* – normally has the sense in Chaucer of 'dead body'. The exceptions to this are three. Firstly, it occurs, perhaps pronominally, in a passage which he acknowledges makes jovial nonsense, and where we should expect to find incongruity:

> I pray to God so saue thy gentil cors,
> And eek thyne vrynals and thy iurdones,

> Thyn ypocras, and eek thy galyones,
> And euery boyste ful of thy letuarie.   (C 304–7)

The second occurrence is again in the rough speech of the Host to the drunken Cook, whom the narrator has previously called a *palled goost*. He has fallen from his horse, and the company dread yet again 'liftyng up his heuy dronken cors' (H 67). Here the associations with a dead weight are obviously appropriate. The third and final example of the use of the word *cors* to refer to the living is in *Sir Thopas* (908), apparently in a similar pronominal use to that found in *Sir Gawain*: 'God shilde his cors fro shonde'. Speculation is hazardous, but it may well appear that Chaucer felt something inappropriate about the use of the word *cors* for the body of a living person. Although it had been so used in the *Kyng Alisaunder* group and is still found in *Piers Plowman*, in the languages of Chaucer and Gower the word is common, but any sense other than that of 'dead body' may well have seemed outdated or perhaps lower class.

As well as particular senses becoming *démodé*, it is possible also that certain forms of words may have become stigmatised as malapropisms. The best manuscripts agree that in the speech of the uneducated carpenter, *hende* Nicholas's landlord in the *Miller's Tale*, there occurs the phrase *Nowelis flood*, apparently as a malapropism. Also in John's speech, the word *astromye* is repeated, whereas elsewhere in Chaucer *astronomye* is used. Is this too a deliberate malapropism intended as a part of the characterisation of a humble carpenter, or is it a variant widely acceptable in contemporary London speech? Both views have been argued by scholars without final decision.[21] Although the precise form is not elsewhere recorded, the derivative *astromien* and forms like it were used both in the immediately preceding London language, and also in the contemporary Wicliffite Bible, and in some manuscripts of the B-text of *Piers Plowman*.[22] The distribution of this form among medieval texts written in the fourteenth century is therefore parallel to that of a number of words which, as we have seen, Chaucer seems to have considered *démodé*. It is therefore very possible that this form has been selected as representing the language of an unlettered and naïve man in a way analogous to the use of dated courtly terminology to characterise and describe Absolon and Nicholas. Such an assumption would fit the general pattern of linguistic usage which we have encountered in Chaucer's works and in contemporary Middle English; it would also match the literary strategy of the poem with its low style parody of courtly concerns; but it is unlikely that we shall ever be certain of our ground on this 'malapropism', since the business of allotting social significance to Chaucerian usage is always so severely hampered by the paucity of unambiguous evidence.

In discussing the grammatical structure of Chaucer's language, it became evident that it was largely of a Midland type, and that this was even more evident in the manuscripts of his poetry than it would have been in the original. His vocabulary also records the growing influence of the Midlands upon London English. This can be most easily traced in Chaucer's employment of words drawn originally from the language of the Scandinavian settlers who occupied northern and eastern parts of England from the mid-ninth century onwards. By his treaty with the Danes in 886, King Alfred had ceded a very large area to Scandinavian rule; roughly, all the land to the east and north of the ancient Roman road Watling Street, which ran from London to Chester. The intensity of settlement varied considerably over this area, and place-names show that the places of origin of the settlers did also, but their numbers seem to have been sufficient in some areas to have brought about a creolised language in which one might have heard a man using Norse phrases into which English words had been substituted, or, alternatively Norse words and grammatical forms employed in English sentences.[23] At any rate, the breakdown of the Old English inflexional system was greatly hastened by these social and linguistic conditions. Nevertheless, whatever the state of spoken communication in the Danelaw, the Old English written language proved remarkably resistant to adoptions from Norse, and it is not until after the Norman Conquest that Norse words begin to spread in large numbers from spoken usage into written language.

In view of the east Midland grammatical influence apparent in Chaucer's language, we might reasonably have expected Scandinavian lexical borrowings to be common. But, even if we take into account the fact that London itself stayed outside the area of direct Scandinavian influence, the proportion of Norse words in Chaucer's vocabulary is quite small. It probably does not exceed about 200. It is a proportion, however, which is echoed in many other Middle English texts. Gower, Chaucer's contemporary and fellow-Londoner, has proportionately slightly fewer (84), and the number given by Serjeantson for Robert Mannings *Handlyng Synne*, a text from Bourne in the heart of Scandinavian Lincolnshire, is an astonishingly low 18.[24] The *Ormulum*, written in an area of Scandinavian settlement by a man with the Scandinavian name Ormin, is well-known as the earliest English text to exhibit the complete Scandinavian paradigm, *they*, *their*, *them*, and shows evidence of Scandinavian phraseology; nevertheless, its tally of Scandinavian-derived words is lower than these circumstances might have led us to expect: Serjeantson estimates 'about 120'. The *Ormulum*, in fact, is something of a special case, since its vocabulary contains few signs of French influence. It is apparent that, as a result of the illiteracy of the Scandinavian settlers, the vocabulary of the Old English literary language was able to preserve itself against foreign influence until after the Norman Conquest, when it was seriously challenged by a language with high literary prestige. Norse influence made itself felt through modifications to English grammar and through influence on the spoken language rather than on the vocabulary of the literature. Even today, the proportion of Norse words is much higher in dialect speech than in the standard written language.

To Chaucer and his contemporaries, those words which we recognise to be of Norse origin were not perceived as foreign. Many had become the common property of all speakers of English, but many more would have seemed to be proper only to the dialects of those areas where Norse settlement had been heaviest: the Midlands and the North. A brief list will give the flavour of the Norse-derived words which had become thoroughly naturalised in the London language by Chaucer's time:

algates 'in every way, nevertheless'; *ay* 'always, ever'; *brennen* 'to burn'; *bresten* 'to burst, break'; *casten* 'to throw, utter';

deyen 'to die'; *rennen* 'to run'; *bothe*; *callen*; *felawe*, *fro*; *geten*; *knyf*; *lawe*; *lowe*; *same*; *wing*; *wrong*; *wyndowe*; *they*; *though*; *til*; *dwellen*.

All these words are used commonly by Chaucer, and were also used widely over much of England. All except *same* may be found in texts copied in London in the generation before Chaucer, and so we may assume that they would have been accepted by his audience as native and familiar. However, this had not always been the case, for in the romances *Kyng Alisaunder* and *Arthur and Merlin* some words, like *callen*, *deyen*, *they*, and *though*, are much rarer than they are in Chaucer. Others occurred alongside variants of Old English derivation, thus: *brennen* beside *barnen* 'burn'; *rennen* beside *ernen* 'run'. The latter (Old English) variants had disappeared by the time of Chaucer. But, in the case of other forms, such variation still existed in his language: *ageyn* alongside the Old English derived *aȝein*. The scribes frequently continued the process by substituting the Norse (and modern) spelling for the poet's original form. It is obvious from such examples that the distribution of Norse-derived words in Chaucer's vocabulary supports the observations made in Chapter 5 on the linguistic history of London, and reflects the continuing influence upon its language of immigration from the Midlands.

From the point of view of Londoners like Chaucer, this immigration resulted in the importation of new words, many of which, with the benefit of our linguistic researches, we can recognise as of Norse origin, but which, for contemporary Londoners, were merely an alternative form of expression coming from outside the language system in which they had been raised. Such words would lack the automatic acceptability that social and cultural prestige afforded to new French borrowings, and they may be suspected of concealed pitfalls both with regard to their essential cognitive meanings, and also their associations. Earlier London romances had, for example, used the word *dwellen* only with the native Old English sense 'live'; Chaucer may have risked misunderstanding by using it in the newly-imported east Midland and Scandinavian sense 'wait, stay'. More strikingly, the verb *hopen* had the Old English sense 'hope, expect' in pre-

Chaucerian London; Chaucer uses it in a few ambiguous passages in the more predominantly northern sense, drawn from Scandinavian, of 'think, believe'. It occurs in the speech of the clerk John in the *Reeve's Tale*: 'Oure maunciple I hope he wol be deed' (l.4029). The ludicrous effect of understanding it with the more common southern sense of 'hope' may here be a deliberate part of the linguistic play which Chaucer makes of northernisms in the poem.

Despite the uncertainty inherent in the use of recently available dialect terms, Chaucer shows a considerable readiness to use them. Many of the Norse words recorded in his vocabulary seem to be relatively new to London texts. Rynell lists *dreme, callen, lathe* 'barn', *leuene* 'flash of lightning', *liften, werre* 'worse'.[25] There are many others which Chaucer uses a mere handful of times, or only once. He does not shrink from the use of rare Anglo-Norse forms any more than he avoided those from French, Latin, or Italian, and indeed he occasionally employs the same means of ensuring that they are understood. The word *forsluggen* 'to neglect, to be slow to act', for example, which the *MED* records elsewhere only in the Kentish of William of Shoreham, is paired in Chaucer's usage (as represented by Ellesmere) in the *Parson's Tale* (685) with a more familiar verb, *forslewthen*. The word *clippen* 'to cut off' has a markedly east Midland distribution, but is used in London English by both Chaucer and Gower. Both apparently felt the need to distinguish it from the more familiar verb *clippen* 'to embrace, surround', and they do this by including in its immediate context the more familiar Old English form *schere*, as a verb or a noun: thus Gower

> And out he clippeth also faste
> Hire tunge with a peire scheres;   (*CA* V 5690)

and Chaucer

> And slepynge in hir barm vpon a day
> She made to clippe or shere his heer away.
>   (B 3256–7)

A few lines later the disambiguating collocation is with *yshaue*:

But er his heer was clipped or yshaue
Ther was no bond with which men myghte hym bynde.

(B 3261–2)

A second collocation occurs with *shaue* (A 3326), and these account for all Chaucer's uses of the verb *clippen*.

Despite its apparent unfamiliarity to Londoners of Chaucer's time, the verb *clippen* has become common in modern Standard English, and indeed its wider adoption may have contributed to the disappearance of its Old English homonym. Numerous other words, used sparingly by Chaucer, have experienced a similar history, moving from a Scandinavian origin, through the east Midland dialect, into London English and the modern Standard. We may quote as examples *banke, odd, dowve, ugly, birthe, kyndelen, lifte, skinne, reyse*.

Certain words of a similar origin seem, however, to have been less acceptable among Chaucer's circle because they referred to aspects of life with which folk of quality could have no concern. Revulsion for the actual referent seems to have attached to the word *myre* itself and is unmistakable in *MED* entry 1c. The dictionary entries show that the phrase *in the myre* had developed a figurative sense connoting a particularly unfavourable situation. The concept was used by moralists to inspire revulsion against sin, as it is used against pride in the *Parson's Tale*:

the superfluitee in lengthe of the forseyde gownes trailynge in the dong and in the myre on horse and eek on foote as well of man as of woman that al thilke trailynge is verraily as in effect wasted consumed thredbare and roten with dong rather than it is yeuen to the pouere.   (I 419–20)

That *myre* is frequently collocated with *donge*, betrays a close conceptual association, and here a rather different moralisation, with a specific social orientation, can be found. It is perhaps best summed up by the advice that it is better to live in honesty and dig in the mire than to have a reputation as a thief.[26] This is the idealisation of the honest peasant who labours in the most unattractive occupation imaginable; but does so honestly. Such a conception is evident in Chaucer's picture of the Plowman, who is willing to *dyke* (another Norse borrowing) for his neighbour, but who is introduced by the information that he 'hadde ylad of donge ful many a foother' (A 530). This aspect of an agricultural peasant's life is thought worthy of mention in *Piers Plowman* also (A-text 7 275). Indeed, it is evident that the association of the peasant with *myre* and with *donge* is a strong one in Middle English literature, and the further implication is that such things are not to be associated with courtly men and women. Not infrequently, the occupational hazards of the churl's job are, however, used against him, so that in the romance *Havelok* the expressions *that mixed cherl* (1.2533) and *fule driht-cherle* (1.682) are insulting allusions to his employment. The latter even becomes a kind of surname.[27] Harry Baily's joking use of the proverbial expression 'Don is in the myre' (H 5), although Chaucer does not state it as would many a French author, may well be the use of a churl's proverb with the contextual meaning here that the business of story-telling has come to a full stop.

To refer to another as a *cherle* may be simply socially-descriptive; nevertheless, it may also be an expression of abuse. The English-derived form of the word, *cherle*, was that used in London in the generation before Chaucer, but immigration had, by the later fourteenth century, introduced another form, *carl*, derived from Norse. Although in northern Middle English this was often the normal referential form, in London and also perhaps more widely, the selection of this form seems to have carried an extra charge of contempt: it was perhaps a deliberately coarse form and, with one exception, (C. 717), Chaucer restricts its use to the description of the coarsest of his characters and the most socially-depressed.

The Millere was a stout carl for the nones;   (A 545)

and in his tale a second *carl* appears, who, it turns out, shares his own remarkable talent for opening closed doors (A 3469). In the *Friar's Tale* (1568) an honest carter whose cart has become temporarily bogged down in the mire is called a *carl* by the devil; an expression which is intended to reflect worse upon its speaker than upon its referent. This device is paralleled among terms of abuse by the Summoner's references to a sick old woman as *old rebekke* (D 1573) and *old viritrate* (D 1582). That *carl* was considered a particularly wounding insult among London commercial society is borne out by the records of a London guild where protests are lodged against one of the members of the fraternity who it was alleged had insulted others by the use of the terms *whoreson*, *harlot*, and *carl*.[28]

The word *swayn*, another Norse borrowing, seems also to carry generally derogatory associations in Middle English, although not so dire as those of *carl* in Chaucer's usage. It is repeatedly used in contrast with knightly status, and can cover a wide range of senses extending downwards from 'page, valet' to 'serving boy'. In Chaucer, the sense of 'servant' is that found in the northern speech of the students in the *Reeve's Tale* (4027). The only other use of the word in his works is in the comic description of Sir Thopas:

> Sire Thopas wax a doghty swayn
> Whit was his face as payndemayn.   (B 1914–5)

It is fairly certain that the choice of the word here is part of the deliberate comic ineptness of the piece, and it may well spring from the kind of humour which made kitchen boys behave like heroes in earlier French epic, and tradesmen like knights in the early fifteenth-century *Tournament of Tottenham*.[29]

This latter poem, which shows an intimate knowledge of the London area, is nevertheless written in a predominantly northern dialect. It describes a burlesque tournament held to select a worthy husband for the daughter of Randolfe the Refe. In it the word *cors* (l.70) is applied to the living body of one of the 'knights' taking part, but more striking is the use of the Norse-derived *capul* 'horse, steed'. The word is derived originally from Latin *caballus*, but seems to have none of the elevated associations that Latin derivation might imply. The precise significance of the evidence is difficult to estimate, since in poems written in the North *capul* may be a perfectly respectable word for 'horse', but in the *Tournament* and in Chaucer it is not free from pejorative associations. Chaucer uses it only in the speech of the northern students, in 'churlish' contexts, and in the *brode speche* of the Host. Evidently, although the word was still quite acceptable to the audience of *Sir Gawain and the Green Knight,* its adoption into London English seems to have coincided with a decline in the social estimation of it.[30]

Finally, in this brief consideration of low status terms derived from Old Norse, we may consider the word *clobbed.* The single use in Chaucer is in the Host's outburst against his wife's lack of prudence, which allows her unconcealed antagonism for their neighbours to become a daily threat to his safety and freedom. Her ill-controlled aggression is directed equally upon their servants:

> She bryngeth me the grete clobbed staues
> And crieth slee the dogges euerichon.   (B 3088-9)

The word *clobbed* seems from the citations in *MED* to be chiefly of East Anglian origin, and, moreover, it seems to be used by Chaucer in a recognised collocation, found in the dictionary entry *clubbyd staffe: fustis,* and also in the works of Capgrave and Lydgate. The *Promptorium Parvulorum* has a further interesting entry *clubbyd or boystous – rudis. Clobbed,* it seems, as well as 'club-shaped or knobbed' can carry a metaphorical sense of roughness or coarseness, for this is the most frequent sense of the word *boystous,* which Chaucer twice uses of coarse language. The circle of associations is closed when we realise that the characteristic weapon of churls and of deformed giants in medieval literature, the enemies of courtliness, is a club. The contrast is with the elegance and prestige of the knightly sword. When, in the *Romaunt of the Rose,* Danger is personified, he is represented as a churl, and his weapon is a club: 'The cherl his clubbe gan shake' (l.4061). Such was the prestige of the *Roman de la Rose* that a detail like this would have been likely to make the possession of a club part of the iconography of churlishness.[31] We can be sure, therefore, that the word *clobbed,* existing as it does within this set of associations, must have a socially-depressed significance. The picture of Harry's domestic scene, then, is of one close to churlishness, and the outlandishness of the word probably contributed to this impression.

Norse-derived and relatively unfamiliar dialect words could belong to ordinary discourse, and also to a level of language which would have been deplored in more polite circles. In view of the over-simplified impression given by many accounts of the status of Norse borrowings, it might be assumed that such represent the totality of their use. This is not so; and to avoid such misunderstanding it will be as well to complete this chapter by a brief account of Norse words in a more elevated context. Among these are a number of words which had become a part of military vocabulary: *sparth* 'battle-axe', *ransake*, *gap*, and *big*. The former two are rare words in Chaucer and have a specifically military significance; the latter two have other significances along with the military. But the military sense of *gap* is clear in the following:

> . . . Here cometh my mortal enemy.
> Withoute faille he moot be deed or I.
> For outher I moot sleen hym at the gappe
> Or he moot sle me if that me myshappe. (A 1643–6)

The word *big* may certainly refer to size in Middle English, but it generally also has an association of violence and aggression, hence Chaucer's phrase *byg in armes* (B 3111), jokingly bestowed upon the Host's wife.

Among other Chaucerian words of Norse origin, some seem to have been given a special technical sense: *hap* is used by Chaucer, Gower, and other London texts to refer specifically to random chance in contradistinction to destiny or fortune. The word *flittynge* is employed by Chaucer, Gower, and Lydgate in philosophical reflections upon the instability of worldly things. The word *hauen*, although not restricted to this sphere, is frequently used figuratively in religious or philosophical discourse, and on three separate occasions the phrase *hauen of refut* is used to refer to the Virgin.

The words *slaughtre*, *on-lofte*, and *bark* all tend to be used by Chaucer in more elevated poetic contexts. The last was evidently a rare word, and most Middle English authors preferred the native form *rinde*. The *MED* shows *bark* to have been used most widely in technical contexts, but Chaucer selects it for a memorable poetic image in *Troilus and Criseyde*:

> And as in wynter leues ben birafte,
> Ech after other til the tree be bare,
> So that ther nys but bark and braunche ilafte,
> Lith Troilus byraft of ech welfare,
> Ibounden in the blak bark of care.   (IV 225–9)

The word *sweigh*, too, seems to be used in displays of 'art poetical'. It is used four times in figurative passages to mean 'momentum'. In three of these passages the context is broadly scientific or philosophical: references to the irresistible motion of Fortune's wheel or, in two cases, of the *primum mobile*, which retards the natural motion of the spheres. A flavour of the contextual company which the word keeps can be had from one of a series of apostrophes in the *Man of Law's Tale*:

> O firste moeuer, cruel firmament
> With thy diurnal sweigh that crowdest ay
> And hurlest al fro Est til Occident
> That naturelly wolde holde another way,
> Thy crowdyng set the heuene in swich array
> At bigynnyng of this fiers viage
> That cruel Mars hath slayn this mariage.

> (B 295–301)

In the Hengwrt manuscript this stanza, through its technicality, was considered to merit a Latin note of explanation.[32] The words *diurnal* and *occident* are rare, each used only once elsewhere by Chaucer, and their Latinate form declares their association with an elevated and technical style. In a fifteenth-century author, they are the kind of words which modern scholars would be likely to describe as 'aureate' and be ready to regard as evidence of decorative superficiality. Such a quality is rarely recognised in Chaucer, and most commentators would be even less ready to find a Norse-derived word playing this kind of role in an aureate context.

It is apparent from all that we have seen of Chaucer's vocabulary that this, like the entire London language of his day, possessed a notable dynamism. To discuss his vocabulary purely in terms of the proportions of French, Norse, or Latin loan-words would be to impose a classificatory order for the sake of etymology which would lack all relevance for the understanding of the use of words in his poetry. The vocabulary was constantly growing by the adoption of words from Latin, French, and Italian, but also from the dialects of the east and north. Although there was a general presupposition that new Romance words would be of an acceptable and elevated kind, this does not necessarily mean that words from other English dialects were shunned. Beyond this general presupposition, the true stylistic structure of the vocabulary consisted of the associations between words in terms of their habitual contexts and collocations, the recognisable dialects to which they belonged, or the social status which they shared. Similarities of reference might also prove to be an associative factor and reference could affect the acceptability of new words: if a dialect word referred to the heavens rather than to mud, it was more likely to be accepted into polite speech or technical discourse. At the same time, inspired by similar social judgements, both French and English terms for hackneyed old ideals, now considered laughable in their pretensions, could be discarded from serious discourse, and found an ironic employment in mimicking the aspirations of the socially-despised.

Chaucer's vocabulary, then, if we are to understand its literary deployment, must not be considered to be monolithic, nor even divided into two or three etymologically-differentiated blocs. It is better considered as a texture, an 'architecture' of associations, wrought by the social values its users and his audience perceived in it, and by their recognition of proprieties to verbal contexts, technical discourse, literary genres, or familiar situations.

7 Register and Propriety

As we have seen in the previous chapter, Chaucer's Host knew how to parrot the technical terms of medicine, how to utter the words *urynals*, *jurdones*, *galiones*, *cardynacle*, or *triacle*. He even seems to have known something of the meaning of some of them, yet he cannot use them competently. Indeed, he implicitly admits that his use of them may not make much sense, and offers as an explanation that 'I kan nat speke in terme'. What exactly does he mean by this phrase?[1] Chaucer does not use it elsewhere in precisely this form, but his use of the word *termes* in general suggests that he understood it to refer to words which were in some way distinct from the ordinary range of vocabulary used in everyday conversation. *Termes* may owe their distinctiveness to their obvious foreign origin, as with the phrases *par consequens* (D 2192) in the *Summoner's Tale*, or *questio quid iuris* in his *General Prologue* description, which, we are told, the Summoner chattered as uncomprehendingly as a jay.[2] Such Latin *termes* were also used by the Pardoner to quicken piety in his congregation, who were much impressed, if not informed, by this practice. The Summoner had learned his Latin tag, along with a few others whose meanings were unknown to him, from the formulaic phrasing of a decree; and it is characteristic of those phrases which Chaucer specifies as *termes* that he often makes reference to their source or proper field of use. Thus, he refers to the *termes of astrologye* (F 1266), *phisik* (*TC* II 1038), *philosophye* (*HF* 857), of the schools (E 1569), and, in some manuscripts, of *lawe* (B 1189). What seems to be implied by these phrases are the special forms and expressions of language which are associated with technical discussion. In the description of the Sergeaunt of Law we are told that he is acquainted with all the cases and judgements in the last three hundred years, and that he recalls them in *termes*, that is, in that very formal, technical language, be it Latin or French, in which they had been recorded. But less institutionalised areas of life could also have their *termes*. Troilus is instructed by Pandarus not to confuse the *termes of love* with those of natural science when writing a love letter (*TC* II 1039), and apparently churls were thought to have linguistic peculiarities characteristic of them as a class, since the Reeve threatens to 'quit' the Miller in his own *cherles termes* (A 3917). This is a sphere of linguistic usage in which Chaucer is careful to deny much competence. Obviously, what Harry Baily meant by his admission was that he was unable to maintain a sensible discourse in the recondite technical language appropriate to medicine.

This brief enquiry into the significance of the word *termes* makes it clear that Chaucer was aware of the possibility of classifying the vocabulary of London English not only according to foreign or dialectal origin but according to the propriety of words to particular uses. Some words and phrases were forms, or were used in senses, which were recognisable as characteristic of special areas of interest or particular social circumstances, such as the condition of being a churl, literally or metaphorically, or that, even, of being a lover. As mentioned in the previous chapter, it is unlikely that Chaucer and his contemporaries would have classified their vocabulary along etymological lines, since such a classification requires a spirit of scientific enquiry which would have been quite foreign to vernacular languages at this period. Yet they were capable of recognising novelty or cultural prestige associated with Romance borrowings, and could equally readily associate words with the area of use to which they were currently proper. Any fully-competent user of any living language is aware without any linguistic training of some terms of restricted usage. But there is some evidence that Chaucer and his contemporaries not only employed these terms with propriety by the exercise of this inevitable linguistic intuition, but that, to some extent, they also formulated their intuitive knowledge. In other words, that a knowledge of the propriety of *termes* was fully conscious, and that, however informally, this aspect of language use was the object of attention. The motivation for this attention will be considered in Chapter 8 but, at present, it is sufficient to argue Chaucer's conscious awareness of this means of discriminating vocabulary. The case is put for us by Thomas Usk, a fellow Londoner, an acquaintance, and an admirer of Chaucer:

In Latin and French hath many soverayne wittes had greet delyt to endite, and have many noble thinges fulfild; but certes, there ben some that speken their poysye-mater in Frenche, of whiche speche the Frenche men have as good a fantasye as we have in hering *as clear an idea* of Frenche mennes English. And many termes there ben in English, of which unneth we Englishmen connen declare the knowledginge. How shulde than a *significance* Frenche man born suche termes conne *jumble-together* jumpere in his mater, but as the jay chatereth English? Right so, trewly, the understanding of Englishmen wol not strecche to the privy termes in Frenche, what-so-euer we bosten of straunge langage. Let than clerkes *foreign* endyten in Latin, for they have the propertee of science, and the knowinge in that facultee; and let Frenchmen in their Frenche also endyten their queynt termes, for it is kyndely to their *natural* mouthes; and let us shewe our fantasyes in such wordes as we lerneden *ideas* of our dames tong.
(*Testament of Love*, 22–38)

Usk's words are primarily an explanation of his choice of the English language in which to write his *Testament*, but his argument is that both the French and English languages possess some *termes* which are obscure even to native speakers, and must therefore be outside the range of the foreigner. He is, in effect, dividing the vocabulary into 'common core' and 'queynte termes'; the latter category including, no doubt, not only rarer technical language but also unfamiliar dialectal forms.

If Chaucer and his contemporaries could divide the vocabulary into the plain, everyday 'common core' and into *termes* relatable to various distinct areas of use, it is apparent that they had, in essentials, pre-empted the modern categorisation of the vocabulary into 'registers'.[3] However, fourteenth-century vernacular writers were not concerned with the description of language; their interest in the subdivision of the vocabulary was stylistic, and often socially-motivated. They were not concerned with integrating their conception of the vocabulary into any linguistic theory, but only with its practical relationship to their literary aesthetic and their social ideals. Chaucer's use of the word *termes*, as we shall see, coincides with, but is not co-extensive with, the kind of linguistic division implied by the word 'register'.

Nevertheless, Chaucer's vocabulary is full of words which he would have called *termes*, and which we should regard as proper to technical registers. In its context, the Arabic word *atazir* 'influence (of a planet)' would send us straight to the Glossary, as also would *equinoxial* and *tables tolletanes*.[4] The legal terms *chevissaunce* 'financial deal' and *amercement* 'fine', or *surement* 'bond' are equally opaque technical words restricted to specific registers, and easily recognisable as such.[5] But other words which had restricted technical uses in Chaucer's time have since entered the common core, so that we might easily overlook their technical status in his text. The words *ascenden, ascendent* and *ascension,* for example, were all used by Chaucer exclusively as astronomical terms referring to the rising of stars or planets. Another group of now-familiar words are also practically restricted to the astronomical register in his works: *aspect* 'relative position expressed as angular distance'; *equinoxial* 'celestial equator'; *perpendicular* 'at right angles to the plane of the horizon'; *tortuous* 'rising obliquely'; *elongation* 'angular distance'; *elevation* 'angular distance above the horizon'. Four others are found only in philosophical contexts: *absolute* 'independent, free from restriction'; *consequence* 'logical tie connecting premises and conclusion'; *demonstracioun* 'certain knowledge produced by logical proof'. The words *suggestioun* 'process of putting an idea into the mind of another, evil prompting' and *affeccioun* 'experience of, or capacity for, emotion' are also used by Chaucer in essentially technical ways. A number of terms proper to mathematics are self-explanatory: *centre*; *cercle*; *distaunce*; *equaciouns*; *equal*; *ligne*. The significance of these words is obvious, but it is surprising for the modern reader to discover that in Chaucer's works they have overwhelmingly technical associations. On the few occasions upon which some of them are used outside technical contexts, an awareness of their technical meaning is still present. Thus the Squire, playing on the senses of the word *stable*, describes his ideal king with mathematical correctness as 'Of his corage as any centre stable' (F 22); and the erudition of this image is acknowledged in both the Ellesmere and the Hengwrt manuscripts by a Latin note explaining that it refers ഠ the still centre of a moving circle.[6] On more than one occasion, a *lyne* is regarded as the epitome of straightness or directness. The fact that a simile is used is a good indication of the technicality of the word:

> And took his leue and neuere gan to fyne
> But to his neces hous as streyght as lyne
> He come . . .   (*TC* II 1460-62)

Certain legal phrases, too, are currently of such familiarity that their technicality in Chaucer's language may be concealed from us. The word *prisoun*, for example, does not necessarily denote a building, but rather the condition of being under arrest or restraint, so that the phrase *in prisoun* is often closer in meaning to the modern English 'in detention' or 'under house arrest' than to 'in gaol'. Legal jargon derived from French took account of various types of *prisoun*. The 'horrible and strong prisoun' which Palamon endures in the *Knight's Tale* is not, as might be imagined, a specially-reinforced building; rather it is what in legal French was known as 'prison forte. et dure', that is, detention aggravated by reduced rations and the deprivation of other comforts.[7] Chaucer tells us that the unhappy young man is 'a prisoner perpetuelly nat oonly for a yer' (A 1457-8). This is the fourth occasion upon which the collocation of *perpetuel* and *prisoun* has been used in the tale. It is intended to send a shiver down the spine of the reader, for it too is a technical phrase denoting an unpleasant means used by medieval rulers of liquidating opposition. Imprisonment of persons of quality captured in battle was usually a temporary matter aimed at extracting a ransom. Their associates may be encouraged to pay up more readily by making their imprisonment deliberately uncomfortable, 'horrible and strong'. However, on occasions, for reasons of vengeance or for political motives, a man may be condemned to *prison perpetuel*, which was intended to continue as long as he lived. It was equivalent to annihilation. This fate was rightly dreaded, and a number of medieval authors employ the allusion. In Middle English, Langland refers to a sentence of *peyne . . . perpetuel* passed upon sinners by strict Justice in the final judgement (B-text, XVIII, 200). A similar image is employed in French by Henry, Duke of Lancaster and father of Chaucer's Duchess Blaunche, in his *Livre de Seyntz Medecines*:

> et touz les enemys qe sont entreez en fourbourk descomfire, tuer et getter en prison perpetuele.   (p.81.30)

Chaucer makes it very plain that his use of the phrase has this precisely technical significance when he twice tells us that Theseus will accept no ransom for the prisoners' release (A 1024; 1176) and:

> For soothly for to seyn this Palamon
> Perpetuelly is dampned to prison
> In cheynes and in fettres to been deed.   (A 1341–3)

Palamon, indeed, is to remain in the chains associated with 'horrible and strong prisoun' until his death.

Even as Chaucer employed technical terms from various areas of contemporary learning, the business in which he himself was engaged, that of creating a sophisticated courtly literature, was developing its own specific vocabulary. A large group of words with restricted literary reference denotes genres of composition or types of verse: *romance, geste, fable, ditty, balade, prologe.* Many such words – *tragedie, comedie, prohemye* 'introductory discourse', *roundel, virelaye, rym dogerel* – are first recorded in his works. Chaucer also furnishes the first recorded use in English of the word *original* in the sense 'work from which a translation is made'.

Although Chaucer exhibits a greater awareness of specifically literary kinds and forms than any previous English author, he also shares with them a rich vocabulary of words whose range of use spans literature and the scholastic arts. The words *glose* 'explanatory gloss', *text*, and *rubrike* 'text-heading written in red' reflect the lay-out of the medieval book. The terms *devise* 'describe in detail', *coloure*, *peynte*, and *enlumine* echo the concern of the medieval author to elaborate his text by the use of the ornaments of rhetoric.[8] Chaucer employs various words in common use to refer to poets and performers: *mynstralles* and *gestiours* are classed together along with musical entertainers in *House of Fame* (1197–8). Clearly these are popular entertainers who chant or accompany their narratives with musical instruments. The *auctor* and *poete* occupy a more elevated position. A *rhetor* is a poet seen in the light of his ability to *faire endite* (B 4397), where the word *endite* implies the skills of formal composition. The word *endite*, indeed, belongs to a rather wider register than the purely literary one, and may be used of lawyers drafting the formulation of a legal document. The Sergeaunt of Law, we are told, 'koude endite and make a thyng/Ther koude no wight pynchen at his writyng' (A 325–6). The word *endite* is broadly usable to refer to poetic composition, legal drafting, and even Philomela weaving her unhappy story into a piece of cloth; but some common literary terms have even wider ranges of use. *Matere* 'subject matter' and *forme* 'formulation of phrases, style' are words derived from the teaching of medieval logic. Although in theory they should have been kept rigidly separate and referred to distinct aspects of literary composition, their reference is commonly confused: no clear distinction is made between content and style in the medieval use of the words.

The precise definitions required by logic were not maintained in the transferred uses of its terms in other fields, but the teaching of the art of disputation in the schools bequeathed a substantial vocabulary to vernacular poetry. In the schools, the reading (*lectio*) from an *auctor* would be the occasion of raising a query (*quaestio*) on his views, and this would be the subject of formal argument (*disputatio*). When completed, the whole would be summed up by the master presiding in a *sententia magistralis*.[9] In Chaucer's works it is noteworthy that when a *questioun* is explicitly posed, it is commonly to a group rather than to an individual, and they are plainly expected to discuss it. In reality, a problem is set rather than a question, in the modern sense, asked, and in the *Second Nun's Tale*, although a simple answer to the question is obviously expected, the interlocutor instead seizes upon an error in the technique of posing the *questioun*:

> 'I axe thee', quod he, 'thogh it the greue
> Of thy religioun and of thy bileue.'
>
> 'Ye han bigonne youre question folily,'
> Quod she, 'that wolden two answeres conclude
> In o demande. Ye axed lewedly.' (G 426–30)

The business of conducting a disputation correctly also furnishes Middle English with an armoury of terms which were originally technical, but which gradually became more widely used. The word *argument* itself, used in the narrower sense, signified an Aristotelian syllogism; its *conclusioun* was the third truth derived from the syllogism, and the *consequence* the logical tie connecting premises and *conclusioun*. In medieval logic, propositions in which the subject and predicate were interchangeable without affecting the truth value were called *convertible*. The word is wittily used by Chaucer in the *Cook's Tale*:

> For sikerly a prentys reuelour
> That haunteth dees, ryot or paramour,
> His maister shal it in his shoppe abye
> Al haue he no part of the minstralcye;
> For theft and riot, they been conuertible.
>
> (A 4391-5)

Chaucer uses the words *diffyne*, *diffinicioun*, and *diffynytyve* in two distinct technical senses; firstly, and more commonly, to refer to the concluding statement of a disputation:

> For, though your love laste a seson,
> Wayte upon the conclusyon
> And eke how that ye determynen
> And for the more part diffynen.   (*HF* 341–4)

In this ironic example from the *House of Fame* the word occurs
in the context of two other technical terms connected with the
authoritative culmination of logical processes: *conclusio* and
determinatio. In *Boece*, however, the narrowly-technical sense of
stating the characteristic nature of a thing is to be found. This
is a technique which we should recognise as that of definition
and classification, and it was a formal process carried out in
medieval logic by the use of the 'five predicables': *genus*, *species*,
differentia, *proprietas*, and *accidentia*.[10] Together, these five were
sufficient to state the nature and affinities of any person,
creature or thing of which a definition might be required.
According to this system, contraries are members of the same
genus whose *differentiae* cause them to be incompatible and
opposed. Chaucer employs much of this vocabulary in
figurative or even proverbial form:

> A whetston is no keruyng instrument,
> But ȝet it maketh sharpe keruyng tolis.
> And there thow woost that I haue auȝt myswent
> Eschuwe thow that, for swich to þe scole is;
> Thus often wise men ben war by foolys.
> If thow do so thi wit is wel bewared.
> By his contrarie is euery thyng declared.

> For how myghte euere swetnesse han ben knowe
> To him that neuere tasted bitternesse?
> Ne no man may ben inly glad I trowe
> That neuere was in sorwe or som destresse;
> Eke with by blak, by shame ek worthinesse.
> Ech set by other, more for other semeth,
> As men may se; and so the wyse it demeth.

> Sith thus of contraries is o lore . . .   (*TC* I 631–45)

Here, as in the *Book of the Duchess*, Chaucer is making witty
play of the logical teaching of the schools, suggesting that

within the same class (*genus*) items are defined by the co-existence of their contraries.[11]

The word *difference*, too, can occur in contexts which recall its technical sense:

> Senec seith a good word doutelees
> He seith he kan no difference fynde
> Bitwix a man that is out of his mynde
> And a man which that is dronkelewe,
> But that woodnesse yfallen in a sherewe
> Perseuereth lenger than dooth dronkenesse.
>
> (C 492–7)

The purpose of this use of the word is not strictly one of definition; indeed, for a moral purpose, it rather suggests an ironic similarity than a valid distinction. The drunken man is placed within the same *genus* as the madman, and the *differentia* is represented as minimal. Indeed, it is noticeable that the majority of examples of the use of this scholastic vocabulary by Chaucer is outside truly technical contexts: it is rather used allusively, wittily, or for moral instruction. Criseyde, for example, tells Troilus why she first loved him, and chooses a clever way of putting it, echoing this technical register:

> And that ȝe hadde, as me thoughte, in despit
> Euery thyng that souned into badde,
> As rudenesse and poeplissh appetit.
>
> (*TC* IV 1675–7)

The phrase *souned into badde* 'was associated with evil' is based upon the scholastic Latin *sonare in malo*, which can be applied to the senses of words. In medieval Latin, for example, the word *astutia* 'cunning' may be said to *sonare in malo*, whereas *prudentia* has predominantly good associations.[12] Earlier in the poem, when debating her course of action in loving Troilus, she employs the technical terms of the *disputatio* of the schools:

> Now sette a caas, the hardeste is, ywys,
> Men myghten demen that he loueth me.
>
> (*TC* II 729–30)

Her words are an echo of those of Pandarus when putting his own argument to her:

> I sette the worste, that ʒe dredden this:
> Men wolde wondren sen hym com or goon.
>
> (*TC* II 367–8)

The phrase *setten a cas (the werste)* forms only part of the range of technical terms, rhetorical, logical, and literary, used by all three major characters in the poem. In Book III a variant of it is used, I *pose* (Latin *ponare*), which Pandarus uses to introduce a hypothesis (III 310). As we have already seen in the case of the word *convertible*, such technical vocabulary can be found in *fabliau*-matter as well as in serious works. It can also form part of the banter of the headlink of a tale:

> 'Ha ha,' quod he, 'for Cristes passion,
> This millere hadde a sharp conclusion
> Vpon his argument of herbergage.' (A 4327–9)

Just as with recondite foreign phrasing, the elevated associations of technical terminology can be used ironically in unexpected contexts.[13]

It is apparent from uses like these that many of these terms of scholastic logic were no longer technical terms in any narrow sense: that is, that they were no longer closely restricted to technical discourse. Frequently, their extension to broader use was accompanied by a decline in the precision of their application, by an increase in the range of their senses, or even by the selection of a particular form for the remaining technical use. Thus, whilst *egal* was used widely, *equal* is restricted in Chaucer's works to astrological and mathematical contexts. But, although these terms had extended the sphere of their uses and adopted senses which often coincide with their senses in modern English, it is important to realise for assessing their stylistic function in Chaucer's language that they still bore with them powerful and often specific connotations. They were still *termes*. The extension of these terms from technical to more common core uses is historically significant as the pathway by which many foreign borrowings – including many of the technical terms we have discussed – became familiar words in modern English; but they are not very far advanced upon that journey.

Medieval commentators on the Latin language were well aware of this tendency for technical terms to shift their reference as they became used more and more generally. Technical terms, used in the ways proper to their technical field of discourse, they called *verba propria*. In uses and senses transferred from such a technical field, they were called *verba translata*, a phrase which could also signify 'metaphor'.[14] Now there is obviously a close parallel between the modern notion of register and the late antique one of *proprietas*, but there are also significant differences. Whereas the term 'register' connotes features of a style proper to a given field of discourse, and takes account of syntax and pronunciation as well as lexicon, *proprietas* is usually understood only as a function of vocabulary. Furthermore 'register' is concerned exclusively with the contemporary state of the language, whereas the distinction between *verba propria* and *verba translata* may involve a historical process as much as contemporaneous description. It had, indeed, a metaphysical aspect, since it could be argued that words possessed original and proper references from which they had become transferred through the process of time. Consequently, it was even considered that lexical study to establish the 'original' meanings of words might enable the scholar to discover those words which might, with propriety, be applied to God, thus leading to a more perfect human knowledge of the divine: a supposition which bears an intriguing resemblance to the modern technological aspiration to penetrate to the beginnings of the universe by the construction of ever-larger radio telescopes, but which is not related to the concept of 'register'.[15]

Furthermore, *proprietas* as a concept of 'appropriateness' or 'belonging' went far beyond the study of language and could be associated with the scholastic techniques of definition mentioned above.[16] When attempting to *devise* or describe anything minutely in the course of a literary work, special attention would have to be paid to its *propria*: those things peculiar to it as a species. Thus, considering the problem from a non-linguistic perspective, as medieval authors mostly did, the description of a geographical area might contain a reference to the variety of language (the dialect) which is seen to be characteristic of it. The presentation of a man seen as a representative of social class, a churl or a courtier, perhaps, would demand care in the selection of language forms proper to that class. Even an individual may be considered to have language features which are peculiar to him, and would therefore be among the *propria* defining him as an individual. This notion of *proprietas* could be extended linguistically to the presentation of lovers, northern clerks, or the style of a sermon. Indeed, if any topic, person, or style had linguistic peculiarities characteristic of it, such peculiarities could potentially be considered *verba propria*, or, in Chaucer's usage, *termes*. It is apparent from this fuller discussion that the medieval conception of *proprietas*, although partly coinciding with the modern conception of 'register' was rather differently oriented, and is not congruent with it.

The prominence in medieval literary thought of theorising on love, and the consequent necessity of the frequent presentation of the lover as a type, led to the recognition of forms of language proper to that type. Undoubtedly, the language derives in part from observation of usage in that situation in real life, but there is also a strong element of literary convention. In *Troilus and Criseyde*, when Troilus is warned against confusing the *termes of love* with those of natural science, we should be immediately ready to accept the latter as members of a distinct register, but probably be less certain of the former. In Chaucer's language, both are equally *termes*; both represent language used with a particular propriety. He lists a few of the *termes* used by Troilus in his letter:

> First he gan hire his right lady calle
> His hertes lif, his lust, his sorwes leche,
> His blisse, and ek thise other termes alle
> That in swich cas thise loueres alle seche.
>
> (*TC* II 1065–8)

A collection of similar *termes* is used by the Man in Black in the *Book of the Duchess*:

> For certes she was, that swete wife,
> My suffisaunce, my luste, my lyfe,
> Myn happe, myn hele, and al my blysse,
> My worldys welfare, and my goddesse.
>
> (*BD* 1037–40)

Similar expressions are to be found on the lips of lovers throughout Chaucer's works, and elsewhere in Middle English, and they are clearly to be regarded as a vocabulary proper to that use. But it should be noticed that some of these are also *termes* of a different kind. That is to say, *suffisaunce* and *hap* are equally words used in moral philosophical discussion: the former means 'contentment', the latter 'chance' (as opposed to destiny). Moreover, the phrase *my worldes welfare* may evoke the possibility of an other-worldly perspective, since it limits *welfare* in a rather curious way. Comparison with a different set of *loves termes* is of interest here. In the *Miller's Tale* the usage is different: *lemman, hony-comb, my faire bryd, my sweete cynamome, sweete bryd, my deerelyng*. These *termes* are a mixture of the comically exotic and the rural and commonplace; two of them are culinary. All these are terms of love, but they belong to different social levels. Just as the modern concept of register is intersected by other varieties of language, so the notion of *proprietas* is also a complex one; *termes* can be re-applied in new uses, shifting their *proprietas*, but often retaining connotations of the old. The reason why Absolon's love-terms are recognisably of a lower social status than those of Troilus or the Man in Black may depend in part upon observation of actual usage among the different social classes, in part upon the conventionalisation of such usage in literary treatments (for example, popular lyric or romance expression which had become dated and unacceptable), and in part upon what was perceived to be the proper 'original' application of the words used. Thus, Absolon's words refer to food and the kitchen, whereas those of the Man in Black refer to the elevated realms of philosophy.

Although we began this discussion of register and propriety with examples which were distinctly technical terms of very restricted usage, it has become more and more apparent in the course of discussion that many words can be considered to have more than one 'propriety': love's terms may also be terms of philosophy, or mathematical terms may be common also in astronomy. Nor are terms narrowly restricted to use in the contexts to which they are considered to be proper; they are often transferred in order to add subtlety to courtly casuistry or ironic impudence to *fabliau* material. In the presentation of character the unexpected appearance of proper terms may add a historical resonance, as when the Wife of Bath employs the school-terms which she may have learned from her fifth husband. A case like this raises a critical problem as to whether it is justified to assume that the use of *termes* by the Wife is intended in a realistic way to reflect her past history, or whether, as so often, it is really a device of the author seeking to reach his audience with a display of witty erudition on the subject he has chosen to discuss through the medium of the Wife. There is no doubt that *termes* which can be used in various contexts, whilst still retaining associations of their proprieties, are of immense value to Chaucer in reaching his audience more subtly, and the remainder of this chapter will be devoted to investigating a few examples of this literary exploitation.[17]

We may begin from the simplest case, in which medieval literary theory considered that the ends of characterisation were served by concentration on the *proprietates* of the type of character which was to be presented. Thus, just as the *propria* of fire were light and warmth, and the *proprium* of mankind as a species was its ability to laugh, so the *propria* of a tyrant were his contempt for the law and his cruelty. One praised the constancy in the faith of a churchman, the beauty of women, and the justice of an emperor.[18] The simplest theoretical approaches in the arts of poetry decried any confusion of these proprieties. The speech of the individual was regarded as a *proprium,* and sermon authors were warned by Thomas Waleys not to make Christ speak the words of Nebuchadnezzar.[19] In the Latin tradition, then, a knowledge of the *proprietates* was considered essential for the poet and preachers, and characteristic or actual speeches were considered a device (*sermonicinatio*) by which, along with other attributes, a character might be realised.

In the formal composition of the *Knight's Tale*, there is an allusion to such means of character presentation. When Arcite undertakes to present a laudatory portrait of Palamon, his choice of language betrays recourse to the rhetorical tradition; he intends:

> To speken of a seruaunt proprely
> With circumstaunces alle trewely,
> That is to seyn trouthe, honour, knyghthede,
> Wisdom, humblenesse, estaat, and heigh kynrede,
> Fredom, and al that longeth to that art.   (A 2787–91)

The list of virtues are the *circumstaunces* which are proper in the description of a noble servant of Venus (A 2235). The origin of the word *proprely* is too obvious here to need comment, but the word *circumstaunces* is derived from Latin *circumstantiae*, which is a form used by rhetoricians to refer to the attributes by which a character may be described.[20] Chaucer, therefore, lists here the *propria* and *attributa* of the character in the best Latin rhetorical tradition, and as he does so he employs an anglicisation of the appropriate *termes* of Latin theory. As a lover, Arcite is further represented by his own use of the characteristic *termes of love*: *faireste of faire*, *O lady myn* (1.2221); *lady bright* (1.2231); *my lady* (1.2247); *my lady sweete* (1.2254); *blisful lady deere* (1.2260).

Although Chaucer uses *termes* in this rhetorically orthodox and appropriate way, much more commonly he uses them in contexts shifted from those to which they were considered to be appropriate. They become, in the words of the medieval theorists, *verba translata*, expressions transferred from their original application, and perhaps also sense, and fitted to new contexts where they can be understood allusively and figuratively. In the *Nun's Priest's Tale*, for example, the fox which carries off Chauntecleer is accused of plotting his crime in advance, with 'malice aforethought'. The legal term which Chaucer uses for this is *by heigh ymaginacioun forncast* (B 4407), and the plan of breaking into Chauntecleer's world and lying concealed is described. Only a few years earlier Thomas Usk had accused his former associates in similar phrasing of plotting the discomfiture of some leading London citizens: 'be fals compassement and ymaginacion to-forn cast'.[21] The use of legal indictment serves to give us a momentary glimpse of a cunning and dangerous enemy resolved on the destruction of the unfortunate Chauntecleer, and this portentous language, by the elevation of the cock to importance as the target of an assassin, finds its place as an appropriate part of the elevated language of mock-epic.

The word *ape* is used by Chaucer to refer to the animal which still goes by that name in modern English, but, more commonly, it is used to refer to a foolish man who has become a dupe. Rather unexpectedly, the latter sense derives from a special use of the word in philosophic discussion. The ape, although more or less like a man in form, differs markedly from him in its lack of the faculty of reason. This similarity, with a crucial difference, was used traditionally by logic books as an example of the application of a *differentia*.[22] This special contextual use was transferred into everyday speech, where the word *ape* became widely used to signify a man who lacks the powers of reason. Traces of the original philosophical contrast between man and ape are apparent in a passage in the *Friar's Tale*, where a third member is added to the basic contrast: an angel too has the form of a man, but consists of pure intellect:

> 'Han ye a figure thanne determynat
> In helle ther ye been in youre estat?'
> 'Nay, certeynly,' quod he, 'ther haue we noon;
> But whan vs liketh we kan take vs oon,
> Or ellis make yow seme we ben shape
> Some tyme lyk a man or lyk an ape
> Or lyk an aungel, kan I ride and go.   (D 1459–65)

Now, although the words *figure* and *determynat* are recognisable as *termes*, one would hesitate to call this passage, which is part of a friendly exchange between a Summoner and the Devil, a truly technical passage. In fact they are using technical terms conversationally to allude to a shared background of learning without indulging in an extended technical discussion. The technicality evident may be naturally appropriate to the actual behaviour of professional men educated in the schools, but the true literary function of the use of *termes* here is to demonstrate the degree of *rapport* which exists between Summoners and the Devil.

A similar function is served by the use of *termes* in Book II of *Troilus and Criseyde*. When broaching the matter of Troilus's love to Criseyde, Pandarus employs all the arts at his disposal. Chaucer makes this clear by the images of how he planned his strategy in advance (I 1058 ff.); and he indicates by his commendation to Janus (II 77) that Pandarus will use what he later will call words 'with two visages' (V 899). Pandarus's skills as a persuader are made clear by the narrator who tells us how he fulfils the rhetorician's injunction to match the difficulty of material to the capacities of the audience:

> Than thought he thus: 'If I my tale endite
> Aught harde, or make a processe any whyle,
> She shal no sauour haue therin but lite.'[23]

> (II 267–9)

His general demeanour also emphasises the importance of his speech, which begins:

> . . . Nece, alwey, lo, to the laste,
> How so it be that som men hem delite
> With subtyl art hire tales forto endite,
> ʒet for al that in hire entencioun
> Hire tale is al for som conclusioun.

> And sithe thende is euery tales strengthe,
> And this matere is so bihouely,
> What sholde I poynte or drawen it on lengthe
> To ʒow that ben my frend so feythfully?   (II 255–63)

The reference to *subtyl art* is clearly to rhetoric, the art of persuasion. The word *endite*, as we have seen, means to compose formally and artificially, and the words *entencioun* and *conclusioun* are to be associated with a traditional classification of works by intention and effect (see p. 221). Taking his cue from the latter word, *conclusioun*, Pandarus connects his argument by the lexical variant *ende*; technically, the final cause, the essential received significance of the piece. The gist, he says, is what matters, and his subject matter (*matere*, from Latin *materia*) is so important that there is no need to expand on it (*drawen on lengthe*; cf. Latin *amplificatio*). The word *poynte*, which seems to be a Central French variant of the more common form *peynte*, is a familiar Latin metaphor, referring to the elaboration of a discourse by 'painting' it with the 'colours of rhetoric'.[24]

This display of technical reference by Chaucer is also a deliberate display of duplicity. Whilst employing all the resources of rhetorical persuasion, Pandarus is denying the necessity of practising such arts on one whom he knows to be a faithful friend who will inevitably share his aspirations without such persuasion. Criseyde is impressed by his skill, but she is not blinded by it. She is sufficiently mistress of herself to think 'I shal felen what he meneth ywis', and encourages him to state his position more clearly. When he advises compliance with Troilus's desires, it is Criseyde's turn to use elaborate apostrophes and seek technical terminology:

> Is al this paynted proces seyd allas
> Right for this fy[n]?   (II 424–5)

The fact that Criseyde recognises Pandarus's game, and indeed is a party to it, is evident from her choice of language. Her phrase *paynted proces* echoes words used by Pandarus, and the word *fyn* is simply a synonym of the words *ende* and *conclusioun* which formed part of his denial of the use of rhetoric.[25] Uncle and niece share a common sphere of allusion, and each understands the role the other has elected to play: Pandarus, the true friend wounded by unjustified suspicion of his motives; and Criseyde, the virtuous widow scandalised by the suggestion of a liaison to which she is in reality not averse. The subtlety of characterisation in Book II as a whole is beyond the scope of a guide to the language, but we should not fail to recognise that the allusive use of *verba propria* is a means used in this scene to achieve that subtlety.

A second example may serve to illustrate the allusive value of Chaucer's use of *termes* which have some stable association with a context thought proper for them. In the *Merchant's Tale*, a study is presented of a marriage contracted for reasons of expedience, and conducted in an atmosphere of inhumanity and infidelity. Critics have commented on the bitterness evident in the tale, and upon the difficulty of discerning any trace of moral perspective. A tale characterised by inhumanity and amorality has seemed un-Chaucerian and unacceptable to the poet's admirers, so that the final recourse of Chaucerian critics, when at their wits' end for ways of reconciling his values with our own, has been invoked: the poem has been regarded as intentionally comic. The extreme of critical embarrassment is laughter.[26] It happens, however, that there is in the *Merchant's Tale* a very consistent stream of allusion to the Christian marriage service and to other aspects of idealising medieval doctrine on marriage, and this allusion serves to provide a clear and striking contrast with the actual marriage portrayed for us. The marriage service is evoked by the use of *termes*, both words and phrases, proper to it and juxtaposed in the context of the tale:

> Wel may his herte in ioye and blisse habounde,
> For who kan be so buxom as a wyf?
> Who is so trewe and eek so ententyf
> To kepe hym syk and hool as is his make?
> For wele or wo she wol hym nat forsake.
>
> (E 1286–90)

In the contemporary marriage service, a wife promised to be *buxom* 'submissive' as well as to keep her husband *syk and hool*, in *wele or wo*.[27] The words were sufficiently widespread and familiar to be regarded as inseparable from associations of the ideal of marriage found in the marriage service, and they serve as an introduction to a tale of the contrast between ideals and their betrayal.

Although it cannot be denied that Chaucer often allotted speeches *properly* to his characters, and as we shall see in the next chapter, he even asserted this, yet from the examples given above it is evident that the observance of simple *proprietas* in language was not his chief concern. Much more could be achieved by breaches of propriety and by the exploitation of the allusive power of *termes*. Indeed the deployment outside its proper sphere of language with a recognised propriety is one of the major ways by which Chaucer's poetry gains in richness of meaning. Far from being the sole prerogative of ancient

Trojans, Summoners, or devils, it is characteristic of the medieval clerk and courtier, and is often the foundation of courtly wit. We should not forget, for example, that much of the terminology used for the discussion of human love by such persons could reasonably have been considered proper to theology or feudal law. A writer on vernacular language of the century before Chaucer, Brunetto Latini, comments that the power of making analogies and comparisons is a characteristic of cultivated people.[28]

The recognition of *proprietas* by Chaucer and his contemporaries was a recognition that English now possessed a vocabulary of sufficient complexity to enable one topic to be seen simultaneously in the light of another, and this opened the way to a literary use of analogy, allusion and irony, enabling Chaucer to write secular poetry of a greater degree of conceptual complexity than any before. If he can truly be called the Father of English Poetry, it is clearly not for his employment of French themes and poetic forms, but more justly for his discovery and exploitation of a newly developed potential in the English language.

8   Levels of Style

Why is it that Chaucer makes his Host embark upon a recitation of the *termes* of medicine, entering upon a register foreign to an innkeeper, from which he ignominiously retreats with the admission that he 'kan nat speke in terme'? He seems jovially to be making a fool of himself as much as criticising the incomprehensibility of medical jargon. A contrast can be made with the remarks about alchemical jargon in the *Canon's Yeoman's Tale*, where it is wryly stated that the use of obscure language makes its user seem wondrous wise (G 750–52). Why does Chaucer feel it to be a worthwhile literary manoeuvre to make his Franklin deny knowledge of rhetoric in the technical language proper to that skill, then follow this statement by a declaration that he 'kan no termes of astrologye' (F 1266) and a *tour de force* of these very *termes*?[1] The characters are comically being made to exhibit knowledge or ignorance of technical terms; but what are the implications of this? The beginnings of an answer can be sought in a manuscript written about fifty years after Chaucer's death, MS Egerton 1995. In it there occurs a list of the properties (*proprietates*) of a greyhound, and another list of the technical terms of hunting. They are prefaced by the following words:

> Note ye the properteys that longythe to a yonge gentylle man to haue knowynge of such thyngys that longythe vnto hym that he fayle not in his propyr termys that longythe vnto hym as hyt shall folowe hereynne wrytynge.[2]

Knowledge of certain accomplishments, together with the technical terms which belong to them, is evidently regarded as the characteristic of a gentleman. The printer of the *Book of St*

Albans (1486) also tells his potential readership that it is intended for 'gentill personys' (p. 57), and that it will inform them of the terms in which to refer to hounds and beasts; moreover, he implies, it will enable them to associate with other men of rank by teaching them how to use 'the gentill termys in communyng of theyr haukys' (p. 3). The fifteenth century, in fact, became obsessed with the need for a knowledge of the technical terms appropriate to the pursuits of an aristocratic life. Manuscripts contain fanciful 'terms of association', listing the names for groups of various animals and birds, and these occur alongside useful hints on choosing a horse. Printers filled blank leaves with such informative material as lists of bishoprics and the technical terminology associated with carving at table. In her introduction to the facsimile of the *Book of St Albans* Rachel Hands lists more than twenty extant manuscripts containing collections of such material. It is apparent that the motive for compiling lists of such terms was one of social aspiration: a knowledge of the language proper to the concerns of a gentleman was equated with the possession of gentility itself. To be heard to speak like a gentleman was half-way to being taken for one. Sir Thomas Malory remarks:

> wherefore, as me semyth, all jantylmen that beryth olde armys ought of ryght to honoure sir Tristrams for the goodly tearmys that jantylman have and use and shall do unto the Day of Dome, that thereby in a maner all men of worshyp may discover a jantylman frome a yoman and a yoman frome a vylane. For he that jantyll is woll drawe hym to jantyll tacchis and folow the noble customys of jantylmen.[3]
>
> (Vol. I p.375)

In the fifteenth century, when courtesy books which promised to inculcate the manners of the gentle flourished, it is not particularly surprising to find an interest in the social significance of language. Nor, at a time when poetic art was preoccupied with lexical splendour, is it surprising to find the ancient association between eloquence and cultural refinement taking the form of a fascination with out-of-the-way terminology. The loss of French had by this time finally removed the traditional linguistic distinction between the *gentil* and the peasant, and no upper-class standard English had yet emerged to fill its role, so that it is apparent that the linguistic situation itself had contributed to this new solution to the problem of maintaining linguistic differentiation between the rulers and the ruled.

The word lists, however, were not an invention of the fifteenth century, although the vast majority date from its latter half. Their origins are to be sought much earlier in bilingual glossaries. The *Nominale sive Verbale*, dated by Skeat at about 1340, is a bilingual collection of expressions loosely organised in terms of conceptual areas.[4] It does not confine itself to those areas which in the fifteenth century were seen as the concerns of a gentleman, but contains such things as parts of the body, technical words for house-building, weather phenomena, and the parts of a cart. To some extent it may be regarded as a French-English dictionary, but it is much more a guide to style and idiom. For example, it shows how the single English word *red* may, according to its application, be rendered variously in French as *roux*, *goules*, *rouge*, or *vermaille*. It also gives lists of 'terms of association' whose communicative practicality must be very questionable. It is probable that the work was intended in the same spirit as later lists of *termes*, but it belongs to a period when a discriminating knowledge of French terminology was still as important in defining a gentleman as an awareness of the English terms of hunting, carving, and the associations of beasts.

That a subtle knowledge of the language proper to aristocratic concerns should carry with it the presumption of aristocracy is easily understood. An ability to speak in dialect presupposes an appropriate regional origin, and the analogy with a knowledge of the register of aristocratic concerns is obvious. But the *Nominale* implies something more than this; that is, that a mastery of technical terms other than those narrowly proper to aristocratic interests was considered desirable in itself. Copiousness of vocabulary, which implies breadth of experience evident in the knowledge of technical language, had long been an ideal of eloquence.[5] However, it is perhaps less obvious that eloquence itself was a part of the valued ideal of *gentillesse*. Courtesy books give no detailed

instruction on the art of language, but they do give hints on the
effective use of language: when best to speak and when to keep
silent; and they praise an ability to speak to the point with
force and polish.[6] And indeed, outside courtesy books, most
medieval authors have something to say about the verbal
effectiveness of their heroes and heroines. A few years after
Chaucer's death, the author of *Mum and the Sothsegger*
approvingly remarks of his blunt-spoken hero:

> He can nat speke in termes ne in tyme nother
> But bablith fourth bustusely as a bern un-y-lerid.
>
> (49–50)

What is implied by this is childish naïveté in speech: deliberate
carelessness of the rules of how to deploy appropriate
language, and when to speak in company. In the *Parliament of
Fowls* a goose, a member of the despised class of water-fowl,
speaks and is greeted by the following reply from a superior
gentil bird:

> 'Lo, here a parfyte resoun of a goos!'
> Quod the sperhauke; 'Neuer mote she thee!
> Loo, such hyt ys to haue a tonge loos!
> Now, parde! foole, yet were hit bet for the
> Have holde thy pes than shewede thy nycete.
> Hyt lyth not in hys wytte nor in hys wille,
> But sooth is seyde, 'a foole kan noght be stille'.
>
> The laughtre aroose of gentil foules alle.   (568–75)

The scornful laughter of the 'gentil foules' is directed at the
social ignorance of the goose, both in terms of what she says
and how she says it. This latter is given point by the fact that
the hapless bird has been elected spokesman for her group on
account of her *facounde gent* (l.558). As we saw in Chapter 6 this
phrase is used ironically, but the word *facounde*, a quality which
is possessed by courtly ladies like the Duchess Blanche, is
worth further attention since it has an illustrious history. It
derives from the Latin *facundia*, which, according to the
rhetorician Chirius Fortunatianus, was the Gaulish regional
equivalent of Roman *facetia*, the ideal of eloquence which

distinguished the urbane man in Roman society.[7] In Chaucer's time *facounde* is a relatively uncommon word, but the *Catholicon Anglicum* glosses *facundia* as *faire speche*, a phrase which is widely used instead. *Gentil* folk use *faire speche* appropriately and at the right time, whereas *boistous* men speak out of turn, without polish, and, we may assume, without knowledge of appropriate terminology and phrasing. This is the significance of the Host's and Franklin's references to *termes*. Harry Baily's inevitable failure in his 'proper terms', by which he refuses to be abashed, carries with it certain social presumptions. But, unlike Sir Gawain, he has no anxiety about a possible failure in the 'forme of his castes'; his lack of concern for social shibboleths places him outside the possible scorn of the *gentils*, for he has the licence of a jester, who, as we shall see, can adopt some of the phrasing of *faire speche* when he wishes. The reference to the language of alchemy in the *Canon's Yeoman's Tale* is to the use of impressive *termes* by confidence tricksters, a device also used by the Summoner and Pardoner, where the necessary prestige is drawn from apparent learning. In the *Franklin's Tale* a man of importance and elevated sentiment is presented, whose tale is a *tour de force* of rhetoric and erudite allusion, but who, in a fine display of false modesty, consistently denies the urbanity which his language blazons forth.

Behind all this verbal play of Chaucer's, and behind Gawain's anxiety too, is the concept of *proprietas* and the belief that the language reveals the man. Chaucer repeatedly questions its validity, but such a belief is elaborated in the translation of the *Roman de la Rose*. The dreamer is congratulated on the courtliness of his speech:

> For nowe I wote wel vtterly
> That thou arte gentyl, by thy speche.
> For though a man ferre wolde seche,
> He shulde not fynden, in certayne,
> No suche answere of no vilayne;
> For suche a worde ne myght nought
> Isse out of a vylayns thought.   (1986–92)

Heart, thought, and language are presumed to be united in proclaiming baseness or courtly elevation. For a narrative poet such assumptions about the propriety of language could lead to difficulties, since the esteem in which poetry was held by its prospective audience owed much to its social acceptability.[8] Indeed, in much of Chaucer's poetry the authorial voice is decorous, as befits a poet speaking to gentle folk; but very often also he deviates from such expectations. In the *Canterbury Tales* the fiction of a pilgrimage contains tales told by churls, and here Chaucer seems comically anxious that the *vileynye* proper to them should not be ascribed to him as a private individual:

> But first I pray yow of youre curteisye
> That ye n'arette it noght my vileynye,
> Though that I pleynly speke in this matere
> To telle yow hir wordes and hir cheere
> Ne thogh I speke hir wordes proprely.
> For this ye knowen also wel as I,
> Whoso shal telle a tale after a man
> He moot reherce as neigh as euere he kan
> Euerich a word if it be in his charge,
> Al speke he neuer so rudeliche and large,
> Or ellis he moot telle his tale vntrewe.

> (A 725–35)

The churls' speech which he is going to relate is proper to them and not to him, he claims, and is dictated by artistic necessity. The tales are of a *fabliau*-type, told by churls about people of low social rank and deeds of unaccustomed grossness, and their language must be appropriate.

In speaking of these churls, Chaucer refers to *cherles termes* and tales told in the *manere* of a churl but in assessing the significance of such expressions we are beset by many ambiguities of fourteenth-century usage, and it will be best to be aware of them before continuing the discussion. Firstly an uncertainty exists as to what extent *termes* and styles regarded as proper to churls are a literary convention. In some cases they certainly are; but, given the close connection between social and literary acceptability, they may also represent a real social distinction. Secondly, both the concept of 'churl' and its contrast with 'courtly' are also deeply ambiguous, since they may both refer to actual social class, but frequently refer instead to social ideals. It is often difficult to distinguish between these possible significances in analysing the relevant vocabulary. In Chaucer's works *gentils* use *faire speche* and are *facounde*. They speak *in forme, faire, goodly, frendly, curteisly, wel, renably,* and *feelingly. Cherles termes* are described as *bold, rude, knavyssh, brode, large, bare and pleyn, vilayn,* and they speak *amys* or *uncurteisly.* We cannot devote space here to analyse the precise significance of all these words, or their relevance to the ideals of courtliness, but we must be warned that there are distinctions to be made between them. Whereas words like *vilayn* and *knavyssh* are essentially socially disparaging, *pleyn* only becomes so by contrast with an assumption that courtly men and women use graces of speech which are felt to be necessary in some circumstances. Some of these words also refer as much to attitudes expressed in speech as to the forms of language itself; hence, just as *pleyn* in certain circumstances may indicate reprehensibly blunt speech, so *faire* may imply not only eloquent language but also solicitude for the interlocutor.[9] It is evident that these words have to be interpreted with care; but, whatever their precise significance at any given occurrence, it is also evident that Chaucer recognised a broad division of language into that which was suitable to the courtly and urbane man, and that appropriate to the churl. So much seems to be beyond dispute. It seems also that, at least in some cases, besides the attitudes represented in courtly or churlish utterances, they could be distinguished by the degree of eloquence displayed. The speech of the socially-elevated would embody his ideals and express them more elaborately, whereas that of the humbler betrayed his social naïveté and was brief and plain.

The existence of such a dichotomy, in which social status and language jointly participate within a literary context, raises an interesting question with regard to the criticism of medieval literature, since critics frequently refer to three levels of style: high, low, and middle. This threefold division of style in medieval writings has authority in Latin texts of the period, but, although it is often applied to Chaucer's works, the basis of the division to be made there is rarely given, and it is worth remembering that the whole schematic theory had been severely criticised in antiquity by Quintilian.[10] How relevant is it, therefore, to the dichotomy between courtly and churlish speech which we find repeatedly in Chaucer's writings?

Firstly, it must be stressed that the theory of three styles belongs essentially to Latin and Greek composition. Secondly, it must be realised that neither Chaucer, Gower, nor any of their contemporaries ever discuss it in English.[11] Nevertheless, it is unlikely that it was unknown to them since reference to it is ubiquitous in commentaries and introductions to Latin authors. The implication seems to be either that they did not regard it as relevant to their own composition, or that they considered it either too trivial or too obvious to mention. A brief account of the nature of the three styles is now required.

Traditionally, the *stylus grandis* 'high style' had been distinguished by a striking choice of words, which might include archaisms and neologisms. It employed hyperbolic expression, metaphor, and those figures of words and thought which bestowed grandeur. Syntactically, it tended to be complex and often sought for balanced effects. However, the tradition of Christian rhetoric stemming from Augustine's *De Doctrina Christiana* tended to regard high style in a rather different light, emphasising primarily its emotional vehemence, a circumstance which might carry with it a considerable degree of syntactical disruption.[12] Hence, the notion of high style is not stable within the tradition, but one enduring assumption about it was that it was a style of composition which devoted attention to a display of artifice and erudition in word-choice and allusion. Its function was to move and to impress.

Stylus humilis 'low style', on the other hand, was intended to make art unobtrusive. It was based upon the grammatical structures of everyday speech, but the everyday expressions were to be purged of hiatuses, grammatical faults, and infelicities of sound combinations which might be expected in real utterance. Its aim was to compress sense into brief expression, and although it used figurative language, it used it unobtrusively. Its choice of words was also from everyday usage, although the author was expected to exclude vulgarisms and indecorous expressions. It was to be clear and readily understandable, and according to Augustine, its main purpose was to instruct.

The middle style (*stylus mediocris*) was considered to be an artistic style whose chief function was to delight. In terms of lexical choice and figurative language, it lay between the other two, and its emphasis was upon elegance and smoothness of syntax.

The art of rhetoric flourished as instruction for making speeches in the Roman courts of law, and originally each style was thought to be appropriate to a particular part of the advocate's speech before the judge. In narrating the circumstances of a crime, the low style was to be used, but when appealing for pity, the high style was recommended. Cicero also states that the level of style should be related to the gravity of the case: thus a lawyer would certainly select the high style for a closing appeal to the judge in a trial for murder, but would use the low style in outlining the facts of the case in a charge of embezzlement.[13] However, in Christian Latin times the connection between the level of style and subject matter became loosened. Isidore refers to it only in the cases of the high and low styles, omitting the middle, and, already, outside the law courts, in late Latin in the commentaries of Servius and Donatus on the works of Virgil, the styles had become associated with the social status of the protagonists.[14] By the twelfth and early thirteenth centuries, when Geoffrey of Vinsauf and John of Garlande wrote their manuals of poetic composition, the three styles had become firmly associated with the social status of the persons who were being described. Indeed, the linguistic-stylistic conception of the three styles outlined above seems to have gone into eclipse and been replaced by what has been described as a 'material' one. In other words, the styles were determined by the social level of the material treated. Writing in any particular style was achieved by observing the *proprietates* (that is, the individual characteristics) of those concerns and persons which form the setting and protagonists of the discourse. Reference to the *proprietates* of elevated persons, therefore, results in *stylus grandis*; style and content are no longer separable.[15] The style is determined by the nature of the world which the story inhabits, and the duty of the poet is to avoid inadvertent fluctuation from a social level and its appropriate language. In theory, therefore, unless special effects are sought, one should not use elevated technical vocabulary in a *fabliau* context, nor the words *donge* or *myre* when discussing chivalric exploits.

If we were to search Chaucer's works for overt references to this theory of three levels of style, we should find none; but there are four references to *heigh stile*. One may be the result of Chaucer using a defective manuscript of Petrarch's story of Griselda; a second is a mere echo of this.[16] The other two are used jocularly. What does Chaucer mean by *heigh stile*, and does he see it in contrast to two other levels of style?

On the evidence of the use of the phrase by Harry Baily we can begin to piece together something of Chaucer's conception of *heigh stile*. Harry begs the Clerk to tell an amusing and simple story:

> Tel vs som murye thyng of auentures.
> Youre termes, youre colours and your figures,
> Kepe hem in stoor til so be ye endite
> Heigh stile as whan that men to kynges write.
> Speketh so pleyn at this tyme, we you preye,
> That we may vnderstonde what ye seye.   (E 15–20)

Heigh stile, it appears, may be difficult to follow; it contains figures of speech (*colours*) and of thought (*figures*) as well as unfamiliar words or phrases (*termes*). It is the product of artistic composition (*endite*), and gives an impression of artificiality distinct from that of *pleyn* speech. Furthermore, it is associated with learned men, who are needed to write and understand it. It is also connected with the ceremonious address of persons of the highest social status. In many respects, it is obvious that Chaucer's reference to *heigh stile* corresponds with traditional notions of *stylus grandis*, but there is a sharp distinction: Harry's reference to *heigh stile* in the above passage refers to an epistolary style, to elaborate language used in letters to commend and impress kings. It is possible, therefore, that this phrase had much narrower and more specific associations for Chaucer than those of a general theory of style.

It happens that in the Guildhall in London is preserved a series of letters dated between 1417 and 1424. They were exchanged between the mayor and citizenry of London and Henry V and the English leaders campaigning in France. In the letters addressed to the king content is minimal, for their purpose is essentially to compliment him and to reassure him of the loyal support of the city:

> Of alle erthely Princes our most dred soueraign Liege Lord, and noblest kynge, we recommaunde vs vnto your soueraign highnesse and riall power, in as meke wyse and lowely maner as any symple officers and pouuere lieges best may or can ymagine and diuise vnto her most graciouse and most soueraign kyng, Thankyng with all our soules your most soueraign excellence and noble grace of þe right gentell, right graciouse, and right confortable lettres, which ye late liked to send vs fro your toun of pount-de-larche, which lettres wiþ al lowenesse and reuerence we haue mekly resceyued, and vnderstonde bi which lettres, amonges al other blessed spede and graciouse tithinges in hem conteyned, for which we thanke hyly, and euer shulle, the lord almighty, ware we most inwardly conforted and reioysed, whan we herde þe soueraign helthe and parfit prosperite of your most excellent and gracious persoune, which we beseche god of hys grete grace and noble pite euer to kepe and manteyne.[17]

This is only half of the letter concerned, and we can already sympathise with the fears expressed by Harry Baily about *heigh stile*. All that has been said in the above passage could have been summarised in a couple of brief sentences. But such brevity would not constitute *heigh stile* fit for a king.

The most noticeable feature of this excerpt is that it consists of only one extended sentence. The letter opens with a formal salutation which functions as a vocative introduction to the commendation formula, and the thanks for earlier letters to which this is a reply are connected to the commendation by the use of the present participle, *Thankyng*, which introduces a lengthy adverbial phrase.[18] No opportunity for qualification is missed, and a favourite connective is the relative *which*. Nouns rarely occur without modifiers, and neither nouns nor verbs occur singly; rather, they are paired in any particular grammatical function with a near-synonym. Thus we find *as meke wyse and lowely maner*, *conforted and reioysed*, and even the duplicated auxiliaries *may or can ymagine and diuise*. The choice of words in this excerpt is less exuberant than that in some other letters, but we find the formula *our most dred soueraign Liege lord* together with uncommon Latinate or French terms like *excellence*, *confortable*, and *prosperite*. It is worth noting also that, although the London citizenry use a simple pronoun of themselves (*we*), they never address the king by anything other than abstract nominal phrases.

Is this the *heigh stile* addressed to kings that Harry dreaded? It seems likely that something like this was in his mind, for this style is well established in commendatory letters in French from the time of Edward III onwards, and features of it had invaded artificial prose such as that found in the *Tale of Melibee*.[19] This is not the place to elaborate on the epistolary high style, but that it was well known to Chaucer, at least in its prototype French form, is confirmed by an evocation of it in the *Squire's Tale*. A strange knight enters the hall, greets all there with unrivalled courtesy, and delivers a message word-perfect, with all the skills of the 'art of speche'.[20] The admiring narrator declines to imitate his speech word for word, since he 'kan nat clymben ouer so heigh a style' (l.106), but he will give the gist of it:

> He seyde: 'The kyng of Arabe and of Inde,
> My lige lord, on this solempne day
> Salueth yow as he best kan and may
> And sendeth yow in honour of youre feste
> By me that am al redy at youre heste
> This steede of bras, that esily and weel
> Kan in the space of o day naturel
> (This is to seyn in xxiiij houres)
> Wherso yow list in droghte or ellis shoures
> Beren youre body into euery place
> To which youre herte wilneth for to pace
> Withouten wem of yow thurgh foul or fair.
> Or if yow list to flee as hye in the ayr
> As dooth an egle whan hym list to soore.

                                                        (F 110–23)

This verse greeting from one king to another is clearly not identical to the letters in Guildhall, but it exhibits sufficient of their features to prefigure them unmistakably. The verse treatment merges the commendation and the salutation of the letters, but echoes some of their phrasing nearly exactly. The phrase *best kan and may* stands out, and the formula *my lige lord* also occurs, but is applied to the sender rather than the addressee, who is regarded throughout as an equal, to be addressed only by the polite plural pronoun *yow* rather than the abstractions of the real letter. Word-pairing is merely suggested: *esily and weel, in droghte or ellis shoures, foul or fair*; and there is only one really unusual technical term, *day natureel*, which is carefully explained.[21] However, the whole of the excerpt quoted consists of a single extended sentence built up by the addition of adverbials and qualifying clauses. The connectives seem more natural to us than the present participle and repeated relative *which*'s of the Guildhall letter; nevertheless, that particular feature of the epistolary style is evoked by *to which* in line 120.

The speech of the strange knight in the *Squire's Tale*, in view of the differences of situation and genre, is not identical with existing letters; however, it displays sufficient of the stylistic peculiarities of the epistolary style to make identification possible. It is a stylistic connection which is wholly appropriate to the narrative circumstances, and, taken with Chaucer's reference at the beginning of the *Clerk's Tale* to the *heigh stile* of royal letters, it indicates for us specifically what Chaucer might have understood by this phrase. It is evident that this *heigh stile* belongs to a world of elevated people and things, as Geoffrey of Vinsauf conceived it, but it is also recognisable intrinsically, and distinct from its reference, and it is therefore capable of being imitated or evoked at the purely stylistic level in terms of characteristic sentence structure and phraseology. Moreover, it is clear from this that Chaucer has a conception of *heigh stile* which was truly stylistic in contradistinction to the material conception of *stylus grandis* proffered by Geoffrey of Vinsauf.

This elaborate epistolary style is what Chaucer calls *heigh stile*, and we have no certain proof that he would have applied the phrase to anything else; however, it is likely that he would have acknowledged *heigh stile* to be an inclusive term applicable to other forms of consciously artificial *endyting* as well. The term refers to complex written composition, deliberately displaying art. Chaucer did not refer to the ordinary *speech* of elevated persons as *heigh stile*, even if it were relatively complex. His literary imitation of such speech, he called *faire speche*, and introduced such speeches with a qualifying adverb: *curteisly* or a near-synonym. What, then, does Chaucer understand when he says that a character speaks *curteisly*? We must consider some examples.

Despite his failure in *termes*, Harry Baily can speak *curteisly* as a maid if he wishes, and in a famous passage he does so to the Prioresse:

> My lady prioresse, by youre leue,
> So that I wiste I sholde yow nat agreue,
> I wolde demen that ye telle sholde
> A tale next, if so were that ye wolde.
> Now wol ye vouche it sauf, my lady deere?
>
> (B 1637–41)

Let us consider first the terms of address which he chooses. The pronoun *ye* is that of respect and formality. The form *my lady* is perhaps not so elevated as the *madame*, which, in the *General Prologue*, the Prioresse had adopted for herself, but there is evidence to suggest that Chaucer could view the latter ironically as an aspiration of *bourgeoise* ladies.[22] Here, however, decorum reigns. It is Harry's purpose to solicit a story from the Prioresse, and here we should recall the circumstances in which it was agreed that stories be told on the way to Canterbury, for it makes his conduct all the more striking. It had been agreed that each participant in the pilgrimage should contribute four stories in all, and Harry had been adopted as master of these revels, with the sanction against dissidents of requiring them to pay for all the expenses incurred on the road. With such executive power, it is remarkable that Harry does not simply require a story from the Prioresse, but in fact he never specifically asks her to tell one. Rather than use imperatives and indicatives, he selects the subjunctive, and verbs of wishing and desiring. Indeed, Harry's whole speech is framed by references to the lady's wishes. He only speaks at all *by youre leue*, and his final unspoken question is in the form *wol ye vouche it sauf?* He *would* judge that she should tell a tale, on condition that she is not inconvenienced by it, and indeed, if she positively wishes to do so. Even his desire to ask her to tell a story is dependent upon the necessity for him to know in advance her attitude to his request: a necessity which reduces his executive power to the level of a hypothetical question.

The outstanding feature of this speech, which Chaucer designates as courtly, is the extraordinary lengths to which Harry Baily goes to avoid coercion. He renounces his agreed right to demand a story, and endeavours to ensure that the lady's wishes coincide with his own. This results in an unusually elaborate sentence structure. Something of the circumstances of this solicitude for the wishes of another can be grasped from the scene in *Sir Gawain and the Green Knight* where the lady of the castle tells Gawain that he is of sufficient strength to force intimacies upon her. He replies:

> . . . þrete is vnþryuande in þede þer I lende,
> And vche gift þat is geuen not with goud wylle.
>
> (1499–1500)

[Coercion is profitless where I come from, and so is every gift which is not willingly given]

As in love, so in asking for a story, concern for the wishes of the other is what constitutes *curteisie*.

Following the scholastic principle that understanding is gained by a knowledge of contraries, let us consider a second request for a story on the road to Canterbury. This is that made by Harry to the Nun's Priest in a speech described as *rude . . . and boold*:

> Com neer, thow preest, com hider, thow sir Iohn.
> Telle vs swich thyng as may oure hertes glade.
> Be blythe though thow ryde vpon a iade.
> What though thyn hors be bothe foul and lene!
> If he wol serue thee rekke nat a bene.
> Looke that thyn herte be murye eueremo.
>
> (B 4000–4005)

The use of the familiar singular form of the pronoun is at once noticeable, and in terms of address it is worth emphasising the contrast between the titles *my lady prioresse* and *thow preest*. *Sir John* is a jocular generic name for priests, not necessarily antagonistic, but not very respectful either. It is noteworthy that Harry's request for a story entirely lacks the elaborate structure of conditionals found in the request to the Prioresse. Instead, there is a series of imperatives: *com neer! com hyder! telle us! be blithe! rekke nat a bene! looke that thyn herte be myrie!* No sentence extends beyond the length of a line, and the word order seems as colloquial as the lexical choice, in which phrases like *rekke nat a bene*, and the reference to the horse as a *jade*, echo the derogatory tone of the whole. Harry's attitude to the Nun's Priest is by no means unfriendly, but it is entirely lacking in social esteem. In its patronising familiarity, its bantering references to personal circumstances, it simply disregards the possibility that the addressee may possess any sensibility to be damaged by such brusqueness. There is a demeaning assumption that he will be unconcerned by a direct demand for a story.

The fact that Harry Baily can speak both *curteisly* and in words *rude and bold* is a considerable advance from the assumption implicit in the earlier quotation from the *Romaunt of the Rose*, which implied that these distinctions of speech were *proprietates* of the social or moral state of the individual; but what is the distinction between these two speeches of Harry's? It lies essentially in the difference of attitude revealed in the speeches. In the first, he maintains a respectful social distancing between himself and the Prioresse; he is solicitous of her feelings and her wishes. As courtly theorising would express it, he is endeavouring to ensure that their wills are one.[23] In addressing the Nun's Priest, there is none of this respect, none of the solicitude for the feelings of a sensitive man, but rather a stream of jovial intrusions upon his private circumstances. No doubt the distinction between *curteisly* and *rude and bold* could be made purely in terms of the attitudes expressed here. So much is neatly demonstrated by a contrast between *feire speche* and chiding in the *House of Fame*:

> . . . ful of tydynges
> Bothe of feire speche and chidynges
> And of fals and that soth compovned.
>
> (*HF* 1027–9)

It is clear that the adjectives *faire* and *curteis*, when applied to speech, can refer to attitudes expressed; but another sense of *faire speche* is demonstrated by the Latin gloss *facundia* in *Catholicon Anglicum*, where the phrase is clearly understood to refer to eloquence. In short, utterances which are conciliatory, friendly, and show special consideration for the addressee will be regarded as *curteis* or *faire* speech; also, artificially elaborate language using recondite terms, complex syntax, and high levels of abstraction, is likely to be regarded as *faire speche*. Two different qualities of the *gentil* man are revealed by these two different aspects of *faire speche*: his natural sympathy and his learning in courtliness. Although references to *curteisie* in speech can usually be referred to the former quality, the expression of feelings and attitudes usually leads to stylistic elaboration, and the nobleman's experience of life leads to the use of terms proper to his station; thus *curteisie* and elaborate modes of expression are closely inter-related, and the concepts of *faire speche* and speaking *curteisly* are often indistinguishable. It is probable that such speech would have been considered a variant of *heigh stile*, but we have no direct evidence that it was. We do, however, have some direct evidence that Chaucer could distinguish between socially-related styles on linguistic grounds, as distinct from the attitudes expressed in speeches. This is most obvious, at least in the case of *cherles termes*, at the level of word-choice.

In the *Roman de la Rose* (6898 ff.), in a passage which Chaucer had obviously read with attention, since he alludes to it in the *Book of the Duchess* and at the end of the *Pardoner's Tale*, Reason, personified as a young woman, falls into an altercation with the Dreamer about linguistic usage.[24] The God of Love has earlier warned him that the ideal lover must not use filthy words or 'ribaudies'. But Reason has used the word *coilles* 'testicles', and the Dreamer objects to such bold language from a young woman. His attitude is not unlike that of the ladies satirised in some French *fabliaux*.[25] Words like *coilles*, *coillons*, *vit* are denounced as 'plein de vilenie', and should not be uttered in polite society. Even those coarse women who act as children's nurses, he says, prefer euphemisms. But Reason is unabashed. Her explanation invokes the concept of *proprietas*: these words are proper terms, the correct and original designations of the genitals, and it is right that Reason should use them in *plein texte* without *glose* rather than the range of ridiculous euphemisms in common use: *borses*, *harnais*, *piches*, *pines*. There is nothing intrinsically *vileins* in the words, Reason claims, for if *coilles* were called *reliques*, then this word too would be regarded as one to be avoided. The courtly objection is simply prudery, and it is right that rational discussion should be unfettered by such prejudices. The courtly dreamer cannot effectively counter these arguments, but neither will he accept them.

In the light of this passage we may reconsider the passage from the *General Prologue* quoted earlier in this chapter. Chaucer defends himself from the imputation of *vileynye* arising from his use of *rude*, *large*, and *brode* speech, and his defence is three-fold. Firstly, he employs the artistic arguments of *proprietas*: he is representing the words of the churls as they spoke them. The second defence invokes similar principles: words must be matched to actions and events. This is evidently an invocation of the notion of low style. Thirdly, his defence is moralistic: Christ himself used *brode* speech in the scriptures, and they cannot be considered indecent. *Brode speche* may be used, and indeed be salutary, when used for a good, instructional purpose. This argument parallels that used by Reason. Yet, whilst apparently accepting the arguments of Reason in the *Roman de la Rose*, Chaucer still pays lip-service to the scruples of the courtly dreamer by warning against the vulgarities of the Miller's and Reeve's tales, and advising sensitive readers to skip them.

In a more covert way, too, Chaucer bows to courtly sensibilities, for many of the supposed *cherles termes* which he uses are in fact rather euphemistic. The robustness of the Wife of Bath has often been noted, but in fact her language is distinguished by a display of conventional euphemisms rather than the equivalents of the words condemned by the Dreamer in the *Roman de la Rose*: *sely instrument*, *quoniam*, *thinges smale*, *bele chose.* Most of these euphemisms can be paralleled in the contemporary French translation of Matheolus's *Lamentations.*[26] Even the form *queynte* may be less vulgar than the Norse-derived modern form of the word, which was contemporaneously available.[27] A recent book devoted to Chaucer's bawdy lists many puns and allusions, and it is a significant fact that none are graceless and direct; Chaucer's bawdy nearly always relies on allusion or *double entendre.*[28] However, greater directness may be used for a definable literary purpose. In the *Merchant's Tale*, for example, when he comes to describe the climactic events in the pear tree, Chaucer gives a warning, begging the pardon of ladies who might be offended at such unaccustomed directness:

> Ladys I pray yow that ye be nat wroth;
> I kan nat glose, I, a rude man.
> And sodeynly anon this Damyan
> Gan pullen vp the smok and in he throng.
>
> (E 2350–3)

The shock of this sounds the knell of any pretensions to courtliness in the conduct of this affair. A moment later, however, Chaucer becomes suddenly decorous again, refusing to tell how Damyan had dealt with May on the grounds that it cannot be expressed except *uncurteisly.* This sudden reservation is odd, but it has a purpose: it avoids the use of the word *swyven*, which is then reserved for Januarie's outraged realisation and accusation a few lines later:

> He swyued thee! I saw it with myne eyen.
>
> (E 2378)

There is a second reason for the refusal of the narrator to *glose* here, in addition to that of characterisation, and this is explicable in terms of the slogan that the 'wordes mote be cosyn to the dede'. Direct and even vulgar speech is proper to immoral actions, since it may demonstrate moral disgust. As the Parson says with reference to confession:

> Thow shalt nat eek peynte thy confessioun by faire subtile

wordes, to covere the moore thy synne . . . Thow most tellen it platly, be it nevere so foul ne so horrible.[29]

(I 1022; Robinson's text)

A similar attitude is found in the *Manciple's Tale* where again the narrator adopts vulgarity, and feigns rude simplicity:

> And so bifel whan Phebus was absent
> His wyf anon hath for hire lemman sent –
> Hir lemman, certes this is a knauyssh speche!
> Foryeueth it me and that I yow biseche.
> The wise Plato seith as ye may rede:
> The word moot nede acorde with the dede;
> If men shal telle proprely a thyng,
> The word moot cosyn be to the werkyng.
> I am a boystous man. Right thus seye I
> Ther nys no difference trewely
> Bitwix a wyf that is of heigh degree
> If of hire body deshoneste she be
> And a poore wenche, oother than this
> (If it so be they werke bothe amys)
> But that the gentile in estat aboue
> She shal be clepid his lady as in loue,
> And for that oother is a poore womman
> She shal be clepid his wenche or his lemman.
> And god it woot, myn owene deere brother,
> Men leyn that oon as lowe as lyth that oother.

(H 203–22)

Although there are no indecent words in this passage, the word *lemman* is considered *knauyssh*, and in the *Merchant's Tale*, May, who considers herself a *gentil womman* shuns the appellation *wenche*.[30] Both words are clearly unacceptable designations of a lady of quality in Chaucer's language. The point of this use of the socially-derogatory terms *wenche* and *lemman* is betrayed by the exhortation of 'myn owene deere brother', references to not being *textueel*, and the exploitation of the question of the *differentia* distinguishing a war-leader from a pirate a few lines later. The narrator has adopted the tones of the preacher. Under the dual pretence of *proprietas* of *termes* and simple-minded directness, a moral position is being taken: the social distaste felt by the *gentils* for *wenches* and *lemmans* is being converted to revulsion for a breach of the moral code. Plain-spoken bluntness of this kind, as well as the presentation of moral baseness in terms of social scorn, are common devices of Christian exhortation in the Middle Ages.[31] The word *lemman* in Middle English is somewhat uncertain in its connotations, since it could still be used without evident irony in some dialects in Chaucer's time; but even in the language of the *Gawain*-poet it can take on strongly pejorative associations, as when in *Cleanness* he mocks the pretentiousness of referring to Balthasar's concubines as 'mony a lemman . . . þat ladis wer called' (1352).

As words considered to be socially disparaging in Chaucer's language, *lemman* and *wenche* may be considered to represent two classes of terms to be avoided in courtly speech. *Lemman* is one of those words, common in earlier literature, which had become associated with a faded romantic ideal, and now was probably used ironically both in much everyday language and certainly in Chaucer's poetry. Collocated with *lotebie* elsewhere in Middle English, it had become associated with the illicit, extramarital affairs of clerks with peasant girls, and so had developed a marked moral connotation.[32] The word is commonly found in literary use in the popular love lyrics which described such encounters, and it is therefore probable that any moral aversion felt to the word would be reinforced in Chaucer's circle by aesthetic and social deprecation. Indeed, the word *lemman* can be classed with other *démodé* and *déclassé* terms like those discussed in Chapter 6: *oore, hende, derelynge, swete brid, ris, drury, worly, dextrer, wonger, auntrous, gent, rode, loue-longynge, gore*, and the words *fetys* and *tretys*.

The word *lemman*, in Chaucer's usage, can have overtones of moral disapproval, social scorn, or artistic patronising as a result of its literary history. The word *wenche*, however, is derogatory on rather different grounds, deriving more directly from its reference. Although both *wenche* and *knave* could be used of children without pejorative implication, they frequently refer to servants, persons of lower class and, in addition, of doubtful morals. The word *malkin*, originally the diminutive of a personal name, has a similarly morally and socially-derogatory sense as *wenche*. *Carl* and *harlot* are frequent terms of abuse for men in Middle English, and both have social implications; the latter exhibiting the common association between social and moral weakness. Words of this kind, except in their proper applications to children or servants, could have been regarded as *cherles termes* in courtly speech. Two other such words whose status is hard to ascertain on the basis of their unique occurrences are *knarre* and *gnof*. Since both seem to have a sense not unlike that of 'lump' applied to a person in modern English, it is evident that they lack respect, and, in view of their relative absence from written texts, it may be that we are here dealing with examples of very rare slang words in Chaucer's English.

We may now summarise our discoveries about the relationship between courtly and plain speech. Firstly, and above all, courtly speech is that speech which exhibits or propagates the ideals of courtliness; speech which reveals its speaker to be ignorant of, or in opposition to, these ideals may be regarded as *uncurteis*, and hence the speech of a *cherle*. This basic opposition is regardless of language choice or patterning and also regardless of the true social status of the individual: it represents only adherence to an ideal, or the lack of it. Beyond this, and more concerned with style rather than content, courtly speech (Chaucer's *faire speche*) may be expected to exhibit the skills of eloquence, including the elaboration of syntax, use of figurative language, and knowledge of *termes*. The knowledge of terms from technical fields is matched by, and indeed often identical with, the choice of words of French or Latin derivation. Certain words which are considered to belong to a discredited intellectual world are avoided, as are words with indecent reference and words whose reference is to things with which courtly people could have no concern. However, there are exceptions to these exclusions, as when the need for clarity of exposition outweighs social display, and then simple terms and plain style may be sought. Chaucer's Clerk speaks briefly and pithily, and his Eagle in the *House of Fame* is proud of the simple lucidity of his exposition:

> Haue y not preved thus symply
> Withouten any subtilite

Of speche, or grete prolyxite
Of termes of philosophie,
Of figures of poetrie,
Or colours, or rethorike?
Pardee, hit ought the to lyke!
For harde langage and hard matere
Ys encombrouse for to here
Attones . . .   (*HF* 854–63)

Usk, too, believed that plain language was most suitable for instruction: 'for rude wordes and boystous percen the herte of the herer to the innerest point, and planten there the sentence of thinges'.

Plain language may therefore be an art, used for a special purpose by those who are capable of more elaborated discourse, and the style of courtly speech may therefore include words which might have been considered proper to churls. It may do this either for an artistic or a moral purpose. However there is a style of speech which is used by genuinely *burel* or *boystous* men, and which is truly *rude, bare* and *pleyn*.[33] It is uncourtly from various perspectives: it is *lewed* since it exhibits neither eloquence nor learning, and so its sentence structures are simple and its word-choice limited and concrete. It may be *vileyn* because it uses indecent reference, and it is *boystous* and *rude* because its speaker knows nothing of the concerns of elevated existence and cannot refer to them: the proper *termes* of *gentilesse* are outside the range of the *boystous* man. In principle, such a man may be of any social class, but in practice, he is usually a simple peasant.

In this discussion of the levels of style in Chaucer's language, we have been able to demonstrate a very tangled skein of stylistic associations, complicated by shifting moral, social, and artistic values. It has been possible to discern in this a kind of polarisation towards two distinct levels: a lower style and a higher style, both of which are further complicated individually. The more elevated style, for example, may consist of a coincidence of courtly ideals and complex language, when it is likely to be called *faire speche*, or it may be simply a matter of complex written composition, when it may be referred to as *heigh stile*.

But it is without much profit, and indeed justification, to try to classify Chaucer's composition in terms of the traditional theory of three levels of style. Although a low style is recognised as the language of churls and peasants, it is never brought into explicit stylistic – as opposed to social – contrast with what he called *heigh stile* or *faire speche*. Plainness of style is in any case ambiguous, since as well as ignorance, it can denote consideration for the capacities of an audience in an instructional style free of all social implication. Neither Chaucer's remarks on the subject of style nor his literary vocabulary give us any secure grounds for distinguishing a middle style. Although there is no proof that Chaucer knew of the theory of three styles, the strong probability is that he did because of its ubiquity in medieval sources. The further implication is that he was not particularly interested in it. It is reasonable, however, to assume that, if he thought about it at all, Chaucer thought of the ascent from low to high style as a rhetorical and social progression of growing elaboration and elevation rather than as three well-differentiated levels of style. The references which he makes to linguistic usage refer somewhat imprecisely to the extremes of this assumed scale. But whatever his attitude to the three-level theory, Chaucer certainly was aware of style in a much more concrete and immediate way, as the characteristic style of sermons, say, or of royal letters, of courtly *dits*, or of *fabliaux*, or even of the linguistic peculiarities of Northern immigrants into London whom he wished to represent as clerks. It is in these more precise proprieties of style, and in the complicated network of social, moral, or artistic associations within which they exist, that we can best see Chaucer exploiting the stylistic resources of his language.

9   The Architecture of Chaucer's Language

If asked 'what does such-and-such a word mean?' there is a very good possibility that we might return the question 'in what context?' For, although we might be able to offer a meaning for the word, we may not be sure that it is the particular meaning sought; and, if we are not certain of the meaning at all, context will probably help us to recall it. This familiar piece of linguistic behaviour should draw our attention to two closely-related facts: firstly, that the meaning of words is somehow dependent upon the context in which they are used; and, secondly, that differences in meaning may be associated with differences in context.

In glossaries intended to help modern students to read medieval authors we everyday encounter the effects of the multiple meanings of words. The simplest glossaries provide a modest range of possible meanings for each word, and it is left to the reader to select the meaning appropriate to the context in which the word is puzzling him. More ambitious glossaries give more meanings, perhaps with a short illustrative context, and line-references to the specific *senses*, as such meanings-in-context are properly called.[1] By this means the reader or translator can be more certain that he is selecting the sense appropriate to the context in which he has found the word. The use of such a sophisticated glossary enables him to choose the right sense from the range possible for a word, and such elaborate glossaries are usually more warmly applauded than the simpler type; yet we should not assume without question that they are superior in all respects. Paradoxically, the simple vocabulary, by its very inadequacy for providing an instant translation, has its own value: it throws a heavier onus upon the reader, forcing him to ponder the context of occurrence of the word, to recall other encounters with it, and to arrive at his own translation. On the other hand, the elaborated glossary provides a satisfactory gloss for every occurrence, and the learner need only slot this into the appropriate place in his translation. Clearly, both kinds of glossaries can fulfil a useful rôle; but let us further consider the worth of the simpler kind.

The new student is very often dismayed by the apparent diversity in the senses of Old English words. But this impression of diversity arises principally from the way in which the senses are presented to him: that is, as a collection of semantically-distinct modern English terms, chosen for their suitability in rendering the meaning of the Old English original in a variety of disparate contexts. In the case of such words the elaborate glossary helps the student to make sense of his set text, but restrains him from learning Old English in the way in which it was known to its original speakers, who knew the significance of a word from repeated use. Seen from the perspective of modern English glosses, no logic may be discernible in the range of senses of an Old English word. Paradoxically, therefore, the strength of a simple vocabulary may be in its weaknesses, in that the reader is forced to worry out contextual senses from a word's occurrences in context, and it may be that, as a result, he will perceive relationships of sense and usage more in the way that they were perceived by earlier users of the language, rather than an apparent chaos imposed by the disparate senses of modern English.

Although the previous paragraph may seem to be ammunition for a covert attack on the practice of translation as a way of learning earlier languages, it is not intended to be anything of the kind, since the capacity to reproduce the significances of another language in the forms of one's own is an important proof of mastery of both languages. Rather, it is intended to urge that the expression system of earlier stages of the language should be seen to possess its own logic and its own structures.[2] Truly competent translation acknowledges this, transforming syntactical structures as well as substituting words, and operating with an awareness of the stylistic implications of both; otherwise, we are deciphering rather than translating. A study of the expression system of a language is valuable as a complement to practice in rendering actual passages of discourse.

It is probably a universal characteristic of languages that their words are capable of taking different senses according to context, and it is equally probable that the range of senses applicable to one word-form is not completely distinct from the sense-ranges of all the others. In other words, all languages will possess synonyms, because the range of senses indicated by two or more word-forms will overlap to some extent. It is worth emphasising at this point that the reference to synonyms is made in terms of the *senses* of words; that is to say to the meanings words have in context. Synonymy is semantic identity seen at the level of words in context; but although semantic ranges overlap, producing contextual synonymy, we should not expect to find many examples of total overlap, or total identicality of all the possible senses of any two words.[3] For example, one would not normally suggest the word *grace* if asked, out of context, for a synonym of the Chaucerian word *destinee*. The overlap of their sense-ranges is far from complete. Yet, quoting both in context, we can show that they can occur synonymously:

> I hadde the bettre leyser for to pleye
> And for to se and eek for to be seye
> Of lusty folk. What wiste I wher my *grace*
> Was shapen for to be or in what place?
>
> (D 551–4)
>
> And if so be thow wolt noght do me grace,
> Or if my *destynee* be shape so
> That I shal nedes haue oon of hem two,
> As seend me hym that moost desireth me.
>
> (A 2322–5)

By contrast, *hyre* and *guerdoun* are quite likely to be suggested as synonyms of *mede* by anyone familiar with Middle English, and they would probably be accepted as equivalent without the need of supporting contexts. But synonymy is, as we have stressed, a context-dependent relationship between senses. Therefore, in order to verify our feelings that these words may be synonyms, we must examine the range of senses of each, and reconsider the extent of synonymy. The account of their sense-ranges set out below is based upon entries in the *Middle English Dictionary* and in the *OED*, and these are supplemented by an independent analysis of Chaucer's usage. Where appropriate, each major sense is illustrated by a context showing the use of the word in that sense; other words used synonymously are represented by line-references.

1. A reward or compensation (for a noteworthy service).

guerdoun   And sire right as they han answered wysly and discretly, right so rede I that they be heighly and souereynly gerdoned for hir noble speche. (B 2462)

mede   (*Bo* IV p.v 24)
hyre   (D 1008)

2.   A payment for services rendered, or employment completed or continuing (often with an implication of a previous contract), wages.

hyre   He wolde thresshe and therto dyke and delue
              For Cristes sake for euery poure wight
              Withouten hyre, if it laye in his myght.   (A 536–8)
mede   (*Scogan* 33)

3. Payment for the performance of a particular task; a professional fee.

guerdoun   At after-soper fille they in tretee
              What somme sholde this maistres gerdoun be
              To remoeuen alle the rokkes of Britayne.
                                                          (F 1219–21)

hyre   (*ABC* 103)

4. Payment for the temporary use of something or someone's time.

hyre   He sette noght his benefice to hyre   (A 507)

5. A munificient gift bestowed without any necessity of a service having been performed.

(This sense, common in early Middle English, with the use of the word *mede*, is not recorded for any of these words in Chaucer.)

A group of subsidiary or derived senses is also found:

6. A spiritual reward; salvation.

guerdoun   But by the pris of ryghtwisnesse and of verray mekenesse we disseruen þe gerdon of the deuyne grace whiche þat is inestimable.   (*Bo* V p.3 193–6)

mede   (*Truth* 27)

(This sense is apparently an extension of both 1 and 5 (above), in which divine grace is perceived as analogous to the largesse of a feudal lord. In popular usage there is often uncertainty about whether it has to be earned.)

7. Undesirable consequences or punishment for some word or deed.

mede   ⎱   This is the mede of lovynge and guerdoun
guerdoun ⎰ That Medea receyued of Jasoun.   (*LGW* 1662–3)

(Apparently an ironic development of 1.)[4]

8. Bribe or financial inducement.

mede   There shul we han a iuge that may nat ben deceyued ne corrupt. And why? For certes alle oure thoghtes ben descouered as to hym, ne for prayere ne for mede he wol nat ben corrupt.   (I 168)

hyre   (TC 504)

9. Consequence, good or bad, of preceding words or actions. A sense closely related to (7).

mede   Is this the verray mede of youre byheeste?
       Is al this paynted proces seyd, allas!
       Right for this fyn?   (*TC* II 423–5; Robinson's text)

guerdoun   (*TC* V 1852)

10. Corruption, graft.

mede   . . . for turned up-so-doun
guerdon   Is al this world for mede and wilfulnesse
       That al is lost for lak of stedfastnesse.

                       (*Stedfastnesse* 5–7)

In Middle English, *mede* may also mean 'material wealth', but this sense is not found in Chaucer.

SENSES	6	7	9	1	3	2	8	4	10	5
guerdoun	x	x	x	x	x	–	–	–	–	–
mede	x	x	x	x	–	x	x	–	x	–
hyre	–	–	–	x	x	x	x	x	–	–

The above list and tabular arrangement of the sense-ranges of the three words *guerdoun*, *mede*, and *hyre* demonstrate quite clearly how their senses overlap, showing that we should be quite justified in regarding them as synonyms. But the sense-ranges, although they overlap, are not identical: the words are not total synonyms. *Mede* alone has the abstract sense (10) of 'corruption', and only *hyre* can have the sense (4) 'payment for temporary use'. Sense (3), according to the table, is represented by *guerdoun* in Chaucer, and not by *mede*. *Mede* exhibits the widest range of senses, but does not include all the senses of the others.[5] But although the arrangement of these words and senses in a table of this kind serves to demonstrate the degree of synonymy in a mechanical way, and it reveals that *hyre* and *guerdoun* are somewhat more specialised in sense than *mede*, yet it cannot show other important aspects of their meaning. Frequency of occurrence, both of the word-form, and frequency in any particular sense, is not represented. In fact, perhaps as the result of its broader sense range, *mede* is the most frequent form, followed closely by *guerdoun*, and, rather less frequently, by *hyre*. The frequency of the senses realised by each word is also interesting and reveals the limitations of tabular presentation. Easily the most common sense of *mede* is (1) 'reward or recompense for a noteworthy service', but the second most common is (8) 'bribery or financial inducement'. Other senses are relatively rare. Of *hyre*, the most common sense is easily sense (2) 'payment for services rendered or employment completed or continuing' but sense (8) 'bribery' is also reasonably frequent. *Guerdoun* overwhelmingly means (1) 'reward or recompense for notable services', and the only other common sense is (7) 'undesirable consequences or punishment'.

It is apparent from this further analysis that, although *mede*, *hyre*, and *guerdoun* may loosely be regarded as synonyms, the varying frequencies of the different senses, and the occurrence of senses peculiar to each word, would tend to differentiate them in use. For a contemporary reader of Chaucer's poetry, we may assume that this differentiation would be more distinct since it would be based upon more prolonged experience of their use. Whether a written corpus such as Chaucer's work adequately represents more general use is an unanswerable question; and another serious question arises regarding the psychological truth of quantitative statements based upon the eccentricities of written texts. The word *mede*, for example, shows such a preponderance of uses with the sense (1) 'reward etc.' over sense (8) 'bribery' in this data solely as the result of the ubiquity of the former sense in a single text, Chaucer's translation of *Boethius*. If we were to set aside this text, the number of uses with the sense 'bribery' would nearly equal those with the sense 'reward'. Evidently, if we are to come to a true picture of the status of a group of words in fourteenth-century usage, we must also take into account the distribution of their senses through Chaucer's works.[6] We may summarise the results of our investigation into the semantic structure of these words in the following terms: although they share many senses, *mede*, *hyre*, and *guerdoun* may be distinguished semantically. In terms of the frequency of occurrence of senses, *mede* is about equally likely to signify reward or bribery; *hyre* is primarily concerned with remuneration for employment, but also with bribery; whereas *guerdoun* is essentially to do with reward. *Guerdoun* is distinguishable from the other two in that it never means 'bribery'; *hyre* is distinct from the other two in that it never means 'spiritual reward' and always implies earned income.

A further serious question now arises as to whether an analysis of word senses on the pattern above bears any resemblance to the kind of knowledge of the expression system possessed by the original user of the language. Since it is based upon his usage, it must obviously be related to his ways of constructing expressions, but is it related to his more conscious knowledge of the meanings of words? If asked, would Chaucer have made the distinction between synonyms in this way? It must first of all be admitted that itemising the senses as in a glossary has tended to obscure relationships between them.[7] For example, the main distinction to be made between sense (1) and sense (6) is one of application; the same basic meaning is applied in different contexts. The use of *guerdoun* in senses (1) and (7) differs largely through ironic application in the latter case. There is a possibility, too, that the unique use of *hyre* with sense (1) occurs for a special stylistic reason, possibly related to the social status of the recipient of *hyre*. There are obviously complex stylistic relationships between the uses of the words and their senses: semantics and contextual use are interdependent. But how real an existence had such relationships for Chaucer? When he wrote the word *mede* in a context in which it meant 'reward', to what extent was he simultaneously aware of the 'ironic' sense 'bribery'?[8] We cannot answer such a question with certainty, but we can assemble the probabilities. By analogy with modern English, we can make a division between connotational and cognitive meaning.[9] The latter term refers to that meaning which at any given moment is considered to be central and essential; connotational meaning is the accumulation of peripheral or associative meanings also attached to the word. To make this distinction more cogently in the light of our earlier discussion, cognitive meaning may be thought of as either the sense in context of a word, or as its primary sense when out of verbal context. This latter is constituted by the most psychologically salient of its range of senses. This may not be absolutely stable, and although frequency of occurrence plays an important part in determining psychological salience, it is not an infallible guide to it. Connotative meaning, then, can be considered to be composed of memories, more or less precise, of other senses and other circumstances of the use of a word than that which currently engages attention. For example, a simple experiment shows that, out of context, the modern English word *beam* has two cognitive meanings which are equally likely to be elicited from informants, 'wood' and 'light'. A third meaning which is frequently elicited is 'smile'. In principle, if any of these meanings is regarded as the central one, the other two may be considered to be probable connotations of the word. The emergence of connotations is not random, however, since most people seem to perceive a close connection between 'light' and 'smile', but none between either of these and 'wood'.[10]

It is reasonable to suppose that Chaucer's language, like any other – since its words had multiple senses and were used in different contexts – was also susceptible of similar structural relationships between potential senses. Chaucer, therefore, could have had an awareness of the sense 'bribery' present in his mind when he selected the word *mede* with the contextual sense 'reward'. Such a meaning-relation existed as a potential in his language; but whether this potential was realised in any particular example can only be argued from a detailed analysis of the context in which the word has been used. Let us consider briefly one of Chaucer's uses of the word *mede*. *A priori*, we should expect its sense to be either 'reward, recompense' or 'bribery, financial inducement', but of course context may impose any of a range of other senses. In the *Miller's Tale* Chaucer gives us an account of Absolon's attempts to gain the favours of the attractive Alisoun:

> He kembed his lokkes brode and made hym gay.
> He woweth hir by meenes and brocage
> And swoor he wolde been hir owene page.
> He syngeth brokkyng as a nyghtyngale.
> He sente hir pyment, meeth and spiced ale
> And wafres pipyng hoot out of the gleede.
> And for she was of towne he profred meede,
> For som folk wol be wonnen for richesse
> And som for strokes and som for gentilesse.
>
> (A 3374–82)

Very urbanely, the editors of the *Middle English Dictionary* give the sense of *mede* in this context as (1a) 'gift, or suitor's blandishment'. Perhaps it does not seem appropriate to call it a bribe. Nevertheless, the context, which deals with courtly refinements, then gifts in kind, moves on to discuss money payments openly. Furthermore, it tells us that a financial inducement was offered 'for she was of towne'. The significance of this phrase is uncertain. The *OED* cites no examples of the modern, sexual associations of the phrase 'man or woman of the town' before 1700, and both Chaucer and Gower use the phrase without apparent pejorative association. Nevertheless, it seems that townswomen, who, like the Wife of Bath, lived among commerce, were considered to have a better appreciation of the value of money than their sisters in the countryside. In such a context, although *mede* may signify a suitor's gift, the connotations of bribery and corruption must inevitably have been powerfully present and have contrasted with Absolon's assumed idealism.

The word *hyre* is not morally but socially disparaging, since it is strongly associated with the need to earn money by labour. Of course, Christian morality has never rejected this necessity, and indeed has willingly espoused it, so that Luke 10.7 is quoted by a friar with reference to his labour of saving souls: 'the werkman worthy is his hire' (D 1973). The word *hyre* therefore is not out of place in the context of Christian humility. It is, however, less to be expected in the context of the favours of a courtly lady. Thus, allegorised as the service of a god, love for such a lady may more properly be expected to result in a *guerdoun* than in *hyre*; and indeed this is one of the most common circumstances of the use of the former word in Chaucer's works. At the beginning of the *Parliament of Fowls*, however, seeking to represent the God of Love as a tyrannous oppressor of his followers, Chaucer ironically alters our perspective on the situation by employing the word *hyre* (*PF* 6). Love is a tyrant who persecutes his servants and demands their loyalty whilst only irregularly and uncertainly paying them their *hyre*.[11] This imagery is used again in *Troilus and Criseyde*, where it is introduced by a reference to Love's servants:

> . . . for the konnyngeste of yow,
> That seruen most ententiflich and best,
> Hym tit as often harm therof as prowe.
> ʒour hire is quyt aʒeyn, ʒe, God woot howe.
> Nought wel for wel, but scorne for good servyse.
> In feith, ʒoure ordre is [ruled] in good wise.   [MS piled]

(I 331–6)

Here, however, the word occurs in a more complicated context, for this passage is immediately followed by an analogy not with secular servants, but with monastic service of God. This is introduced by the last line above, and is continued in the stanza following:

In veyn, certeyn, ben alle ȝoure observaunces,
But if it a sely fewe pointes be;
Ne no thing asketh so gret attendaunces
As doth ȝoure lay, and that knowe alle ȝe.

(I 337–40)

The use of the word *hyre* is now seen to evoke not merely the familiar analogy of lovers as servants, but rather a contrast between two such analogies: those of lovers and monks as servants respectively of the God of love and of Christ. In its entirety, the passage functions along with others in Book I of *Troilus and Criseyde* to point a contrast between *love celestial* and *love of kynde*.

'Scorn for good service', which is so often the lot of the courtly lover, explains why so many of the uses of *guerdoun* are ironic ones. Its commonest sense is, of course, that of rich reward, but its use by those disappointed of such a recompense for their service is so common that the *Middle English Dictionary* records a separate sense 'punishment, retribution, retaliation'. This suggestion of a distinct sense seems inappropriate for the Chaucerian use of the word; indeed such a division of sense between 'reward' and 'retribution' is implicitly denied by a brief passage in the *Summoner's Tale*:

Lazar and Diues lyueden diuersly
And diuerse gerdon hadde they therby   (D 1877–8)

The rich man who lived careless of the sufferings of the poor suffered the retribution of hell; the beggar, however, was comforted by the recompense of heaven: but both concepts, recompense and retribution, are covered by the same occurrence of the one word *guerdoun*. It is truer to the semantic structure suggested by Chaucer's usage to regard *guerdoun* as equivalent in meaning to 'reward, recompense', and, instead of positing a second distinct sense, to be aware that the word may be used ironically, especially with regard to love service. Chaucer completes the theme of the uncertain rewards of secular ideals in *Troilus and Criseyde* by just such an ironic usage:

Lo here, thise wrecched worldes appetites;
Lo here, the fyn and guerdoun for trauaille
Of Ioue, Appollo, of Mars, of swich rascaille.

(V 1851-3)

We can expect to find such an ironic dimension in the use of many words which denote high ideals and things of value, and this irony is best thought of as a contextual modification to the sense of a word: ironic contexts are common for words like *curteisly*, *gentil*, *kynde*, *honeste*, *purveiaunce*, *war and wys*, *dangerous*, and a number of other words denoting aspects of human behaviour.[12]

Our analysis of the senses and uses of the words *mede*, *hyre*, *guerdoun* reveals that, although they have senses in common, they also have senses which are characteristic and distinct. These latter senses, it appeared, might lend them distinctive connotations, so that, although a particular context might seem apt for the use of any one of these synonyms, yet such connotational distinctions might make the choice of one or other of them more satisfactory: *le mot juste*. In the examples we have discussed, the choice of each word – *mede* for the suitor's blandishment, *hyre* for the reward of workmen, lovers, and monks, and *guerdoun* to evoke the disgust of the disappointed idealist – must be considered to be a significant one. It is a choice made by a man eloquent in the English of his time and able to exploit the semantic structure of its words in concert with a network of associations drawn from habitual usage. This is not to exaggerate the creativity of Chaucer as a poet, or to represent his poetic technique anachronistically. The sentence urges no more than it says. That conception of the poet's language which is appropriate to Chaucer is one which acknowledges that it differs from that of men of his time in degree rather than in kind. He had an unusually full and creative grasp of the 'architecture' of his London English, and could achieve more with what the language and its uses offered to him.[13]

The architecture of Chaucer's language does not, however, consist simply of the association between particular larger contexts and senses. As we have seen, sense itself is dependent upon context, and context should be taken to include verbal context. Since repeated situations tend to call forth the same expressions, and since these latter may be embedded in similar sentences, it is inevitable that words will become associated not only with their synonyms, with particular stylistic levels, or with characteristic situations of use, but also with other words and phrases with which they habitually tend to co-occur. A word will tend to collocate with a characteristic range of other words, as well as in familiar lexico-grammatical environments. For example, a common lexico-grammatical context of the word *grace* is *God sende*; a common collocation of *destine* is *shapen*.[14] It is a feature of the style of much medieval writing – without reaching the extremes of *heigh stile* letters – that synonyms are linked together, thus reinforcing synonymic associations between words by collocational ones. As we saw in Chapter 4, such semantic and collocational associations can be used for purposes of coherence in less syntactically-ordered passages. Indeed, analysis of the contexts of *mede*, *hyre*, and *guerdoun* in order to determine their senses also brings to light a number of collocations with words which are near-synonyms: *wages*, *fee*, and *shepe*. The area of vocabulary of which *mede* is a part is now seen to consist of six words rather than the original three, bound together in usage by both semantic and collocational ties. The words *shepe* (sense 2) and *fee* (sense 3) have very restricted sense ranges. *Wages*, although a rare word, is recorded with senses 1, 2, 4, and 7, and is semantically well integrated, although the rarity of its use makes judgements of its stylistic status hazardous.

Collocational ties in the architecture of a language may extend in their degree of fixity from lexico-grammatical formulae like *quit . . . his hyre/mede/guerdoun* to a mere tendency to co-occur, like the word *socour* with words denoting the Virgin, or *servisable* with squires.[15] Collocation may be associated with particular senses, or contextual developments of sense, rather than with word-forms alone, as for example the ironic use of *hende* with *clerke*, or with Nicholas, who is a clerk. Sometimes the collocational tie is so firmly established that breaking it can itself constitute a literary device. The word *buxom* 'obedient, submissive, patient' is habitually collocated in both Chaucer and Gower with *wyf*. The very condition of being a wife is regarded in the *Merchant's Tale* (1287) as being the epitome of buxomness. Yet, in the *Shipman's Tale*, in a passage which recalls the quest of the unfortunate knight in the tale of the Wife of Bath, we learn:

> . . . that wommen naturelly
> Desiren thynges vj as wel as I:
> They wolde that hir housbondes sholde be
> Hardy and wise and riche and therto free
> And buxom vnto his wyf and fressh abedde.
>
> (B 1363–7)

This passage, which echoes the final words of the Wife's tale, also echoes her desire for dominion over her husband, who, she argues, should patiently accept such rule (D 1257–60). It also, of course, contrasts with the prevalent medieval conception of the proper hierarchy in marriage. Thus the misapplication of the word *buxom* to the husband exploits the reversal of linguistic expectations to give greater impact to the supposed reversal of the natural order. All this is given added force by the fact that the ordinary collocational tie between *buxom* and *wyf* is one which is to be associated with a very particular situation context: that of the contemporary marriage service, in which the wife promised to be 'bonere and buxsum in bedde and atte borde'. Other authors inevitably participated in the same world of experience as Chaucer, so that we find the author of *Speculum Gy de Warewyke* scornfully condemning uxoriousness by a similar device when he remarks 'boxsmere he was to his wif þan to god' (233).[16]

In the discussion of the relationship between husband and wife which recurs in the *Canterbury Tales*, as elsewhere in Middle English, the selection of the word *buxom* in preference to a synonym like *meke* or *pacient*, seems not to have been a random one. In the *Merchant's Tale*, in particular, it is collocated with other words and phrases which together constitute a precise reference to the contemporary marriage service. In short, a minor feature of linguistic architecture can be shown to have been dependent upon a single specific influence upon the culture in which Chaucer lived. Nor is this an isolated event, since that kind of ordering in the language which we have called its architecture – a system of perceived associations between semantic structure, collocations, language varieties, and other patterns of usage – is inevitably dependent ultimately upon the history and culture of the world in which the language exists, and has existed.[17]

The word *camuse*, for example, which occurs only twice in Chaucer's works, is restricted to use as a modifier of the noun *nose* in the *Reeve's Tale*:

> Round was his face and camuse was his nose;
>
> (A 3934)
>
> This wenche thikke and well ygrowen was,
> With camuse nose and eyen greye as glas.
>
> (A 3973–4)

The description of the nose forms part of a static and formal description of the hero or heroine in many medieval romances. In the *Romaunt of the Rose* the measured proportion of a lady's nose is stressed:

> And by mesure large were
> The openyng of hir yen clere;
> Hir nose of good proporcioun,
> Hir yen grey as is a faucoun.   (*RR* 543–6)

Simkin's daughter, too, has grey eyes, and it is apparent that her description is a paradigm of that in the *Romaunt*, but her nose is *camuse* 'snub' rather than being of good proportion, and instead of a lady, she is a *wenche*. Both *wenche* and *camuse* are in this context socially disparaging, and the use of the latter word to deflate Simkin's pretensions depends on an analogy with prestigious French literature in which nobility is associated with physical proportion and both are celebrated in formal description. Chaucer seems to have been fascinated with the possibilities for satire which these circumstances offered him, for, as we have seen, of the words used to modify the noun *nose* in his works – *heigh* (A 2167); *tretys* (A 152); *semely* (B 1919) – the latter two may also be suspected of ironic usage.[18] The portrait of Malyn, then, depends upon the inversion of a courtly physical ideal, coupled with a prefiguring of the contrast made in the *Manciple's Tale* between a *lady* and a *wenche*; it is a portrait which, like that of the Prioress or of Sir

Thopas, is made possible only by familiarity with a literary device of French romance and by the language which is appropriate to it.

If the architecture which Chaucer can exploit in this way extends into the literary practices of Old French, certain features of the use and sense relationships between the words *herte* and *corage* are equally dependent upon distinctions made in Latin. The two words are partial synonyms: both can mean 'heart' in the more abstract sense to do with feelings and innermost being. The actual physical organ, however, is never called *corage*, except when it is viewed as the recipient of sense impressions. There is also a marked difference in the distribution of the words through Chaucer's works. *Herte* is one of his most frequent nouns, but occurs relatively rarely in *Boece*. By contrast, *corage* is more common in *Boece* than anywhere else, although it too is used fairly widely outside *fabliau* contexts. Such a distribution may be sufficient to warn us that *corage* has a special, technical sense; and indeed analysis of its occurrence in *Boece* quickly reveals that the vast majority of its uses are as translations of the Latin word *animus*. The bond between Latin *animus* and Chaucer's *corage* is further demonstrated by the information that on three-quarters of the occasions on which *animus* is used in the original Latin, it is rendered *corage* in Chaucer's translation. To render *animus* as *herte* is relatively rare, but the words *thought*, *soule*, and *wil* are also used as translations. The only word other than *animus* which Chaucer translates as *corage* is the word *mens*; but this is on one occasion only. *Corage*, then, is the established translation of *animus* in technical contexts, although there is some slight overlap with the use of *thought*, which itself seems to be the established translation of Latin *mens*.[19]

Animus is a word used in philosophical writings of the rational part of the soul; it is that part of the soul which is in contact with the world around us by way of the senses. In it, perceptions are ordered, desires formed, and courses of action are decided. Although these functions may be ascribed to the *herte* by Chaucer, in his translation of Boethius the word *corage* is chosen by preference. Here, it is clearly one of the *termes of philosophie*; outside this context, less care is evident: the word can mean 'courage, valour'; 'inclination, desire'; even 'lust'.

It may also be used to refer rather vaguely to the heart as the seat of affections and perceptions. Nevertheless, its technical propriety may be restored. Criseyde's famous *slydynge . . . corage* contrasts within the sphere of moral philosophy with the ideal king, who, in the Squire's imagining, is 'benigne and honurable/Of his corage as any centre stable' (F 21–22). This 'stablenesse of corage' the Parson defines as the virtue of *constantia* (I 737); a virtue which is the subject of the Clerk's allusion to steadfastness in his tale:

> This wyl is in myn herte and ay shal be.
> No lengthe of tyme or deth may this deface
> Ne chaunge my corage to oother place. (E 509–11)

Although it would be incorrect to assert that the words *corage*, *herte*, *thought*, *soule* and *spirit* are clearly distinct in Chaucer's usage as a whole, it is apparent that in some contexts, and consequently in their connotations, they can be distinguished in ways patterned upon the usage and senses of Latin words like *animus*, *mens*, and *anima*. In short, the semantic relationships, the circumstances of use, of these words are directly affected by the architecture of the Latin texts upon which all organised knowledge was based. That the architecture of Chaucer's language should partly coincide with that of French romances and with Latin philosophical texts in this way should not surprise us, for linguistic architecture is largely the product of cultural history, and Chaucer's cultural values, as we have seen, were formed by the fusion of French chivalry and Latin scholarship.[20]

That Chaucer had a fully competent grasp of architecture developed in Latin is further indicated by his handling of the moral symbol of the tyrant. In the philosophical tradition, the tyrant was conceived of as an irrational and cruel ruler who disregards laws and oppresses his people with a passion allied to madness. In Latin works his furious raving attracts the epithets *saevus*, *furibundus*, *rabidus*, and he is *crudelis* and *ferox*. He murders men who are *sine labe* 'without stain' and is overwhelmed with *ira*. He never shows pity, and his heart is *induratum* 'hardened'. Chaucer, too, has a vocabulary which is characteristic of the tyrant and it is obviously based upon that of Latin, but its range of epithets is more restricted. Repeatedly the tyrant is called *wood* or *cruel*; he is *hard* or *daungerous*, possessed by *ire* and *wratthe*. He murders his victims *giltelees* or *withouten gilt*. The word *ire*, as a chief characteristic of the tyrant, may have been adopted directly from Latin, but the form of the word *cruel* indicates a French intermediary. *Wood*, *wratthe*, and *gilt* are derived from Old English.

In his translation of Boethius, for which he employed Jean de Meun's French version, Chaucer uses the adjective *felonous* of tyrants. This and the nouns formed from it, *felonye* and *felon*, are relatively rare in Chaucer outside *Boece*. Their frequency in the translation is the direct result of Jean de Meun's predilection for the word. If we were to check Chaucer's uses of it in *Boece* against the French text, we should find that on every single occasion he was merely adopting the verbal suggestion of Jean de Meun. Jean was simplifying a much broader vocabulary in Latin: *nefas*, *scelus*, *saevus*, *torvus*, *nequitia*, *ferox*, *improbus*, *perniciosus*, *iniquitia*, *facinus*. Such a process of simplification is found also in the case of other words, as a table will show:

CHAUCER	JEAN DE MEUN	BOETHIUS
tyraunt	*tyrant*	*tyrannus*
ire *wratthe* }	*ire*	*ira*
wood	{ *enragiez* *forsenez*	{ *rabidus* *furiosus/furibundus* *saeviens/saevus*
cruelte	{ *cruelte*	{ *saevus, torvus,* *crudelis, inmites* *atrox, iniustus* *severitas*
	{ *felonye* *justise*	*saevus, ferox* *severitas*

That Chaucer should render *justise* as *cruelte* can be explained in terms of the special use of *crudelitas* by Seneca in a discussion of justice and mercy. The Middle English word *wood* had a sense range extending through madness, anger, and ferocity, and thus satisfactorily renders two words which Jean de Meun had kept rigorously apart, perhaps more from a scholastic's regard for etymology than any real distinction in their use.

In summary, then, Chaucer had a vocabulary proper to the discussion of the traditional concept of the tyrant. It was distinguished by a group of words which tended to collocate in discussions of tyranny, some of which were also partially synonymous. The actual words were variously of Old English and Old French origin, but the topic was essentially one of Latin moral philosophical literature, and the typical uses of the words imitated usage in Latin. The discussion of the subject of tyranny in English, then, demonstrates an architecture which is paralleled in French but which originates in Latin. In employing a word like *wood* to refer to a tyrant, Chaucer was not using an isolated lexical item, but was selecting a word incorporated into an architecture of collocations, sense relations and associations. There is no need to assume that all these were called into consciousness whenever the word was used in any context whatever, but, in order to understand Middle English in the way that Chaucer did, we should be aware of this potential in his words.

That the architecture of English, at least among men of some learning, was affected by that of French and Latin is undeniable. But this is probably too weak a claim. Gower's ability to discuss the topic of tyranny, and use its appropriate vocabulary in both English and Latin indicates that for him the architecture of his linguistic competence extended through three languages. If we consider the matter not from the point of view of the differentiation of languages, but that of the total competence of the individual, it is apparent that in many cases it is less a matter of the influence of Latin or French upon English than of the interpenetration of the three languages.[21]

A final example will serve to illustrate this organisation of the architecture of Chaucer's language by Latin technical vocabulary. This is in the language which Chaucer used to describe his work as *auctour* and *poete*. Although he did not accept all its implications, Chaucer wrote against a background of Christian Latin literary theory which, although allowing that literature could serve to entertain, yet asserted that its primary purpose was one of moral education: to draw

Christians to virtue and salvation by example, persuasion, and instruction. In such a formulation, *poetes* and *rhetors*, those who concocted fictitious tales or elaborated and *enlumined* their *enditynges* with the *coloures of rhetorike*, were naturally in an ambivalent position. Chaucer's *Retractions*, genuine or not, acknowledge this. The sober works of authenticated authors were solemnly classified according to their assumed beneficial intentions and effects. An introduction to the works of Lucan, for example, would state the supposed *intentio auctoris* 'author's purpose' and its *causa finalis* 'significance to, or effect upon, its audience'. Intention and effect were traditionally the yardsticks by which the morality of any act was to be judged, so that it is apparent that literary works were being morally classified in the same way as any ordinary action. Chaucer uses the same method of estimating the moral value of actions:

> . . . How many oon may men fynde
> That noght for werk sometyme but for th'entente
> To doon this synne been outher slayn or shente.
>
> (B 929–31)

The intention is as important as the deed; and this is a plea which Chaucer continually makes with regard to his poetic compositions.[22]

The origins of the methods of classification of Latin authors lay in twelfth-century introductions to classical authors prepared for the direction of young scholars, but, in the thirteenth century, the Aristotelian four causes began to be used as a means of classifying the works of philosophers. Poetic works were introduced in the earlier period, by their title, genre, some biographical details of the author, his assumed intention in writing (*intentio auctoris*), the number and order of the books comprising the work, and perhaps a few interpretative remarks (*explanatio*). The later Aristotelian method with which this coalesced can be illustrated by Robert of Basevorn's categorisation of his own work, *Forma praedicandi* (1322). The *causa formalis*, he tells us, is the orderly arrangement of the work; the *causa materialis* – its subject matter – is preaching; the *causa efficiens* is the author, Basevorn himself; and the *causa finalis* is God, or strengthening by God.

This last is a little cryptic, but other authors made more subtle and explicit distinctions. The internal final cause is in fact the product of the author's ordering of his work, and is equivalent to the *causa formalis*. This refers to the author's compositional skills. The external final cause can be understood in three ways, and these are exemplified by Robert Kilwardby's remarks on Priscian's grammar.[23] Firstly, the immediate final cause (or, as we should say, the result) is knowledge of grammatical structures; secondly, the distant final cause is the interpretation of literary texts and the promotion of eloquence; thirdly, the ultimate final cause is that of all formalised knowledge, the cultivation of virtue and morality.

The coalition of the two ways of characterising a work was not carried out in any systematic way, so that individual instances may vary considerably; ordinarily, in introducing a work of literature some reference may be expected to be made to the title, the author, the *intentio auctoris*, the *causa materialis* or (in abbreviated form) *materia*, the *causa finalis*, and perhaps also the *causa formalis*. Precisely how available information about an author and his work was distributed under these headings varied somewhat, and indeed the distinctions between the headings were not always rigidly maintained: a poem is a very complex kind of action in which it may not be easy to keep the author's intention distinct from the external final cause, so that confusion of the two is common. The *causa finalis* itself was known by a series of alternative expressions, some of which suggest Kilwardby's division of it, although this is not always evident in the use of these words: *finis*, *effectus*, *utilitas*, and metaphorically, *fructus* (*finalis*), are all used as alternatives to *causa finalis* in Latin texts.

Now, although Chaucer never attempts to classify any literary work by the use of such schemata, it is evident that this Latin tradition has contributed heavily both to the vocabulary in which he discusses his authorial role and the way in which he visualises it.[24] His subject matter, he calls *matere*, a form derived through French from the Latin *materia*. He constantly uses words derived from alternative designations of the *causa finalis*: *fyn*, *ende*, *conclusioun*, *fruyt*. These are not always kept very distinct from those derived from references to the intention of the author: *entente*, *entencioun*, and, unparalleled in

Latin, but common in Old French, *purpos*. Ordinarily, Chaucer's use of this vocabulary is not very discriminating. Effect and intention are repeatedly confused; for example, the phrases used by Chaucer to indicate a return to his principal topic after a digression, or to refuse the temptation to embark upon such a digression in the first place, will illustrate such confusion:

> Now to th'effect turne I of my matere;   (*LGW* 2403)

> But now to purpos of my firste matere.   (*PF* 26)

Here *purpos*, which is author-oriented and associated with intention, is used in a way identical to *effect*, which is audience-oriented and associated with final cause; both, however, seem to have the shifted sense 'gist, essential content, purport'. The word *ende* can be used in a similar way:

> This is th'effect and ende of my prayere:
> Yif me my loue, thow blisful lady deere.
>
> (A 2259–60)

And the word *entente* too can be used to signify the purport of a piece of literature:

> Who made this song now with so good entente?
> (*TC* II 878)

Habitually, then, Chaucer uses a technical vocabulary originating in the scholastic classification of literature, but he often fails to make the conceptual distinctions which it should properly imply. The meaning of a piece of literature is notoriously Janus-like, since it may be considered to possess the meaning intended by its author as well as a possibly quite different meaning attributed by its reader. However, the fact that Chaucer often overlooks this dichotomy by no means suggests that he was unaware of it, and indeed, as we have seen, there is considerable discussion of his individuality as author both in terms of the distinction between intention and effect and the use of 'proper' terms. Few authors are so concerned to assert their individuality. A peculiar feature of the usage of this vocabulary is also significant in this respect: for this confusion is apparent only in reference to literary works. Dreams, which, of course, are narratives without an author, but which are still regarded as potentially significant, are never referred to in terms of *entencioun*: their meaning or outcome is always their *fyn* or *effect*. These two words, the first of which is used neither by Gower nor the *Gawain*-poet, and the second of which occupies distinctly philosophical contexts in Chaucer and Gower, seem to be more recognisably technical than others in this field. Usage in fourteenth-century London English shows, then, that although the distinction between intention and effect was often blurred, the resources existed to restore technical propriety if need be. In the *Canon's Yeoman's Tale* a dichotomy is acknowledged between intention and text (*speche*):

> Lat no man bisye hym this art for to seche
> But if that he th'entencioun and speche
> Of philosophres vnderstonde kan.   (G 1442–4; El.)

And in *Troilus and Criseyde* effect is contrasted with intention in the manner of a commonplace:

> ʒet preye ich ʒow, an yuel ʒe ne take
> That it is short which that I to ʒow write;
> I dar nat, ther I am, wel lettres make,
> Ne neuere ʒet koude I wel endite.
> Ek gret effect men write in place lite;
> Th'entente is al, and nat lettres space.
>
> (*TC* V 1625–30)

The use of such phrases as *fyn of his entente* and *effect of his entente* are further illustration, if any be needed, of a conceptual and linguistic distinction between intention and its actualisation.

To tease out any further the synonymic senses and the subtle distinctions between these words, which have entered Chaucer's vocabulary from many different spheres and with a wide range of senses already confused in Latin, will be impossible within the space available. However, it is sufficient to recognise the existence of this literary vocabulary, the fact that the words are related to one another by sense and collocation, and that they pattern together in this way as the result of their association in a particular conceptual area in Latin scholastic culture. Although their adaptation to English and the ubiquity of their use has extended their sense range and modified the architecture proper to their technical use in Latin, occasionally the technical distinctions of Latin can be seen to be restored in English contexts. They are evidence, living in the language of Chaucer and Gower, of the impact upon English of the structures of Latin thought and linguistic usage.

Finally, before closing this chapter, we should consider briefly Chaucer's use of the word *fruyt*, derived through French from Latin *fructus*. Like other words which were associated in Latin with the *causa finalis*, the word can refer to actions as distinct from the intentions which precede them (I 115–16). In the *Tale of Melibee*, Melibee is advised to analyse the counsel he receives according to the Aristotelian four causes. They are represented figuratively:

> Thanne shaltow considere of what roote is engendred the matere (*materia*) of thy counseil and what fruyt (*fructus*) it may conceyue and engendre. Thow shalt eek considere alle thise causes from whennes they ben sprongen.
>
> (B 2400–2401)

Fruyt is also used, like the other words, to indicate the gist or essential meaning of a speech or work of literature. Inessential meanings and artistic elaborations are then denoted by a figurative extension of the use of *fruyt* into an opposition between *corn* or *whete* and *chaf* or *draf*:

> Me list nat of the chaf, or of the stree,
> Maken so long a tale as of the corn.
> What sholde I tellen of the realtee
> At mariages, or which cours gooth biforn,
> Who bloweth in trompe or in an horn?
> The fruyt of euery tale is for to seye:
> They ete and drynke and daunce and synge and pleye.
>
> (B 701–7)

In discussing the art of the poet, *fruyt* and its synonym *corn* indicate the basic essential meaning of the work, the *effect* or *purpos* to which Chaucer keeps telling us he will limit himself, or wishes to return. However, in the tale told by the Parson a somewhat different significance is allotted to the opposition *whete:draf* (I 30–38). The distinction he wishes to make is between empty fables and 'moralitee and vertuous matere'. Whete in this conception is that literary art which has a morally instructional purpose and effect. Such, also, although he is unlikely to have esteemed the same teaching, is the implication of the god of love's use of the opposition between *corn* and *draf* or *chaf* in the *Legend of Good Women* (Text G 312; 529). However, the best known of the oppositions with this significance is, without doubt, that at the close of the *Nun's Priest's Tale*:

> But ye that holden this tale a folye
> As of a fox or of a cok and hen,
> Taketh the moralitee, goode men.
> For seint Poul seith that al that writen is
> To oure doctryne it is ywrite ywis.
> Taketh the fruyt and lat the chaf be stille.
>
> (B 4628–33)

Precisely what *moralitee* one is expected to draw from this tale may be debatable, but it is related to that *fruyt* of literature which was defined by Bernard of Utrecht: 'fructus finalis in correctione morum legentis est'; the remote cause, the morally beneficial effect of a work upon its reading audience.[25]

Thus, behind the language of some of the most familiar lines in the *Canterbury Tales*, whose general significance is apparent to all who read them, there is a subtle architecture of sense-relations and associations which derives ultimately from scholastic Latin culture. Much of Chaucer's writing is like this: its sense is immediately obvious, or quickly becomes so with the help of a little grammatical knowledge and a good glossary. But to read Chaucer by these means alone is to experience his work as semantically flat and featureless, and to deny oneself the pleasure and satisfaction of perceiving the stylistic perspective which the fourteenth-century London language had acquired from its multi-cultural background. Worst of all, it threatens a proper appreciation of the subtle effects which the most urbane poet of the period could summon up from the opportunities offered to him by his language. An appropriate awareness of stylistic subtlety will, of course, develop naturally in the sensitive reader from repeated readings, but that awareness can be advanced and encouraged by learning the possibilities inherent in the language, and by discussing particular examples of their literary exploitation. This book has sought to offer a guide to such useful activities.

Notes

1 CHAUCER'S GRAMMAR

1. On the Chancery language and its relationship to other London languages, see M. L. Samuels, 'Some Applications of Middle English Dialectology', *ES*, XLIV (1963) 81–94. Reprinted in R. Lass (ed.), *Approaches to English Historical Linguistics* (New York, London: Holt, Rinehart, 1969) pp. 404–18. Also, John H. Fisher, 'Chancery Standard and the Emergence of Standard Written English in the Fifteenth Century', *Speculum*, LII (1977) 870–99, and 'Chancery Standard and Modern Written English', *Journal of The Society of Archivists*, VI (1979) 136–44.

2. On these 'petrified datives', see Ruth B. McJimsey, *Chaucer's Irregular -e* (New York: King's Crown Press, 1942) pp. 69ff. A considerable degree of freedom existed in both the pronunciation and writing of final *-e* in such cases.

3. The conditions under which the *-es* genitive singular might be extended to the plural also are explained by S. T.R. O. D'Ardenne in her edition of *þe Liflade ant te Passiun of Seinte Iuliene*, EETS OS, 248 (London: OUP, 1961) pp. 208–10. See also J. A. W. Bennett and G. V. Smithers (eds), *Early Middle English Verse and Prose*, 2nd edn (Oxford: Clarendon Press, 1968) pp. xxiv–v.

4. The ambiguity arises from the fact that the word *love* gives no semantic prompting as to whether *of frendes* should have subjective or objective reference (that is, 'friends love me' or 'I love friends'). The Chaucerian significance is subjective and qualitative: that is, it refers to the kind of love which friends have for each other.

5. *Thilke* is strictly speaking a contraction of the determiner *the* and the modifying adjective *ilk*, but since it is formally indivisible, and behaves structurally like a determiner, it is here considered to be one.

6. J. D. Burnley, 'Inflexion in Chaucer's Adjectives', *NM*, LXXXIII (1982) 169–77. For information on polysyllabic adjectives, see Delores E. Topliff, 'Analysis of Singular Weak Adjective Inflexion in Chaucer's Works', *JEL*, IV (1970) 78–89.

7. M. L. Samuels, 'Chaucerian Final -E', *NQ*, CCXVII (1972) 445–8.

8. Also in legal phrases in which native terms render the French (*the saides* for *ledits*) and in the curious *thise oldes dotardes holours* in the *Parson's Tale*, 857 in the Ellesmere MS.

9. The existence of variant forms in spelling and pronunciation is an important feature of Chaucer's London language. The symbol ⁓ is used to

mark alternative forms which may be selected to serve identical structural functions. Although such variant forms may perform the same role in phonological, grammatical, or lexical structure, they may well be differentiated by social, dialectal, or communicative implications, as for example the choice of *you* or *thou* as pronouns with singular reference.

10. This usage seems to have developed in Middle English under the influence of French. It continues into the language of Shakespeare, and, in its essentials, is found in some Northern dialects of modern English. On the general background, see R. Brown and A. Gilman, 'The Pronouns of Power and Solidarity', in T. A. Sebeok (ed.), *Style in Language* (MIT Press, 1960) pp. 253–76. The use of these pronouns in Chaucer's works has most recently been studied by N. Nathan, 'Pronouns of Address in the *Canterbury Tales*', *MS*, XXI (1959) 193–201.

11. A discussion of anaphoric and exophoric reference may be found in M. A. K. Halliday and R. Hasan, *Cohesion in English* (London: Longmans, 1976) pp. 31–37. See also C. Novelli, 'The Demonstrative Adjective *This*: Chaucer's use of a Colloquial Narrative Device', *MS*, XIX (1957) 246–9.

12. In R. W. Chambers and M. Daunt (eds), *A Book of London English, 1384–1425*, 2nd edn (Oxford: Clarendon, 1967) pp. 33–7. In his *Appeal* (*ibid.*, pp. 22–31), Usk uses *thilk* and *the forseyde* rather than the cohesive chain of personal pronouns. The use of *the forseyde* is limited in the Mercers' Petition to major changes in topic.

13. It might perhaps be argued that even in anaphoric use the demonstrative robs proper nouns of their unique reference, implying familiarity with the referent as one of an undistinguished group, and that this is therefore demeaning; but this semantic mechanism is certainly dependent upon contextual cues.

14. Care must be taken to distinguish indefinite uses of *who* from true relatives. In such examples as the following, *who* is indefinite: 'Ther seen men *who* kan juste and *who* kan ryde' (A 2604).

15. T. F. Mustanoja, *A Middle English Syntax,* Memoires de la Société Néophilologique de Helsinki, XXIII (Helsinki, 1960) pp. 196–7.

16. The form *catch; caught* represents a formal and semantic confusion between the Norman French *cachier* 'to chase' and the Old English *læccan; lahte* 'to catch, seize'.

17. Jan Svartvik and Randolph Quirk, 'Types and Uses of Non-finite Clause in Chaucer', *ES*, LI (1970) 393–411. For the function of variant forms of the infinitive as a metrical device, see pp. 122–3.

18. G. V. Smithers, 'A Middle English Idiom and its Antecedents', *EGS*, I (1947–8), 101–13. Smithers' translation is: 'I do not choose to wish you . . .'.

19. Mustanoja, *Middle English Syntax*, pp. 536–7. A similar, although not identical, structure, in which the infinitive is replaced by the present participle, is found in Old French. John Orr, *Old French and Modern English Idiom* (Oxford: Blackwell, 1962) p. 16.

20. F. T. Visser, *An Historical Syntax of the English Language*, 3 vols (Leiden: Brill, 1963–69) vol. I, pp. 36–9.

21. Despite the loss of many Old English impersonal constructions, many

new ones were coined in Middle English. These are asterisked in the above list.

2 TIME AND TENSE

1. See the remarks of Uriel Weinreich and Joseph B. Casagrande in their papers in Joseph H. Greenberg (ed.), *Universals of Language*, 2nd edn (Cambridge, Mass: MIT Press, 1966) pp. 154–6 and 287–8. Whorf's contrast between modern Western European quantifying concepts of time and the durative concept in the Indian language, Hopi, have become famous. B. L. Whorf 'Science and Linguistics' in John B. Carroll, (ed.), *Language, Thought and Reality* (Cambridge, Mass.: MIT Press, 1957).

2. A good brief account of aspect is that in John Lyons, *Semantics*, 2 vols (Cambridge U.P., 1977) vol. II, pp. 703–18. More detailed accounts, with specific application to English, may be found in F. R. Palmer, *A Linguistic Study of the English Verb*, 2nd edn (London: Longman, 1974) and G. N. Leech, *Meaning and the English Verb* (London: Longman, 1971).

3. Johannes Scheffer, *The Progressive in English*, North Holland Linguistics Series, XV (Amsterdam and Oxford: North Holland Publishing Co., 1975) pp. 77–86.

4. Leech, *English Verb*, p. 2.

5. Visser, *Historical Syntax*, III, pa. 1483; pa. 1562.

6. Cf. Phyllis Hodgson (ed.), *Chaucer: The General Prologue to the Canterbury Tales* (London: Athlone Press, 1969) p. 71.

7. Cf. D. R. Howard, *The Idea of the Canterbury Tales* (Berkeley: University of California Press, 1976) pp. 139–58.

8. This variation in narrative tenses raises important questions of a literary nature, which cannot be answered with confidence through the lack of sufficient suitable non-literary data for comparison. To what extent would switches in tense in the description of the knight be perceived to be related to Chaucer's capacity to manipulate temporal perspective in a realistic and dramatic way? The simple preterite is that of description within the sphere of reminiscence, and would tend to deprive the Knight of his own individual chronology, making him part of an exemplary portrait gallery; the use of the pluperfect, however, restores his own personal history and contributes to a sense of actuality, since it implies events or states in the past with continuing relevance to the time of the pilgrimage. This duration is, of course, also implied by the adverbial *fro the tyme that*.

9. Note the durative and iterative aspect of *romed* in this quotation. The verb 'to be' is commonly used in Middle English with intransitive verbs indicating change in state (*was risen*). Other such verbs are: *comen, gan, befallen, growen, waxen, turnen*.

10. See, for example, the well-known account of Cynewulf and Cyneheard in the *Anglo-Saxon Chronicle* annal for 755: þā cuǣdon hīe þæt hīe hīe þæs ne onmunden 'þon mā þe ēowre gefēran þe mid þām cyninge ofslægene wǣrun'. [Then they said that they did not care any more for that

'than your companions who were slain with the king'.] Notice how the construction *pæs. . . mā* spans the switch from indirect to direct speech.

11. G. G. Sedgewick, 'The structure of the Merchant's Tale', *UTQ*, XVII (1948) 337–45. Alternatively, the passage may be considered to be the prejudices of Januarie ironically reflected by the Merchant: E. T. Donaldson, 'The Effect of the Merchant's Tale', in *Speaking of Chaucer* (London: Athlone Press, 1970) pp. 30–45. J. M. Manly believed that the lines were out of character for the Merchant, but did not question that they were intended as the reflections of *some* fully-characterised narrator on the Canterbury pilgrimage: *Chaucer's Canterbury Tales* (New York: 1928) p. 596.

12. That the use of the 'historical present' is to lend vividness to narrative is argued by L. D. Benson, 'Chaucer's Historical Present: Its Meaning and Uses', *ES*, XLII (1961) 65–77. The opposite view, that it is simply a metrical convenience, is best put by Visser, in *Historical Syntax*, II, pp. 705–26. J. Kerkhof accepts Visser's view with regard to rhyme, but not metre, and is disposed to accept a stylistic function in narrative. *Studies in the Language of Geoffrey Chaucer* (Leiden U.P., 1966).

13. The scribe of MS Gg 4.27 repeated several passages, most notably one in the *Man of Law's Tale*, where in line 985 the verbs *wepen* and *syghen* were changed from preterite to historic present in the second copying. *The Poetical Works of Geoffrey Chaucer: A Facsimile of Cambridge University Library MS Gg 4.27*, with an introduction by M. B. Parkes and Richard Beadle, 3 vols (Cambridge: D. S. Brewer, 1979–80) vol. I, folio 208r. See also the discussion of this and the other repeated passages in vol. III, pp. 48–54.

14. R. Quirk and J. Svartvik, 'Non-Finite Clauses', state that 2/3 of the complements of *ginnen* occur in rhyme position (p. 400). H. M. Smyser gives a figure of 73 per cent in 'Chaucer's use of *Gin* and *Do*', *Speculum*, XLII (1967) 68–83. Smyser's article is critical of the arguments for a semantic interpretation of the use of *ginnen* put forward by E. R. Homann, 'Chaucer's use of "gan" ' , *JEGP*, LIII (1954) 389–98. He argues convincingly for the metrical use of the *gan* and *do* periphrases. Nevertheless, to prove that they are a metrical convenience typical of popular poetry is not to deny the possibility of semantic implications in their use in suitable contexts. See also T. F. Mustanoja, 'Verbal Rhyming in Chaucer', in Beryl Rowland (ed.), *Chaucer and Middle English Studies in Honour of Rossell Hope Robbins* (London: Allen & Unwin, 1974) pp. 104–10.

15. Clear causal significance is evident in the lexical verb *do* in: 'And do that I tomorwe/may haue victorie' (A 2405). Such causal significance is probably encouraged by French constructions with *faire*. See Smyser, 'Chaucer's use of *Gin* and *Do*', p. 75.

3 NEGATION

1. Randolph Quirk and Sidney Greenbaum, *A University Grammar of English* (London: Longman, 1973) pp. 184–6.

2. W. Labov, 'Negative Attraction and Negative Concord in English Grammar', *Language*, XLVIII (1972) 773–818. See also George B. Jack,

'Negative Concord in Early Middle English', *SN*, L (1978) 29–39. Jespersen's discussion of negation in 'Negation in English and Other Languages' is still interesting. Reprinted in *Selected Writings of Otto Jespersen* (London: Allen and Unwin, 1962), pp. 3–151.

3. In referring to 'deletion' here, I do not intend to imply any historical development, but merely a convenient way of discussing Chaucerian usage. George B. Jack finds that Chaucer's London language is conservative in its continued use of a high proportion of double negatives. Other contemporary prose texts rarely use *ne* except in a few restricted contexts. 'Negation in Later Middle English Prose' *Arch. Ling.* IX (1978) 58–72.

4. Variation in the form of negation is common between Hg and El: for example, *he ne was nat gay* (A 74) in Hg is *he was nat gay* in El. Hg's *whoso that nyle be war by othere men* (D 180) is *whoso that wol nat be war . . .* in El. The following is a list of variations in the A fragment:

	Hg		El
A 74	*ne . . . nat*	⌐	*nat*
A 205	*was nat*	⌐	*nas nat*
A 288	*was noght*	⌐	*nas nat*
A 404	*was noon swich*	⌐	*nas noon swich*
A 428	*was noght*	⌐	*nas net*
A 1610	*I nyl nat faille*	⌐	*I wol nat faille*
A 2287	*It nere no charge*	⌐	*It were no charge*
A 2322	*thow wolt noght do me grace*	⌐	*thou wolt do me no grace*
A 3510	*I nam nat lief to gabbe*	⌐	*I am nat lief to gabbe*

5. Jack, Negation in later ME points out that there was a sharp decline in the use of *ne* and *ne . . . noght* after about 1400 (p. 59).

6. Such forms are characteristic of the South and West Midlands in Middle English, and may be considered a conservative feature of Chaucer's linguistic usage (Mustanoja, *Middle English Syntax*, p. 339).

7. See Jack, 'Negative Concord' for similar usage in early Middle English.

8. Morton Donner, 'Derived words in Chaucer's Language', *Chau. R.*, XIII (1978) 1–15.

9. This view, together with the example (D 500) is quoted from E. T. Donaldson, 'Gallic Flies in Chaucer's English Word Web', in Donald M. Rose (ed.), *New Perspectives in Chaucer Criticism* (Norman, Oklahoma: Pilgrim Books, 1981) pp. 193–202.

10. Visser, II, p. 733.

4 TEXTUAL COHERENCE

1. W. Haas, *Phono-graphic Translation* (Manchester: Manchester U.P., 1970) pp. 7–16.

2. The verb 'to go' is not recorded by *OED* in the sense 'to utter'; however sound-echoic adverbials (for example *pit a pat*) are recorded with the

verb from the late eighteenth century. That the modern uses with a personal subject and a direct quotation as adjunct are derived from this use is suggested by the fact that there is usually a marked effort at precise imitation in the quotation. Features like intonation and tone of voice are carefully duplicated.

3. A. Martinet, 'Le Mot' in *Problèmes du Langage* (Paris: Gallimard, 1966) pp. 39–53; R. H. Robins, *General Linguistics: an Introductory Survey*, 3rd edn (London: Longmans, 1980) pp. 148–54; S. Ullmann, *Semantics: An Introduction to the Science of Meaning* (Blackwell: Oxford, 1969) pp. 26–53. This last contains a useful bibliography on the question of the linguistic definition of the unit *word*.

4. Systemic grammar, indeed, has adopted the word as a unit of grammatical analysis. The theory is classically stated by M. A. K. Halliday in 'Categories of the Theory of Grammar', *Word*, XVII (1961) 241–92. A more recent and accessible statement is that by Margaret Berry, *Introduction to Systemic Linguistics*, 2 vols (London: Batsford, 1975–7). See also the notion of lexical word, or 'lexeme', in J. Lyons, *Introduction to Theoretical Linguistics* (Cambridge U.P., 1968) p. 197.

5. The word is derived from the Latin verb *texo* 'I weave'. It is used by Quintilian (IX, 4, 17) to refer to the cohesive quality of written composition.

6. The use of 'coherence' as a technical term is condemned by W. Gutwinski, *Cohesion in Literary Texts* (The Hague: Mouton, 1976) pp. 26–8. He prefers the more precise definitions of 'cohesion' derivable from Halliday and Hasan's *Cohesion in English*. I have here used the term 'coherence' deliberately to indicate that my discussion of connective features, although based upon Halliday and Hasan, includes marginally-linguistic phenonema which they do not discuss. For a recent survey of this field, see R. de Beaugrande and W. Dressler, *Introduction to Text Linguistics* (London: Longman, 1981).

7. The cohesive function of some pronouns and demonstratives has already been discussed in Chapter 1.

8. But see the discussion in Chapter 1.

9. In order to emphasise possible differences between the coherence of the medieval text and that imposed upon it by modern scholars, the texts in this chapter are quoted with MS punctuation only.

10. Exophoric reference to the disparate details of a scene imagined to be actually taking place before one's eyes is a favourite device of epic, and especially of the description of battle in alliterative poetry. On the reputation of alliterative style as battle poetry, see G. Shepherd, 'The Nature of Alliterative Poetry in Late Medieval England', *PBA*, LVI (1970) 57–76. Also T. Turville-Petre, *The Alliterative Revival* (Cambridge: D. S. Brewer, 1977) pp. 100–101.

11. Deixis is that feature of language which fixes the utterance in time and space. Lyons, *Semantics*, II, pp. 636–724.

12. Halliday and Hasan, *Cohesion in English*, pp. 274–92.

13. By hyponymy is meant a semantically inclusive relationship: thus, for example, the sense of the word *red* may be said to include those of the words *crimson*, *scarlet*, and *flame*, which are its hyponyms. Lyons, *Structural*

Semantics, Philological Society Publications, XX (Oxford: Blackwell, 1963) p. 69.

14. A 'lexical set' is that group of words which habitually recurs in the same context, or 'collocates' together. Inevitably, words referring to the same situation will tend to co-occur, as will words used to discuss particular ideas. In the latter case, lacking a clear, concrete referent, semantic assimilations will take place more easily. R. Quirk has pointed out the way in which alliterative metrical connections carry with them semantic and lexical presuppositions in 'Poetic Language and Old English Metre', in Arthur Brown and Peter Foote (eds), *Early English and Norse Studies presented to Hugh Smith* (London: Methuen, 1963) pp. 150–71; reprinted in R. Quirk, *Essays on the English Language Medieval and Modern* (London: Longman, 1968) pp. 1–19. On the relationship between meaning and collocation, see also J. McH. Sinclair, 'Beginning the Study of Lexis', in Bazell, Catford, Halliday and Robins (eds), *In Memory of J. R. Firth* (London: Longman, 1966).

15. A formalised account of the battle-motif is given by Susan Wittig in *Stylistic and Narrative Structures in the Middle English Romances* (University of Texas Press, 1978) pp. 81–101.

16. H. A. Gleason has referred to such cohesive phenomena as 'enation' and 'agnation'. The former denotes the relation between sentences with identical grammatical structures, the latter the relationship between sentences containing similar lexical items and whose grammatical structures, although different, can be simply and systematically related (for example, active or passive). For a discussion of these and some examples, see Gutwinski, *Cohesion in Literary Texts*, pp. 75–9.

17. For the significance of the word *circumstantiae* see p. 171, (note).

18. Ruth Finnegan points out that repeated patterns and parallelisms are found in all poetic composition. Nevertheless such devices are perhaps especially prominent in oral poetry. See her discussion of style and performance in oral poetry: R. Finnegan, *Oral Poetry: its Nature, Significance and Social Context* (Cambridge U.P., 1977) pp. 88–133.

19. Diane Bornstein, 'Chaucer's *Tale of Melibee* as an Example of the *Style Clergial*', *Chau. R*, XII (1978) 236–54.

20. Square brackets indicate additions from Ellesmere where the text of Hengwrt seems to be incomplete.

21. See p. 501.

22. See p. 46.

23. On the use of doublets, see I. Koskenniemi, *Repetitive Word Pairs in Old and Early Middle English Prose*, Annales Universitatis Turknensis, Ser. B, Tom. 107 (Turku, 1968).

24. The benefits bestowed upon a man during his life were often categorised by moralistic writers into those of *nature* (that is, hereditary gifts); those of *grace* (spiritual gifts of God); and those of *fortune* (temporary benefits from worldly concerns). Other arrangements can also be found and the *MED* entry *god* 9c is a useful preliminary index to them.

25. W. O. Ross (ed.), *Middle English Sermons from MS Royal 18B xxiii*, EETS OS 209 (London, 1938) pp. 175, 180, 217, 235 etc. The phrase 'here may ye see' is a common introduction to the *moralizatio* of the *exemplum*.

5 LINGUISTIC DIVERSITY

1. Modern ethnographic linguistics sees the inter-relationship of dialects as forming a 'continuum'. The word seems to have been regularly applied to a concept of dialects which had become widespread in the late 1950s. See J. Gumperz, 'Speech Variation and the Study of Indian Civilisation (1961)', in Anwar S. Dil (ed.), *Language in Social Groups* (Stanford U.P., 1971) pp. 77–96.

2. A full discussion of the development of mixed languages in Middle English texts may be found in Michael Benskin and Margaret Laing, 'Translations and *Mischsprachen* in Middle English Manuscripts', in Michael Benskin and M. L. Samuels (eds), *So Meny People, Longages and Tonges: Philological Essays in Scots and Medieval English presented to Angus McIntosh* (Edinburgh: Benskin and Samuels, 1981) pp. 55–106.

3. However, the form *yzene* is found in the *Ayenbite of Inwit*, written as far away from London as Canterbury.

4. The sound-change resulting in the form *strāte* extends beyond London over a small area of the south-east Midlands, including Middlesex, Essex, Hertfordshire, and parts of Bedfordshire, Huntingdon, and Cambridgeshire. That development which gives the plural *man* is found in east Middlesex, south and east Essex, Surrey, East Sussex, Hertfordshire, south Bedfordshire, and Cambridgeshire. Karl-Gustav Ek, *The Development of OE ǣ (i-mutated a) before Nasals and OE ǣ in South Eastern Middle English*, Acta Universitatis Lundensis Sectio I Theologica, Juridica, Humaniora, XXII (Lund: Gleerup, 1975). It is apparent that so-called Essex-London forms are forms proper to the area of East Saxon influence rather than the modern county of Essex.

5. These forms are designated London forms by W. Heuser, *Altlondon mit besonderer Berücksichtigung des Dialekts* (Osnabrück: Liesecke, 1914) p. 45.

6. For an account of the development of London English in the fourteenth century, see M. L. Samuels, 'Some Applications of Middle English Dialectology', *ES*, LCIV (1963) 81–99. And on the development of Standard English in the fifteenth century, Arthur O. Sandved, 'Prolegomena to a renewed study of the use of Standard English', in Benskin and Samuels, *So Meny People*, pp. 31–42.

7. Quoted from Bede, *A History of the English Church and People*, translated with an introduction by Leo Sherley-Price (Harmondsworth: Penguin, 1955) pp. 102–3.

8. Sylvia L. Thrupp, *The Merchant Class of Medieval London* (Chicago: University of Chicago Press, 1948) p. 1.

9. Chambers and Daunt, *Book of London English*, p. 237.

10. The maps on pp. 112–3 are based on the researches of E. Ekwall as reported in *Studies on the Population of Medieval London* (Stockholm: Almqvist and Wiksell, 1956). They represent schematically, county by county, the origins of identified London immigrants in three generations from 1270–1359. Each dot represents five persons. The importance of East Anglia is apparent throughout, as is the growing importance of the counties of

Bedford and Northampton in the fourteenth century. Unfortunately, in the face of various technical difficulties, Ekwall did not pursue his research beyond 1360, so that the triumph of south-east Midland forms evident in the development from Samuels' Type II to Type III is not fully represented. The decision to represent immigrants schematically, county by county, rather than by their presumed place of origin, hides the fact that most Lincolnshire immigrants were from the north of the county, and most Yorkshire immigrants were from East Yorkshire. The southern counties are omitted, but immigration from Essex, Middlesex, Surrey, Hertfordshire and Buckinghamshire was very high throughout the period. For a map showing the places which contributed to the population of London in the years 1147–1350, see P. H. Reaney, *The Origin of English Surnames*, (London: Routledge and Kegan Paul, 1967) p. 344.

11. G. V. Smithers (ed.), *Kyng Alisaunder*, 2 vols, EETS OS 227 and 237 (London: OUP, 1952; 1957); O. D. Macrae-Gibson (ed.), *Of Arthour and of Merlin*, 2 vols, EETS OS 268 and 279 (London: OUP, 1973, 1979). This poem is referred to in the text by its shorter title, *Arthur and Merlin*.

12. Macrae-Gibson gives the following figures for the proportion of *an* to *en* rhymes in *Arthur and Merlin*: 32:28; and in *Kyng Alisaunder*: 11:41 (*Of Arthour and of Merlin*, II, p. 61).

13. On the use of *-ande* in *Arthur and Merlin* and related texts, see O. D. Macrae-Gibson, 'The Auchinleck MS: Participles in *-and (e)*', *ES*, LII (1971) 13–20. Macrae-Gibson notes that the form is recorded in place-names as far south as Northampton and Cambridge, and in view of immigration from these counties and from Norfolk, it must have been familiar to Londoners throughout the fourteenth century.

14. According to Kittredge, among the early MSS he studied, (that is, MSS Campsall, Cambridge Gg 4.27, and Harley 2280 and 3943) only 3943 exhibits the forms *them*, *theym*. 'Observations on the Language of Chaucer's *Troilus*', Chaucer Society, 2nd Series, XXVIII (London, 1891).

15. J. Frieshammer, *Die sprachliche Form des Chaucerschen Prosa: ihr Verhältnis zur Reimtechnik des Dichters sowie zur Sprache der älteren London Urkunden*, Studien zur Englischen Philologie, XLII, (Halle: Niemeyer, 1910).

16. See, for example, the variation in the language of the Appeal of Thomas Usk, which he says he wrote with his own hand, Chambers and Daunt, pp. 18–31.

17. Thus words like *schoon* and *foon* are widespread, as are *oxen*, *eyen*, and 'double plurals' like *bretheren* and *children*.

18. *Complaint of Venus* (79–82).

19. Rhymes of /k/ with /t/, /n/ with /m/, /v/ with /ð/, and /f/ with /x/ are common. However, M. Mills shows that Thomas Chestre, a hack-writer active in the later part of Chaucer's career, is prepared to sacrifice sense and also to borrow from outside his own linguistic system in order to obtain pure rhymes. *Lybeaus Desconus*, EETS OS 261 (1969) pp. 33–6.

20. Some idea of the regularity of eye-rhyme in Chaucer MSS can be gained from the fact that in the first 500 lines of Book III of *TC* in Corpus 61, eye-rhyme fails on only 31 occasions. In the first 500 lines of *CT* in both Hg and El, there are only 14 failures.

21. W. W. Skeat, 'On Chaucer's Use of the Kentish Dialect', in *Essays on Chaucer*, Chaucer Society, 2nd Series, VI, pp. 659–71.

22. The extent of the area in which *e* and *y* may be expected to have been co-variants can be deduced from Karl-Gustav Ek, *The Development of OE ȳ and ō in South-Eastern Middle English*, Lund Studies in English, XLII (Lund: Gleerup, 1972).

23. These *-s* inflexions are commented on by G. V. Smithers in his edition of *Kyng Alisaunder*, vol. II, pp. 50–1. In that text, *-s* forms usually follow a dental and may be conditioned by this fact. That they are rapid-speech variants existing in Chaucerian London English is argued by Kenneth Shields, Jr. in 'Fast Speech and the Origin of the Standard English Verbal Suffix *-s*', *JEL*, XIV (1980) 24–35.

24. A valuable insight into those northernisms a Southerner of Chaucer's time found to be unacceptable is given by the revisions made to the Middle English translation of Robert de Gretham's Anglo-Northern *Miroir*. See Thomas G. Duncan, 'A Middle English Linguistic Reviser', *NM*, LXXXII (1981) 162–74.

6 CHAUCER'S VOCABULARY

1. T. H. Kaplan, 'Gower's Vocabulary' *JEGP*, XXXI (1932) 395–402.

2. J. Mersand, *Chaucer's Romance Vocabulary* (Brooklyn: Comet Press, 1937) pp. 37–43. Mersand's estimate of Chaucer's vocabulary is 8430 words.

3. *Beowulf*, 259.

4. In Caxton's translation of the *Book of the Knight of the Tower* (ed. Offord), p. 40, a warning is issued not to contend with those who are 'langageurs and full of wordes'. Lydgate (*Siege of Thebes*, 47) gave Chaucer himself the honour of introducing the art of *wel-seyinge* into English. His reference echoes the traditional description of rhetoric as *ars bene dicendi*.

5. For a recent and illuminating discussion of lexical borrowing in the medieval period, see W. Rothwell, 'Lexical Borrowing in a Medieval Context', *Bulletin of the John Rylands Library of Manchester*, LXIII (1980) 118–43.

6. These phrases are collected from the romances *Kyng Alisaunder* and *Of Arthour and of Merlin*.

7. This point is raised by N. F. Blake in *The English Language in Medieval Literature* (London: Dent, 1977) pp. 57–8.

8. Mersand, *Chaucer's Romance Vocabulary*, p. 43. The necessity of knowing the contemporary stylistic status of a word as well as its ultimate etymological origin is forcibly put by N. Davis in 'Chaucer and Fourteenth Century English', in D. S. Brewer (ed.), *Geoffrey Chaucer* (Writers and their Background) (London: Bell, 1974) pp. 71–8.

9. A similar point is made by Ralph W. V. Elliott in '"Faire subtile wordes": An Approach to Chaucer's Verbal Art', *Parergon*, XIII (1975) 3–20.

10. The way in which written French gradually adopts the phrasal

patterning and syntax of English can readily be followed in the pleas recorded in the Rolls of Parliament. An increasing anglicisation is notable throughout the thirteenth century. The influence of French upon English phrasing is treated, with many detailed examples, by A. A. Prins, *French Influence on English Phrasing* (Leiden U.P., 1952).

11. *Ars Poetica*, 46–59. Quoted by Geoffrey of Vinsauf, *Documentum de Arte Versificandi*, II 142–4.

12. Isidore of Seville, *Etymologiarum*, edited by W. M. Lindsay (Oxford: Clarendon, 1911), II xx. L. W. Daly and B. A. Daly (eds), *Summa Britonis* (Padua, 1975), s.v. *Ambigo*. *Chaucer's Troylus and Cryseyde compared with Boccaccio's Filostrato*, translated by Wm. Michael Rossetti, Chaucer Soc. First Series, XLIV (London, 1873) p. 264.

13. 'amphibologia est constructio non manifestans sensum perfecte: puto te socium superare. hoc fit multotiens, quia non determino plene affectum mentis defectu praepediente, sive duplex sensus ex verbis possit haberi'. D. Reichling (ed.), *Das Doctrinale des Alexander de Villa-Dei*, Monumenta Germaniae Pedagogica, XII (Berlin: Hofmann, 1893), lines 2399–2403.

14. Since most of the authors in Halm's *Rhetorici Latini Minores* discuss ambiguity in the same legalistic terms, often using the same examples, and since the words *ambages* and *amphibologia* are found in such important reference works at Brito and Alexander of Villadei, it is a fair presumption that both words and concepts were familiar to Chaucer's first audience, many of whom seem to have received some legal training.

15. Gower (*CA* V 6236) glosses *amadriades* as 'wodemaydes'; Chaucer explains *fauns* as 'halue-goddes . . . of wildnesse' (*TC* IV 1544); and Lydgate (*Troy Book* II 5652) refers to the invisible gods of the green wood. *Fauns* are referred to by Trevisa (*Bartholomew's Encyclopaedia*), Capgrave and *The Gest Hystoriale of the Destruction of Troy*, but *MED* cites only Chaucer, Gower, and Lydgate as users of the other two words.

16. Hence Chaucer's repeated explanations that he must speak words as they uttered them (that is, *proprely*). See Chapters 7 and 8.

17. Edmund Reiss, 'Chaucer's *deerne love* and the Medieval View of Secrecy in Love', in Edward Vasta and Zacharias P. Thundy (eds), *Chaucerian Problems and Perspectives: Essays presented to Paul E. Beichner C.S.C.* (Notre Dame University Press, 1979) pp. 164–79. The phrase *deerne love* is shown to be morally pejorative. The word *hende* had been used in pre-Chaucerian London romances to mean simply 'close by, at hand', and it may be that it still has some associations of this kind. Gower uses the word (*CA* II 644) as a term of endearment used by an irrational lover. It is one of the terms of popular poetry discussed by E. T. Donaldson in 'The Idiom of Popular Poetry in the *Miller's Tale*', in *Speaking of Chaucer*, pp. 13–29.

18. In Béroul's *Tristan* Isolde calls herself Tristan's *dru* (l.2815), but denies this to her husband, King Mark (l.2857). Elsewhere, *druerie* is associated with *vilanie* (l.2229) and *folie* (l.3048) by other members of the court.

19. John L. Lowes, 'Simple and Coy: A Note on Fourteenth Century Poetic Diction', *Anglia*, XXXIII (1910) 440–51.

20. As with other originally-idealising terms, *fetys* is given an ironic, morally pejorative interpretation in the *Pardoner's Tale* (C 479), where it is used of the neat figures of dancing girls who associate with *baudes* and notoriously immoral *wafereres*. The choice of the word here may reasonably be considered to represent the Pardoner's own point of view. Here social mockery turns into moral satire.

21. The form *Nowelis* occurs also in the language of the narrator, but as an obvious (mocking?) echo of John. For the view that *astromye* is an old-fashioned, countrified form in Chaucer's eyes, see Jeffrey F. Huntsman, 'Caveat Editor: Chaucer and Medieval English Dictionaries', *MP*, LXXIII (1975–6) 276–9. N. F. Blake, ' "Astromye" in "The Miller's Tale" ' *NQ,* CCXXIV (1979), 110–11, argues that *astromye* is an unremarkable variant in Chaucer's London English, and has been reproved for it by T. W. Ross in 'Astromye in the Miller's Tale Again', *NQ,* CCXXVI (1981) 202.

22. *Of Arthour and of Merlin* (l.585); *Kyng Alisaunder*, (l.136), and other uses of the variant *astromien* recorded by *MED* under *astronomien*. See also the variant readings cited by Kane and Donaldson for the B-text of *Piers Plowman* (XV 370).

23. R. I. Page, 'How long did the Scandinavian language survive in England? The epigraphical evidence', in Peter A. Clemoes and Kathleen Hughes (eds), *England Before the Conquest: Studies . . . presented to Dorothy Whitelock* (Cambridge U.P., 1971) pp. 165–81.

24. Mary S. Serjeantson, *A History of Foreign Words in English* (London: Kegan Paul, Trench, and Trübner, 1935), p. 81.

25. A. Rynell, *The Rivalry of Scandinavian and Native Synonyms in Middle English . . .* Lund Studies in English, 13 (Lund: Gleerup, 1948) p. 363.

26. Idley's *Instructions to his Son* quoted in *MED* s.v. *mire*.

27. *MED*, s.v. *drit* 3b.

28. Sylvia L. Thrupp, *The Merchant Class of Medieval London (1300–1500)* (London: Cambridge University Press, 1948) p. 166.

29. In W. H. French and C. B. Hale (eds), *The Middle English Metrical Romances*, 2 vols (New York: Russel and Russel, 1964) vol. II, pp. 989–98. Compare also the mock-epic hero Reneward, a kitchen-boy with a club, in Duncan Macmillan (ed), *La Chanson de Guillaume*, 2 vols, SATF 74 (Paris, 1949) lines 2648–2717.

30. That *capul* is at once a Northern word and a vulgarism in Chaucer's language is suggested by Ralph W. V. Elliott, *Chaucer's English* (London: Deutsch, 1974) pp. 199–200; 392.

31. As it did in the illustration in the Morgan manuscript of the *Roman*. Douglas Gray, 'Chaucer and "Pite" ' in Mary and Robert T. Farrell (eds), *J. R. R. Tolkien, Scholar and Storyteller* (Ithaca: Cornell U.P., 1979) p. 174

32. On the origins of this and some other learned glosses to the *Man of Law's Tale*, see Lotario dei Segni, *De Miseria Condicionis Humane*, edited by Robert E. Lewis, The Chaucer Library (University of Georgia Press, 1978) pp. 32–9.

7 REGISTER AND PROPRIETY

1. A fuller discussion of this question may be found in J. D. Burnley, 'Chaucer's *Termes*', *YES*, VII (1977) 53–67.

2. The statement that a jay can call 'Watte' as well as the Pope (A 642–3) refers to the fact that jays, magpies, and jackdaws were commonly taught to 'speak' in medieval times. Their cries were, of course, merely imitative, without understanding or intention, and this fact is enshrined in the schematic expression 'janglen as a jay, pye etc.' The verb *janglen* carries with it a strong connotation of speech without thought or purpose, and is cognate with Old French *jongleur*. The *jongleurs* were that class of performer who merely repeated the literary compositions of other creative artists, who were known in contrast as *trouvères*.

3. The concept of a dichotomy between 'common core' features and those with some form of restriction to a particular variety of language is ancient and pervasive. In lexical terms, it is present among early rhetoricians (for example, Chirius Fortunatianus) and is evident in the diagram in the *NED*, vol I, p. xvii. Certain words used in all dialects, styles, or varieties of English, are there called 'Common Words'. The phrase 'common core' itself is used by C. F. Hockett to refer to linguistic features shared by two or more idiolects or dialects: *A Course in Modern Linguistics* (New York: Macmillan, 1958) pp. 331–7. It is applied to stylistics in David Crystal and Derek Davy, *Investigating English Style* (London: Longman, 1969) pp. 64–6, where it refers to those features which are common to all styles of English.

The term 'register' refers to stylistic varieties of language, distinguished by use rather than user, and therefore distinct from social or geographical dialects. See M. A. K. Halliday, Angus McIntosh and Peter Strevens, *The Linguistic Sciences and Language Teaching* (London: Longman, 1964) p. 77. The generality of this definition is criticised by Crystal and Davy (pp. 61–2), but it corresponds well with traditional stylistic perceptions.

4. *A Chaucer Glossary*, compiled by N. Davis, et al. (Oxford: Clarendon Press, 1979). *Equinoxial* is glossed as 'celestial equator', and *tables tolletanes* are separately listed as 'tables (for calculation)' and 'of Toledo'. For further enlightenment one must turn to the notes in the edition by Phyllis Hodgson of *The Franklin's Tale* (London: Athlone Press, 1960) pp. 125–30.

5. See R. Blenner-Hassett, 'Autobiographical Aspects of Chaucer's Franklin', *Speculum*, XXVIII (1953), 791–800; and further, Marie Collins, 'Love, Nature and Law in the Poetry of Gower and Chaucer', in Glyn S. Burgess (ed.), *Court and Poet* (Liverpool: Francis Cairns, 1981) pp. 113–28.

6. This note is found in many good Chaucer MSS, and may perhaps descend from the poet himself, but certainly from a very early copy of the *Canterbury Tales*. J. M. Manly and E. Rickert, *The Text of Chaucer's Canterbury Tales*, 8 vols (Chicago: University of Chicago Press, 1940) vol. III, p. 511.

7. F. Pollock and F. W. Maitland, *The History of English Law*, 2 vols, 2nd edn (Cambridge U.P., repr. 1968) pp. 651–3. More generally, see also R. B. Pugh, *Imprisonment in the Middle Ages* (Cambridge U.P., 1968).

8. The words *coloure*, *peynte* and *enlumine* are figuratively related to those

devices known by the rhetoricians as the flowers or colours of rhetoric (*colores rhetorici*), by which a work was given stylistic embellishment. Geoffrey of Vinsauf wrote a short work entitled *De Coloribus Rhetoricis*. Cicero frequently refers to style being 'painted' (*pingere*) and Quintilian refers to the *lumina* of style. However, Chaucer may well have derived this latter usage not from Quintilian, but Brunetto Latini. The word *devise* has strong associations of graphic visualisation, either unexpressed within the imagination, or expressed in circumstantial description or narration. It was the usual French word equivalent to the scholastic Latin *distinctio*.

9. G. Paré, *Le Roman de la Rose et la Scolastique Courtoise* (Paris and Ottawa, 1941) pp. 33–4.

10. The basic source for medieval discussion of the predicables was Boethius's commentary on the *Isagoge* of Porphyry. This latter is available in English translation: *Porphyry the Phoenician, Isagoge*, translated with notes and introduction by Edward W. Warren (Toronto: Pontifical Institute of Medieval Studies, 1975).

11. Latin *contrarium*. In *BD* 996–8 Chaucer plays with the notion of definition by contraries when he says: 'I sey not that she ne had knowynge/what harm was; or elles she/Had koud no good, so thinketh me'.

12. For example, Alberti Magni, *Quaestiones super de Animalibus*, XV, qu. xi.

13. The scholastic element is apparent in the very plot of the *Summoner's Tale*. J. Bédier pointed out long ago that the *fabliau* genre was the product of clerks. *Les Fabliaux*, 5th ed. (Paris: Champion, 1925) pp. 389–90.

14. The sense 'metaphor' is found ubiquitously in rhetorical handbooks, and usually refers to metaphor arising from a shift in habitual application or reference. Cicero, *Topica*, VII, 32; Matthew of Vendôme, *Ars Versificatoria*, III, 19, and Geoffrey of Vinsauf, *Poetria Nova*, IV, 765–99. Geoffrey furnishes such examples at 'flowers *are born*' (*verbum translatum*) and 'flowers grow' (*verbum proprium*). The conception of propriety of use which is analogous to 'register' occurs, however, in Chirius Fortunatianus, III, 3; *Rhetorica ad Herennium* IV, 17; and is fully explained by Quintilian, VIII, ii, 8. Geoffrey of Vinsauf makes only a brief reference to it, *Poetria Nova*, IV, 1087–93.

15. J. Jolivet, *Arts du langage et theologie chez Abelard* (Paris: Vrin, 1969), p. 278 n. 178.

16. Douglas Wurtele discusses *proprietas* with reference to Chaucer's *Man of Law's Tale*, but only in relation to the Ciceronian concept of decorum and without reference to its pervasiveness in scholastic thought. '*Proprietas* in Chaucer's *Man of Law's Tale*', *Neophilologus*, LX (1976) 577–93.

17. The Wife's *Prologue*, which we are apt to read as the naturalistic outpourings of a turbulent and rebellious woman, is treated by Chaucer as a text on marriage to which the reader is jocularly referred in the *Merchant's Tale* and the *Envoy to Bukton*.

18. Matthew of Vendôme, *Ars Versificatoria*, I, 64–6.

19. Thomae Waleys, *De Modo Componendi Sermones*, in Th.-M. Charland, *Artes Praedicandi* (Paris and Ottawa, 1936) pp. 348–9. Thomas is not concerned with verisimilitude, but with the moral and scholarly responsibility of the preacher. However appropriate to Christ the words may seem when taken out of context, they were used in a different spirit by

Nebuchadnezzar, who is a type of the Devil, and this fact must be made clear if they are to be related to Christ.

20. Quintilian, V. x, 104; V, xii, 4. Aulus Gellius, *Noctes Atticae*, edited and translated by John C. Rolfe, 3 vols, Loeb Classical Library (London: Heinemann, 1928). Gellius says that the *circumstantiae* are details of life, character and disposition of individuals in a legal case (XIV, 1, 15).

21. Chambers and Daunt, *A Book of London English*, p. 26. See also J. D. Burnley, *Chaucer's Language and the Philosophers' Tradition* (Cambridge: D. S. Brewer, 1979) pp. 105–15, and Karl P. Wentersdorf, 'Heigh Imaginacioun in Chaucer's *Nun's Priest's Tale*', *SN*, LII (1980) 31–34.

22. The distinction between Man and Animal was made in the logical tradition by means of the *differentia* of the former's possession of reason and the *proprium* of his ability to laugh. The contrast was often made in terms of Man and Horse, but in Aristotle's *Categoriae* was also made in terms of Man and Ape. (III.2, 117b).

23. Compare Geoffrey of Vinsauf's instructions in *Poetria Nova*, IV, 1084–6: 'Regard not your own capacities, therefore, but rather his with whom you are speaking. Give to your words weight suited to his shoulders, and adapt your speech to the subject'. Quoted from *The Poetria Nova of Geoffrey of Vinsauf*, translated by Margaret F. Nims (Toronto: Pontifical Institute of Mediaeval Studies, 1967).

24. The form *poynte* is discussed as a technical term by J. A. Burrow in *Ricardian Poetry* (London: Routledge and Kegan Paul, 1971) pp. 69–79. He does not make explicit a connection with *peynte* (cf. Latin *pingere*), but takes 'pointing' to refer to the accumulation of significant detail, sometimes narrative or descriptive, but also in selection of the *mot juste*.

25. The technical nature of this discussion has recently been noted by Ian Bishop in *Chaucer's Troilus and Criseyde: A Critical Study* (University of Bristol, 1981) pp. 53–4.

26. Martin Stevens, ' "And Venus Laugheth" : An Interpretation of the *Merchant's Tale*', *Chau. R*, VII (1972) 118–31.

27. For the form of the vows in the contemporary marriage service, see Henry Littlehales (ed.), *English Fragments from Latin Medieval Service Books*, EETS ES 90 (London, 1903). Further examples are given in J. D. Burnley, 'The Morality of the Merchant's Tale', *YES*, VI (1976) 16–25.

28. F. J. Carmody, *Li Livres dou Tresor of Brunetto Latini* (Berkeley: California U.P., 1948): 'ceste maniere de parler est mout bele et mout bonne et cortoise et de bon sentence, et mout le puet on trouver es dis de sages homes'. (p. 331).

8 LEVELS OF STYLE

1. Chaucer's extravagant use of rhetoric in the *Franklin's Tale* has been studied by Benjamin S. Harrison in 'The Rhetorical Inconsistency of Chaucer's Franklin', *SP*, XXXII (1935) 55–61.

2. See John Hodgkin, *Proper Terms*, Supplement to the *Transactions of the Philological Society*, 1907–10, p. 7.

3. Hunting skills and their technical terminology are part of the conception of social elegance in the romances of *Ipomadon*, *Sir Gawain and the Green Knight*, the *Parlement of the Thre Ages*, as well as *Sir Tristrem*. Malory repeatedly refers to Tristram's role in the establishment of these gentlemen's skills. See T. Malory, *Works*, edited by E. Vinaver, 2nd edn, 3 vols, (Oxford: Clarendon, 1967) II p. 571; pp. 682–3.

4. W. W. Skeat (ed.), 'Nominale sive Verbale' *TPS* (1906) 1–50. The *Nominale* is derived from Walter of Bibbesworthe's treatise and probably served a similar purpose of instructing Englishmen in French. It was apparently written by a French scribe, but its errors suggest an English author. W. Rothwell, 'The Teaching of French in Medieval England', *MLR*, XLIII (1968) 37–47.

5. For example, Chirius Fortunatianus, *Artes Rhetoricae III Libri*, III, 3 in C. Halm (ed.), *Rhetores Latini Minores* (Leipzig: Teubner, 1863) pp. 80–134.

6. In addition, the works of Chaucer, Gower, Hoccleve, and Lydgate are praised as a schooling in eloquence in Caxton's *Book of Curtesye*, ed. F. J. Furnivall, EETS ES III (London 1868) lines 274–427. See also F. J. Furnivall (ed.), *The Babees Book etc*, EETS OS XXXII (1868). Most of these books are intended for the instruction of children in social proprieties.

7. Chirius Fortunatianus, III, 4. On ideals of *urbanitas*, see Edwin S. Ramage, *Urbanitas: ancient sophistication and refinement* (Norman, Oklahoma: Cincinnati Univ., 1973) pp. 56–64.

8. The social expectations of a poet may lie behind the frequent adoption of a *persona* and other similar distancing devices. R. F. Green, *Poets and Princepleasers: Literature and the English Court in the late Middle Ages* (University of Toronto Press, 1979) pp. 112–3.

9. The word *plat* is often used synonymously with *playn*, and indeed often collocated with it, to describe direct and unadorned expression. That *brevitas* could be an ideal of weighty expression is suggested by Chaucer's famous description of the Clerk's speech as 'short and quyk and ful of heigh sentence'.

10. Quintilian, XII, x, 58. Quintilian accepts the notion of three styles but points out its arbitrariness: style is infinitely variable in level. Although the relevant passage is missing from the mutilated copy which circulated before 1416, knowledge of Quintilian's teaching was passed on to the Middle Ages by a number of minor authors; but it is difficult to find any clear echo of his criticism of the theory of three styles.

11. It has been argued that no specifically rhetorical teaching was available in England in Chaucer's time, although a knowledge of some of its devices could have been gleaned from grammar books. J. J. Murphy, 'Literary Implications of Instruction in the Verbal Arts in Fourteenth Century England', *LSE*, NS I (1967) 119–35.

12. On the traditions of ancient rhetoric, see J. J. Murphy, *Rhetoric in the Middle Ages* (Berkeley: University of California Press, 1974). Also, more generally, J. W. H. Atkins, *English Literary Criticism: the Medieval Phase* (Cambridge U.P, 1943). The most detailed study of the history of the three styles is that by F. Quadlbauer, *Die Antike Theorie der Genera Dicendi in Lateinischen Mittelalter*, Österreichische Akademie der Wissenschaften.

Philosophische-Historische Klasse-Sitzungsberichte, 241, Band 2 Abhandlung (Vienna: Bohlau, 1962).

13. Cicero, *De Oratore*, III, lv; *Rhetorica ad Herennium*, IV, 8; Julius Victor, XXII (Halm, *Rhetores Latini Minores*, p. 438).

14. *Etymologiarum*, II, xvi–xvii. According to Isidore, the low style is for small matters; the high for matters to do with God and salvation. He repeats the Augustinian idea that the low style is for instruction, the middle for praising or blaming, and the high for the persuasion of reluctant Christians. Servius and Donatus associated the three styles with the works of Virgil: high style (*Aeneid*); middle style (*Georgics*); low style (*Bucolics*). They thus laid the foundation for the Carolingian interpretation of this as an association with ways of life and levels of society, the *Aeneid* being associated with the warrior aristocracy, the *Georgics* with farmers, and the *Bucolics* with shepherds (Quadlbauer, *Die Antike Theorie*, pp. 35–9).

15. Geoffrey of Vinsauf, *Documentum de arte et modo versificandi*, II, 149 and John of Garlande, *Parisiana Poetria*, V, 5.

16. In some MSS of Petrarch's story of Griselda the phrase *in alto stilo* has been substituted for *in alio stilo*. J. Burke Severs, *The Literary Relationships of Chaucer's Clerke's Tale*, Yale Studies in English, LXIX, (New Haven, 1942) p. 288. Also Manly and Rickert, *Canterbury Tales*, III, p. 275.

17. Chambers and Daunt, *A Book of London English*, pp. 72–3.

18. On medieval epistolary style, see N. Davis, 'The *Litera Troili* and English Letters', *RES*, n.s. XVI (1965) 233–44. And, on the formal structure of a letter, J. McKinnell, 'Letters as a Type of the Formal Level in *Troilus and Criseyde*', in M. Salu (ed.), *Essays on Troilus and Criseyde*, Chaucer Studies, III (Cambridge: D. S. Brewer, 1979) pp. 73–89.

19. See, for example, letters in H. Ellis (ed.), *Original Letters*, 2nd series, (London, 1827) and also in M. D. Legge (ed.), *Anglo Norman Letters and Petitions*, ANTS, III (Oxford: Blackwell, 1941). The development of the 'curial' style into other prose writing is noted in French by J. Rasmussen, *La prose narrative française de XVᵉ siècle étude esthétique et stylistique* (Copenhagen: Munksgaard, 1958) pp. 32–8.

20. The convention of the oral delivery of a message by a messenger is found in the Anglo-Norman *Romance of Horn*, lines 1350–52; 2426–7. In the latter example the perfect delivery of the messenger is jokingly complimented by an enquiry as to whether he is reading from a parchment. A similar scene in which Jason delivers a message replete with the skills of rhetoric occurs in Lydgate's *Troy Book*, I, 1397–1448. I am indebted to Jean Moorhead for this latter reference.

21. *MED*, s.v. *natural* 2b. A 'natural' day is one of twenty-four hours and is thus distinct from that sense of *day* which contrasts with *night*.

22. See *General Prologue*, A 376; *Reeve's Tale*, A 3956; and *Wife's Prologue*, D 296.

23. On the importance of the union of wills in *amicitia* and in courtly theorising, see J. D, Burnley, 'Fine Amor: Its Meaning and Context', *RES* n.s. XXXI (1980), 129–48. Also *Chaucer's Language and the Philosophers' Tradition*, pp. 134–170.

24. E. Langlois (ed.), *Roman de la Rose*, 6928–7230. The dreamer has

previously been warned by the God of Love that he should not utter the names of base things (2111). That Chaucer had read this passage with some attention is suggested by a quotation of line 6924 in *BD* 1114, and an allusion in *Pardoner's Tale*, 948–55 to lines 7109–15 of *RR*.

25. Per Nykrog, 'Courtliness and the Townspeople: The Fabliaux as a Courtly Burlesque', in Thomas D. Cooke and Benjamin L. Honeycutt (eds), *The Humor of the Fabliaux: A Collection of Critical Essays* (Columbia, Miss.: University of Missouri Press, 1974) p. 68. A few *fabliaux* have as protagonists precious young ladies who cannot bear to hear any mention of sexual organs.

26. Z. P. Thundy, 'Matheolus, Chaucer, and the Wife of Bath', in Edward Vasta and Zacharias P. Thundy, *Chaucerian Problems and Perspectives, Essays presented to Paul E. Beichner C.S.C.* (Notre Dame U.P., 1979), p. 36. See also *instrument* and *chose* in Godefroy, *Dictionnaire de l'Ancienne Langue Française* and Tobler-Lommatzsch, *Altfranzösischer Wörterbuch*.

27. *A Chaucer Glossary*. ed. Davis, et al. s.v. *queynte*.

28. Thomas W. Ross, *Chaucer's Bawdy* (New York: Dutton, 1972). Often bawdy reference requires a very sharp eye for a pun.

29. The injunction to make confession in *pleyn* or *plat* terms is a commonplace to which Gower alludes in the lover's confession to the priest Genius: '. . . let nothing be forsake/Telle pleinliche as it is befalle'. *CA* I 210–11.

30. This passage from the *Manciple's Tale* is discussed in the context of the medieval teachings on verbal discretion by John Scattergood, 'The Manciple's Manner of Speaking', *Essays in Criticism*, XXIV (1974) 124–46.

31. The idea that the sinner is the slave of his passions, or, as Chaucer's Parson puts it, the *thral of synne*, can be traced back to popular moral philosophy in Hellenic times, and it was adopted by the Fathers of the Church. A. Oltramare, *Les Origines de la Diatribe Romaine* (Lausanne, 1926).

32. Distaste for this word is apparent in almost all Chaucer's uses of it. In *LGW* (F) 1772 and B 917 it is used by rapists of their intended victims. It is used by religious narrators in a disapproving way; by the Parson of priests' mistresses (I 900) and by the Monk of faithless lovers (B 3253; 3309). In *Mum and the Sothsegger*, 1351 and in *Piers Plowman*, A-text, 3.140, *lemman* is alliteratively collocated with *lotebie* to refer to the mistresses of priests.

33. The word *burel* emphasises the connection between *curteisie* and learning, since its metaphorical sense is 'unlearned'. See *Summoner's Tale*, D 1869–75 and *Franklin's Tale*, F 716–20.

9 THE ARCHITECTURE OF CHAUCER'S LANGUAGE

1. The word *sense* implies that kind of meaning which is defined by its contrast with other possible senses of a word. It occurs only in contexts. But contexts are understood as being either *syntagmatic* (that is, the verbal context in ordinary utterance) or *paradigmatic* (that is, those words which are semantically related or substitutable for a word in syntagmatic context). See further John Lyons, *Semantics*, vol. I, pp. 197–206.

2. That languages have their own characteristic 'architecture' is well known to teachers of foreign languages, but may often be ignored in approaching earlier stages of our own. See E. Coseriu, 'Lexical Structures and the Teaching of Vocabulary', in *Linguistic Theories and their Application* (London: Allen and Unwin, 1967) pp. 9–90.

3. On synonymy as a context-dependent sense relationship, see John Lyons, *Theoretical Linguistics*, pp. 446–53.

4. That this is best viewed as an ironic sense development is suggested by a statement that 'good and yvel, and peyne and mede ben contrarie' (*Bo* IV p. 3, 60). The implication of this is that penalty and reward are opposites within the same *genus* of repayments for a service. The ordinarily understood sense of *mede* is therefore said to contrast with penalty or punishment, that is, to be sense 1 (above). The ironic use of words in a diametrically opposite sense is a common feature of linguistic usage.

5. The notion of conceptual areas delineated by an appropriate vocabulary, whose items gained their meaning from their limitation by other items, was first promulgated in Germany by Jost Trier. The study of semantic fields has been largely a feature of European Linguistics, flourishing in Germany, and to a lesser extent in France and Eastern Europe. A brief account may be found in W.v. Wartburg, *Problems and Methods in Linguistics,* trans. E. Palmer (Oxford: Blackwell, 1970).

6. An outstanding problem of any limited corpus of data – as historical data generally is – is that results will be 'skewed' by that data being in some way 'atypical'. Here, it seems that the preoccupation in *Boece* with rewards and punishments has disturbed the statistical basis for assumptions about the characteristic senses of *mede*. It is easy to imagine circumstances in which the inclusion of a technical text into a corpus of data would give an uncharacteristically prominent place to technical senses of words. The degree to which word-meaning as a whole – and thus our conception of medieval culture – is affected by the partial nature of surviving data is imponderable, but salutary to remember.

7. The point is that made at the opening of this chapter: glossaries function by making distinctions, but connexions are as important as distinctions in actual usage.

8. This question relates to a more general problem of the gradual nature of semantic change.

9. Connotational meaning is not currently well-regarded by theoretical writers on semantics, since connotation is regarded as a vague, catch-all term. Nevertheless, it is undeniable that words carry with them a possible range of associations derived from earlier experience of their uses. An analysis of this connotational meaning may be beyond the legitimate bounds of semantics, but falls within the sphere of stylistics.

10. One hundred and two students of English at the universities of Sheffield and Liverpool were asked to write down all the meanings of *beam*. Forty-two placed 'light' at the top of their list, forty-one 'wood', and nineteen 'smile'. The implication is that the former two are equally psychologically salient meanings in modern English. When either 'light' or 'wood' occupied first place, then second place was taken by the other

member of this pair about four times as often as by 'smile'. However, when 'smile' was placed first, although one might have expected 'wood' and 'light' to have occupied an equal second place, in fact 'light' appeared in second place about three times as often as 'wood'.

11. J. D. Burnley, *Chaucer's Language and the Philosophers' Tradition*, pp. 29–30.

12. The contextual modification of the senses of words so that they become directly opposed to their central sense – *mede*'s synonymy with *peyne*; or *guerdoun*'s sense of 'punishment' or 'retribution' – is such a persistent feature of Chaucerian usage that any true account of the 'architecture' of his language must take it into account. Here is a sharp distinction between semantic structure and the sense-listing of the dictionary. A recent study of Chaucer's use of the adjective *sely* is of interest in this connection: Geoffrey Cooper, ' "Sely John" in the "Legende" of the *Miller's Tale*', *JEGP*, LXXIX (1980) 1–12.

13. The term 'architecture' is used by Coseriu in 'Lexical Structures and the Teaching of Vocabulary', but was borrowed from an article by L. Flydal, 'Remarques sur certains rapports entre le style et l'état de langage', *Norsk Tidsskrift for Sprogvidenskap*, XVI (1951) 240–57.

14. 'Collocation' which refers to the tendency of certain words to co-occur in verbal context, was a term introduced by J. R. Firth. Following his own practice (although not his theory) I have made no distinction here between 'collocation' and 'colligation'. The latter refers to words co-occurring in grammatical relationships. J. R. Firth, 'Modes of Meaning', *Essays and Studies*, n.s. IV (1951) 118–49.

15. The word *servisable* is used on two of its four occurrences in Chaucer's works in application to squires; *socour* is applied in nine out of twenty-three occurrences (outside *RR*) to the Virgin.

16. Margery Kempe also seeks a variation of these familiar words when describing her vision of her spiritual marriage to Christ: 'I take þe, Margery, for my weddyd wyfe, for fayrar, for fowelar, for richar, for powerar, so þat þu be buxom and bonyr to do what I byd þe do.' Sanford B. Meech (ed.), *The Book of Margery Kempe* EETS OS 212 (1940) vol I, p. 87. Cf. the form of the oath in Littlehales, *Medieval Service Books*, p. 6.

17. Coseriu stresses the connection between history and architecture ('Lexical Structures and the Teaching of Vocabulary', pp. 33–7).

18. The Prioress reaches for food in a *semely* way (A 136) and has the word applied to her three times in the course of a short description. Sir Thopas has a *semely* nose (B 1919) and the word is used of two of the most villainous traitors in the *Legend of Good Women*, Theseus and Jason (*LGW* 1603; 2074). Indeed *semely* is as nearly restricted to satirical use in Chaucer's works as is the word *hende*.

19. J. D. Burnley, 'Criseyde's Heart and the Weakness of Women: An Essay in Lexical Interpretation', *SN*, LIV (1982) 25–38.

20. A point made at some length in Burnley, *Chaucer's Language and the Philosophers' Tradition*.

21. The fallacy of regarding English, French and Latin as separate languages in medieval England is noted by W. Rothwell, 'Lexical

Borrowing in a Medieval Context', *Bulletin of the John Rylands Library*, LXIII (1980) 143. See also Burnley, *Chaucer's Language and the Philosophers' Tradition*, pp. 1–9.

22. For example, *LGW* (F) 470–4; A 3172–5; B 2144–54. Characters like the Pardoner (C 432), Pandarus (*TC* II 295), and the Wife of Bath (D 192) also discuss their intentions in preaching, speech-making, or telling tales.

23. R. W. Hunt, 'The Introductions to the "Artes" in the Twelfth Century' in *Studia mediaevalia in honorem admodum Reverendi Patris Raymundi Josephi Martin* (Bruges: Societas edit. 'De Tempel', 1948) pp. 85–112; reprinted in R. W. Hunt, *The History of Grammar in the Middle Ages: Collected Papers*, edited by G. L. Bursill-Hall, Studies in the History of Linguistics, vol. V (Amsterdam: Benjamins, 1980) pp. 117–43.

24. A number of studies of this material have been published by A. N. Minnis: 'Discussions of "Authorial Rôle" and "Literary Form" in Late-Medieval Scriptural Exegesis', *Beiträge zur Geschichte der deutschen Sprache und Literatur*, XCIV (1977) 37–65; 'The Influence of Academic Prologues on the Prologues and Literary Attitudes of Late-Medieval English Writers', *MS* (forthcoming).

25. R. B. C. Huygens, *Accessus ad Auctores*, 2nd edn (Leiden: Brill, 1970) pp. 78, 86 and 99.

Sources and Further Reading

This list is limited to book-length works and monographs relevant to the study of Chaucer's language. References to some important articles can be found in the Notes and by recourse to standard bibliographies such as GEORGE WATSON (ed.), *The New Cambridge Bibliography of English Literature*, vol. I; *The Year's Work in English Studies*; the *Annual Bibliography of English Language and Literature*; and the *MLA International Bibliography of Modern Languages and Literature*. A bibliography of writings on Chaucer is published annually by the New Chaucer Society in *Studies in the Age of Chaucer*, and *Neuphilologische Mitteilungen* and *Chaucer Review* annually publish details of current research. Four specialised Chaucer bibliographies can be recommended: D. D. GRIFFITH, *Bibliography of Chaucer 1908–53* (Seattle: University of Washington Press, 1955); W. R. CRAWFORD, *Bibliography of Chaucer 1954–63* (Seattle and London: University of Washington Press, 1967); LORRAYNE Y. BAIRD, *A Bibliography of Chaucer, 1964–73* (Boston, Mass. and London: Hall and Prior, 1977); A. C. BAUGH, *Chaucer*, Goldentree Bibliographies in Language and Literature, 2nd edn (Arlington Heights, Illinois: AHM Publishing Corporation, 1977).

Facsimiles and editions cited in the text

RUGGIERS, PAUL G. (ed.), *The Canterbury Tales, a facsimile and transcription of the Hengwrt Manuscript*, with introductions by Donald C. Baker and A. I. Doyle and M. B. Parkes (Norman, Oklahoma: University of Oklahoma Press, 1979).

The Ellesmere Chaucer, Reproduced in Facsimile, 2 vols, (Manchester: Manchester University Press, 1911).

Troilus and Criseyde, a Facsimile of Corpus Christi College Cambridge MS 61, with introductions by M. B. Parkes and Elizabeth Salter (Cambridge: D. S. Brewer, 1978).

Bodleian Library MS Fairfax 16, with an introduction by John Norton-Smith (London: Scolar Press, 1979).

The Poetical Works of Geoffrey Chaucer: A Facsimile of Cambridge University Library

MS Gg 4.27, with an introduction by M. B. Parkes and Richard Beadle, 3 vols (Cambridge: D. S. Brewer, 1979–80).

The Auchinleck Manuscript, Facsimile with introductions by D. A. Pearsall and I. C. Cunningham (London: Scolar Press, 1977).

SKEAT, W. W. (ed.), *The Complete Works of Geoffrey Chaucer*, 7 vols (Oxford: Clarendon Press, 1894–7).

ROBINSON, F. N. (ed.), *The Works of Geoffrey Chaucer*, 2nd edn (London: OUP, 1957).

MANLY, JOHN M. and RICKERT, EDITH (eds), *The Text of the Canterbury Tales*, 8 vols (Chicago: University of Chicago Press, 1940).

BLAKE, N. F. (ed.), *The Canterbury Tales by Geoffrey Chaucer* (London: Arnold, 1980).

MACAULAY, G. C. (ed.), *The English Works of John Gower*, EETS ES 81 and 82 (London, 1901).

SMITHERS, G. V. (ed.), *Kyng Alisaunder*, 2 vols, EETS OS 227 and 237 (London: OUP, 1952, 1957).

MACRAE-GIBSON, O. D. (ed.), *Of Arthour and of Merlin*, 2 vols, EETS OS 268 and 279 (London: OUP, 1973, 1979).

CHAMBERS, R. W. and DAUNT, M. (eds), *A Book of London English, 1384–1425*, 2nd edn (Oxford: Clarendon Press, 1967).

Books on Chaucer's Language

BURNLEY, J. D. *Chaucer's Language and the Philosophers' Tradition* (Cambridge: D. S. Brewer, 1979).

DAVIS, N., GRAY, D., INGHAM, P. and WALLACE-HADRILL, A. *A Chaucer Glossary* (Oxford: Clarendon Press, 1979).

ELIASON, NORMAN E. *The Language of Chaucer's Poetry: An Appraisal of the Verse, Style, and Structure* (Copenhagen: Rosenkilde and Bagger, 1972).

ELLIOTT, R. W. V. *Chaucer's English* (London: Deutsch, 1974).

HÉRAUCOURT, W. *Die Wertwelt Chaucers, die Wertwelt einer Zeitwende* (Heidelberg: Winter, 1939).

KARPF, F. *Studien zur Syntax in den Werken Geoffrey Chaucers* (Vienna, 1930).

KENYON, JOHN S. *The Syntax of the Infinitive in Chaucer* (London: Chaucer Society, 1909).

KERKHOF, J. *Studies in the Language of Geoffrey Chaucer* (Leiden U.P., 1966).

KITTREDGE, G. L. *Observations on the Language of Chaucer's Troilus* (London: Chaucer Society, 1891).

KIVIMAA, KIRSTI *The Pleonastic* That *in Relative and Interrogative Constructions in Chaucer's Verse*, Commentationes Humanarum Litterarum: Societas Scientiarum Fennica, 39.3 (Helsinki, 1966).

————— *Clauses in Chaucer Introduced by Conjunctions with Appended* that, Commentationes Humanarum Litterarum: Societas Scientarum Fennica, 43.1 (Helsinki, 1968).

KÖKERITZ, HELGE *A Guide to Chaucer's Pronunciation* (New York: Holt, Rinehart, 1961). This pamphlet has been reprinted by the University of

Toronto Press (1978) in association with the Mediaeval Academy of America.

McJIMSEY, RUTH B. *Chaucer's Irregular -e* (New York: King's Crown Press, 1942).

MANLY, JOHN M. *Observations on the Language of Chaucer's Legend of Good Women*, Studies and Notes in Phil. and Lit., 2 (Cambridge, Mass.: 1893).

MASUI, MICHIO *The Structure of Chaucer's Rime Words* (Tokyo: Kenkyusha, 1964).

MERSAND, J. *Chaucer's Romance Vocabulary* (Brooklyn: Comet Press, 1937. Reprinted, New York: Kennikat Press, 1968).

PETERS, R. A. *Chaucer's Language*, *JEL* Occasional Monographs, I (Bellingham: Western Washington University, 1980).

REMUS, HANS *Die kirklichen und speziell-wissenschaftlichen romanischen Lehnworte Chaucers*, Studien zur engl. Phil., 14 (Halle: 1906).

ROSCOW, GREGORY *Syntax and Style in Chaucer's Poetry* (Cambridge: D. S. Brewer, 1981).

ROSS, THOMAS W. *Chaucer's Bawdy* (New York: Dutton, 1972).

TATLOCK, J. S. P. and KENNEDY, A. G. *Concordance to the Complete Works of Geoffrey Chaucer and to the Romaunt of the Rose* (Washington, D.C: Carnegie Institution, 1927. Reprinted, Gloucester, Mass.: Peter Smith, 1963).

TEN BRINK, B. *The Language and Metre of Chaucer*, trans. M. B. Smith (London: Macmillan, 1921).

WILD, F. *Die sprachlichen Eigentümlichkeiten der wichtigeren Chaucer Handschriften und die Sprache Chaucers* (Vienna: 1915).

Background and Reference

BAUGH, A. C. and CABLE, T. *A History of the English Language*, 3rd edn (London: Routledge and Kegan Paul, 1978).

BLAKE, N. F. *The English Language in Medieval Literature* (London: Dent, 1977. Reprinted Methuen University Paperbacks, 1979).

BOURCIER, GEORGES *An Introduction to the History of the English Language*, English adaptation by Cecily Clark (Cheltenham: Stanley Thornes, 1981).

BRYAN, W. F. and DEMPSTER, GERMAINE (eds), *Sources and Analogues of Chaucer's Canterbury Tales* (University of Chicago Press, 1941).

BRUNNER, K. *An Outline of Middle English Grammar*, trans. G. K. W. Johnston (Oxford: Blackwell, 1963).

FISIAK, J. *A Short Grammar of Middle English* (London: OUP, 1968).

JORDAN, R. *Handbook of Middle English Grammar: Phonology*, trans. and rev. by Eugene Crook (The Hague: Mouton, 1974).

MUSTANOJA, T. F. *A Middle English Syntax* (Société Néophilologique de Helsinki, 1960).

SAMUELS, M. L. *Linguistic Evolution* (Cambridge U.P., 1972).

SCRAGG, D. G. *A History of English Spelling* (Manchester U.P., 1974).

SERJEANTSON, M. *A History of Foreign Words in English* (London: Kegan Paul, 1935).

VISSER, F. T. *An Historical Syntax of the English Language*, 3 vols (Leiden: Brill, 1963–74).

Index of Lines Quoted

This index lists all lines – and substantial parts of lines – quoted as illustration. Shorter quotations are not separately listed if they are included within a longer passage already listed, but page references are given under the entry for the longer passage.

Index of Words

Subject Index